TOXIC DECEPTION

A JORDAN REED MYSTERY

K.C. GILLIS

Chesterfield Press

Copyright © 2019 by Chesterfield Press

First edition.

ISBN: 978-1-7333924-1-9

www.kcgillis.com

For my family and my readers.

THE GILLIS CLAN

The Gillis Clan is a virtual community for those who enjoy the Jordan Reed mysteries and want to keep up to date with all things Jordan Reed.

Members of the Gillis Clan will get exclusive access to free books and other insider information.

Please look for the link to sign up at the end of the book.

I can't wait to see you in the Gillis Clan!

1

WHAT THE HELL IS THAT?

Jordan reached the top of the stairs and paused before grabbing the doorknob. A large white envelope was taped to the door of her walk-up. It had no specific addressing and no postage, just "*JORDAN REED*" written in large block letters. Since it obviously wasn't a check from Publishers Clearing House, Jordan really wanted nothing to do with it. She had planned a very relaxing Sunday, and whatever was in that envelope was more likely to ruin her day than make it more enjoyable. She seriously considered throwing the envelope into a garbage can. But the natural curiosity that made her a good reporter compelled her to peel the envelope off her door and bring it inside.

It didn't mean she was going to open it.

She dropped her purse on a chair and tossed the envelope on the kitchen table. It landed beside other documents she didn't want to deal with. Namely, bills. Jordan didn't earn much as a junior staff reporter, and rent in Boston wasn't cheap. But her financial struggle wasn't a result of simply living in Boston. It could be traced back to her mother's illness and death.

Her mother's cancer diagnosis while Jordan was in college meant that her parents' contribution to her education expenses never materialized. Jordan had to find her own college financing and now had a small mountain of debt she was trying to chip away at. Making her financial situation worse were the medical bills from her mother's treatments. Her mother had died years ago, but the bills were far from paid off. Despite Jordan's resentment toward her father for forcing her mother into a risky medical trial, she still helped him as much as she could. If it weren't for the checks she sent her father, they'd have no communication at all.

Jordan went about the rest of her morning. A good swim always made her hungry, and this morning's workout was harder than most. Part of her Sunday routine was breakfast at the Green Clover Diner a few blocks away, but her hunger demanded immediate taming. A yogurt did the trick.

Jordan's apartment needed some tidying up, so she puttered around a bit, gathering laundry and putting dishes in the sink. But the envelope sitting on her table begged attention. She knew if she opened it, her day would be shot.

She had to either deal with the envelope and what was inside or get rid of it. She toyed with the idea of torching it in the sink. But not knowing what the envelope contained, and why it had been given to her, was too tantalizing to ignore. Jordan had to look inside.

Dammit.

Jordan sat down at her two-seater kitchen table and ripped open the envelope.

Inside was a single page from a newspaper, the *Lexington Post*. She expected to see a particular news story, maybe something she had written, or perhaps a story related to some of her work. Instead, she found an obituary page, with one obituary near the middle circled with a red marker. The rather long obituary was for someone named Eric Smith, a husband and father of two young children. He died last month. As Jordan read the obituary, a single line stuck out: "While his end came much too soon, we trust that time will not only help us overcome our loss but allow for a full reckoning."

That's odd. Who puts that kind of sentence in an obituary?

A few questions immediately came to mind. Was Eric Smith's death intentional or the result of negligence? Did someone put him in a position that led to his death? Did he have an underlying disease that went unnoticed by a doctor?

All potentially valid questions, but so what?

From Jordan's perspective, if there had been a crime, the local police should handle it. A lawyer would be the best bet for negligence. Jordan reread the obituary. Nothing else jumped out at her. While a father's death was certainly tragic for a family with young children, her reporter instincts didn't sense much of a story.

Jordan tossed the obituary on the kitchen table and leaned back in her chair, balancing on its two back legs. She thought more about what she had read. The most important question was: Who'd put this on her door? Perhaps equally important was: Why had someone chosen her? Jordan didn't live in Lexington and had no connection with the Smith family. She didn't even write for that newspaper. Her reporter home was the much larger *Boston Courant*. She also spent no time on homicides. Most of her reporting was aimed at exposing city corruption.

Somebody obviously thought this death wasn't just chance or bad luck. That person also thought Jordan should be involved. Either because of a personal connection that wasn't clear yet or a corruption angle concealed somewhere. Or both. Maybe neither.

Now what?

Jordan left her one-bedroom walk-up on Pacific Street and headed to her favorite diner on foot. The Green Clover had the best eggs Benedict in Boston. The South Boston neighborhood was jammed with three-story walk-ups, with red brick being the predominant color and style. This trademark look conveyed a sense of the neighborhood's old age. There weren't a lot of families with kids. Residents were either younger singles trying to get by or older couples who couldn't afford anything more.

The gray autumn morning had that dry and crisp feeling of a nice fall day. The street was largely empty of cars, with only a couple of people visible in any direction. Trash blew around, a lot of it packaging from fast-food joints, making the grungy sidewalks seem dirtier than usual.

Jordan wore her typical black leather jacket and black jeans, her hair still smelling like chlorine from the pool. A cool, light breeze blew through her jet-black hair, giving her pale cheeks just a hint of red. With her hands in her pockets to keep them warm, her mind returned to that one line in the obituary, pausing on "full reckoning." The mystery was maddening. She hoped that by the time she'd finished brunch, her curiosity would have subsided.

"Hey, Marcus," Jordan called as she entered the diner. She had been a Sunday regular for years and knew or recognized the entire staff. Marcus, who was in his sixties and sported the physique of someone who had worked his whole life in a diner, handled the counter. Jordan parked herself in her usual counter spot. Dining alone was her specialty.

"Hey yourself," Marcus said. "You're late today. Did you give yourself some extra beauty sleep? You're not getting any younger, you know. Those good looks need maintenance if you expect them to last until you get yourself a man."

"Hilarious, old-timer. No, I didn't sleep in today. There was an unexpected interruption to my morning." Jordan leaned forward on her stool. "Do you have any eggs Benedict today? You didn't have them the last time I was here, so I hope I don't have to take my business elsewhere."

"Yes, I do. I couldn't bear to hear your complaining again."

"Think of it as me helping you serve your customers better. How are the grandkids?"

"Growing too fast to keep track. Seems like every time I see them, they've skipped a year. It can make a man feel older than his days."

"Well, make sure they don't forget who you are."

"No danger of that. My kids like the free babysitting my wife and I provide."

As Marcus poured her a cup of coffee, Jordan reflected on how her family had drifted apart and how she hadn't seen her grandparents in years. Her dad's father had died several years ago, and his mom lived in Arizona. Her mom's parents lived in Florida, and she hadn't seen them since her mother had died. They spoke several times in the weeks after her death, but only once in the past year. Jordan's brother and sister kept closer touch with all the grandparents than she did, providing just one more reason to duck calls from her siblings. Secondhand guilt felt just as bad as firsthand guilt, and her brother was a master at laying it on.

While waiting for her brunch, she pulled out her phone to check in on what had been happening in the world. A quick scan of her news feed showed more of the same crap that came with the current presidential administration. While not a fan of any politician, since they were all just what their donors wanted them to be, she missed the days when basic facts weren't disputed. The constant stream of lies and misdirection was a shitty way to lead. Politicians cared more about their parties than the country. To Jordan, that was a recipe for disaster.

Jordan used Twitter to keep abreast of local news and events. It had helped her crack what was her most successful story to date. She'd exposed how a state senator had been funneling campaign contributions to the personal holdings of his brother-in-law. He wouldn't hold office again thanks to her. Jordan suspected a bigger conspiracy involving multiple elected officials and several high-powered business leaders. But she wasn't able to break through the "old boys'" wall of silence. Her editor, Tom Winters, told her she did a great job on the story, but Jordan figured most of the criminals were still out there, breaking the law under the guise of capitalism.

Jordan's food still hadn't arrived, so she delved deeper into her news feed. She rarely noticed much on the medical side, but one headline caught her eye. A hospital in Greece had had over a dozen fatalities in the past month where patients had developed bacterial infections that didn't respond to antibiotics. The news story said the infections were *staph* infections, which were common in hospitals.

Jordan continued to read the article. It mentioned that drug-resistant infections were on the rise globally and that new treatments weren't being developed fast enough to deal with antibiotic-resistant bacteria. The author speculated that humanity was entering a period where the inability of traditional antibiotics to treat common infections would lead to an increase in deaths from minor infections that we currently assume we can easily treat.

Jordan had a basic understanding of antibiotic resistance but didn't have a strong enough science background to understand all the complexities. Like most people, she figured that some combination of government and industry would find a technological solution.

"Eggs Benedict are up," Marcus announced, setting a platter down in front of Jordan. As always, they looked delicious and came with a heap of home fries and toast. All for $9.99, including the coffee.

"Thanks, Marcus, it looks as good as ever." Jordan dove right in. She ate half of the platter before pausing. Marcus topped up her coffee, and Jordan took a sip, enjoying the aroma of the freshly brewed java. She finished the second half of her brunch, but at a slower pace than she'd devoured the first half. She indulged her coffee addiction with one more refill before leaving fifteen dollars on the counter.

"See you next Sunday, Marcus," Jordan said.

"Yes, you will, young lady."

As Jordan headed back to her apartment, the morning sunshine gave way to thick clouds. The stiff breeze made it legitimately cold. She had hoped her curiosity about the obituary would have subsided, but it continued to gnaw at her. She needed to figure out its significance. She hustled along and decided that her afternoon at the movie theater would have to wait.

Back in her apartment, she grabbed the obituary and her laptop and got comfortable on the sofa.

So, Eric Smith. Who are you, and why do you matter?

So far, all Jordan knew was that he was a husband and father and likely lived in Lexington.

Jordan made an effort not to drink in the mornings. It wasn't a rule but rather a guideline. After all, she wasn't an alcoholic. But it was almost noon, so she wouldn't really be drinking in the morning. A vodka and OJ seemed appropriate. The orange juice allowed her to classify the drink as healthy.

Googling "Eric Smith" was predictably not very helpful, given how common the name was. The number of hits was staggering. Even filtering the search to "Eric Smith in Lexington, MA" didn't return a manageable number of hits. Unfortunately, there was no actual story about Eric Smith's death. Finding an easy answer to how he died wasn't going to happen. Eric Smith proved surprisingly hard to learn anything about. Not a thing about his occupation or anything else that left a convenient record. Nothing so basic as a time for a local 5k.

It looks like you're trying to hide from me, Eric. I guess you don't know that hiding from me only makes me look harder.

Jordan switched gears and moved on to searching social media platforms. Facebook had no shortage of people named

Eric Smith—so many that Jordan couldn't bear to go through them right away. Same problem with Instagram, Snapchat, and Twitter. Jordan hoped for better luck with LinkedIn, but there was no Eric Smith from Lexington. There were lots of people named Eric Smith elsewhere, even in Massachusetts, but not an obvious candidate for the Eric Smith in the obituary.

It perplexed and annoyed Jordan to strike out so easily. Eric Smith had no readily findable public footprint. It seemed unlikely for someone with a family. Moms and wives often shared pictures of their kids through Facebook.

Jordan went back to Facebook and took a slightly different tack. She knew the first names of Eric's family, and as long as they had the same last name, she could search for them. If his wife, Laurie, had a Facebook account and posted family pictures, she should be able to find them. After about ten minutes, Jordan found a Facebook page for a Laurie Smith who was from Massachusetts and had children named Jack and Samantha. Jordan wasn't good at judging the ages of kids, since she never spent any time with them, but Jack and Samantha looked to be four and two. Way too young to lose a parent. At least she'd been much older when her own mother died.

An afternoon of digging didn't get Jordan much farther than when she'd started. Jordan had established that Eric Smith and his family lived in the Lexington area, but that was it. She uncovered nothing about how he'd died or where he'd worked. This could all be on the up-and-up, but now Jordan's reporter instinct kicked in. It was just a bit too convenient how absent Eric Smith was. If he really were that private, his wife wouldn't share family pictures on Facebook. Why was he so hard to find?

Well, Eric Smith, you've piqued my curiosity. It looks like I'll invest more than a Sunday afternoon into figuring out why someone wants me to investigate your death.

2

JORDAN'S MONDAY WAS ONE OF THOSE DAYS SHE LOVED TO HATE. She was working to find contacts for a story that her editor had assigned but wasn't having any luck. Not to mention it was super boring. Perhaps it was that the story was looking into changes in zoning regulations to open more land for commercial development. With Boston continuing to be attractive to many industries and having a lot of success luring companies from neighboring Connecticut to the area, commercial land was getting more scarce—unless a company was willing to set up shop in one of the many Boston suburbs that still had room for expansion. Her lack of progress was more likely because of Eric Smith. She couldn't push his obituary out of her mind, and her inability to find anything insightful was frustrating.

By the time the clock read five p.m., she was more than ready to pack it in. As Jordan headed out to the street, she wondered what to do. On Mondays, she usually worked in the office until seven or eight, so punching out early left her a bit at odds. She could head home and hope to find something edible for dinner, an unlikely proposition. Or she could grab fast food, an option that was budget friendly.

What she wanted was a legitimate reason to walk away from

the Eric Smith situation. Despite her curiosity, homicide, or something like it, wasn't her area of expertise. Her strength was working contacts and connections to uncover corruption, or at least the hint of corruption. The thought of dealing with a violent crime made her nervous. Not that she was particularly scared for her well-being. She just didn't have the experience.

Jordan needed the opinion of someone who could assess what she did or didn't know and tell her if it seemed fishy. She didn't want to ask her editor. This wasn't her beat. He might tell her to stop pursuing it. She didn't want to ask another reporter in the event it became a real story and she'd end up having to work with them.

She considered running it by her brother, Mark. He was a marine captain and could analyze any situation and give an objective opinion. At least he could if he and Jordan were on good speaking terms. Since the death of their mother, tension in the family had been high, putting a lot of stress on Jordan's relationships with Mark and her father. She and her sister Rachel still got along well. Rachel had a knack at understanding different points of view and didn't fault Jordan for her opinion. Plus she liked having a little sister. That she blamed her dad for her mother's death was the primary source of tension. Her father's poor financial situation, caused by the mountain of medical bills, just made everything worse. Not the best time to call Mark.

Without fully realizing it, she was walking toward Darcy's Pub. Subconsciously, she must have figured that Travis could help. Or maybe she wanted a good stiff drink. Either way, she was heading to the right place.

Travis Sparks was the smartest person she knew. He didn't just work at the pub. He was the owner—or, rather, a part owner. A few excellent financial decisions coupled with an unexpected opportunity had enabled him to buy a share of the place from his aunt, who had needed the money. It was the love of his life.

Actually, it was the second love of his life. Jordan was the first.

Their relationship was tricky. Jordan had known Travis since high school, and they had always been close. But during university, their relationship had moved from friendship to romance. Before they graduated, they had gotten engaged. But Jordan called if off. She still didn't know exactly why she'd done it. It wasn't that she didn't love him. But in the aftermath of her mother's death and her father's role in her death, the whole "till death do us part" bit just seemed fake. Maybe if her mother hadn't died and if her family hadn't fractured, she would have been happier and more willing to commit. The lesson she learned was that relationships and commitment weren't worth the effort. While she was still close to Travis, their relationship had a constant undercurrent of tension that both acknowledged but rarely talked about.

It was a good fifteen- to twenty-minute walk to Darcy's Pub. By the time Jordan arrived, her brisk pace had warmed her up. She unzipped her jacket and grabbed a spot at the bar. At five thirty p.m. on a Monday, the pub was almost empty. That would change once the Monday Night Football crowd packed the place. But Jordan expected to be on her way home by then.

Travis was hooking up a new keg at the other end of the bar —Allagash White, by the look of it. He noticed Jordan when he glanced up after installing the keg and gave a quick nod of his head and came over. He was your typical tall, dark, and handsome man, with a face like a young Denzel Washington. He still sported the build that helped make him an All-American basketball prospect in high school. Were it not for destroying his knee in the state championship game, he could have had a real shot at going pro.

Good thing he had always prioritized education over sports. He had devoted himself to his education and double-majored in business and computer science. He was a very smart dude.

Maybe too smart. He had used his computer science skills in some not-so-appropriate ways and had been suspended as a junior, which nearly cost him his degree.

Jordan hadn't talked to Travis in more than a week, as their last discussion had ended up an argument about her refusal to visit her dad. Like her siblings, Travis thought she should try to patch up that relationship. She still blamed her dad for his pressure to enroll her mom in a clinical trial for a new cancer treatment. The family was drowning in medical bills, and the trial, though experimental, provided some coverage for treatment and hospital costs. It turned out that the treatment was much riskier than anyone outside the drug company knew. The experimental drug caused her mother's death.

Her dad had gambled with her mom's life and lost. Their family shattered in the aftermath.

Jordan felt tension building as she recalled her last exchange with Travis. Her mouth was dry. Her stomach felt tight. She was sweating, made worse by her brisk walk to the pub. She didn't want to have another argument. Travis was still her closest friend, and the recent disagreements were draining.

"Imagine seeing you here," Travis said. "Gin and tonic, I assume?"

"Not tonight. I feel like a beer, maybe what I saw you hook up. Is it ready to pour?"

"Sure, but I can't remember the last time you had a beer."

"Just trying to keep you on your toes." Jordan watched Travis as he got an ice-cold glass and angled it under the tap, slowly filling it without generating a lot of excess foam.

"Here you go," said Travis, placing the fresh brew on a coaster in front of her.

"Thanks."

"So, what brings you here on a Monday, especially so early? I'm guessing you don't want to pick up where we left off last time?" Travis's smile told Jordan he had moved on from their argument.

"That's for damn sure. How about we agree to disagree on that topic?"

"Works for me. I'm also guessing you didn't stop by to apologize? After all, you were the one who stormed off."

"You know I don't know how to apologize. It would mean admitting I was wrong. I rarely do that, even if it's true."

"So, back to my original question," Travis said. "Why the visit?"

"I need an objective opinion on something without getting a shitload of judgment and analysis. If you can do that, I'll tell you. Otherwise, I'll drink my beer and go home."

"Ouch. You need to find a nicer way to ask people to do something for you. Just a little less edge would go a long way. But, yeah, I'll do my best to provide an objective opinion."

"Thanks. So, I received something out of the blue yesterday. It might be a real story, but I can't see how yet. I'd prefer to leave it alone, as it might be out of my league, but something about it won't let me let it go."

"Well, we can't have that. Tell me what happened."

"When I got home after my swim yesterday, there was an envelope taped to my door with my name on it. No other writing or markings at all. When I got around to opening it, there was a page from a newspaper inside with one obituary circled. It was for someone named Eric Smith. There was nothing else in the envelope. No notes, no other information, no address, nothing." Jordan stared hard at her glass as if it had the answers she needed.

"OK. So, knowing you, I'm sure you did some digging. What did you find?"

"That's what's bugging me. Almost nothing. He had a wife, two young kids, and lived somewhere around Lexington. Otherwise, he seems almost invisible, which isn't easy to do in this day and age. There are lots of people named Eric Smith out there, but I couldn't find anything that looked like it ties to this guy. Except for his wife's Facebook page. No one should be so hard to find anymore." Jordan felt herself getting louder, so she forced herself to use her quiet voice.

Travis paused before speaking. "Someone picked you to get this information and you want to know why? Either they know little themselves or they aren't sharing what they know. Or maybe it's a trick or a joke."

Jordan dismissed the trick or joke theory. "I think they meant it for me. There're lots of reporters better and more well known than I am that they could have picked."

"What about the obituary itself? Anything odd?"

Jordan smiled. Travis always asked the right questions. "As a matter of fact, yes. The only reason I spent any effort on this at all was because of one line in the obituary. Something about some kind of reckoning." Jordan pulled out her iPhone and showed Travis the picture of the obituary, giving him time to read it.

"Damn," he said. "That's not the kind of thing you'd expect someone to say in an obituary. I get the bit about loss and dying too soon, but to hope for a reckoning implies that not everything here is kosher."

"I know," Jordan said. "That's what got my attention. Eric Smith's invisibility just makes the whole thing more curious."

"You said you want to leave this alone. Why?"

"If there's something rotten about Eric Smith's death, this might be a case of negligence or, worse, homicide. That's way out of my comfort zone and something the cops should handle. Not some local reporter who looks for crooked businessmen or officials."

Travis leaned over the bar toward Jordan and shook his head. "As always, you're selling yourself short. You're not a corruption expert. You are an expert at solving puzzles, at finding the pieces and fitting them together. It doesn't matter what the problem is—you can solve it. If there's something fishy in the death of this Eric Smith, you'll be able to figure it out. But only if you want to. Don't get involved if you don't feel like it. It's not specifically your job, and no one expects you to do anything about it." Travis paused, looking right at Jordan. "But you could make a difference."

Jordan slumped down onto the bar. "Thanks for the subtle fucking guilt trip. Well played."

"It's not a guilt trip. It's the truth. You always sell yourself short, acting like you can't take on something big for fear of failing or losing. You're too smart for that. I'm not saying you should take a crack at this story. But you can find out what happened if you set aside whatever is holding you back."

Jordan sat in silence for a moment. Her immediate reaction was to lash out again, but Travis was genuinely trying to help, so she held back. "What do you suggest? Head to Lexington and see what I can stir up?"

"Yep. At this point, you should get some firsthand information. I'd start with the wife."

"Good thing I don't have a deadline coming up. I hope my car still starts."

"If not, you can borrow mine," Travis said, giving Jordan a quick wink to let her know there were no hard feelings. "Before I forget, do you have your laptop with you?"

"Sure, why?"

"There're some updates I should make for you. Nothing you'll notice. Just some security and backup stuff."

"Is that really necessary?"

"You said you wanted me to look after your computer. Well, this is me looking after your computer. You'll thank me someday when your computer dies but everything is safely backed up."

"Fine. Do what you want. Just get me another beer first."

"Coming right up."

3

Kisumu. The third-largest city in Kenya. Situated on Lake Victoria, it was a vibrant port city supporting trade with neighboring coastal towns. The city center was under the watchful eye of the famous town clock, unveiled in 1938 in memory of a local humanitarian businessman who'd died of malaria. A disease that preyed on the African continent, it was far from the only one.

HIV and AIDS had infected fifteen percent of the population in some cities. Perhaps less of a headline, but often more deadly, was tuberculosis. This bacterial infection could take root in the lungs of its victims and had a propensity to be resistant to many of the antibiotics used to treat it. Any new treatment could save hundreds of thousands of lives a year. The health imperative was unequivocal. So was the profit imperative.

Kenya, like many African nations, had felt the brunt of nearly the whole range of tropical and subtropical pathogens. Part of the response to these diseases had been the continued deployment of medical research infrastructure to support the clinical development of new treatments. This was often done or funded with support from the commercial drug industry.

Kisumu was the home of a health research center that partnered with developers from around the world to test new treatments. As antibiotics became less effective with each passing day, novel antibiotic treatments were increasingly important.

Dr. Simon Kemboi was an infectious disease doctor who'd been educated and trained in Nairobi. Though he was a junior physician, his firsthand experience with TB taught him how fragile the human body could be when fighting an infection. He had seen hundreds die from TB because standard treatments no longer worked. The reason for this was antibiotic resistance, a situation that arose when the bacteria causing the infection developed mechanisms to defeat conventional antibiotics.

One such example was when bacteria developed a molecular pump that could eliminate antibiotic molecules that had entered the bacterial cell, never giving them a chance to work. While deadly for patients, it was an exquisite mechanism of self-preservation for the bacteria.

An organism's ability to find a means to survive had always impressed Simon. So when Dr. Gideon Jebet invited him to join the staff of a clinical trial of a novel antibiotic treatment, he didn't hesitate.

The trial was now well underway, and dozens of patients had begun treatment at their site. While he didn't know all the specifics of the treatment, Simon knew it was a gene therapy directed at the TB bacteria themselves.

Each mechanism of antibiotic resistance, such as a molecular pump, required at least one specific gene that bestowed a resistance mechanism to a cell. Disrupting such genes could thwart antibiotic resistance. An effective method of disruption was to insert foreign genes into the bacteria that would render the resistance mechanisms useless. The new treatment platform being tested could deliver several genes to TB cells with something called bacteriophage, or phage. While the genes could in principle be for any purpose, the clinical trial was testing genes to combat antibiotic resistance.

The easiest way to think of phage was as a specialized virus that had evolved to infect bacteria. Simon appreciated the elegance of using one infectious agent to infect another. He suspected there were a lot of hidden complexities in the treatment, but as long as it worked, he didn't care.

Dr. Jebet had briefed Simon on the inclusion and exclusion criteria for selecting patients. They made intuitive sense to him. But he had noticed that Dr. Jebet personally selected each trial patient. While the patients he chose each met the trial-inclusion criteria, they were all from outlying areas and had limited financial means. Dr. Jebet didn't strike Simon as being particularly humanitarian, so the choices he made seemed off. There were definitely candidates much more affluent that weren't selected. Dr. Jebet, and whichever company supported the trial, also didn't communicate this trial widely in the community, unlike most other trials. Dr. Jebet's control was tight.

On a typical weekday, a boy of about eleven or twelve raced into the clinic asking for Dr. Kemboi. Simon recognized him from a few days prior, when his father had undergone a treatment cycle of the new TB antibiotic. The boy was breathing hard, as though he had just sprinted a mile.

After taking a moment to catch his breath, he yelled, "Dr. Kemboi, Dr. Kemboi." The boy took another breath. "It is my father. He is very sick and feels like he is on fire. He is sweating and shaking and breathing very fast. Please help him."

Simon was accustomed to seeing people very sick, but the boy's panic got his adrenaline pumping. He bolted for the doorway and yelled for a nurse to come with him. As he and the boy ran outside, he noticed a woman, presumably the boy's mother, standing by the open rear door of a car. The man, Simon thought his name was Ezra, was in the back seat and

Bonus.

She hadn't been out to Lexington in years but knew how to get to the downtown and could then easily find the office of the *Lexington Post*. She figured she'd start there and talk to whoever managed the obituaries. She wanted an address for the Smith family. If that didn't work, she'd have to resort to going to locations she could recognize from Mrs. Smith's Facebook posts. That wouldn't be an efficient way to spend her time.

Fortunately for Jordan, she was traveling against the main flow of traffic. She pulled into the parking lot at the newspaper's offices around 11:30. She expected most of the staff to be in, giving her a good chance of getting an address. The *Post* occupied the main floor of a three-story office building. Jordan climbed the stairs to the building entrance and walked in. Like most newsrooms, even small ones like this, there was a natural verve in the room, with people buzzing from desk to desk. There were scattered discussions happening in glass-walled meeting rooms. Jordan could feel the energy instantly.

There was an information desk just inside the office. Jordan had her press identification in her hand as she approached the desk.

Jordan put on her best smile. "Good morning. I'd like to speak with whoever handles the obituaries section of your paper."

The woman at the desk looked to be close to retirement age, if not already past it. She reminded Jordan of her middle-school librarian. Not a positive association. The woman stopped what she was doing on a computer, looked up at Jordan, and adjusted her glasses. The librarian meme was reinforced.

"Is the purpose of your visit to place an obituary? If so, there's paperwork you must complete," the woman replied.

"Actually, I'm here on business," Jordan said as she showed her press card. "I need to speak to a person who placed an obituary in your paper a few weeks ago. I hope someone can provide me with the contact information."

The woman didn't look pleased. Dull, pale eyes. Lips as straight as a line drawn on her face. Jordan stared hard at her as the woman processed how she would respond to Jordan's request.

The librarian receptionist didn't take long. "It would be appropriate to first make an appointment. I'm not sure we can help you today."

"Look. I need this information right away. It will take a grand total of sixty seconds for someone to get it for me. I'm not some random person off the street. I'm a reporter, just like most of the people in this office. I'd appreciate some professional courtesy." Jordan paused and said, "Please," but with a heavy dose of sarcasm.

Jordan's abruptness took the woman by surprise, rocking the control she had over her own little world. Jordan doubted anyone talked to her like that. She didn't appear to know how to respond, but after a moment gave in. "Very well," she said. "Marco handles obituaries. Let me get him."

The woman came back about two minutes later with a short, chubby man of about fifty.

"Good morning," he said. "I believe you'd like to know more about an obituary we ran?"

"Yes, I would. If we can go to your office or desk, I can explain what I'm looking for." Jordan's request wasn't really that confidential, but she didn't want to give the librarian receptionist the satisfaction of knowing what this was about.

"Absolutely," Marco said. "Please follow me."

They walked toward the northeast corner of the office, passing desks occupied by people working hard at the start of the week. They came to a desk by the windows, and Marco motioned for Jordan to take a seat.

"So, how can I help?" Marco said. "I know the *Courant* runs its own obituaries section, so I'm not sure why you need our help."

Jordan pulled out the newspaper page with the circled obituary and showed it to Marco. "I'd like to speak to the person who paid to have this obituary run in the paper," she said, pointing to the one for Eric Smith circled in red. Jordan felt the need to embellish. "My editor heard there may be a negligence claim for the death, and he asked me to get some background information. Unfortunately, we don't have the contact information for the family."

That's close to the truth.

Marco gave this a moment of thought. "As you know, we're not in the habit of giving out information on our customers. I see this as a professional request and would like to help, but officially I can't."

"How about unofficially?"

"Unofficially, I always try to help a fellow reporter. There will come a day when I need a professional favor, so I try to do the right thing. But I'll deny ever helping you with this. Got it?"

"Absolutely. A hundred percent."

Marco typed on his computer and stopped when he apparently got to the transaction record for the obituary. "This is strange," he said. "This obituary was a walk-in and paid for in cash. We usually get a full name, address, and phone number, but for this one, we only have a mobile number and a contact name of Laurie."

Jordan frowned. She needed an address. But she knew Laurie was the name of Eric's wife. "That should be enough for me, as long as the phone number isn't a fake. Can I see it?"

Marco turned the computer monitor so Jordan could see. Jordan copied the number.

"Thanks a ton," Jordan said as she got up. "You've been a big help."

"You're welcome," said Marco. "If something interesting

comes out of this, let me know. Not to print it or to tell anyone. Just to satisfy my curiosity."

"You bet," Jordan said as she headed for the door. Walking by the front desk, she glanced at the less-than-friendly receptionist. Jordan stuck out her tongue at the woman. She didn't wait to see a response.

NEXT CAME THE HARD PART. Jordan had experienced her share of grief. She could only imagine how Laurie Smith felt so soon after the death of her husband. She dreaded cold-calling her to ask about Eric's death. But if Laurie was responsible for the wording in the obituary, she might want to talk.

Jordan went to her car to make the call. She dialed the number, put the phone on speaker, and set it down on the console to her right. The phone rang three times before it was answered.

"Hello," said a tired voice.

"Is this Laurie Smith?" Jordan asked.

"Yes, it is. Who's this?"

"My name is Jordan Reed. I'm a reporter with the *Boston Courant*, and I was hoping I could talk to you about your husband, Eric."

Moment of truth. Will she hang up on me or will she talk?

"I have nothing I can say to you or anyone else about Eric." She hung up.

Shit. I can't believe she actually hung up on me.

While Jordan sat and contemplated her next move, her phone rang. She glanced at the number. It was Laurie.

"Hi, Laurie," Jordan said as she answered the call. "I'm sorry for the out-of-the-blue call, but I had no other way to reach you."

"I figured as much," Laurie said. "It's not that I really don't want to talk to you. I actually can't talk to you about Eric. I can't talk to anyone about Eric. At least not about his death."

This caught Jordan by surprise.

Why can't she talk to anyone?

"I'm sorry," Jordan said. "Did I miss something? Did you say you can't talk to anyone?"

"That's right. I had to sign something called a confidentiality agreement about Eric's death." Laurie paused, apparently waiting for Jordan to speak.

One of the first things Jordan had learned as a reporter was that when you want someone to talk, just let the silence build. Nine times out of ten, they'll continue. Jordan was right.

"If I speak to anyone about it, we'll lose the settlement."

That was unexpected. A settlement meant someone had screwed up. Or broke the law. Jordan had a ton of questions.

"Who's the settlement with? The city? Eric's employer? Someone else?"

"I'm sorry, Ms. Reed, but I can't say any more about this. I really should go."

"Wait," said Jordan. "If you can't speak about Eric's death, can you tell me anything about Eric? Where he worked, what he did when he had free time? The names of his friends? Favorite hangout?"

"I shouldn't, because it could come back to hurt me and my children. The only thing I'll say is that he liked to watch the Bruins at a place called the Meeting House. He had a few hockey buddies from his beer league that would meet there to watch games when they could. Usually on Saturday nights but sometimes during the week." Laurie paused and then continued. "Why do you want to know about Eric's death, anyway? There wasn't any publicity on it. I'm surprised anyone is asking."

Jordan gathered her thoughts. She had to answer this carefully. "That's not easy to answer. Someone shared Eric's obituary with me. There was a comment in it about a full reckoning that caught my attention. It seemed like a strange line, so I was curious. I felt obligated to do some due diligence in case something was being covered up." Jordan held her breath, worried about how Laurie would respond.

"What obituary? We never published one. You must have the wrong person."

"Really? You didn't publish one in the *Lexington Post*?"

"No. Nothing public. We did one for the funeral. Printed it out with a nice photo. Maybe you made a mistake? Maybe there was another Eric Smith who died?"

Jordan was stunned. This made no sense at all. The obituary was the genesis for her investigation. There was no way she'd made a mistake this big. "Are you sure no one in your family published one? Maybe a sibling or his parents? Maybe an uncle?"

"No. I made it clear to the family that there would be no public obituary. I really do have to go."

Jordan wished she could see Laurie's face and body language. She couldn't get a read on whether Laurie was lying just from her voice. "I understand. Thanks for your time, Laurie. Sorry to have interrupted your day."

"I'd appreciate it if you didn't call me again."

JORDAN'S HEAD was buzzing after the call with Laurie. The obituary confusion was troubling, but whether or not Laurie was lying, an obituary for her husband had been published. The real surprise was that Eric Smith's death had come with a settlement attached. Someone had something to hide, and that someone was most likely at the center of all this. That would tell her who she really needed to investigate. Jordan wondered how big the settlement was.

As she replayed the conversation in her head, she realized Laurie had sounded nervous. Maybe the settlement was large? It was hard to speculate what may have happened to Eric without knowing whom the settlement was with. But if it was with an employer or the government, then negligence was the probable reason. If it was with the government, it would be possible to track down.

Jordan had to decide on her next move. She needed to learn how Eric Smith had died. Laurie wouldn't, or couldn't, tell her how. But Laurie had given Jordan one good piece of information. The Meeting House. When the Bruins were playing.

Jordan didn't want to wait until the next Saturday game to go to the Meeting House. She hoped the Bruins would be playing before then. Jordan grabbed her phone. She was in luck. The Bruins were playing that night against the Canadiens from Montreal. She was a solid hockey fan and knew this would be a popular game. Local bars would be packed. She knew where she'd be that night.

The Bruins game was scheduled to start at seven thirty p.m., but Jordan wanted to get to the Meeting House well before that. She rolled into the parking lot around five p.m. and grabbed a spot at the bar. She had spent a lot of time in bars and preferred a stool at the counter. You could learn a lot sitting quietly and keeping your ears open.

It was quiet inside, with just a few customers at tables and two men on the opposite side of the bar. Jordan was slim, fit, and taller than average. Her jet-black hair, pale skin, and blue eyes made her hard to miss. She was always noticed when she entered a room. This place was no different. The men opposite her gave her a good long look, and the bartender flashed her a big smile as she sat down. She hoped this was not the opening salvo of an evening trying to fight off would-be suitors.

The bartender sauntered over. "What'll you have?"

"Gin and tonic on ice, with lime," Jordan said. "Open a tab, please."

"You got it." He eyed her while he made her drink. "I don't remember seeing you in here before. Are you visiting or new to town?"

Jordan considered making up a story, but not knowing anything about Eric Smith, she worried the bartender would recognize it as fake. She stayed close to the truth but played a hunch. She flashed the most attractive smile she could muster. "I'm doing some research on cases of wrongful death in Massachusetts. My boss gave me the name Eric Smith. Someone told me he came here a lot with his hockey buddies. Did you know him?" Jordan let what she said hang in the air and watched the bartender intently for a reaction.

He looked like he was organizing clean glasses in anticipation of a busy night, but Jordan thought he was just moving them around. He kept his head down when he replied. "Eric Smith I know. But I think you're mistaken about his death. He got real sick, I think with some kind of flu or something. Had to go to the hospital. Things got bad real fast, and he died within a couple of days. I don't know anything wrongful about it. Just bad luck."

Jordan took this in. The bartender didn't meet her gaze, but he otherwise didn't seem like he was lying. Jordan thought he believed what he said.

"So you never heard rumblings there was more to his death than just getting sick?"

"Nope. Even if I did, I wouldn't be volunteering it to some stranger. We look after each other around here. Laurie, Eric's wife, asked his friends not to talk about how he died. Said it would make it harder for her and the kids. No offense."

"None taken." Jordan could see the local "standing strong" attitude kicking in and knew she wouldn't be able to push her way through. "I get it. If I were you, I'd protect my friends and family from people snooping around. I mean no harm to Eric's family. I'm just trying to make sure someone didn't get away with hurting Eric."

The bartender finally met her gaze. "Are you some kind of reporter or something?"

"Something like that," Jordan said.

"You're welcome to stay. But no more questions about how Eric died. You won't find anyone here that'll talk about it."

Jordan changed tactics. Her hunch was that Eric's employer provided the settlement, and maybe she could get the bartender to fill in that blank for her. "Deal. I heard Eric was a hockey player. Was he any good or was he a typical beer-league player?"

The bartender let a small smile appear. "I didn't know him back then, but everyone says Eric was a standout at UMass Amherst. All-American as a junior. But in his senior year, he got a concussion three times before Christmas. Apparently, the last one was a doozy. He had to be stretchered off the ice and didn't play again that season. He had been a draft pick of the Rangers but never signed. The concussions forced him to stop playing competitive hockey. So, yeah, he eventually became a beer-league player. But he could still skate circles around anyone else. He was so smooth you wondered if his feet even touched the ice."

Jordan felt the bartender relax his guard as he talked about hockey and Eric. He was a fan of one or both. She was moving him where she needed him to go.

"That must have been quite a blow for Eric. To be close to the top of the sport, only to have to give it up. I guess he had something to fall back on."

"He sure did. Eric was a brilliant guy and worked his ass off in college to make sure he could do something besides hockey. I know he was some kind of engineer. Worked at one of those drug company plants around here."

Bingo.

"Good for him. I guess he was helping to make one of those super-expensive drugs that are all over the news these days. What was the latest? Some pill for the elderly that most of them don't even need? Sometimes these big companies piss me off."

The bartender jumped in, happy to pile on. No one really liked drug companies. "Me too. Trying to get rich on other people's suffering. But he worked for a small company. Making a new drug for people in Africa or something like that. I can't remember the company name. Gene-something. It's out near the air force base. Eric seemed happy, so maybe it was a good place to work."

That's probably all I'll get from him.

"Well, it's nice to know there may be a few good drug companies out there. We'll all need them one day."

"That's for sure. Besides, they employ a lot of people around here. Definitely helps keep me in business."

"Good for us both. How about another?"

"Coming right up."

WHILE JORDAN and the bartender continued to chat about nothing much, the bar got some new customers. A man in a Bruins hat sat down at the bar five seats to Jordan's left, right at the end. He kept to himself and had ordered a beer at some point, brought to him by one of the other bartenders. Jordan paid him no attention, even though he was close enough to hear her conversation with the bartender. When Jordan eventually left, she vaguely noticed the man get up at the same time, looking at his phone.

THE MAN in the Bruins hat followed Jordan into the parking lot, taking a picture of her car as she got in.

He came back inside and ordered another beer, specifically from the bartender Jordan had spoken to. "Well, she was something to look at. Who was she?"

"I don't know. She was just passing through town, stopped in for a drink."

"I heard her asking about that guy Eric who died recently. Was she an old girlfriend?"

"Nah. Just heard about him. She asked how he died, what he was like as a hockey player. Nothing much. I think she's heading back to the city."

"Too bad. I would have liked to take a pass at her."

He picked up his mobile phone and made a call. "You have a problem," he said.

JORDAN NEEDED to find the name of Eric Smith's employer. But pulling out her laptop in the bar would have drawn unnecessary suspicion. She headed to a Starbucks a couple of blocks down the road. She could get some caffeine while she worked.

Jordan had the place practically to herself. She turned on her laptop and opened Safari. Eric Smith's employer was a local drug company, probably not a big one, from what the bartender said. It had the word "gene" somewhere in its name, and it was close to Hanscom Air Force Base.

Searching for a company with "gene" in its name wasn't very helpful. Almost every company talked about genes, making the search results overwhelming. Instead, she searched for a list of all Massachusetts drug companies. It was a long list, but she figured she could go through it quickly. The list was alphabetical, and she went right to the names starting with G, hoping that "gene" was the first part of the company name.

There were four candidates, but only one was near the air force base. This company had two addresses, both in Massachusetts. One was in the Seaport District. Probably a headquarters building. The second address was for a site on Wiggins Avenue in Bedford, about a mile from Hanscom. The company name was GenPhage.

5

NEIL FOLEY WAS NEARING THE END OF HIS WORKOUT AT EXECUTIVE Sports in the Boston Seaport District. He started every workday here unless he was traveling. The studio was on the top floor of a twenty-story building. Two walls were entirely made of glass, providing a stunning view of the Atlantic Ocean. The view alone was worth the three-hundred-dollar monthly membership fee.

This morning, he was doing a high-intensity interval workout in a class of five. The last exercise was reverse lunges while holding a dumbbell straight in front of his body. Neil glanced in the mirror to his left. He focused on perfect form and a fast, steady pace, alternating legs lunging backward, keeping the weight perfectly positioned. Sweat streamed down his forehead and into his eyes. After the last lunge, he popped up and returned the dumbbell to the rack.

Another solid workout was in the books. In his opinion, he was the strongest of the group. He didn't say much during workouts, letting his fitness speak for him. He knew the others would talk about him, saying he was like a machine. That he was the oldest person in the class just made his fitness level more impressive.

"Thanks, Pam," he said to the instructor. "Another great

workout. You'll have to step it up next time. I've still got something left in the tank." Neil was actually serious, but Pam seemed to think he was just kidding around.

"Sure, Mr. Foley. I'll find a workout that breaks you. I promise."

"You're most welcome to try. See you tomorrow."

Neil showered and dressed in his typical business attire. For him, that meant a navy-blue Brooks Brothers suit, custom tailored to his lean frame. He could wear an off-the-rack suit, but he was too picky. Neil demanded a perfect fit. He typically accented his suit with a sharp color in his shirt or tie, or both. Today it was a bright-yellow shirt and a striped blue tie. The different shades complemented his blue eyes and red hair. His eyes and hair hinted at his Irish heritage, and he had unnaturally perfect teeth and skin. He always believed he could have been a model or actor had he been interested. For sure he knew he was better looking than that Damian Lewis guy.

Near the locker room exit was a bin for used towels. Neil tossed his clump of three towels at the bin but missed, the towels landing on the floor. He didn't hesitate or break stride. There was someone who worked at the gym whose job it was to pick them up.

The morning was crisp and cool, the sun hidden behind a thick layer of clouds and lingering fog. Neil slung his backpack over his right shoulder and headed to his office, just a few minutes' walk away. At 7:30, the sidewalks were just getting busy with people heading to work in the Seaport District. This was perhaps the nicest part of downtown Boston. It benefited from hundreds of millions of dollars of investment to entice companies to move their businesses here. Unlike much of the city, this area was free of the dirt and grunge one came to expect. Sidewalks and street cleaning happened regularly in the never-ending battle against decay.

The GenPhage headquarters occupied four floors of a just-completed building overlooking the Main Channel. This was a trendy location for biotech companies, despite the high real-estate cost. GenPhage was flush with cash, having achieved several successful rounds of financing in the last two years. They were close to completing the third and final phase of clinical trials for their lead treatment. They would then file for approval with the FDA in the United States and with health authorities around the globe.

At about the time they expected to have their first product approved, the company planned to go public, offering shares for purchase. This was common for small biotech shops that hadn't yet been acquired by one of the big pharma companies.

The major investors in the company would reap the biggest rewards from the initial public offering, but the senior executives at GenPhage would also make out well. Depending on exactly how much money the IPO raised, GenPhage C-suite executives like Neil could net up to $40 million. This would definitely meet the financial measure of success Neil set for himself.

Another measure of Neil's success was to become a CEO, possibly of GenPhage, but any good company would do. To become a biotech leader at one of the most exciting, young companies would make him the envy of the industry. It would also be a fantastic stepping stone for his longer-term ambitions, which went well beyond leading a company.

Neil knew GenPhage's treatment had the potential to be a game changer. With one of the greatest fears of modern medicine being bacterial resistance to antibiotics, the company's new antibiotic platform was poised to deal with most forms of antibiotic resistance. Though not yet the CEO, as chief operations officer, Neil oversaw all of the company's day-to-day activities. The actual CEO, Helmut Grainger, was a seasoned biotech leader the board of directors had brought in to guide the young company to its IPO. Grainger didn't focus on operational details at all. He was just a friendly leadership face, one that had earned the trust of the industry and investors during his nearly four decades in the field. He would not hang around long after GenPhage went public.

Neil entered his building through a revolving door. He normally needed his key card to gain access to the foyer where the elevators were. Before he got there, a security guard, who was watching specifically for Neil, triggered the gate to let him through. Neil didn't so much as say thanks to the man. It was the guard's job to let him in. Neil had important work to do, and the staff's job was to make sure he had as much time as possible to be productive.

He arrived at the GenPhage headquarters before much of the staff. Neil took in the wide-open welcome area and saw Carter Nash sitting on one of the high-backed leather chairs. He was sporting a dark-gray suit, a white shirt, and a navy-blue tie. He always wore this outfit whenever he visited the GenPhage headquarters. Neil imagined Carter having a huge walk-in closet in his home with seven identical outfits. His patent leather oxfords displayed a high shine, no doubt a result of habits picked up from his time in the army.

Carter was not officially part of the GenPhage corporate security team, but he was the head of a security team that reported directly to Neil. Officially, Carter was a security consultant. While he provided occasional guidance to the GenPhage security team, Carter directed his efforts to specific tasks assigned by Neil. Carter and his team of ten were all ex-military, each one having been a member of at least one specialized branch of the military. Carter himself was a former US Army Ranger. He based six of his team members in the Boston area. The others worked overseas to be able to reach GenPhage clinical trial sites quickly.

Neil knew he didn't have an appointment scheduled with Carter and that it wasn't like him to show up unexpectedly. Especially at headquarters.

"Good morning, Carter," Neil said. "I didn't realize we had an appointment."

"We don't," Carter said, standing up. "There have been two recent developments. We need to decide on a course of action for each of them."

Neil felt the leading edge of a wave of frustration. Carter wouldn't be here if it were something minor. They reserved one-on-one meetings in the headquarters for serious discussions. "Let's head upstairs. I'll grab a coffee, and then you can brief me. Go to my office, and I'll be there in a minute."

There were several conveniences in the executive suite, including a top-of-the-line Nespresso machine. Neil prepared a ristretto, the strongest available, and went into his office.

Neil's office was spacious, sparse, and efficient. His desk had a docking station for his MacBook Pro with two twenty-four-inch monitors attached. His keyboard and mouse were wireless, leaving just two cables for the monitors and one cable for power.

His walls had a small selection of art depicting architectural masterpieces.

This included a photo of Frank Lloyd Wright's Fallingwater, in Bear Run, Pennsylvania. The building was an exquisite piece of architectural design with clean lines and layers of stacked rectangular balconies. It projected an image of structure and strength. On the side of Neil's office opposite his desk sat a coffee table with a black leather sofa and two matching chairs.

Carter sat in one of the two chairs. Neil sat in the other, taking a sip of his coffee.

"So, tell me what's going on. You wouldn't be here if it weren't important."

Carter sat upright and began in his direct, army-officer style. "We have two issues. First, the Kisumu trial site is ahead of schedule."

"That doesn't sound like an issue. What's the problem?"

"The lead investigator at the site is getting skittish. He called in yesterday to say one of his staff was asking questions about a patient's death. The investigator said it was hard to deflect the questions. The staff doctor was suspicious."

"Well, one thing we pay him for is to deflect suspicion. And we pay him very well."

"Agreed. However, he's now asking for more. An additional monthly installment for each of the remaining four months."

"Are you shitting me? We're paying him as much in a month as he would otherwise make in a year. Did you approve the request?"

"Not yet. But I think we should."

"Why? Because he's nervous? He needs to do his job. As we agreed in advance."

"In principle, I agree. But there's a significant risk if we don't increase his payment. He and the other site leads could expose what's happening within the trials. That could damage GenPhage. Or worse. Plus, they'll get to keep what you've already paid them. You have much more to lose than they do."

"What's your recommendation?"

"Give him half of what he's asking for."

"You spoke to him. Do you think that'll be enough?"

"By itself? Maybe not. But a visit from my team will remind him of what he should really fear. The situation will stabilize."

"Is your team close by?"

"Yes. They're in Nairobi. I can have them in Kisumu tomorrow morning."

Neil pondered the situation for a moment. He was being blackmailed and couldn't really do anything to stop it. The trial was almost done, and Kisumu was a key test site. He couldn't afford for it to go off the rails now. "Fine. But I want that greedy bastard to know some real fear. He can't fuck with me like this and expect everything to be peaches and cream."

"We'll take care of it."

"You said there are two issues. What's the second?"

"Our second issue is new and possibly more serious. One of our contacts in Lexington called in to my site surveillance team. He said there was a woman asking questions about Eric Smith at a place called the Meeting House. That's a bar where Eric Smith spent a lot of time with his friends. The source didn't know her name or why she was asking. But he got her license plate number. I had the plate run. The car is registered to a Jordan Reed. She's a reporter with the *Boston Courant.*"

"That's fucking great. A reporter sticking her nose where it doesn't belong. Especially when we're so close."

"It doesn't appear she learned very much, at least not from the bartender. He wouldn't talk about how Eric died, only about how Eric was a star hockey player in college."

Neil stood up and paced around his office, continuing his questions. "Does she know there was a settlement with his family? Did she figure out where he worked? If she learned either of those, she'll dig deeper."

"I don't know yet. I may need to pay a visit to Mrs. Smith to ask her if she spoke with this reporter. If so, I'll remind her about the settlement we have in place and that it would disappear in an instant were she to speak about her husband's death."

"You talked to her when she signed the settlement. Do you think she's the type to drop the money and try to expose the company?"

"No," Carter replied. "She has two young children and is a substitute schoolteacher. The settlement sets up her family for life. While it may not be a lot of money to you, two million dollars over five years is a hell of a lot of cash for a middle-class family with a mortgage. Plus, she got the life insurance Eric had through GenPhage, another five hundred grand."

"All right. So, what's our next play with the reporter, this Jordan Reed?" Neil asked.

"I'm already taking steps to contain her. We've got it under control."

Neil crossed his arms, one of the few signs he was not satisfied with a situation. He knew he shouldn't worry. Carter would handle the situation efficiently. Carter had an exemplary military career that ended only because he occasionally used tactics that were too direct. Security was more a calling to him than a job. He was the type to take any security failure personally. Besides, Neil paid him extremely well and supported his team. In fact, Neil doubted that any security team at any other drug company was as well resourced as Carter's. His ex-military team had a full arsenal of electronic surveillance gear, and each member was trained and equipped with multiple weapons. GenPhage had clinical trials running in several dangerous countries, and Carter's team needed to be ready for anything that could go wrong.

Neil was finished with this discussion. "Thanks for the updates. Make sure you handle these situations effectively. This reporter can't be allowed to dig any deeper. Keep me informed of her activity, and brief me when you learn her backstory. I want to have at least one viable alternative to act on if she gets too close to the truth."

"Absolutely."

6

Jordan spent her Wednesday morning tying up loose ends on a project her editor had assigned her. This did a good job of keeping her mind occupied and not dwelling too much on the Eric Smith story. The amount of information she didn't know was frustrating, and she needed to either get some real traction on what this story was about or pack it in and move on.

As she left her office desk buried in stacks of papers and notes, she headed outside to grab something from one of the food trucks that showed up every day at lunchtime. The day was cloudy and damp, with a near continuous drizzle, reducing the number of people looking for food. Even the street traffic seemed less heavy than usual.

She passed on the fried-food options, settling for a hummus wrap from a Greek food truck. This was one of her favorite trucks. Its options were less unhealthy than the alternatives. She added a Mountain Dew to wash the food down and maybe give her a little jolt of energy. She sat on a bench to eat and revisited the Eric Smith story.

In her mind, she was working with the hypothesis that the settlement was with GenPhage. From what the bartender said, Eric had gotten sick and died within days. While a tragedy, it didn't sound like something that required a settlement. There had to be more to Eric Smith's death. And she needed to know exactly how he died.

Laurie Smith wouldn't be much help. She wouldn't risk jeopardizing whatever the settlement provided. Jordan didn't know where Eric Smith died or who the treating doctor was. Besides, Jordan couldn't expect the doctor involved to talk to a reporter, especially if it could violate patient confidentiality. But she could learn a lot if she had a copy of the death certificate.

In principle, Jordan knew it would be difficult to get a copy of, or even see, Eric Smith's death certificate. She wasn't an immediate family member or heir, nor did she have permission from one. But she might be able to talk her way into getting a copy at the Registry of Vital Records and Statistics. It would require some fast talk, but she could play a public health angle. If she was lucky, there'd be a man working the help desk that couldn't resist helping an attractive woman. She recalled the scene in *Erin Brockovich* where the guy managing a town's water records took one look at Julia Roberts's long legs and in-his-face breasts and let her have whatever files she wanted. At least for a while.

There was only one way to find out. She got in her car and headed for the Registry of Vital Records and Statistics in Dorchester. It would be much harder for them to say no to her face than it would be on the phone.

Traffic wasn't too bad at midday. It took about twenty-five minutes to get there. She parked in the large parking lot and got ready to go in. She applied some red lipstick, gave herself a light spray of a nice floral perfume, and plumped up her cleavage. She kept her leather jacket unzipped to make sure her T-shirt-clad figure was front and center. Then she went inside.

What she needed was on the main floor. She located where one could order birth and death certificates. There was one person at the desk.

Shit.

Not only was it not a man, but the woman looked like she was from the TV show *The Golden Girls*. Not the one who slept around. Most grandmothers wouldn't appreciate Jordan's current look. There wasn't much she could do except zip up her jacket and take her place in line.

When it was Jordan's turn, she walked up to the counter. "Hey there. I'm trying to find out how to get a copy of a death certificate." The nameplate on the counter read "Mildred."

That's exactly the name I would have guessed.

The woman adjusted her glasses and grabbed a form from a small filing cabinet beside her. "You need to fill out this form and provide identification. I assume that you're looking for a death certificate for a family member?"

"Actually, I'm looking for one for someone I don't know but who may have died as a result of something dangerous."

"That's going to be a problem," Mildred said. "You must be a family member or have their written permission. Death certificates are not subject to the Freedom of Information Act. If you really want this, you must get permission."

There probably weren't many ways to entice Mildred to bend the rules, but she had to try. Jordan did her best to look distraught. "I understand. I'm a reporter with the *Courant* and am doing a report on the rise of deadly communicable diseases. The individual about whom I'm inquiring may have died from one. The family of the man who died is going through a tough time, especially with two young children. I don't want to make their grief any worse by getting them involved in my investigation. Unless it's necessary."

Jordan hoped the embellishment might create just enough compassion to encourage Mildred to help. "Oh," said Mildred. "That would be terrible if there was something dangerous involved. Unfortunately, I still can't help. If the family learned that I shared the death certificate without their permission, I'd lose my job."

Jordan's first thought was that Mildred was old enough that she should let someone else have her job. Someone young who needed the work. She held back that response. "Fine. But there must be someone besides family who can access death records."

"Yes," Mildred said. "But not the press. State and federal government agencies can access death records if there is a public health reason. The CDC maintains a database of all deaths, and that gets updated each year. I believe it's called the National Death Index, or something like that. I think the CDC could get any death certificate they wanted. But I can't give you what you want without permission of the family. I'm sorry."

"OK, thanks anyway."

JORDAN HEADED BACK to her car, frustrated at how bureaucracy always managed to get in the way. But all wasn't lost. Jordan knew someone at the CDC. Charlie Choi. Even better, Jordan and Charlie were close and had even gone on a few dates. Nothing much had materialized from those dates from a romantic point of view, but she and Charlie had become good friends. He was a brilliant guy who just wanted to help people. He was really too nice for Jordan. When it came to relationships, being nice wasn't a benefit.

Charlie was a CDC epidemiology field officer in Burlington, Vermont. Jordan first met him during the last Ebola outbreak in Africa, when every news agency in the nation was trying to learn as much about Ebola as they could. The *Courant* had tasked Jordan with building an Ebola fact base they could reference. Jordan had reached out to a few individuals across the CDC and Massachusetts Department of Public Health, and Charlie was the most interested in helping. That was even before he saw how attractive Jordan was. Charlie's Good Samaritan nature and Jordan's great looks made his helping her a foregone conclusion.

Jordan was confident she could convince Charlie to help her get a copy of the death certificate. Her real dilemma was how much to tell him. Charlie was the type to want to jump right in and help. He would be the perfect Robin for any Batman. Jordan preferred to do things herself and wasn't good at teamwork. She could just ask for the favor and promise to tell him more later. Or never. Or she could just share the basics on the death she was investigating, leaving out the family, the settlement, and the employer. Just keep it medical.

The time was around 1:30. She could get to Burlington by five if she left now. She called Charlie from her car.

He answered right away. "Jordan," he said with a friendly warmth in his voice. "It's been a while. What's going on?"

It surprised Jordan to feel happy hearing Charlie's voice. It had been a couple of months since they'd last spoke. "Hey, Charlie. Yeah, it has been a while." Jordan felt sheepish. "It turns out I need to ask a favor for a story I'm working on. I want to run it by you in person and am driving up to Burlington now. How about I treat you to dinner and tell you how you can help?"

"Wow," Charlie said. "This must be important. Lucky for you, I have no plans. My dating calendar has been pretty empty since we had our last date."

Jordan knew this comment wasn't really a dig, just a reminder that Charlie would be open to trying again with Jordan. "Can you meet me at that Tex-Mex place we went to before on Main Street? I can be there by six."

Jordan breathed a sigh of relief. "Thanks a ton, Charlie. You're the best. See you soon."

She pulled out of the parking lot and headed to I-93 North.

IN HER HASTE TO get on the road, Jordan barely noticed a black Chevy Suburban parked at the edge of the lot, facing the building entrance. She also didn't pay attention to a tall, athletic man wearing sunglasses who sat in the waiting area of the Registry of Vital Records and Statistics office. Apart from being perfectly groomed, he was rather bland in appearance, wearing black jeans, a thick gray sweater, and a black jacket. One of those light puffy ones.

He left about ten seconds after Jordan and got into the passenger side of the Suburban. "It looks like she left empty-handed," the man said to the driver. "Let's see where she goes next."

JORDAN HAD BEEN at the restaurant for about forty-five minutes by the time Charlie arrived. He was slim, but not a lot taller than Jordan, maybe five ten. He was a first-generation American, his family coming to the US from South Korea in the early eighties. When he entered the restaurant, he stopped and looked around for Jordan. He spotted her at the booth she had grabbed at the far end of the diner and flashed a big smile. Charlie always walked as though he was in a hurry. Today was no different.

As he approached, Jordan stood up. "Thanks, Charlie, for making time on such short notice." Jordan gave him a quick hug.

"No problem at all. It's great to see you." Charlie's smile told Jordan it really was no problem for him. She could tell he still had feelings for her and would do just about anything she asked. They sat down opposite each other in the booth. Jordan already had a margarita and knew what she would order for dinner. She slid the menu over to Charlie.

Charlie didn't let the silence persist for more than a moment. "How have things been?"

"Kind of boring," Jordan said. "It's not easy to expose the bad guys, so I spend a lot of time banging my head against a wall. How about you? Any new outbreaks keeping you up at night?"

"Nothing big since Ebola. But those exotic diseases are unlikely to be a real threat here. I lose more sleep worrying about the flu, or more precisely, the flu we haven't seen yet. There's always a new one lurking out there, just waiting for its chance. Some chicken, pig, or bat is carrying the next big killer. It's only a matter of time."

Charlie was an infectious-disease epidemiologist, and to Jordan, he seemed to be an expert on pretty much anything medical. As a field epidemiologist, Charlie would go to sites of infectious outbreaks to figure out where they started and how they spread. Jordan knew he was young to have this job, which confirmed that Charlie was damn smart.

After they ordered, Charlie leaned back so he could stretch his legs. "So, what's so important that you had to race up here?"

Jordan needed specific help from Charlie. At the same time, she didn't want to create the impression that prolonged help was necessary. She had decided she'd share what she had pieced together about Eric's death but leave out the bits about the settlement. At least to start. Charlie's expertise was medical, so Jordan kept the focus there.

"I don't know a lot yet, but the story goes something like this. A man died unexpectedly after getting sick. People said it was like a bad cold or flu. He was young and healthy, he played hockey, but he went from sick to dead in a couple of days. No one who knew him is saying much of anything, and I got a tip that there might be more to this. Without knowing the specifics of how he died, I can't determine if there's a story here. It may be nothing, but it smells like there's something wrong. No one's cooperating, so I'm stuck."

Charlie made the leap for her. "So you need to see the death certificate. And since I work for the CDC, I can access the record. Ideally, you'd want me to give you a copy. This will provide the location and cause of death, the name of the physician who treated him, and the hospital. How am I doing?"

Jordan felt like a kid trying to trick her parents into letting her do something they wouldn't normally approve of. "Not bad," Jordan said. "I thought the CDC could access death records if they believed there was a public health risk. Given that this guy seemed to have died as a result of some kind of infection, or a cold or flu, I don't know, it couldn't hurt knowing the specifics. Just in case." That was her best pitch.

Please, please, please.

The waitress brought Charlie's beer and he

sat forward and took a nice long drink. "What you're asking is not exactly within the guidelines of what I can do. If one of the treating physicians reached out to the CDC, then I could definitely get involved. If the family was concerned we could get involved, since they could provide the death certificate and names of doctors, hospitals, and anyone else involved. But a reporter asking for this, with no actual proof or cause, is at best in the gray zone. My management would most likely say it's not within our guidelines. If I did this and your hunch was wrong, it would damage my credibility for sure. It might even cost me my job. As much as I'd like to help, I don't think I can give you the death certificate. I hope you know I would if I could."

Jordan felt like Charlie had punched her in the stomach. She knew this was a possibility, but she really thought Charlie would come through for her. "What if there is something dangerous out there, and this guy was the first one? Wouldn't you want to know for sure?"

"Of course I would. But there are guidelines for doctors and hospitals to follow when there are deaths where a potentially dangerous pathogen is involved. If a treating doctor didn't report such an event, that doctor is lazy, stupid, or covering it up. And if the doctor is at a hospital, not reporting a suspicious death would put the hospital at risk."

Something Charlie said struck home. No one was willing to talk about Eric Smith's death, and that, paired with the existence of a settlement, showed real potential for a cover-up of the cause of death. It wouldn't have to be some big cover-up. Just a cause of death not likely to raise any red flags.

"All right," Jordan said. "I get that you don't really have just cause to request the death certificate and that if there were really something suspicious here, someone should have reported it. But what about glossing over the cause of death, making it seem like it was something not dangerous? How hard would that be?"

Charlie paused to think about this. "Well," he began. "Let's say this person contracted some kind of virus or some virulent bacterial infection. He likely would have died because of some major organ failure or from excessive swelling in the brain, which happens with meningitis. A doctor or hospital could dumb down the cause of death and keep it as simple as, say, kidney failure. But I can't think of a good reason a doctor would do this. If it was something like meningitis, it would have to be reported so public health agencies could take action. There's no real reason for the family to not talk about it, so it seems unlikely that there's something sinister going on. Sorry."

"I guess that makes sense," Jordan said as the waitress brought their food. Jordan and Charlie both ordered another drink. As it stood right now, Charlie wouldn't help her. Jordan needed to give him a better reason. She had to tell him about the settlement.

"There's one more thing you should know. I wasn't planning on sharing this part because it needs verification. I talked to the wife of Eric Smith, the man who died. She said she couldn't talk about Eric's death because it would violate a settlement agreement."

"Really?" Charlie said. "That's peculiar if the rest of what you said is accurate. Death settlements are usually with a company or employer or with some branch of government, depending on how the person died. It could also be with the hospital if there was negligence. If he died just a few weeks ago, then I'd rule out hospitals and government as providers of the settlement. They're not able or willing to move that fast to pay people. If this Eric Smith got sick, rapidly deteriorated, and died, then the cause of the illness is likely the basis for the settlement. If it's something infectious, we may have something to investigate."

Jordan didn't like Charlie's use of "we" but couldn't push back, not since she could see Charlie coming around. "See," Jordan said. "You have to trust me. I wouldn't get you into any trouble."

"Maybe not on purpose," Charlie said with a smile.

"Good point. So, what do you think? Will you help me get a copy of the death certificate?"

"Possibly. If all your facts are correct, then there may be something worth looking at, especially from your point of view. But maybe not from a public health perspective. So here's what I'm willing to do. I'll get a copy of the death certificate on the grounds of an anonymous report that the individual died from an infectious disease of some sort. This is true, though technically you aren't anonymous. I'll review the death certificate and maybe talk to the treating physician. If the situation seems in any way suspicious, I'll let you have a copy. If everything looks perfectly appropriate, then I'll destroy my copy of the death certificate. Not even a peek for you. Deal?"

"Deal," Jordan said. "Now let's eat. I'm starving."

Jordan and Charlie enjoyed their dinner and got caught up on each other's lives. They didn't revisit the discussion on Eric Smith's death, other than Charlie telling Jordan it might take a couple of days to get back to her. Jordan figured that was fast, given that there must be layers of bureaucracy he would have to slice through. As Jordan and Charlie were getting ready to leave, Jordan reflected that the day had gone pretty well. What started out as a series of brick walls had given way to some actual progress.

———————

As CHARLIE and Jordan got into their respective cars and drove out of the parking lot, neither noticed a black Chevy Suburban parked near the entrance of the restaurant. Its side windows were impenetrably dark. Inside were two well-groomed men who were intently watching Jordan and Charlie as they left. The men noted Charlie's license plate. They'd know the identity of the Korean guy within the hour.

7

WITH GENPHAGE'S INVESTOR DAY COMING UP, NEIL'S WEEK WAS beyond hectic. Events like that required a lot of preparation and review, much of it useless. It was usually an exercise in death by PowerPoint. The worst part was that most of the work wasn't necessary. But the CEO and several other executives just couldn't make decisions. Not really. Though GenPhage was a private company, they did periodically share information publicly to ensure the marketplace knew key progress. The company fully intended to go public, and sharing information was good PR. Even if it was a carefully orchestrated performance meant to reveal as little as possible.

In parallel, the GenPhage executive team was also preparing briefings with their lead commercial investors. With phase III trials now well underway, the future of the company was riding on the trial's success. With their first treatment designed to target drug-resistant TB, most of the patients were in developing countries where TB was most common. All earlier trials supported the expectation that phase III would succeed. Getting approved for drug-resistant TB required a very high response rate, with minimal adverse side effects.

Conducting trials in African countries made control of

patient records much easier than in the US and Europe. Official patient data would appear appropriately safe.

GenPhage had several investors, but three were key. First was a global venture-capital firm that had a very broad investment base across many sectors of health care. OmniVentures was a diverse and stable firm that took pride in building a portfolio that offered the potential for strong short-term returns and long-term growth.

At the other end of the spectrum was the hedge fund Newman Brothers. The firm was heavily biotech focused and was the largest GenPhage investor. It stood to make hundreds of millions of dollars when GenPhage went public. It might generate a billion dollars in value in the first year, depending on how well the stock performed. Financially, no one had more at stake than Newman Brothers.

The third key investor didn't have a high financial stake in GenPhage. It also didn't have a publicly known stake. But its investment had been a critical one early on when seed money for biotech was scarce. When GenPhage first tested its antibiotic platform, the US Army became very interested and provided funds and some lab space to support several preclinical studies. These enabled optimization of the treatment platform. The army was interested in the potential to have a guaranteed antibiotic treatment when there was a high risk of soldiers contracting infections unresponsive to conventional antibiotics. Supporting GenPhage guaranteed certain rights to use the technology in the future. But the US Army investment had been virtually silent, hidden in a purposeful mess of Senate appropriations activities. It would be difficult for anyone to follow the money trail.

The army also had another application in its sights, one GenPhage had agreed to support. Their treatment platform delivered genes directly to bacterial cells to counter antibiotic resistance. One could also do the converse: deliver antibiotic resistance genes to nonresistant bacterial cells, rendering an infection untreatable. As a weapon, this could destabilize small localized populations, such as camps of combatant soldiers or terrorists or even towns and small cities. Neil didn't know the full extent of the army's intentions to develop and use this as a weapon platform, but GenPhage's role was to test the technology. The testing would bring Neil a sizeable bonus.

Neil was heading to meet Carter on the Harborwalk by Daily Catch Seaport around nine p.m. Carter usually waited by the seawall beside the US Federal Courthouse for the First District. Neil didn't like this location, but being in the shadow of the law offered some irony. The Harborwalk was a perfect location to have a conversation with little chance of being overheard.

Carter noticed Neil coming his way and waited as Neil came up beside him. "Long day?" Carter asked.

Neil took the chance to vent. "Yes. Aligning with those executive-team morons on how to message our progress and expectations for the next twelve months is tedious. We don't have to share anything with the public, so I see no reason to communicate more than some basics on our trials and FDA filing timeline. But some of these assholes who come from the so-called big pharma companies feel obligated to be more forthcoming than we need to be. Nothing positive can come from some fancy Investor Day, at least not until we're closer to approval. By then, we'll want to build excitement that will carry over into our IPO. Balancing what we share publicly with what we have to share with our key investors is tricky. Our important investors expect to know more than anyone else outside the company."

"My news won't put you in a better mood."

"That's what I expected. Spit it out," Neil said.

They walked briskly along the Harborwalk as Carter summed up what he'd learned in the past forty-eight hours. "My team has made progress regarding Jordan Reed and her activities. First, we know for a fact she spoke with Laurie Smith. Laurie guaranteed she said nothing about her husband's death and apparently told Reed she wouldn't talk about it. I pressed her on if she said 'wouldn't' or 'couldn't.' She thinks she said 'wouldn't.' If she said 'couldn't,' then Reed may have picked up on the difference. I don't think it was a coincidence Reed ended up at Laurie's husband's favorite bar the same night. She must have felt Laurie was hiding something."

"Did you remind her that the settlement was conditional on her keeping her mouth shut?"

"I did," Carter said. "Laurie assured me she didn't talk at all about the settlement. For now, we have no evidence to the contrary."

Neil processed this. "We assume Jordan Reed was suspicious and went to Eric Smith's favorite hangout. Laurie must have somehow revealed that fact. But we think no one there shared anything incriminating, at least according to your source."

"That's what we believe. Our source heard some of their conversation but heard nothing about Smith's death. Just him as a hockey player. The bartender didn't even know the name of Smith's employer."

"Ah," Neil said. "Reed must have tried to get this out of him somehow. She must suspect something was wrong in Smith's death, and we have to assume the worst—that she knows there's a settlement involved. To her, this looks like a story hiding in these bits of information. What else do we know?"

"My team followed her to the Registry of Vital Records and Statistics. We think she was trying to get Eric Smith's death certificate. It looked like she didn't get anything."

Neil nodded. "Some minor good news. Bureaucracy to the rescue. That's a fucking first."

"Maybe. But Reed didn't give up. She then made a beeline for Burlington, Vermont."

Neil stopped walking and turned to face Carter with a puzzled look. "Why Burlington? Something personal?"

"That's what I thought at first. She went directly to a local restaurant and was joined by a man we now know is Chung-Ho Choi. He goes by Charlie. Based on their reaction to seeing each other, they're at least friends. Our team thought it might have been an old flame."

"So he's nothing to worry about?"

"I'm afraid not. He's a CDC field epidemiologist."

"Jesus Christ. That could be a problem."

"You're right. Death certificates aren't covered under the Freedom of Information Act, which is why Reed wasn't able to get a copy. But the CDC can pretty much get any death certificate they want under the auspices of public health. Either Jordan Reed meeting with Charlie Choi was a coincidence, or she asked for his help."

"Perfect. Now we have to assume she could get her hands on the death certificate?"

"Yes. Not to mention that she now has an epidemiologist to help her. He'll be able to come up with scenarios for how Eric Smith died. If they connect this to the company and to the settlement for the Smith family, GenPhage could face serious regulatory and legal trouble."

Neil felt the need to add one more log to the fire. "Let's not forget that the treating doctor at the hospital where Smith died is a paid speaker for GenPhage. And an old college classmate of mine. He'll need to be able to handle pointed questions."

"He will."

"Fuck, fuck, fuck." In Neil's mind, it seemed unfair that everything he had built at GenPhage could unravel so easily. Aside from the fact that the company was doing things both illegal and unethical, Eric Smith was only exposed to a highly dangerous material because of a stupid accident. As part of the engineering staff, he'd responded first. But he wasn't responsible for that particular location of the facility. Neil had a special team assigned for any incidents that may have occurred there. And Eric Smith saw something he shouldn't have.

"Neil," Carter said. "Let's align on how to handle this. We need to anticipate Reed's next moves."

"You're right." Neil knew Carter was now refocusing him. "We have to assume she'll see Smith's death."

"Yes. That's not enough on its own to cause us any trouble. However, if she learns who Eric Smith's employer was and figures out what we do, which wouldn't be too difficult, she may conclude he got infected at work. If she knows there's a settlement with the Smith family, then the pieces start to fit together rather well."

Neil had already reached this conclusion. It seemed probable that Jordan Reed and Charlie Choi would uncover these facts. The real question Neil had to answer was what it meant for GenPhage. Neil motioned for Carter to sit down on a nearby bench. The evening was chilly, just above freezing, and Carter hesitated before sitting.

"Without some specific intervention, Reed will link Eric Smith's death to GenPhage." As Neil spoke, a plan began to take shape. "But all she would really have is a story on a company trying to cover up the accidental death of an employee. This wouldn't be a great story for GenPhage. But it wouldn't be something that would have a long-term impact. As long as the overseas events remained invisible to her."

"Are you saying to leave her alone and let this play out?" Carter asked.

"Absolutely not. We'll continue to maintain twenty-four-seven surveillance to ensure we're not surprised. She may piece together enough about Smith's death to publish a damaging story. But maybe we can pull the rug out from under her when she thinks she has everything she needs. What if there is no real cover-up, nothing illegal, by the time she gets her story together? Yes, Eric Smith died because of a workplace accident. But if we appear to have addressed the accident cause and compensated the family, the story will have no teeth. And if the story has no teeth, Jordan Reed will probably move on and never learn about what we're doing in Africa. That is what we have to prevent at all costs."

Carter nodded. "That's one approach."

"What do we know about Reed's day-to-day activities? Does she have any routine? Breakfast at the same place every morning or a regular evening hangout? Does she have any hobbies we know of?"

Carter handed Neil an envelope from his inside pocket. "Here's the initial report. We can go deeper, but this is a good start. Once you go through it, let me know where you want to dig in more. As for habits, the only thing somewhat regular in her schedule is swimming. Most mornings, she hits the pool at the local Y around six fifteen. She finishes in about an hour and goes back to her apartment."

"Thanks for this. I'll review it later."

8

_____

CHARLIE HAD CALLED JORDAN FRIDAY AFTERNOON. HE HAD ERIC Smith's death certificate and would share it with her. He didn't elaborate on the details but said he felt comfortable letting her read it. He would drive down to Boston Saturday morning, and they could go through it then. Jordan gave Charlie the address of her favorite local diner, and they agreed to meet at eleven.

Charlie was already there by the time Jordan arrived and was sipping a coffee. A second cup and a pot of coffee were on the table. "Hey," he said. "I arrived here early and got us some coffee."

"Thanks," Jordan said. "I could use one." She took off her jacket and sat down opposite Charlie.

"How was your week? Did you do any more research on the Eric Smith story?"

"I did some research on GenPhage, the company that I think Eric worked for. I had planned to do more, but Tom asked me to help run down some sources for another story. Besides, it makes sense to see what the death certificate says before we spend a ton of time on the story." Without intending to, Jordan said "we" instead of "I." She didn't mean to make her and Charlie a team

61

on this, but it had just come out that way. It felt wrong to shut Charlie out.

"I don't blame you. You could have spun your wheels all week and not really gotten anywhere. Pour yourself a cup of coffee, and we can talk death certificates."

While Jordan poured her coffee, the server came to take their orders. Without looking at the menu, Jordan ordered a turkey club. Charlie ordered the same.

Jordan leaned over the table toward Charlie. "Tell me what it says."

"OK. We have some basic facts of his death you weren't able to get from anyone you talked to." Charlie laid out a copy of Eric Smith's death certificate on the table so Jordan could follow along. He pointed at section 32 of the form. "Here's the important information. You can see that the immediate cause of death is listed as acute renal failure. His kidneys just stopped working."

Jordan took this in. "What does that mean? Did he have kidney disease or a bad kidney or some kind of infection? Could GenPhage have exposed him to some kind of toxic chemical?"

"Yes, to pretty much all of that. In theory. But if you look at the next line, it would rule out some toxic compound exposure. Here it states acute respiratory distress syndrome as the first underlying cause of death. This shows that the lungs were also in distress and leaking fluid. They were losing their ability to deliver oxygen to the bloodstream, which affects basically all organ systems, including the kidneys. Eric Smith was heading toward multiple organ failure."

"What would cause that? Eric was young and healthy."

"I'd expect someone in this condition to have an underlying infection, maybe pneumonia, a staph infection, something. I'm surprised not to see any infection-related cause or even mention of a trauma that could have triggered this series of complications."

"There's nothing like that mentioned?"

"Nothing. From my point of view, this death certificate is lacking. Either the doctor who completed it didn't know enough about Eric Smith's death, he was being lazy, or he was being purposefully vague and misleading. For a healthy person to die of multiple organ failure without a documented infection or trauma is practically impossible. And there was no autopsy done, so we have no blood or tissue samples we could test. To me, this isn't an acceptable death certificate."

Jordan processed what Charlie said. "If Eric died of multiple organ failure, what would you expect to be the cause?"

"For someone who is otherwise healthy and had no recent trauma or surgery? I'd go with septic shock as a strong possibility."

"But isn't that what someone gets after they go to the hospital?" Jordan had heard of examples of hospital-acquired infections, sepsis being one of them.

"It often is," Charlie said. "If a dangerous infection gets into the bloodstream, then a person can quickly become sick, often in days or hours. You told me the bartender said Eric Smith apparently went downhill fast? That would be expected if he had sepsis."

"It smells funny to me," Jordan said. "If I update my working hypothesis based on the death certificate, I'd state that Eric Smith died because of something that happened at work. His employer either felt responsible or negligent and made a settlement with the family. The settlement came quick and was probably large enough that Eric's wife never considered declining it. The more I think about the settlement, the more it feels like a cover-up. As you've said, governments wouldn't move so fast on a settlement. Especially if they knew they could be in trouble if whatever caused this death became known to the public."

"I don't disagree," said Charlie. "But I know little about how fast companies could get a settlement in place. Do you know what GenPhage does?"

"Not much. They're developing a kind of gene-delivery technology."

"Hmm," mumbled Charlie. "I wouldn't automatically link gene therapy with an infectious disease."

"I'm sure there's more to it," said Jordan. "This isn't my area of expertise. They're a private company, and I remember something I quickly read on a biotech website. I need to do some more research on them."

"Fair enough."

"What do you think about my hypothesis?"

Charlie thought for a moment. "It's plausible. It's also possible that the treating doctor, a Dr. Jonathan Hauptman, just did a poor job on the death certificate and didn't care. It's almost like the death certificate is vague on purpose. It's worded in such a manner so as not to arouse interest or suspicion. For a presumably healthy young person, this cause of death is unexpected. At least without an underlying trigger."

"So you don't think I'm nuts?" Jordan asked.

"Not at all. At least not about this." Charlie delivered the last part with a big smile. "You're the investigative reporter. What's next?"

As long as she had the kernel of a story, Jordan could always figure out at least one next step. This story was no different.

"First, I need to do a deep dive on GenPhage. I'd like some kind of confirmation that this was Eric Smith's employer. For now, I'll assume this is correct. I also need real ideas about what could have happened that led to his death and why the company would want to provide a settlement so fast. While I'm at it, I should confirm the settlement somehow."

"That all sounds like it's right in your wheelhouse," said Charlie. "Is there anything I can do to help?"

"There is. If you're suspicious about the death certificate, then I am as well. Are you able to talk to the certifying doctor about the cause of death? You might assess if the doctor was just lazy, incompetent, or part of a cover-up. We know the hospital where Eric died. Maybe you could talk to one of the nurses who treated him as well?"

"As an employee of the CDC, I may interview caregivers for patient cases where I'd like to know more details. That's an accepted role of the CDC and wouldn't draw undue attention. I need to make sure my management has a heads-up as to what I'm working on, so I'll give them a few details. Not a lot, just that someone flagged a death where the cause seemed unclear and warranted asking a few questions. Just in case there's a concern to public health agencies. To answer your question, yes, I can do this."

A wave of relief washed over Jordan. Charlie's help with the medical stuff was critical. She was way out of her league and would have gotten nowhere without him. "You're my savior."

"Don't get too excited. This still could be a lot of nothing. But I'll give it a shot. I'll call the doctor who provided the information for the death certificate Monday morning."

"Perfect. By then I should know more about the company."

———

JORDAN HAD DEDICATED MUCH of her Sunday to digging into GenPhage. What she needed was to confirm that Laurie Smith had received a settlement from them. Following the money was always the best way to get to the bottom of a crime or cover-up. But that would take some dedicated personal attention and would have to wait. She should be able to learn a lot without leaving her apartment.

She ate a light breakfast of Greek yogurt, blueberries, and strong coffee and dove into her research. Dressed in thick baggy track pants and a hoodie, Jordan sat on her sofa with her feet up, her laptop on her lap. Her budget didn't support much in the way of furniture and extras, but she made sure she had one good sofa and Wi-Fi with the maximum bandwidth available.

She began with the GenPhage home page. Within ten minutes, she'd learned two key things. First, she hadn't accurately characterized to Charlie what GenPhage did. She was right that they worked on gene delivery. But they targeted it at bacteria, not at humans.

The second thing she learned was more important. Not only did GenPhage target bacteria, but it also looked like the first product they were planning to take to market was a treatment for drug-resistant TB. She knew that was an infectious disease and that it was more common in poorer countries.

Did you get exposed to TB at work, Eric? Is that what made you sick?

GenPhage didn't disclose much about their technology or their clinical trials, but there was a good deal of company coverage. Industry experts expected the company to file for FDA approval of their first product by the middle of next year. That put them on the radar of investors and industry experts.

As she read through several stories written in the past year, she learned that people expected GenPhage to go public after their first product got approval. Many biotech companies went public before having a product because they couldn't afford the phase III trials. But if they had the cash to get a product to market, they could really cash in when they later went public.

Jordan followed the financial thread. GenPhage was a private company, and it was expensive to run clinical trials. Unless they had a large personal fortune from a company executive, they would need serious investor support to take a product through clinical trials. Thanks to her experience investigating fraud, Jordan knew how to find investors.

The key was venture-capital investment in GenPhage. Without much effort, she came upon a few sources that listed all the financing rounds for GenPhage. It was impressive. There looked to have been seven distinct rounds, each raising at least $10 million and some as much as $50 million. The report listed the lead investors for each round. These included firms called OmniVentures and Newman Brothers, among others. Jordan looked at each one. OmniVentures appeared to be very large and diverse, while Newman Brothers was smaller and focused on the biotech sector. There were a few smaller investors, but Jordan prioritized the big ones. If nothing panned out from those, she could come back to the smaller ones.

Every one of these investors, big and small, stood to make a large profit if GenPhage had a successful IPO. After more research, Jordan learned that some biotech companies raised hundreds of millions of dollars in their initial public offerings while selling only a fraction of the company shares. One company ended up with the total value of all shares worth nearly $3 billion after the first day on the stock market. She came upon one instance where a biotech founder made almost $500 million after selling his stake in the company.

That fact disgusted Jordan. She couldn't justify anyone getting that much money, especially for making a drug. No wonder drugs were so expensive. These drug companies made out like bandits.

Jordan shifted her focus to who controlled GenPhage. Their leaders were setting themselves up for a major payday. Fortunately, this information was easy to find. The CEO was a man named Helmut Grainger. Based on press releases, he'd been brought in recently after the original CEO passed away. Grainger had a long track record at drug companies, and most industry insiders thought the board of directors had selected him because of his success at taking companies public. In Jordan's mind, he was a serial profiteer for the drug industry.

I wonder how many people had to sell their homes to make him rich?

There were two other big dogs at GenPhage. One was the chief scientific officer, Robert Perlman. He had been at GenPhage since the beginning and likely had a sizable stake in the company. The second was Neil Foley, the chief operations officer. It looked like he had been at the company almost since the beginning. Something about him was familiar, but Jordan couldn't place it. She pushed that thought aside.

These three men would make a small fortune with a successful IPO. Anything that damaged the company or put them in jeopardy could rob them of their payday. This provided a motive to cover up a workplace death where the company had some culpability.

Jordan set her laptop down on the sofa. She liked to walk when she was problem-solving. She got up and paced around her small apartment. Her mind kept coming back to the possibility that Eric Smith had been exposed to something at GenPhage.

Jordan knew not to dismiss her instincts. They'd told her there was something here. Now, she was sure. She didn't know nearly enough yet, but GenPhage played a role in Eric Smith's death. She could expose their role and, in the process, prevent the company's leaders from profiting from their actions.

Jordan wondered what must drive people like the ones running GenPhage. Was it greed or bragging rights in the old boys' club? Was there an element of power and control at play? Probably all the above. But Jordan believed it was greed more than anything else. She had seen enough examples of money being the most powerful motivator. When one considered tens or hundreds of millions of dollars, what wouldn't someone do to get it?

Jordan almost forgot that seeing Neil Foley's name had triggered a memory. She still couldn't remember why but felt it was worth it to identify the connection. She went back to her sofa, grabbed her laptop, and did some digging on Neil Foley.

She easily found useful information using LinkedIn in combination with various business news outlets. Neil Foley was a Harvard grad, but not for just one degree. After his undergrad, he got his MD, followed by an MBA. So he was probably smart. He had specialized in oncology, and after several years of real-world practice as a clinical oncologist, he'd jumped into the investment banking world. The firm he'd joined was now familiar to Jordan. Newman Brothers. One of the largest GenPhage investors.

That can't be a coincidence.

Neil Foley eventually took his skill and expertise to the drug industry, moving to a small company called OncoTherapeutics, where he was the clinical program lead for a breast-cancer drug. That company name also seemed familiar. She made a note to check it out.

A little more digging uncovered that Newman Brothers had also been an investor in OncoTherapeutics. This reinforced her "not a coincidence" theory. Neil Foley's first investment bank job was as a leading investor in two companies with which he had important jobs. After OncoTherapeutics, there was a bit of a gap in Neil Foley's timeline before he resurfaced at GenPhage.

Jordan wanted to know how an oncologist went from an oncology drug company to a company that worked on infectious diseases. She found several news stories that talked about the stunning failure of a major phase III clinical trial for a breast-cancer drug.

Jordan's breath caught in her throat. Her heart felt like it would explode through her chest. Her throat tightened, and she felt a wave of shock pass through her.

This can't be the same company. There's no way.

Jordan's mother died not long before these stories were published. She had been in a breast-cancer clinical trial for an aggressive tumor type, and the experimental treatment had appeared to be working. But a side effect of the drug had caused excessive blot clotting, and her mother died from a massive stroke.

One news story stated the experimental drug was being developed by the company OncoTherapeutics. It came out that the company had known about the risk of blood clots but hadn't disclosed this to doctors or patients. The FDA halted the trial after the deaths of several patients. The company, already operating with a significant amount of debt, declared bankruptcy, so there was nothing left of the company for the victims' families to sue. There was talk the Southern District of New York would charge key executives, but charges were never laid. No one at the company had had to pay for what they'd done.

Reality started to sink in for Jordan. Neil Foley had been in charge of the OncoTherapeutics breast-cancer program that had killed her mother. He had worked at what was a major investor in the cancer company. Now he was the chief operations officer for GenPhage, also heavily funded by his former investment firm. From where Jordan sat, GenPhage was trying to cover up the death of an employee. The connections and patterns couldn't be coincidental.

Any doubt she may have had about GenPhage hiding something evaporated in an instant. Neil Foley was at the center of all this shit.

Jordan grabbed a bottle of gin, a glass, and sat down at her small kitchen table. She poured a drink and drank the first half. The alcohol burned her throat as it went down, the sensation having the desired effect of moving her thoughts away from what she'd just realized. The relief lasted only a few moments, her mind quickly returning to Neil Foley. As much as she wished she could, Jordan couldn't go back and change what had happened to her mother. But she could prevent Neil Foley from doing any more damage.

I'm coming after you, Neil Foley.

9

JORDAN HEADED TO DARCY'S PUB. SHE WAS TOO WIRED TO DO much else and wouldn't be able to give proper attention to anything until she calmed down.

Neil fucking Foley.

Jordan pondered how it could be that the same person who'd overseen the clinical trial that had killed her mother was also a leader in the company she was investigating for a cover-up. It was too much. Jordan had originally assumed that Laurie Smith had somehow sent her the obituary. But this coincidence made her reconsider. Her selection had been connected to Neil Foley and OncoTherapeutics' clinical trials.

She walked into Darcy's Pub. Her nerves were frazzled. She could almost feel the individual molecules of adrenaline tightening her blood vessels, priming her body for a fight. Her hands were shaking. She needed another drink. And she needed to tell someone what she'd learned. Someone she could trust.

There was only Travis.

It was pathetic that the only person in Jordan's life she could turn to was the man she'd dumped. She never thought she'd be someone that didn't have many friends. But it was true. Somehow along the way, she ended up alone. Except for Travis.

She grabbed a seat at the bar and took off her jacket. There was a good crowd, bigger than expected. Jordan saw that the Patriots were playing the Jets, providing the reason for the large crowd. Jordan needed that drink.

She made eye contact with Travis as he emerged from the kitchen. A look of concern grew on his face, clearly in response to Jordan's obvious distress.

He poured a gin and tonic and brought it over to her.

"Twice in one week," Travis said. "You really must not have a life."

"Piss off," Jordan said. "I'm not in the mood for any smart-ass remarks. One more, and I'm out of here."

"Wow. If this is the mood you're bringing, maybe you should take it somewhere else."

Jordan stood up and started to put her coat on.

"Wait," Travis said. "Sit down. I'm sure there's a reason for the acidic mood. Give me a few minutes, and then you can tell me all about it."

Jordan sat back down. "Fine."

It took Travis ten minutes to free himself. He had a fresh drink for Jordan, and she followed him to an empty booth away from the TV screens.

"You look like you've seen a ghost or something close to it," Travis said.

"You don't know how close you are to the truth."

"Does this have anything to do with that obituary someone left on your door?"

"Yep. It looks like that guy, Eric Smith, died of kidney failure. That's strange for a healthy middle-aged man. Plus, his family has already gotten a settlement from someone. I bet something happened to him at the biotech company where he worked."

"OK. So you think there's a cover-up. Any idea why someone would want to do that?"

"Not yet. But there's more to this. A lot more." Jordan locked her hands together to keep them from shaking. "When I dug into the leadership of this company, I found a guy named Neil Foley. He's some Harvard hotshot running the operations of the company. A few years ago, he was in charge of a breast-cancer clinical trial that failed." Jordan paused to see if Travis made the connection.

"OK," Travis said. "So what?"

"The trial failed because people in the trial died from blood-clot complications. The company went bankrupt." Jordan paused again.

Travis leaned forward on the table, tilting his head. He looked Jordan straight in the eyes. "Your mom." Travis was quiet for a moment, the tears in Jordan's eyes telling him he was correct. "She was in that clinical trial when she died. Are you saying that the guy in charge of that trial is involved in the cover-up of the death of this Eric Smith?"

"That's exactly what I'm saying."

"Shit. That seems like way too much of a coincidence. How sure are you?"

"If I got Eric Smith's employer correct, then a hundred percent."

"Damn."

"It can't be a coincidence, Travis," Jordan said. "Someone gave me that obituary on purpose. *Me*." Jordan's hands trembled.

"How could someone know this Neil Foley was tied to your mother's death? And that you'd figure out that the same guy is covering up the cause of a death at his company?"

"I totally have no clue. But there has to be a connection."

"I don't know. It seems like a hell of a stretch."

"Does it really matter what you think?"

"Calm down. I'm not the enemy here."

"It doesn't sound like you're on my side."

"I'm always on your side. I just question the likelihood of you being selected for this on purpose."

"Like I said, you don't have to believe it."

"OK. We can agree to disagree for now. We're good at that."

"Whatever."

"So, what now?"

"What I'd like to do is find this asshole Foley and confront him about the cover-up. Then tell him how I'll fuck him up for what he did to my mother and the family of Eric Smith."

"If you do that, his lawyers will be all over you. They'll shut you down."

"I can handle myself."

"Can you really? Remember that story you worked on where you figured out a city councilman was getting sex in exchange for government contracts? You made the mistake of confronting him before you confirmed your sources would go on the record. He threatened to destroy your career if you published anything that wasn't a hundred percent accurate. Your key source backed out, and you had to back down. I bet he kept right on doing the same thing. I don't want that to happen to you again. You're great at figuring out these stories, but you need to get them across the finish line to make a difference."

"That was one bad example."

"Yeah, but it would have been your best story had it made it to publication."

"Thanks for the vote of confidence."

"Sorry. But sometimes you get ahead of yourself and fuck things up. Go at this with a plan. What do you need to get the story out there?"

"I need to confirm some things. First, I need to know for sure there was a settlement paid from GenPhage to Laurie Smith. Second, I need to know more specifically how Eric Smith died. I have help with this one and hope to know more tomorrow. The last thing I need may not be possible. I need to get confirmation from inside the company that Eric Smith died because of his job. I need an insider."

"Good luck with that last one. Do you have any financial tools to uncover the settlement payment?"

"Not without knowing something about it. It could be a simple onetime payment, or it could be an annuity. They could have set it up as a trust. Without knowing something about its structure, it would take a lot of favors to figure out."

"So, what's your plan to confirm the settlement is from the company?"

"I think my best bet is Eric's wife, Laurie Smith. If she sees we have a common enemy in Neil Foley, she may open up enough to at least confirm that the settlement for Eric's death is from GenPhage. That would be enough to support the actual cover-up."

"Do you plan to tell her about your mother?"

"If I have to. We've both lost loved ones because of the actions of Neil Foley. If that doesn't work, I'll have to ask my editor to hire a forensic accountant. He'll never approve."

Travis realized something Jordan had said earlier and backtracked. "You mentioned you had information about Eric Smith's cause of death. Where's that coming from?"

Jordan had hoped to avoid this question. Travis didn't know about Charlie. Not that he had helped her do some Ebola research or that they went on a few dates. She wanted to keep it that way. "I know an epidemiologist, who got me a copy of the death certificate. He'll try to talk to the doctor who certified Eric Smith's death to see if he was hiding anything. He suspects that the doctor was incompetent, lazy, or maybe part of the cover-up. Either way, we need to know why a healthy, athletic guy's kidneys failed. His lungs, too, apparently."

"Can you get the story done without knowing exactly how Eric died?"

"Maybe. That requires an insider. If I can get confirmation that something happened to Eric at work and that GenPhage paid his family a settlement, then I have a cover-up. Knowing specifically how he died should answer the 'why' of the cover-up."

"How the hell are you going to get a company insider to help you?"

"I don't know yet. I don't know much about the drug industry, and I have no real connections I can leverage."

"Can you find any recently fired employees?"

"Maybe. If people are quick to update their employment status on LinkedIn, that might be an option. But most people don't update the fact that one job ended until they have another one, so I may not find someone who was let go in the past month. But I'll check."

"Is there a way to get into the company and interact with some people?"

"Funny you should mention that. I saw that they're having something called an 'Investor Day' on Friday. I think it's possible to get a pass to go to the headquarters for presentations. I could ask my editor to request access for me. That would let me talk to some people and see if there's someone who could be convinced to help."

"Feels like a long shot, but I don't have any better ideas," Travis said.

"I know. But I have some time before Investor Day to plan my approach. First, I need to find definitive proof that there was a settlement with GenPhage."

"Let me know how it goes."

THE GUYS from the Chevy Suburban were in Darcy's Pub. They sat at the end of the bar closest to the booth where Jordan and Travis were sitting. They couldn't hear everything they said with the sporadic cheering and swearing at the football game.

But they picked up on two things.

They caught that Jordan planned to confirm the settlement. They also heard mention of GenPhage's Investor Day. So although they didn't hear specific details, the fact they were talking about it was likely important info to share with Carter.

They followed Jordan long enough to confirm that she was going home and then phoned in their update. They would be stationed again in front of Jordan Reed's apartment before sunrise.

10

_____

Jordan's alarm went off at 5:30. She reluctantly slipped out from under her blankets and made her way to her dresser, where her alarm sat. She could hear the wind howling outside and saw rain pelting against the bedroom window. She did not feel like hitting the pool. When it was cold, rainy, and dark outside, the last thing she felt like doing was getting into a cold pool. She turned off the alarm and toyed with resetting it to 7:30 and getting back into bed. But in those few seconds, she woke up enough to remember she always felt better after a good workout. If she skipped it, she'd be grumpy all day. She headed to the kitchen to microwave some of yesterday's leftover coffee. It would help warm her up, and the caffeine would give her a much-needed jolt of energy.

On the pool deck was the usual 6:30 crowd. The first lane was for the fastest swimmers. Jordan was a strong swimmer and usually swam in the second lane. She could hang with most of the speed demons but didn't have the competitive drive to race this group. She usually had three others in her lane, two men and a woman. She loosened up and sat on the edge of the pool as she put her goggles on. Her typical warm-up was five hundred yards.

78

After a few laps, she noticed another woman waiting on deck to join her lane. Jordan didn't recognize her and assumed she was a newcomer. She looked like she could be close to Jordan's age, but it was hard to tell with the swim cap and goggles. The woman looked to be in excellent shape. She was tall, slim, and muscular with a nearly perfectly shaped body.

Great. A supermodel.

The woman sat on the edge of the pool, her legs in the water. It was polite to wait for a gap before joining the flow of swimmers. With several people in one lane, it was customary to swim counterclockwise within the lane, each swimmer managing their spacing. After Jordan finished four hundred yards, she took a moment to stretch, standing against the wall in the shallow end of her lane. She made sure not to interfere with the other swimmers.

The new girl was about to finish a lap. Jordan was impressed by her graceful swim stroke. It looked like her swimming ability matched her looks.

She's probably rich and dating Jared Leto.

When the new girl reached the wall, she stood up. She wasn't even breathing hard.

"Thanks for letting me join your lane," she said to Jordan with a big smile. "It's my first time at this pool, and I wasn't sure how crowded it would be. Looks like this is a busy time."

"Yep. There're a lot of early risers around here," Jordan said.

"Are you a regular?"

"I try to be." Jordan didn't like to chat when she should be swimming. She pulled her goggles back over her eyes and pushed off.

Jordan had planned to do a few sets of one-hundred-yard repeats, pairs of out-and-backs in the twenty-five-yard pool. She really didn't like all-out sprinting, but one hundred yards was a good distance to push hard. She did three sets of five. More than enough to get a good burn in her shoulders. Instead of the longer cooldown her body needed after the sprints, she opted for a quick one and hit the shower. She was eager to get her day going.

Jordan stood under the stream of hot water face-first, eyes closed, letting the water run from her forehead and face down her body. The water felt great on her muscles. She could have stood there for hours. She eventually turned the water off and grabbed her towel. She hadn't noticed before, but the new girl had come into the shower after her and had also just finished.

"How was your workout?" the new girl said.

"No complaints, I guess," Jordan said.

"Well, you looked good in the pool. Were you a competitive swimmer before?"

"In high school. Until I was a sophomore." Jordan still didn't feel much like chitchatting. She was mostly dry, so she headed to her locker.

The new girl stayed with her. "Why didn't you finish out high school swimming?"

Why won't she leave me alone?

Jordan wanted to say it was because of annoying and pushy people like her. She tried to be polite instead. "There was too much prima-donna bullshit on my swim team. I just wanted to swim, but no one would let me do my own thing. Everything was about the team and the star swimmers."

"I get it. High school girls can be real bitches, especially if they're great at something like swimming. I quit for the same reason."

Maybe she's not so bad.

As they were getting dressed, Jordan couldn't help notice how perfect the new girl's body was. Jordan was attractive, but the new girl was something else. She carefully glanced back and forth between the new girl's body and her own, doing a quick comparison. While Jordan's figure was trim and athletic, the new girl was in a different league. And despite her supermodel good looks, she wasn't as stuck up as Jordan originally thought.

"Are you going to be a regular here, or was it just for today?" Jordan asked.

"This location is convenient, and the group is large, which makes for better workouts. I'll try it for a while."

"I guess we'll be sharing a lane, then. I'll have to get faster to keep up with you, though."

"I don't think that'll be too hard. Your swimming style is really efficient."

"Thanks. But I bet you have speed to burn."

"I'm Emma, by the way."

"Jordan."

"Great to meet you. Will I see you tomorrow morning?"

"If I can drag my ass out of bed."

"Well, I prefer to swim with someone I know, so if you want to give me your number, I can text you around five forty-five to make sure you're up. It would be for me as much as you."

Jordan wondered if she should share her number with someone she'd just met. It wasn't like she had an army of friends. She decided it couldn't hurt. "I guess so."

"Great." Emma seemed pleased, like she was the one who needed a new friend. She typed Jordan's number into her phone. "I'll text you later so you'll have my number. See you tomorrow."

Somehow Emma had gotten dressed before Jordan and was out the door before Jordan had finished. She must have been in a hurry.

***

JORDAN HAD to swing by the office before trying to meet with Laurie. She needed to ask Tom to get her access to GenPhage's Investor Day. She wasn't sure how hard that would be, but she had to get into the event to find someone with a conscience who could help her. She also owed him an update on the story, especially since it was keeping her out of the office and incurring travel costs.

She got into the office at eight a.m. and went in search of her editor. Tom was an old-school news guy who had spent nearly thirty years in the business. He had started out in New York and at one point was an assistant editor at the *New York Times*. He once told Jordan that he didn't like living in New York City, but Jordan thought Tom realized he wasn't cut out for that hyper-competitive environment. He moved to Boston about twenty years ago and had been a cornerstone at the *Courant* ever since. But he never quite made it to the top.

Tom started his days early. Jordan found him in his office reviewing proofs for the next print run. His overweight frame more than filled his chair, which he had pulled in tight to his desk. His eyes were sharp and bright, a sign of the intelligence hidden in his large frame.

"Well, well, well," Tom said as Jordan knocked on his partially open door. "Are you really going to do some work this week? Or at least today? If not, let me know so I can stop paying you."

"You wouldn't be able to replace me if I left. You should know that by now."

"Like hell I couldn't. I could get two fresh kids to take your place and still save money. Plus, they might even give me some stories to run. As an editor, that's kind of important to me."

"You know I'm working on one now. And when it's finished, you won't be able to print it fast enough."

"Really? Don't bullshit a bullshitter, Jordan."

"Trust me."

Jordan gave him a quick summary of the Eric Smith story, pointing out the suspicious cause of death, the mention of a settlement by the widow, and that it looked like GenPhage was covering up the death. She left out any reference to her mother. Tom wouldn't like the personal connection.

"Interesting," Tom said. "You may actually have something. And on a drug company to boot. If this is all true and you can show it, then it'll be another PR disaster for that industry. Too bad GenPhage is a local success story."

"Tough shit. If I'm right, they'll have to pay for the crime. These drug executives are greedy bastards that make their fortunes on the backs and bodies of the sick and dying. I don't just want to embarrass them. I want to open the door for real charges."

"If that's your goal, you'll need to prove whatever they're trying to cover up."

"I know. This story will be a slam dunk if I get confirmation of a settlement from GenPhage paired with evidence the company is responsible for Eric Smith's death."

Time for the request.

"This is where I need your help."

"What do you need? Am I going to hate it?"

"I need inside information. I want to get into their Investor Day on Friday so I can try to find someone who can corroborate what happened to Eric Smith. I know it's a long shot, but everyone there can't be a criminal."

"So, you need me to pull some strings to get you in? Get you a guest pass?"

"That would be perfect. You can spin it that we've heard great things about the company and want to share what they're doing with our readership. Give them some fluffy bullshit."

"Well, you're in luck. I know their head of corporate communications, Erin Macdonald. She used to work in the governor's office a few years back, and we helped each other out. I may owe her a favor for this, but I don't think she'll object to granting a press pass so we can tell everyone how great their company is."

"Perfect. I'll assume I'm going and will plan to pick up the pass at their headquarters on Friday morning. If this all works out, I might even let you continue to be my editor."

"Smartass. Don't let the door hit you on the way out."

11

JORDAN NEEDED TO GET LAURIE TO CONFIRM THAT THE settlement was with GenPhage. She was betting Laurie wouldn't be able to say no in person. She had the address from Eric's death certificate and headed to her home in Chelmsford, roughly a thirty-minute drive away.

The drive was pretty much traffic-free since she was heading against the general flow of commuters. The bright sun was behind her, perfect for driving. As Jordan headed toward Laurie's neighborhood, she pondered whether to call first or just ring the doorbell. If she called, Laurie would likely decline to meet in person. Ringing the doorbell risked getting the door slammed in her face.

I came all the way up here. I may as well try face-to-face.

Jordan navigated through the residential area where Laurie lived, easily finding her house. It was a nice Cape Cod in a middle-class neighborhood of similarly sized homes. Jordan guessed this neighborhood was less than twenty years old. All the homes and properties were well maintained.

There were three cars in the Smith driveway. Laurie likely had family staying with her, maybe her parents.

As Jordan parked on the side of the street in front of Laurie's house, she pondered how to start the conversation. Best not to beat around the bush—be honest and direct. Most important was for Laurie not to slam the door in her face. Jordan walked up the steps and rang the doorbell.

After a moment, a woman too old to be Laurie opened the inner door. She gave Jordan a quick once-over. The woman was much shorter than Jordan, neatly dressed with wire-rimmed glasses. Her expression said she most definitely wasn't happy to see Jordan, as if she knew Jordan was a reporter or someone more likely to cause trouble than not.

The woman opened the screen door a few inches. "May I help you?" she said.

Jordan did her best to sound nonthreatening. "My name is Jordan Reed. I was hoping I could speak to Laurie for a few minutes."

The woman's facial expression said "not a chance." She responded with curt politeness. "Is she expecting you?"

"Uh no, she isn't. I spoke with her on the phone the other day. I only need five minutes of her time. Then I'll be on my way."

"What's this about?"

"I'd rather speak to Laurie."

"I'm sorry," the woman said. "But I don't think you really know her, and I don't want anyone causing trouble for her or the kids. Good-bye."

She shut the screen door and was closing the inside door when it paused. Jordan heard some words spoken between the old woman and someone else. Then the inner door opened again. A woman close to Jordan's age opened the screen door and came out onto the porch. She was maybe five-foot-five, had long, straight brown hair. She was maybe just a few pounds overweight. but it didn't take away from her girl-next-door beauty. She had deep-brown eyes and round cheeks. Her broad, thin mouth wasn't smiling. Her arms were crossed tightly in front of her body.

"I don't appreciate you coming to my home," Laurie said. "I thought I made myself clear when we spoke that I have nothing more to say. You should leave."

"I understand, and I'm really sorry to bother you. I don't mean to cause any harm or grief for your family. But I think something bad and potentially illegal happened to your husband, and if I'm right, the people responsible will get away with it. Unless I can prove what they did. You don't have to say anything if you don't want to. Just give me a few minutes. I'll do all the talking and tell you what I know."

Laurie gave it a moment's thought. "You can have five minutes. Max."

"Perfect. You mentioned you had to sign a confidentiality agreement and that there was a settlement involved. Given how soon the settlement came, I assumed it was from a company, probably your husband's employer. You at least indirectly pointed me to the bar where Eric and his hockey friends hung out. The bartender wouldn't talk about Eric's death, but I learned he was a great hockey player and an engineer. Apparently, he worked for a small drug company near the air force base. I could only find one likely candidate. A company named GenPhage. I also learned that Eric died from organ failure, both lungs and kidneys, which is strange for a healthy person unless he contracted a dangerous infection or experienced major trauma. There doesn't appear to be evidence of either. My current conclusion is that something happened to Eric at work and that GenPhage felt responsible. They gave you a settlement as compensation. Your obligation is not to disclose the details." Jordan paused for a moment. "What do you think?"

"I think you've spent too much time poking around," Laurie said. "I told you there was a settlement, and that was my mistake.

But I can't risk losing it. My family needs it for their future. Nothing can bring Eric back. I need to move on."

This conversation wasn't heading where Jordan needed it to go. Laurie had to know it meant something to Jordan besides just solving a puzzle. "Laurie," Jordan said. "Can I share one other piece of information? It might make you consider answering one or two questions."

"I don't see how it could make a difference, but go ahead. You haven't used your five minutes yet."

"A few years ago, my mother died. She was in a clinical trial for a breast-cancer drug, and the treatment was working. But the drug had side effects that hadn't been disclosed. She died from one of these side effects. The company that made the drug went bankrupt. The man in charge of the clinical trial was Neil Foley. He's now the chief operations officer at GenPhage. If I'm right that GenPhage was responsible for Eric's death, then Neil Foley took a loved one from us both. I don't want to jeopardize your future, but knowing GenPhage offered the settlement may help to expose the company. And Neil Foley."

Jordan held her breath. Laurie's eyes welled with tears, one drop rolling down her right cheek.

Laurie wiped the tear with the cuff of her sweatshirt.

"It was GenPhage." More tears flowed. "They never said exactly what happened, but Eric got sick one day, and two days later, he was dead. Three days after that, two people from GenPhage came to see me. One was a lawyer, and I don't know who the other guy was. He didn't really speak and looked stern the entire time. He didn't seem like a lawyer or businessman. Anyway, they said it was remotely possible Eric got sick from something at work. You know they do something with infectious diseases? Anyway, they wouldn't admit any fault, but they told me that they take care of their employees. I can't say any more. If they find out, we'll lose the money."

Bingo.

"Thank you, Laurie. That confirmation was really all I was hoping for. I understand how hard that was for you."

"It was harder than you think. But I'll never testify to this. I'll never admit to anyone that we spoke. You now know the truth about the settlement, but I won't do any more to help. They can't find out I told you this."

"If I do my job, you won't have to do anything else." Jordan still had two lingering questions. "Laurie, can I ask you two things, not about GenPhage and the settlement?"

"I suppose. I'm not sure I'll be able to help."

"We'll see. About the obituary for Eric that I mentioned the first time we talked. Is it true you really knew nothing about it?"

"Definitely not." Laurie paused and glanced around quickly. "I wasn't allowed to do one. Another part of the agreement with GenPhage was to not publish anything about Eric's death. Not even an obituary. They also made me remove what I could from social media."

"I can't believe they wouldn't let you publish an obituary for your husband. The social media bit is actually creepy. It makes no sense."

"I know. But they didn't give me a choice. We needed the money."

Jordan pulled out her phone and opened the picture of the obituary. "Is this Eric?" she said, passing Laurie the phone.

Laurie looked at the screen and read the obituary. More tears welled up in her eyes. "Oh my God. Is this for real? You saw it in a newspaper?"

"Yes. In the *Post*, right here in town. You really didn't know?"

"No. I didn't do it, and I don't really read the paper. I can't explain this at all. I hope GenPhage didn't see this."

"I'd be willing to bet that if they did, you'd already know. They don't seem like they wait around when something needs their attention."

"What does this mean to you?"

"Well, it tells me that there's someone out there who not only stuck it on my door but also wrote it and got it published. Using your phone number. Someone wanted me to investigate this. Somewhere along the way, I'll have to figure out who and why."

"What a mess. I'm sorry you got dragged into this. But please keep me out of it. I need to move on with my life."

"I won't bother you again. You have my word. Thanks for your time today. It was a huge help. Please call me if there is anything you think I can do for you. I mean it." Jordan reached out and gave Laurie a quick, tight hug.

"Thank you, Jordan."

As JORDAN LEFT, she drove past the same black Suburban that had been parked on her street in Boston. Now it was parked across the street from Laurie's house, behind Jordan's car.

Chris dialed a number on his phone as the driver pulled out and did a U-turn to follow Jordan Reed. "Carter, this is Chris. We're outside Laurie Smith's house. Jordan Reed just paid her a visit. They stayed on the steps and talked for a few minutes. We don't know what they said, but it was more time than needed for Laurie to tell her to go away."

"Thank you," Carter said. "Sounds like Mrs. Smith may have forgotten our agreement. I'll take care of it." Carter hung up and headed to his car. Something would have to be done.

12

JORDAN SCRATCHED TWO QUESTIONS OFF HER LIST. SHE NOW HAD confirmation that Eric Smith worked for GenPhage and that GenPhage had provided the settlement to his family. Now she needed to know what had happened at GenPhage to cause his death. It must have been the fault of the company for GenPhage to mobilize on a settlement so quickly.

I hope Charlie comes through.

Before heading back to Boston, Jordan wanted to talk to Charlie, but not while she was driving. She drove back to the Meeting House, as good a place as any to park herself.

The Meeting House had just opened for lunch as Jordan pulled in. She parked close to the entrance, noticing a black Suburban pass by. Jordan grabbed a booth by the windows. It felt just a bit too early for a gin and tonic, so she opted for a coffee. She wasn't sure if she would stay for lunch but kept the menu just in case. She was desperate to find out if Charlie had made any progress with the doctor who'd certified Eric Smith's death certificate. It could be hard to get time with any doctor on short notice. But Charlie worked for the CDC, likely speeding up access. Or it might slow it down, depending on the guilt of the doctor.

Jordan drummed her fingers on the table while she waited for her coffee. Once it arrived, she called Charlie. He may not have made any progress yet, but she needed to know. He picked up right away.

"Hi, Jordan," he said. "I see you're still as impatient as ever."

Jordan detected Charlie's ever-present joviality in his tone. "You know reporters are the most impatient people you'll ever meet. You're lucky I'm not sitting on your doorstep right now."

"I might like that," Charlie said. "I don't get a lot of visitors, so having you come by would break up the monotony."

Even though he was trying to be nonchalant, she knew Charlie was serious. If she thought she could really handle being in a grown-up relationship, she might try it. But when it came to relationships, she wasn't a grown-up.

"As we figure out more pieces of this story, we should meet up to put it all together," Jordan said.

"You're assuming I'll be able to help you answer some important questions. Quite a gamble, if you ask me."

"I have faith in you, Charlie. You wouldn't give up unless you felt that there was nothing to find."

"Yeah, you're probably right. So do you want to learn the meager information I've already uncovered?"

"You know I do, meager or not."

"OK. Let me say up front that I haven't figured if our Dr. Hauptman is covering up something or if he's just incompetent. I spoke to him this morning. There's nothing like a call from the CDC to get a doctor's attention."

"What did you learn? Did he seem nervous?"

"To your second question, it was hard to tell on the phone. He definitely hesitated to answer questions and struggled to find the words he wanted. But that could just be him. I told him that someone mentioned Eric Smith's death to the CDC and that I wanted to understand if there was a potential public health concern. He told me Eric Smith came into the hospital very sick.

He had a high fever and low blood pressure. He was exhibiting signs of septic shock. Dr. Hauptman said there had been no obvious triggering event. He put Eric on a series of IV antibiotics. He didn't respond and deteriorated rapidly. Ultimately, he had multiple organ failure."

"Hmm," Jordan said. "Did they do any tests to identify the infection?"

"No, and I challenged him on this. He said they ordered cultures, but Eric's condition went downhill so fast they didn't come back before he died. He canceled the tests before they completed the report. Convenient if one is covering something up, but also plausible. The IV antibiotics used were standard procedure for someone in Eric's condition when an infection could be at play."

"So, no obvious triggering event? Then why the settlement?"

"My thought exactly. There was no obvious reason for a settlement. Especially since there were no records for Eric Smith having had another medical event."

"How do you know?" asked Jordan.

"I requested copies of Eric's medical records for the last three months. There was no record of treatment for anything."

"What does that mean?"

"Two possibilities. Either he never had a problem or had one but didn't seek treatment. Or they treated him for something onsite at GenPhage and we don't have the record. I wouldn't expect a company to include workplace-injury records in someone's general medical records, so we could have a blind spot there."

"Something happened at GenPhage. They must have medical support available, since this was a manufacturing site."

"Right. And for the record, since I've seen his medical records, I can confirm GenPhage is his employer. You can move that from the assumption column to the fact column."

"Thanks, Charlie. It looks like we confirmed that fact at the same time. I met with Laurie Smith this morning. After I shared what I knew, she opened up and confirmed that Eric worked for GenPhage and that they provided the settlement."

"Wow. I didn't think you'd convince her to break the confidentiality agreement. You must have the Midas touch."

Charlie didn't yet know about the connection between her mother's death and Neil Foley, and Jordan didn't want to get into it over the phone. Not right now. It was an emotional topic for her, and she didn't feel like crying right now. "Well, she may have confirmed it with me, but she'll never publicly confirm it. I know the truth but can only use her as an anonymous source. It may weaken the story."

"Still, that's great progress. Sorry I couldn't sniff out a smoking gun. Dr. Hauptman's description and explanation are minimally plausible. I have a list of the staff that worked Eric Smith's case, and I could interview them at some point if you think it could help."

"You've been a big help, Charlie, don't sweat it." Jordan's mind was working through what Charlie had just said, and something came to her. "Could we find out if this Dr. Hauptman has any connection to GenPhage or Neil Foley? He doesn't immediately seem to be playing a role in covering something up, but if there's a connection, we may have to push harder."

Charlie thought for a moment. "Well, there's the basic stuff you could do, looking for educational or professional overlaps. Maybe Dr. Hauptman worked with Neil Foley or others at GenPhage. That's one thread to follow. We can also look to see if there's a specific financial tie between Dr. Hauptman and GenPhage. As it's a private company, we won't be able to see if Dr. Hauptman is an investor. But if he's done any work for the company as a hired medical contractor, GenPhage must report it as part of the Sunshine Act. Basically, every dime a drug company pays or gives a doctor is tracked and reported. This includes everything from giving them a pen to paying them to speak on the company's behalf."

Jordan digested this. "That's an option if we need it. It won't immediately help to figure out exactly what happened to Eric Smith, but if we show a connection between Dr. Hauptman and GenPhage or Neil Foley, we might be able to exploit it."

"That's definitely an option. I wish I had more."

"This is great, Charlie, really. I wouldn't have gotten this far without you."

"Glad to help. Just say the word if there's anything else I can do."

"You know I will."

"So, what's next?" Charlie asked.

"I need to regroup and lay out the story. See if it holds together. Identify the gaps."

Jordan had a four-by-eight-foot whiteboard in her apartment where she laid out every story she worked on. She kept an archive of photos of the board so she'd always have a record of her research portfolio. Eric Smith was next up for her big board. "Then I'm hoping to get into GenPhage's Investor Day on Friday. I need to find someone on the inside who will help."

"Do you think you have much of a chance, especially since you'll only get to meet a few people?"

"I know it's a long shot. I'll do some prep in advance to identify potential targets, people senior enough to be part of Investor Day and who may also know what's happening at the manufacturing site. I'll let you know how I make out."

"You better. As an FYI, I'm heading down to New York tomorrow to attend the International Conference on Emerging Infectious Diseases. It's a great forum to hear from on-the-ground experts from around the world about what diseases they're witnessing and how they're dealing with them. It won't help your story, but I hope it'll make me smarter."

"Jesus, you're smart enough already. Any smarter and I won't be able to take it. I'll talk to you after I crash GenPhage's Investor Day. Later."

"Bye, Jordan."

Jordan decided against lunch. She wanted get this story up on her board. There was also some research she needed to do on Dr. Hauptman, not to mention trolling LinkedIn for potential GenPhage employees she should meet. She left three bucks on the table, went to her car, and headed home.

13

NEIL HEADED TO THE HARBORWALK TO MEET WITH CARTER. THE location meant the update would be significant and require some decisions. As he reached the Seaport District, he could see Carter about fifty yards away, heading to the same destination. The sun was setting, and the western horizon was bright pink and purple against a darkening sky. Photo worthy, if he cared about such things.

Carter was carrying a small black duffel bag in his right hand. That gave Neil some sense of a pending decision.

"I'm glad you could make time to meet. There have been some developments," said Carter.

"Let me guess. Our favorite reporter, Jordan Reed, hasn't given up and will become a bigger pain in my ass."

"That's a fair statement. This morning, she paid a visit to Laurie Smith at her home. We don't know what they said, but their discussion was several minutes long. Laurie is extremely familiar with the specifics of her confidentiality agreement, but my gut tells me she told Reed something she shouldn't have."

Neil could feel his frustrating building. "How dare that bitch? If she spilled anything, I'll yank that settlement back so fast she'll forget she even had it. You know, I tried to show some consideration for Eric's family, despite the fuckup that led to his death. If he'd done his fucking job—which, in that case, was nothing—we'd be fine."

"You'd be perfectly within your rights to do that. But if you do, Laurie's confidentiality terms disappear, and this story will be all over the news. You'll be royally fucked. I'll pay her a visit and apply pressure. She'll tell me what she told Reed. I'll make sure she reveals nothing else."

"Do you think you'll be able to convince her to shut the hell up?" Neil said.

"Absolutely. Everyone has a weakness, a pressure point, that if accessed will force them to agree to almost anything. I also think we can have her promise that if Jordan Reed offers any story that directly or indirectly cites Laurie Smith as a source, she'll renounce it. This will give you a way to neutralize any story Reed tries to publish about Smith's death."

"Good idea. The more difficult we make it for Reed to develop a credible story, the better."

"Right. There's a second development that may require your intervention. We overheard a call between Reed and Charlie Choi. Based on hearing some of Reed's side of the call, we believe Charlie talked to Dr. Hauptman. Whether he suspects Smith's death wasn't an accident, or he was just probing, is hard to say. But Hauptman is potentially a weak link. The cause of death he endorsed didn't raise any red flags at the hospital, but if Charlie keeps digging, he may cave in."

"That would be disappointing. He only made it through medical school because of me. He owes me his career. I need him to follow through on the one thing I've asked for in return."

"How strong is he? Do you think he'll hold up under pressure?"

"He said he'd keep this confidential. He knows I have pull at the hospital and could suggest he be removed. After all, I was the one who recommended him in the first place."

"I don't doubt you. But an intervention is needed."

"What kind of intervention?"

"If you think money is a motivator for him, that's the easiest. We could take a more extreme approach, if you prefer."

Neil looked at Carter. It was clear he considered eliminating Hauptman no different than paying him off. To him, each was just an option with an associated action to take.

"We don't need to go that far. He can be convinced to stick to our agreement with a cash incentive."

"I'm sure you're right. If you think money is sufficient, the solution is simple. But if he feels like he's in jeopardy, he may try to strike some kind of deal to save himself."

"I'll pay him a visit. I assume that duffel bag has what we need?"

Carter passed Neil the bag. "Yes. I expected you'd need this. There's a hundred grand here. That should be enough to get Hauptman to keep his mouth shut until we deal with Reed."

"This is getting more and more expensive. We need to shut it down. Before Jordan Reed learns that Eric Smith is just the tip of the iceberg."

"We will. I'll pay Laurie a visit tomorrow. Good luck with Hauptman."

"I don't need luck."

LATE THE NEXT MORNING, Carter headed for Laurie Smith's neighborhood. He needed to have a very direct conversation with her, and she needed to understand there would be repercussions if she ignored her agreement. As Carter approached her house, he noticed three cars in the driveway. He parked on the side of the street, four houses down, facing the Smith house.

Carter knew Laurie's mother was staying at the house and didn't want her to be part of the conversation. No reason for

Laurie to have any support to make her feel more confident than she should. He needed to isolate Laurie from her mother. He thought of a few elaborate ruses to get the mother or Laurie out of the house, but he wasn't feeling very creative. The most efficient approach was to simply go to her door and ask to speak with her in private for a few minutes.

Carter stepped from his car, went to the front door, and rang the doorbell. Fortunately, Laurie answered. Partway through opening the door, Laurie's face betrayed her recognition of Carter. Logical, since Carter had been present when the GenPhage lawyer walked her through the settlement and confidentiality agreement.

She looked tired and was dressed for a day inside with young children. Sweatpants, baggy sweatshirt, and hair in a ponytail. "May I help you?" she said as she opened the door.

"Mrs. Smith," Carter began. "My name is Carter Nash. I was present when you met with a GenPhage lawyer regarding the settlement for your husband's death. I was hoping to speak to you for a few minutes about a matter that has come up."

Laurie's eyes opened just a bit too wide. She must have known why Carter was on her doorstep. She looked behind her before speaking. "I suppose that would be all right. Would you like to come in?"

"I think you'd prefer a private conversation. If your mother is still here, perhaps you could come outside, where we can speak alone."

"Um, yes, my mother is here. I won't ask how you know that. Let me grab my jacket." Laurie went inside. Carter heard her talking to someone, presumably her mother. He couldn't make out much but heard Laurie say: "Just stay out of it, Mom."

Laurie returned and came outside to stand with Carter on the top step. "Let's take a short walk down the street," Carter said. "It will be warmer if we keep moving."

Carter let Laurie go down the stairs first and followed behind.

"Mrs. Smith, I have two questions for you. First, do you fully understand the terms of the confidentiality agreement you signed with GenPhage?"

Carter watched Laurie closely for her reaction. She continued to look straight ahead, her face tilted slightly down toward the ground. She spoke with an edge in her voice. "Yes, I understand completely. The terms are very clear."

"Good." Carter made sure he could see most of her face as he continued. "Second, did you break any terms of that agreement when you spoke with Jordan Reed yesterday?"

Carter heard a sharp intake of breath from Laurie. Her stride broke the tiniest amount, just enough to be noticeable. He expected her to try and buy time for her brain to think of a way out. "Who's Jordan Reed?" she said. Her voice rose in pitch and cracked just slightly.

"Don't be stupid, Laurie. You know perfectly well who she is."

Laurie hesitated before answering. It didn't take long.

"All right, fine. I know she's a nosy reporter who's been hounding me about Eric's death. She won't take no for an answer. But I haven't told her anything about Eric's death. Honest."

Carter noticed she was a reasonably good liar. But anyone who felt the need to say "honest" was most likely not being honest. "What specifically did she want to know?"

"She wanted to know how he died. Even I don't really know exactly what happened, just that he got sick. She also asked who he worked for, but I told her I didn't want to talk about his death at all."

"You realize that if I think you're lying, GenPhage will revoke the settlement. We'll also nullify Eric's company-sponsored life insurance. We'll prove that his own negligence led to his death and that the insurance policy is therefore void. In fact, GenPhage may have grounds to sue his estate for damages." Carter knew most of this wasn't true. Laurie Smith had never engaged a lawyer, so he expected her to believe what he was saying.

Laurie's lower lip quivered. "Please, I'm not trying to cause trouble. I'm trying to do what's best for my kids."

"They'll be fine, as long as you hold up your end of the agreement. Can GenPhage count on you to maintain confidentiality?"

"Yes. Absolutely."

"Very good, Laurie."

They turned around and headed back toward the Smith house.

"Laurie, you mentioned how important the settlement is to your children's future."

"Yes. Without Eric's income, it'll make all the difference. We're not exactly set for life, but I'll be able to pay for our home and set money aside for education."

"Children are the most important people in the lives of parents," Carter said as he pulled a small object from a pocket.

The object was a glass ampule about two inches long. It was completely sealed and contained a gelatinous liquid that was bluish purple in color. It seemed to change color continuously, depending on the angle of light hitting it. He held it up between his thumb and forefinger, allowing Laurie to see it. "Do you know what this is?"

Laurie examined the glass ampule, a look of confusion on her face. "Uh, no."

"It's a breakthrough gene therapy that can change the genetic profile of infectious bacteria. It was designed to defeat drug-resistant genes, allowing antibiotics to kill bacteria. But it can also work in reverse. It can make bacteria become drug resistant, killing the host. It's an amazing technology."

Laurie's face bore the look of fear people experience maybe only a few times in their lives. "Why do you have that here?"

"I like to have a reminder of what I'm working for. Plus, I feel that carrying something that might kill me, were I to break the glass, keeps me on my toes. I know what's important to you. Make sure you continue to do the right thing. There's no need for anyone else in your family to get sick."

Carter observed the horror in Laurie Smith's eyes. The color had drained from her face. She was as pale as a ghost. Mission accomplished.

"I won't talk to anyone," she said. "I promise. Now please leave, and take that with you."

"Thank you, Laurie. Go hug your kids." Carter waited until Laurie went inside and then returned to his car, satisfied with the visit.

NEIL HAD CALLED the hospital to find when Dr. Hauptman would be on the floor and learned he wouldn't be there in the morning but would start a shift at two p.m. That would work fine. Time enough to eat something before intercepting Jonathan before the start of his shift.

After grabbing some barely acceptable hospital cafeteria food, Neil returned through the entrance of the emergency room and went outside. Jonathan would most likely enter through the main doors of the ER, so Neil grabbed a seat on a bench off to the left, about twenty yards away. He had a good view and would easily be able to see Jonathan approach. It was 1:15, and Neil figured Jonathan should arrive in the next fifteen minutes for his two p.m. shift.

Neil's relationship with Jonathan had been up and down since they graduated. While they had both excelled early in medical school, Jonathan's ability to keep up and perform well faltered, while Neil performed better the heavier the workload. Jonathan had barely passed and struggled to get a desired hospital. Neil used his connections to get him an internship at Mass General, which eventually turned into a full-time position. Until recently, they hadn't spoken in years.

When Neil knew Eric Smith would end up in a hospital, Neil called in a favor, asking Jonathan to help. After all, he owed his job to Neil. He had been reluctant, but Neil made it worth his while with a small but potentially lucrative number of GenPhage shares. A good IPO would net Jonathan perhaps $300,000. Now Neil had to make sure Jonathan stayed on script.

Neil saw Jonathan approaching the entrance. He was at the opposite side of the roadway that led to the ER. Neil got up and crossed over. As he got to within forty feet of the ER, Jonathan noticed Neil and stopped in his tracks. "Neil," he said. "I wasn't expecting to see you."

"Nor was I expecting to be here myself. But something came up, and I wanted to discuss it with you privately."

"It'll have to be quick. My shift starts in thirty minutes."

"I know. It won't take long. Let's go to that bench across from the entrance for a few minutes," Neil said.

"Sure."

Once they sat down, Neil proceeded. "I want to ask you about a discussion you had with Charlie Choi from the CDC. I believe he was asking about Eric Smith and how he died?"

"What the hell, Neil? How could you possibly know that? Are you following me? Is my phone tapped?" Jonathan showed signs of panic.

"Nothing so sinister. We know of someone with whom Charlie is sharing information, and I learned of the call from them. Regardless, I find it troubling that the CDC is poking around. I hope you didn't somehow tip them off. That would not bode well for you."

"Absolutely not," Jonathan replied strongly. "He called me

out of the blue, saying someone told him Eric Smith's death may be relevant for public health reasons. I assured him that the cause of death was multiple organ failure and that we had no evidence of any specific pathogen being involved."

"Did he know something specific, or was he just fishing?"

"Just a fishing trip. He didn't know much at all."

"Do you think you satisfied his curiosity?"

"He didn't say he'd need any additional follow-up and requested no additional records. It looks like I satisfied him."

"What if he contacts you again?"

"What do you mean?"

"Well, if he tries again, or perhaps learns something else that makes him think you're hiding something, how strong is the death certificate? Will it stand up?"

"Of course it will. Look, it's unusual for someone as young as Eric Smith to have multiple organ failure, but it happens. It doesn't necessarily require any additional workup unless requested by the family or law enforcement. Which is the situation we have here."

"All right, Jonathan. As this interaction with Charlie Choi from the CDC wasn't part of our original agreement, I have some additional compensation. When you get up for your shift, take the duffel bag by my feet with you. Put it in your locker. When your shift finishes, take it home with you and then open it. I'm sure you'll find the contents acceptable."

Jonathan glanced down at the duffel bag and then back up to Neil. "This isn't necessary. Really. I don't need more compensation."

"Don't be stupid. You've earned it. Buy a new Porsche."

"You're not asking for anything else?"

"No. Just to honor our agreement. But do let me know if anyone else comes calling about Eric Smith."

Jonathan stood up and grabbed the duffel bag. "I will." He turned and went into the hospital.

14

Jordan's alarm gave her the bad news. It was 5:30.

Ugh.

She repeated her daily ritual of considering crawling back into bed but again fought it off. She convinced her half-asleep body to go to the kitchen for some coffee. A text from Emma arrived just before she headed out the door.

"Hope you got up and are on your way...see you soon."

Jordan gave a minimal response.

"On my way," Jordan texted back.

Emma was already at the pool when Jordan arrived. She was just stepping into her black one-piece suit as Jordan came up beside her in the locker room. "Good morning," Emma said.

"Hey there."

"I guess you didn't need my text to get you going."

"I guess not. I managed to get my ass out of bed on the first try. Maybe because I knew you were expecting me."

"Nothing like a workout buddy to make you show up. Guilt's a powerful motivator."

Jordan slipped on her royal-blue swimsuit, and they both headed out to the pool deck. The scent of chlorine seemed particularly strong. A few others were already on deck, but no lifeguard yet. She usually showed up right on time. Not a second before. Teenagers.

"So, what are you doing after the swim?" Emma asked.

"I have work to do from home, so I was just going to get back and dig in."

"Do you have time to grab breakfast or a coffee? My treat."

Jordan thought about what she needed to get done to prep for Investor Day. There was no way she could prepare perfectly. Besides, she needed to eat. Especially if someone else was paying. "Sure," she said. "Why not?"

"Great. I saw a nice little bakery close to here. I can take us there and drop you back here or at your place."

"My place will be fine."

The lifeguard arrived on deck, and everyone piled into the pool. Jordan did her workout pretty much without interruption. When she finished, she signaled to Emma that she was getting out. A minute later, Emma finished her lap and got out. They hit the showers and changed back into their regular clothes. Jordan wore her usual Nike sweats from Kohl's, while Emma had on the latest from Lululemon. She looked as though she'd walked right out of their catalog.

"I parked my car on the street around the corner," Emma said. "Let's go." They left the building and turned right, walking into the morning's first rays of sunlight.

They turned right at the first intersection. About halfway up the street, Jordan saw the lights flash on a car up ahead. As they approached the car, she saw that it was a red Audi S4. It looked practically new. "Nice car," Jordan said.

"Thanks," said Emma. "It was my dad's, but he gave it to me when he realized he really liked a larger car. He got a big old Lincoln instead."

They climbed into the car. Emma pushed the ignition button, and the engine roared to life.

This thing must really move.

They pulled into the parking lot of a place called Mama's Bakery and headed inside. They obeyed the sign that said "Please seat yourself," grabbing a table in the back. The smell of fresh-baked bread permeated the place, making Jordan's mouth water. She had hunger pains, not helped by just having burned several hundred calories in the pool.

A woman in her forties came over. Her name tag said "Carrie."

"Fresh coffee, ladies?" she asked.

"Yes for me," Jordan said.

"Me too," said Emma. "Do you have any skim milk?"

"Yes," Carrie replied. "Let me grab some." She poured two cups of coffee and grabbed a small carafe of skim milk for Emma. "I'll be back in a few minutes to take your orders. The menus are beside the condiments."

It pleased Jordan to see eggs Benedict on the menu. She felt she'd earned it after her hard workout. "What are you getting?" she asked Emma.

"Egg-white omelet with peppers and mushrooms. You?"

"Eggs Benedict. It's my usual eat-out breakfast, especially after a swim."

Carrie returned, took their orders, and topped up their coffee.

"So," Emma began. "What do you do for fun?"

"Not much. I let work take up a lot of my time and then spend the rest of my free time watching movies. I guess I'm a bit of a loner."

"No man in your life?"

"Nothing serious in a while. Relationships and I don't get along well. I barely get along with myself." Jordan felt herself starting to relax with Emma. There was something disarming about her, if not exactly friendly.

"Don't blame yourself. Most men are assholes and just want to get us into bed. I can't remember the last time a man actually seemed interested in me as a person. It seems every guy just wants to hit on me. Once that happens, I get turned off. I wish I could do without them altogether."

Carrie returned with their food. It smelled great. Jordan and Emma dug in right away.

"So I guess you're single at the moment?" Jordan asked.

"A hundred percent. I was engaged before, but the guy was cheating on me with his old high school girlfriend. When I found out, I threw all the stuff he had at my apartment onto the street. He was pissed, but some neighbors came out and told him to get lost. He picked up his shit and hit the road. It was beautiful."

"That's a story you'll never forget," Jordan said. "Since you already went there, I was engaged before."

"Really? What a coincidence. What happened?"

"I ended it. Travis, my fiancé, didn't really do anything wrong. But the pressure of a long-term relationship at a time when my family situation was a disaster was more than I could manage. I couldn't do it."

"Do you still keep in touch with him?"

"Actually, yeah. I see him all the time. He's part owner of a bar, and I like to do my drinking there. He's probably my best friend. Even if he is a bit judgmental."

They had both finished eating. Emma set forty dollars on the table to cover the check. Jordan thought this was way too much but said nothing. "Ready to go?" Emma asked.

"Yep. That hit the spot. Now I need to fight off a nap so I can get to work."

"Let's go, then. By the way, I have an early start at work tomorrow and won't make the pool. See you Monday?"

"Sure. I've also got a busy morning tomorrow. My swim will have to wait."

IN THE EXECUTIVE suite at GenPhage, Carter sat on a black leather sofa, waiting for Neil. He sat with his spine pressed against the back of the sofa, his posture perfect. He never slouched. It was a sign of laziness, and laziness was a weakness. He hadn't become a highly-paid corporate security professionals by luck. All of his training and experience had taught him what he needed to know. His effort, focus, and dedication made him one of the best.

Carter thought the situation at GenPhage was riskier than Neil realized. Taken alone, either the clinical trial situation or the Jordan Reed investigation could be managed to reduce risk. GenPhage couldn't easily be tied to the deaths in Africa, assuming anyone even tried. Money went a long way there. Carter knew one of the main reasons companies studied drugs in developing countries was the ease with which they could manage documentation to keep the trial records clean. Deaths rarely got investigated, and the right financial incentives made unwanted deaths vanish.

But no solution was perfect. Carter knew many examples where a plan thought to be 100 percent effective blew up, sometimes literally. If Jordan Reed got one whiff of any overseas death that resembled Eric Smith's in a country where GenPhage operated, she would make the connection. She may have already identified other sites around the world where GenPhage had a presence. Connecting the dots could be easier than Neil thought.

What concerned Carter specifically was that Reed now had help. And not just help from anyone. Someone from the CDC. Charlie Choi would be more likely to notice potentially suspicious deaths happening anywhere in the world. Worse, he also appeared to be close to Reed, so they should expect him to go the extra mile for her. He may require some special attention if they didn't quickly shut down the Eric Smith story.

Carter knew Neil had a morning of reviews and rehearsals

for GenPhage's Investor Day. When Neil entered the executive suite, his face was a cloud of frustration. Carter personally hated all forms of bureaucracy. That was the main reason he had left the army. He could appreciate how Neil felt.

Neil walked past Carter and motioned for him to follow. Carter closed the door to the office and sat down opposite Neil.

"Well," Neil said. "Any updates?"

Carter leaned forward and folded his hands together, resting his elbows on his knees. He needed to make sure Neil was engaged, so Carter infringed on his personal space, forcing Neil to give him his full attention.

"The Jordan Reed situation has been calm since Monday. She hasn't attempted to contact Laurie Smith and hasn't ventured far from her apartment. But I reviewed the guest list for tomorrow's event. She has a pass. Apparently, her editor and your head of corporate communications are friends. She did him a favor."

"Should I tell her to revoke the pass?"

"I don't think so. It would be too suspicious. Better to just manage the situation."

"What do you think she hopes to achieve?"

"I have no information on what her specific aim is. It could be as simple as her doing surveillance and learning who's who. She doesn't know much about drug companies, and this is a chance for her to peek inside. At the other extreme, she could be planning to come in here and ask some very direct questions about Eric Smith. Given the public nature of the event, there's risk if she does this. However, if she brings this into the public forum, other reporters will pick up on the story and she'll have competition."

"So, what do you think she'll do? What should I expect?"

"I was getting to that." Carter maintained his composure. No matter how impatient a client or business partner became,

Carter could set aside his own feelings and focus on what he needed to do. He brushed off Neil's impatience and continued.

"I think she'll try to find a contact. Someone who she feels could be a weak link and help her figure out what happened to Smith."

Carter observed as Neil sat there quietly. Neil was decisive but not impulsive. Carter was getting used to Neil thinking before speaking. It reminded him of general he knew. One who rarely made a mistake.

"That sounds manageable. Have your team keep an eye on her. I'll do the same"

15

GenPhage Investor Day. Tom had come through for Jordan and arranged for her to attend. She felt like she had a lot riding on this. She needed to uncover the triggering event that had led to Eric Smith's death. Without knowing this, she didn't have a complete story.

Jordan didn't own a lot of clothing for business events such as this, and she needed to blend in. She decided on a slim knee-length gray wool skirt, which she wore with a solid indigo-blue top. The top was slim fitting with buttons down the front and three-quarter-length sleeves with a small cuff. She completed the outfit with black leather pumps with two-inch heels. The outfit complemented her pale skin and blue eyes.

She stuck with her black leather jacket since it matched her shoes. Taking the bus was the easiest way to get to GenPhage in the Seaport District, but she wanted her car in case she needed to get somewhere else after the event. Investor Day would start with breakfast and an open meet and greet at 8:30. Jordan gave herself an hour to get there. The sunny November morning was beautiful, but it meant Jordan had to drive right into the rising sun.

There was a designated parking area for GenPhage guests.

Jordan found it easily and took a spot a few rows into the lot. It was 8:15. She waited ten minutes before heading to the entrance. She used the time to quickly review her list of potential targets. There were both too many and not enough. Her chest felt tight. Small beads of sweat were forming on her neck, despite the cold. She began to doubt if she could find anyone who would help. At the moment, it felt like more of a long shot than she'd originally thought.

I don't know if I can do this.

GenPhage occupied the top four floors of a new twenty-story office building on Seaport Boulevard. The building itself was a beautiful amalgam of steel and glass with an abundance of windows. Its round shape ensured that it was always catching and reflecting light. Jordan walked through the set of double doors at the main entrance that led to a cavernous reception area. The ceiling was so high, it looked like the space could be used as a concert hall. The steel-and-glass motif permeated the interior of the building as well. A reception desk fronted the large, round space.

Jordan went to the desk and showed her identification. They gave her a temporary access badge and told her to take the elevators to the seventeenth floor.

As Jordan waited for the elevator, a man and a woman joined her. They both had temporary access badges and were most likely attending Investor Day. They chatted like they knew each other. Jordan took one look at them and classified them as bankers. She assumed they worked for investment banks or perhaps a finance news agency. She didn't watch CNBC, so if they were finance news celebrities, she wouldn't know. All she could say for sure was that the man wasn't Jim Cramer. He was the only business personality she could recognize.

The elevator didn't stop on the way up, and the door opened on floor seventeen. Jordan let the two bankers exit first. She followed behind them, fighting the feeling that she didn't belong.

Jordan wasn't expecting a space like the one that greeted her. It was striking. Unlike the steel and glass on the main floor of the building, GenPhage's decor was tasteful and modern. The furniture was a sleek combination of white leather and polished aluminum. It reminded Jordan of what she might see in IKEA, though more luxurious.

The reception desk was about twenty feet long. Instead of a basic rectangular shape, it instead bowed outward, tapering off on each side. One receptionist sat in the center on a high stool. On each side was a security guard with a computer console equipped with cameras.

Jordan's two elevator companions went ahead of her to check in. The man worked for TD Waterhouse. The woman was from Chase. Definitely here to make sure their banking companies missed nothing. Jordan noted their names.

It was Jordan's turn. "Good morning," the receptionist said. "Welcome to GenPhage."

"Thank you," said Jordan. "I'm here for Investor Day. But I guess you probably knew that."

"Yes, all our guests today are here for the event. Let me scan your badge. It will allow you to be here until two p.m. If you try to use it after that time, we'll be notified here."

"Wow," said Jordan. "You take security seriously."

"Yes, we do." The receptionist gave her a sly smile. Jordan looked closely at the woman as she stood up to scan her badge. She couldn't help but think she looked like a CrossFit trainer. Jordan could see well-toned muscles in her upper body. The woman moved with a sense of strength and fluidity. Jordan wondered if she was really another security guard posing as a receptionist. In fact, all three individuals behind the welcome desk looked as if they would be more at home engaging in hand-to-hand combat than processing visitors.

I wonder where GenPhage found these folks. They don't look like they came from Monster.com.

The receptionist/CrossFit trainer handed Jordan back her access badge. "Here you go. Enjoy your visit."

"Thanks."

The access badge allowed Jordan to pass through the main company entrance doors behind the welcome desk. As she walked in, the first thing she saw was a large flat-screen displaying "Welcome to the Annual GenPhage Investor Day." The screen wasn't Texas-stadium size, but it had to have been at least a dozen feet tall and almost twice as wide. It was impossible to miss.

The main floor space was expansive. She could see that the ceiling for much of it extended up to the next floor, with windows along the back wall. To her right was a collaboration space with tables and chairs. Farther back was the company cafeteria, configured for buffet-style breakfast with the cash registers somewhere out of sight. Or maybe food was free.

It was possible for several hundred people to mingle in this space. Over to her left, she saw an entrance to a large room. Some kind of auditorium. The ceiling extended into what otherwise would have been the eighteenth floor.

There were already several dozen people milling about. Jordan saw the bankers from the elevator among the minglers talking to other like-employed people or perhaps employees from GenPhage. Jordan noticed several nearly identically dressed men spread out in the space. They didn't look as though they were there to watch the presentations. They stood still, continually scanning the room.

More security in here? What a paranoid bunch.

Jordan went to the buffet and grabbed a fruit kabob and a coffee. She picked a convenient spot to stand from which she could observe the room.

She scanned the faces of the guests for any that looked like those she'd profiled. It was harder to do than she'd thought from people's LinkedIn pictures. Their headshots were probably many years old. After going through about two-thirds of those in the room, she finally recognized a face. Patrick Jackson from Investor Relations. It made sense for him to be here, but he wasn't the one most likely to answer questions about Eric Smith. Jordan meandered over near Patrick and the person he was talking to. Sounded like family chitchat.

Jordan walked to a trash can to dispose of her fruit kabob stick. Out of the corner of her eye, she caught sight of someone she recognized. She almost dropped her coffee.

Holy shit, is that Emma?

Jordan looked closely at a woman turned mostly away from her. The height was right. The woman's exposed shoulders, shapely body, and long legs confirmed it. It was Emma.

She looked amazing in a slim-fitting black dress that failed to reach her knees. Before Jordan could decide what to do, Emma turned in her direction. Jordan expected Emma to look as surprised as she felt. That didn't appear to be the case. She walked over, smiling broadly.

"Jordan, what a surprise," Emma said. "I have to say I never expected to run into you here. What are you doing here?"

Jordan regrouped. "You and me both. My editor asked me to cover this for someone who couldn't make it. It's a new gig for me."

"Your editor? You're a reporter?"

"Yeah, I am. For the *Courant*. Do you work here?"

"I do. I guess we never talked about each other's jobs. It's kind of funny we end up here at the same time."

"Definitely a weird coincidence. You didn't seem surprised to see me."

"It takes a lot to surprise me. Besides, when I'm at work, I make sure never to let my expressions and reactions give away what I'm thinking. I need to maintain an edge, especially when I work with so many men."

"What do you do here?"

"I'm on the commercial strategy team. I say 'team,' but there's only three of us. We map future options for the company and quantify what they could mean to the business. We're supposed to help the bosses make the best decisions."

"Sounds important."

"Sometimes it is. Other times, it's a complete pain in the ass. Creating scenario after scenario, knowing damn well the company won't do any of them."

Running into Emma sparked a new idea. Jordan set aside her plan to make contact with the strangers she'd researched. She actually knew someone at GenPhage, and she and Emma were friends. Sort of. Emma may be the person who could help, as long Jordan teed it up properly.

"How busy are you with the event today?" Jordan asked.

"Not insanely busy. A lot of the work has been done. Now it's just a matter of leadership doing what they're supposed to do and the rest of us looking professional. Why do you ask?"

"There's something I want to talk to you about if you have time later. Maybe during a break?"

"Absolutely," Emma said. "Anything you need. I gotta run and get more welcome kits, but I'll see you later."

Jordan felt an immediate sense of relief. She had a much better chance of getting Emma to help her than someone she'd just met. How she pitched it to Emma would be key. Jordan would need a soft approach, one with no perceived threat. The complete truth would make the threat to the company obvious. That likely wouldn't get Emma on her side.

The best approach would be to leverage any sympathy Emma may have for the Smith family. Emma may not have known Eric, but Jordan could set up the request as somehow being on behalf of Laurie Smith. It would be a lie that could be found out, but it was the least threatening option. If Emma hadn't known Eric, Jordan could even say Laurie was a family friend. Jordan really didn't want to lie to Emma, but she wouldn't let one or two small untruths get in her way.

It was time for the first presentations. Jordan went into the auditorium. She didn't want to be too visible, picking a seat near the back that still allowed her to see the presenters.

I want to see what you look like, Neil Foley. Just in case I ever have the chance to run you over.

Jordan allowed herself a small smile at the thought.

The entire GenPhage executive team took the stage, but it was the CEO and chief medical officer who did most of the talking. Not a surprise, since the presentations focused on the threat of antimicrobial resistance and the science behind it. They painted a stark picture of what life could be like if we lost the ability to treat common infections. Routine procedures like tonsillectomies and C-sections would become high risk. People could die by the millions from things we typically didn't worry about. It seemed surreal.

As the presentation moved from the big picture of global disease and increasing antimicrobial resistance to the relatively narrow focus of GenPhage's flagship treatment for drug-resistant TB, Neil Foley took over. As chief operations officer, he oversaw the execution of all aspects of the business, from clinical trials to manufacturing to preparing a commercial team to launch the product once approved. In the pre-approval period, all focus was on the trials and expanding the manufacturing capacity.

Jordan wanted him to look like an ogre, but the opposite was true. Neil was a great-looking man, his Irish heritage showing through in his complexion and hair color. He looked fit, and he dressed impeccably well. He spoke clearly in front of an audience, deploying perfect energy and tone. No slip-ups, no filler words, and just a hint of joviality. The kind of guy you'd want to go for drinks with. Jordan would have been enthralled if she hadn't known the truth.

Neil Foley engaged the entire audience, making eye contact across the crowd. He was a pro. He made eye contact with Jordan as well. And not just once or twice, but every minute or two. A few times, he seemed to want to hold her gaze. Jordan felt a shiver go down her spine when he smiled directly at her.

Not much of what the presenters said really caught Jordan's attention. But when Neil provided a summary of the company's clinical trials, she learned that the phase III trials were running predominantly outside of the US. In fact, they were mostly held in countries that Jordan thought of as developing: Kenya, Ethiopia, South Africa, Bangladesh. Obviously, these were countries with a high prevalence of TB, but it surprised her not to see many developed countries on the list.

I really need to learn more about how these drug companies work.

At the beginning of a scheduled forty-five-minute break, Emma met Jordan just outside of the auditorium. "How about I take you to my office to chat? Think of it as an informal tour."

"Works for me." Jordan followed Emma through a door at the far end of the room and up the stairs to the nineteenth floor. The modern office motif continued, and Jordan saw a mix of open seating spaces and small offices that all had at least one glass wall. There were also meeting rooms of different sizes, presumably to compensate for the scarcity of offices.

Emma had a corner office. Though it was small, it had two glass walls, which offered a spectacular view. The office was sparse, with a single picture of Emma on some modern sailing ship on one wall. Her desk was uncluttered, with a laptop and dual monitors. Jordan wondered if such an office was typical for someone in Emma's position.

Emma pulled her chair around from behind her desk to face the only other chair in her office. She and Jordan both sat down.

"Very nice office you have. It looks brand new," Jordan said.

"Just about. We've been in here less than a year."

This was Jordan's opportunity.

Focus. Don't screw it up.

"I have something I want to ask you. I hadn't considered it before today because I didn't know you worked here. But since you do, I think you'd be the perfect person to ask."

"I'm intrigued. Go ahead."

"Did you know someone named Eric Smith who worked for GenPhage?" Jordan's throat tightened as she asked the question.

"You're referring to the Eric Smith who died recently? Yes, I did."

Since Emma knew him, Jordan had to be careful mentioning Laurie, in case Laurie and Emma were close. "Did you know him well?"

"No, not really. He worked at our manufacturing site, and our paths didn't cross often. But we're a small company and have a lot of company activities, so we had spoken several times in the past year."

Good. She's probably not too close to Laurie. Time for my story.

"Well, I learned Eric Smith's wife and I have a mutual acquaintance. Apparently, Laurie doesn't really know how he got sick. She knows there was some kind of incident at GenPhage, but she didn't get a complete picture of what happened. Our acquaintance said she's not angry or anything like that. Eric had excellent life insurance, and the company has been kind. But she'd like to get some closure. Especially for her kids. They're young right now, but one day they'll start asking questions. She'd like to have answers." Jordan held her breath. She had embellished the story more than she had intended.

Emma appeared to be taking this in. "So, are you asking me to find out what happened? To be able to tell Eric's wife?"

"Yes. But I don't want to put you in a tough spot at work. If this is something you could do without too much effort, it would be a big relief for the Smith family."

"You're sure that this isn't for some lawsuit? That she's not using you to write something that could help her case?"

"I'm a hundred percent sure. Laurie is absolutely not intending to sue anyone for Eric's death. I'm helping as a courtesy."

With the settlement Laurie accepted, she couldn't sue.

"I get it. I can imagine not knowing exactly what happened is tough on the family. Let me see what I can find out. I have a good friend in the HR department. He should be able to access Eric's personnel file. No promises, but I'll give it a try."

Jordan almost couldn't believe her luck. "That's great. Thanks a ton, Emma. This would mean a lot to Laurie and her kids."

"Remember, no promises. I won't violate any company policies here. I'll ask for a favor and see what I can learn. If my HR friend says no, then you're out of luck."

"I understand. I'll keep my fingers crossed."

"Today's busy with the event, but I should have time tomorrow morning. I'll call you once I have something to share." Emma stood up. "We should head back to the auditorium. The next session will start soon."

Jordan felt excitement coursing through her body. She could feel things coming together. But in the back of her mind, it worried her how this would impact Emma. If Jordan got what she wanted, then the story she would tell could kill what could be a great friendship. She decided to worry about that later. First, she needed to know what had happened to Eric Smith. If that looked bad for GenPhage, then Jordan would find a way to deal with the Emma situation.

Jordan and Emma returned to the main floor of GenPhage and walked out into the open space between the buffet and the auditorium. Jordan was just about to beg off to go to the restroom. She stopped dead in her tracks.

Neil Foley was twenty feet away, walking straight toward them. There was no way she could hide her surprise.

Oh shit.

She almost tripped over her feet, having to put a hand on Emma's right shoulder to prevent herself from falling. Emma gave her a startled look but then noticed Neil approaching.

"Emma," Neil said, flashing a bright smile. "Don't you look perfectly beautiful today." He came in close and gave her a quick hug and a kiss on her left cheek.

"Thank you, Uncle Neil. You're such a flatterer."

Oh my God. They're related. How did I not know this?

Jordan couldn't move. She was sure her mouth was wide open.

Deep breath. Don't panic.

"Who's your lovely companion here?" Neil asked, gesturing toward Jordan.

"This is Jordan Reed. She works for the *Boston Courant* and is here to share positive news about the company. I hope. She recently started covering biotech and is getting to know the local companies. I hope we impressed her today," Emma said and threw a quick wink at Jordan.

Neil turned slightly to face Jordan. "Very nice to meet you, Jordan. I hope you learn a lot about us today. Our future is very bright. We're going to save a lot of lives."

"Pleased to meet you as well, Mr. Foley." Moving past the shock of discovering close family ties between Neil and Emma, Jordan saw an opportunity to tilt the playing field in her favor. "May I quote you on saving a lot of lives? That sounds like a prediction people would want to put their money behind."

Neil's eyes flashed a hint of something. Maybe surprise. Maybe anger. It passed as quickly as it appeared. "Please call me Neil. But let's keep things off the record for now. We haven't submitted our product for approval yet. I wouldn't want the regulators to think GenPhage was presuming to do their job. Perhaps we'll do a real interview in the future."

"I look forward to that. Just say the time and place."

"Absolutely. I must excuse myself, as we're about to recommence. Lovely to meet you, Jordan. Emma, I hope you can join the family for dinner soon." With that, he was off.

Jordan turned to Emma. "He's your uncle? I had no idea. I thought your last name was Donovan?"

"It is. Neil is my mother's younger brother. He was the one who encouraged me to study science and business and ultimately get into biotech. He's been my biggest supporter."

"Very nice. Now I have an inside track on GenPhage," Jordan said, returning a quick wink back to Emma.

16

AFTER THE GENPHAGE EVENT, JORDAN LAID OUT HER STORY. HER working title was "Local Biotech Company Hides Deadly Workplace Accident." She wrote the story with the assumption that there was an accident at GenPhage because of company negligence. For the moment, she didn't dwell much on the specific cause of Eric Smith's death from multiple organ failure, as it so far seemed plausible.

The real emphasis was on the secrecy around the accident and that GenPhage never shared what happened with Eric Smith's family. Jordan didn't use the real names of the Smith family, and she didn't directly quote Laurie to protect her settlement. Jordan also assumed there was nothing specifically illegal with whatever the accident was. If that were the case, she'd need to regroup with Tom on a different approach.

By noon the next day, Jordan had heard nothing from Emma. The suspense was killing her. If she wasn't able to come through, then the story was a dud. Either way, she'd have to let Emma know about the story before it got published. Hopefully, she'd understand that the cause of a workplace death shouldn't be hidden.

As if on cue, her phone buzzed, announcing the arrival of a text message. It was Emma.

"can U come downtown?"

"yes...where?"

"Starbucks across from GenPhage...will B there @ 1"

Jordan exploded off her sofa, grabbed her things, and headed out. She got to Starbucks with ten minutes to spare. She went inside, hit the restroom, and claimed a table.

Emma walked in at 1:02. Jordan waved her over. "Do you want a coffee?" Emma said.

"Sure."

When the coffees were ready, they added milk and sugar and returned to their table.

"I'm here to report success," said Emma. "My HR friend had no problem looking for, and sharing with me, the accident report for Eric Smith. I even have a hard copy. Sort of. I can't give it to you, and I can't even keep it myself. I need to return it before four p.m. today." She set down the report.

"What's that thing stuck to it?" Jordan asked. There was a small dark square, kind of metallic looking, in the top right corner of the page. It was maybe an eighth of an inch in each direction.

"It's a digital tracking device. Think of it like a bar code or QR code. That's why I can't give it to you. We have a kind of high-tech document-management system. Digitally, it's easy to track where documents reside and who has viewed them. For hard copies of documents with some kind of protected information, we're required to check them out digitally."

"Are you serious? Doesn't your company trust its employees?"

"Security comes before trust."

Jordan couldn't wait any longer. "So, what does the report say?"

"Well, there's nothing that warrants a lot of secrecy. Apparently, there was an incident with one of the manufacturing bioreactors. Some kind of temperature malfunction that triggered an alarm. Eric responded and apparently shut down the bioreactor. There's a standard protocol for that, by the way. He was taken to the on-site medical facility and was released later the same afternoon."

That doesn't sound very dangerous. Or incriminating.

"What's involved with shutting down a bioreactor? Does it involve opening it or anything?"

"I don't think so. It's a self-contained unit and can be shut down without having to worry about what's inside. Bioreactors are usually used when working with bacteria or yeast, sometimes viruses. It could be risky to require opening the bioreactor to shut it down."

"I guess that makes sense. I wonder why they took Eric to the medical facility?"

"I'm sure it's standard procedure for any incident. I wouldn't worry about it."

Jordan wasn't worried. From what Emma said, the incident sounded about as safe as an incident could be. She couldn't explain how Eric had been exposed to something that led to septic shock if the bioreactor was never opened.

If that's what really happened, why would GenPhage offer a settlement?

Jordan didn't share this observation with Emma. "OK, that seems straightforward. There must have been something else that sent him to the hospital a day or two later. What was the date of the accident?"

"November eleventh. Why?"

"Just thinking about the timing. Eric went into the hospital on the thirteenth and died on the fifteenth, so the timing makes sense."

"Did you think it wouldn't?"

"No. I like to map out events in sequence to make sure they

seem logical. A reporter habit, I guess. I don't know why this wouldn't have been shared with Laurie Smith. It sounds pretty benign."

"I asked my HR friend. He thinks it was an oversight. One of the senior managers from operations, or perhaps from IIR, should have offered to share this with Laurie. It seems someone missed it. This kind of thing happens in small companies. Our processes are still a work in progress. This was the first site accident we had. Also the first active employee death. Not an excuse but a reality."

"I know. It sucks when those who are already suffering are also the victims of corporate oversight. At least Laurie will be able to get past this knowing it was bad luck."

"I guess so," Emma said. "I was wondering why Laurie Smith reached out. Do you know?"

Jordan had to maintain her lie. "I think it was just opportunistic. Our mutual acquaintance suggested I could help. Apparently, she'd tried to reach out to Eric's boss but got nowhere. She thought nothing bad had happened but didn't know what else to do, short of hiring a lawyer. So here we are."

Not the truth, but believable.

"I suppose that makes sense," Emma said. "Anyway, that's it. Mystery solved."

"Thanks for going out on a limb. I owe you one."

"Anytime. I hope this high-tech paper didn't record our conversation. Then I'll be in big trouble," Emma said with a smile.

"I better take off. Lots to finish up today. Thanks for the coffee."

NEIL SAT with Carter in his office.

"Eric Smith's accident report was checked out today," Neil said.

"Is it safe to assume it will get in front of Jordan Reed?"

"It is. Why else would it be checked out?"

"That's fair. Do you still believe Reed will proceed with her story about a covered-up employee death at GenPhage?"

"I don't see another play for her. She has the core elements of what would be a readable story. The negative PR for us would be significant. It might even trigger an investigation by the authorities. If they publish it."

"Right. If they publish it." Carter shared a small smile with Neil.

"We need to act fast. I want this shut down today. By five p.m."

17

JORDAN RECEIVED AN ANGRY CALL FROM TOM AT 3:40.

She could hear him yelling before she even got the phone to her ear. "Jordan, what the hell did you do at GenPhage yesterday? They're sending a team of lawyers over. Get your ass down here ASAP."

What the hell's going on? I was just with Emma, and everything seemed fine.

Jordan got in her car and headed to the office. She wasn't exactly panicked, but it was obvious that something significant had happened. How often does a company send a legal team to the office of a local newspaper? It had to be pretty serious.

She parked as close to the entrance as she could and sprinted inside. Gail, who worked at the front desk, said, "They're waiting for you in Bob's conference room." Bob was the senior editor. Not a good sign if he was involved.

It was 4:10 as Jordan approached the door to the conference room. She slowed her pace to catch her breath, trying to calm her racing pulse. It was a useless exercise.

She opened the door. Bob and Tom sat on the far side of the large conference table. Sitting with their backs to Jordan were five individuals, all dressed in dark suits ranging from navy blue to black.

"Jordan," Bob said. "Nice of you to make it." There was just a hint of sarcasm, and his face betrayed his unhappiness. This was his professional home, and he deeply resented having some gang of corporate lawyers intrude.

"Sorry, Bob. I left as soon as Tom called." Jordan went to the other side of the table and sat down next to Tom. He didn't meet her gaze, signaling he didn't know what exactly this meeting was about. She took in the view of the five men across from her.

"Fine," he said to Jordan. Facing the row of guests, he said, "How about you tell us what this is about? It had better be worth my time."

The guest in the middle responded. "I assure you it is. First, quick introductions. I'm Gary Jacobsen, senior counsel for GenPhage. To my right are members of our legal team, Francis Doherty and Dylan Hughes. To my left are Neil Foley, chief operations officer, and Carter Nash, GenPhage security advisor."

"I'm Bob Goldsmith, senior editor. Tom Winters here is our business editor. I couldn't get anyone from legal on short notice. The reporter who just entered is Jordan Reed. According to you, she's the reason we're here, correct?"

"Correct," Gary said. "Let me jump right in. It has come to our attention that Ms. Reed is working on a story that would cast GenPhage in a negative light. We believe her story is neither adequately nor accurately sourced. At least not for a reputable newspaper." Gary said "story" as though Jordan was a child doing a poor job on a class project. "We're here to request that the *Boston Courant* cease and desist work on this story. If you continue and publish the story, we will use all legal means at our disposal. This would include filing an injunction, demanding a retraction and apology for any incorrect facts published, and seeking damages commensurate with the perceived damage to our reputation."

Jordan knew Bob wasn't someone to be pushed around. He had no doubt dealt with his fair share of lawyers over the years and wasn't going to roll over. At least not without an understanding of how solid the story was.

"Let's back up a bit," Bob said. "There's no need to throw out a bunch of threats before we even review the facts. Can you excuse us for a minute? I need to ask Jordan a few questions."

Bob and Tom stood up and headed to the door. Jordan followed. They went into Bob's office beside the conference room. Bob looked at Jordan. "What the hell are they talking about? Give us a rundown of the story."

Jordan swallowed hard. Her mouth was dry. She wasn't prepared. Not even close. "Well," she began, "the story isn't complete yet. I have a couple more facts to track down." She was thinking about how the GenPhage accident report didn't mention anything dangerous, and yet somehow a healthy guy had become deathly ill.

"It goes like this. GenPhage, a local biotech company, is covering up their role in the death of an employee who died from a workplace accident."

"What information do you have on the accident?" Bob was going to walk her through it.

"I've seen the accident report."

"Do you have a copy?"

"No."

"A confirmed source?"

"Anonymous. She can't go on the record."

"Was there something incriminating in the report?"

Jordan glanced at Tom for guidance, but his face didn't give her any sign of how to proceed. She was on her own.

She didn't want to answer the question but really didn't have much of a choice. "Well, the report doesn't say anything happened that was remotely dangerous. It seemed like a straightforward incident where Eric Smith shut down a bioreactor. Yet they still gave him some kind of medical treatment, which makes no sense. Especially with how quickly he got sick. Three days after this innocuous incident, he was dead."

"Did you talk to the doctor who saw him in the hospital? Will he go on the record?"

Jordan wasn't the one who'd talked to Hauptman, and she didn't want to bring Charlie into this. "He was interviewed. So far, his comments are off the record."

"OK. What else supports your cover-up theory?"

Jordan had to be careful with her phrasing. She couldn't jeopardize Laurie's settlement. "GenPhage paid a settlement to the family of Eric Smith and included a confidentiality agreement. Plus, this all happened within a week. Why would a company offer a settlement, especially that fast, if they weren't trying to hide something?"

"That supports your hypothesis. What do you have proving there's a settlement in place?"

"I have a confidential source that told me personally about both the settlement and the confidentiality agreement. The source won't go on the record, but I can keep the real name hidden. I've done that before."

Bob summed up. "You have a suspicious workplace accident, and you have what is probably a record for the fastest-ever settlement. Especially given that this so-called accident seemed pretty tame. If you can get sources on the record, you have a story. Not a Pulitzer. But a story that I wouldn't want to see in print if I were at GenPhage. Let's get back to our guests."

The trio reentered the conference room.

"I was beginning to wonder if you were going to come back," Gary said.

"You're the one who sprang this meeting on us without warning. We needed to get up to speed on why the hell you're here."

Gary's face betrayed a hint of contempt. People probably

didn't speak to him that way. "Now that you're up to speed, shall we continue?"

"Absolutely. I think you're here prematurely. Jordan definitely has the components of a newsworthy story. She still needs to lock in some things. When she does, I'll give you the courtesy of telling you when we'll go to print. I'll even give you the chance to comment. On the record. If she doesn't lock things down, we won't have a printable story."

Gary smiled smugly. He had restrained himself, but now the floor was his. "Actually, our timing is perfect. We can save your staff a lot of useless effort and at the same time ensure this frivolous story never sees the light of day."

Jordan didn't know what the GenPhage team had up their sleeve, but she felt like someone trapped on railroad tracks with a train coming. Fast.

Gary continued. "First, the death certificate for the victim is perfectly clear." Gary passed a copy to Bob. "He died of multiple organ failure. Period. The GenPhage accident report shows that the victim felt perfectly fine and went home at his own request. There's no connection between the workplace incident and Mr. Smith's cause of death. There is nothing in the death certificate regarding GenPhage." Gary reached out for the death certificate, and Bob returned it.

"How does GenPhage explain the settlement?" Bob said.

"We assert there's no evidence of any settlement. I believe Ms. Reed spoke to someone who said GenPhage paid the victim's family a settlement. We have here a signed affidavit from the spouse of the victim attesting that she told no one her family received a settlement from GenPhage. Any story that intends to use the spouse as a source, confidential or otherwise, won't be factual, and we would have to proceed with litigation for libel."

Gary crossed his hands and leaned against the back of his chair, pleased with himself. Neil looked as if he could barely contain his laughter.

They fucking got to Laurie. And they got her to sign that she never told me about a settlement. My story's dead.

"Can I see the affidavit?" Bob said.

"Certainly."

Bob read it quickly and took a deep breath. He leaned in toward Tom and said something, but Jordan couldn't hear what it was. Bob nodded in response.

"If what you say is true, then we've got a gap. For now, we won't print anything on this topic."

The smug look on Gary's face mirrored the triumph he must have felt. "I'm glad you recognized there's nothing newsworthy here. I trust we can consider this matter closed?"

"As I stated, the current situation doesn't support going to print. If circumstances and sources were to change, we'd reconsider. But, yes, this is currently closed."

"Perfect," Gary said. "We're done here." The GenPhage team got up and began to leave the conference room.

Neil approached Jordan. "Please don't take this personally, Ms. Reed. I'm merely fulfilling my company's obligation to ensure we have the best chance for success. Perhaps we'll have an opportunity to collaborate on an important story, one that will show the great benefit GenPhage will bring to people suffering from deadly diseases."

He sounded almost genuine.

Jordan felt her embarrassment showing in her expression. But the smugness of these assholes, especially Neil Foley, allowed her to briefly forget that fact.

"I appreciate the sentiment. Like you, I was doing my job to uncover a lie that hurt people." Jordan saw an opportunity to test a theory. "I really hope you're acting in the best interest of patients. I seem to recall a trial failure for a breast-cancer drug. Several women died. Women who were wives and mothers. No one responsible for those deaths was ever held accountable. I see my job as one that can hold such people accountable. That's what makes me go to work each day. To make sure companies like yours don't get away with hurting people under the guise of trying to help them."

Jordan didn't flinch as Neil glared at her. She hoped he got the reference. And that it made him sweat. Just a little.

Neil leaned in, close enough that she could smell the mints he had recently finished. He spoke so only Jordan could hear him. "I see you've done some homework. Make sure you're ready for the game you're trying to play. There's no room for losers." Neil turned and followed Carter out of the room.

Once the GenPhage team left, Bob, Tom, and Jordan stood looking at each other.

"What was that about?" Tom said.

"Something I came across in my research. Neil Foley has a history that's not well known. I wanted to let him know it wasn't as well kept a secret as he thought."

"Don't antagonize him further. We escaped with some bruised egos. Let's keep it at that."

Bob closed the door to the conference room. "Can someone tell me what the hell just happened?"

Jordan stood motionless, head down. "I don't know. I think they set me up."

"They set you up? You're the reporter. Did the spouse give you any indication she'd sign an affidavit that would kill your story?"

"None at all," Jordan said. "In fact, she was open to discussing what she knew. She wouldn't have let me use her name, but I could have used her as a confidential witness. They must have pressured her to sign that affidavit."

Bob asked the question Jordan hadn't had time to consider. "Jordan, how did GenPhage even know you had confirmation of the settlement? I can't imagine the spouse voluntarily calling them to let them know she violated the confidentiality agreement."

How did they know? I was at her house, not out in public.

"I honestly have no idea. I was operating pretty much under the radar, at least until yesterday. Even then, I only asked a GenPhage employee I met about an accident report. She didn't even know I knew about the settlement."

"Well," Bob said, "it doesn't matter now. They've us locked out. Unless you have any other sources?"

Jordan lowered her gaze in defeat. "No. And the way GenPhage has closed ranks, I can't imagine getting someone from inside to confirm anything."

It was obvious to Jordan that Bob was pissed that his turf had been invaded. And that he had lost. When he spoke, his voice was even and measured. "This is for both of you. Unless an actual smoking gun shows up, you are to stay out of GenPhage's business. I'm not risking getting sued or fired unless we have a story that's bulletproof. You may not know this, but their CEO is a close college friend of the governor. I don't want any heat from him. None. Do I make myself clear?"

"Perfectly," said Tom.

"Crystal," said Jordan.

"Good. If there's a repeat of this fucking scenario, you're both done here."

18

JORDAN WENT RIGHT FROM THE OFFICE TO DARCY'S PUB. THE traffic was worse than normal, but she accepted this as more of her reward for fucking up the story. There was no amount of drink that would cure how shitty she felt. After meeting Emma this morning, she had been on top of the world. The core pieces of the story were coming together, and she had reliable sources identified or in place. That had changed in an instant. Now the story was dead. Maybe not completely dead, but Bob made it crystal clear that Jordan had to keep her distance from GenPhage. Her failure was the kind one felt in the pit of their stomach.

Jordan parked her car and started for the entrance to Darcy's Pub. She could almost taste that first drink.

The ringing of her phone proved fate really was conspiring against her. Why couldn't the world leave her alone for five minutes? She pulled her phone out of her jacket pocket to see if she recognized the number. It was blocked. She started to put it away but hesitated. Given the day she'd had, there was no telling who was calling. Her gut told her it wasn't a wrong number or a telemarketer. She reversed course and took the call.

"Hello," Jordan said. "Who's this?"

"My name isn't important, but you can call me Ben."

"Well, Ben, I'm busy. You have five seconds to tell me what I can do for you."

"I have one question. Are you going to continue investigating GenPhage?"

Jordan stopped in the middle of the parking lot. "What the hell? How do you know about that?"

"Let's say I'm a concerned citizen who hopes to see justice. I thought you were making progress with your investigation. But something changed this afternoon, correct?"

"First, I have no idea who the hell you are. For all I know, you're a buddy of Neil Foley checking up on me. Second, how the hell do you know about this afternoon? That wasn't even an hour ago."

"I'm afraid I can't disclose exactly how I know what I know. But I can assure you that I'm not out to protect Neil Foley. In fact, quite the opposite."

"Assuming you're telling me the truth, which, by the way, I don't believe, what business is any of this to you?"

"I have a connection to this situation and played a role in how it got to this point. I didn't act when I could have, and now I need to influence events from behind the scenes."

"Really? Are you Neil Foley's father? Is this some sort of reverse Darth Vader scenario?"

"Nothing so simple. All you need to know is that I had a part to play in Neil getting his current job. A mistake on my part. Now I hope to rectify that mistake."

Jordan's mind raced, trying to figure out Ben's role in this. Her roller-coaster day didn't put her in a frame of mind to easily process new information. "Great. You want Neil Foley to get fired. That doesn't help me understand how you know my role in this."

"Maybe not, but there's an obvious connection if you allow yourself to think about it."

As Ben said this, it hit her. There was one way he could know she was investigating GenPhage. He was the one who had left her the obituary.

"Son of a bitch. You stuck that obituary to my door."

"Yes. That was me."

"Why? What possible reason did you have to pick me?"

"Again, you now know enough to answer that question. The connections you need to make are within your grasp."

Jordan liked puzzles on most days. Solving one was not what she wanted to do at the end of this day. But something about this man's demeanor made her want to understand why he'd picked her.

"Let me give it a try. You know Neil Foley and have some reason to get him fired or something. That part I get. You chose me to investigate this story, even though I know nothing about biotech. Not to mention that I'm a junior reporter. You didn't pick me because of my experience and credentials. Right or wrong?"

"Right."

There's a connection I'm not seeing.

"Your name and voice aren't familiar, so I don't think I know you. I had never heard of Neil Foley before, so you can't be trying to tap into some relationship between him and me."

"Are you sure about that? You never heard of Foley before this?"

Jordan considered this. She was positive she hadn't known Neil Foley before this. But she did have a previous connection to him.

Shit. I knew of him but didn't realize it.

"My mother." Jordan let her words hang in the air.

"Very good. That's precisely why I picked you."

"How did you even know about my mother? Were you a friend? Are you a doctor?"

"None of those. All you need to know is that I knew Neil

when he was in charge of that clinical trial. I later learned that the company hid the side effects of the drug from patients. But I learned it too late to prevent what happened to people like your mother. I also inadvertently enabled whatever he and GenPhage are doing today. Though I don't know exactly what that is, it can't be good. I'm in a position where direct intervention is personally risky. But a trained reporter, one with a connection to Neil Foley, is a much better option than doing something myself."

"Well, if you know anything about this afternoon, you know they've shut me down. Neil Foley and his legal team killed the story in front of my editors. They removed any sources I had and threatened to sue the paper. It's over."

"That's disappointing."

"That's what lawyers do."

"You misunderstood. I'm not disappointed that they stopped your investigation. I'm disappointed you're giving up. I really thought you had more fight in you."

"What gives you the right to talk to me like that? You know nothing about me."

"I didn't intend to be offensive. But you're giving up too easily."

"*Too easily*? I have no sources to confirm anything about Eric Smith's death. My editors told me to back off. I have no leverage."

"I don't believe for a minute the story is the death of Eric Smith. I'm sure it's part of something bigger."

This made no sense to Jordan. "What do you mean by bigger? You were the one who pointed me at Eric Smith in the first place."

"I don't know the full extent. But I can guarantee it's much bigger than Eric Smith. Investigating his death was just a means to get you looking at GenPhage. The real story lies deeper. For Neil Foley and GenPhage to shut you down with such precision is confirmation there's much more to the story than Eric Smith."

"Well, unless you know where else I need to look, I'm done. I have no other leads."

"Be patient. There's always someone who knows a piece of needed information. It'll come out. Don't give up and be ready when it does."

"Thanks for nothing. If that's all you've got, I'm going to have that drink I need."

"Fair enough. But let me leave you with one last thought. How did GenPhage so expertly cut you off at the knees? Just when you thought you had the Eric Smith story, they ripped it out of your grasp. Surely, it can't have been dumb luck?"

"What do you know?"

"Nothing factual. But I know Neil Foley. I'm certain he has been managing the entire situation since you got on his trail. He has no shortage of resources at his disposal."

"You think he knew I was on to him?"

"How else could he have intervened the way he did?"

"It doesn't matter. GenPhage is now off-limits."

"Be patient. And keep your eyes open."

"Is that all you can tell me?"

"For now, yes. Be careful, Jordan. I'll be in touch." With that, he hung up.

Jordan returned the phone to her pocket and replayed the call with Ben. Jordan didn't want to trust him. But he hadn't said or done anything to make her think he was working on behalf of Neil Foley. Ben's question of how Neil knew to intervene when he did reminded Jordan that Bob had asked the same thing.

How did they know I talked to Laurie and that she told me about the settlement?

The more she thought about being set up, the more stupid Jordan felt. She had missed something. Something important.

19

JORDAN WENT INSIDE DARCY'S PUB. A SOLID HAPPY-HOUR CROWD had gathered. She took one of the three open seats at the far side of the bar, trying unsuccessfully to spot Travis. One of the other servers said Travis would be in by six. Jordan ordered a gin and tonic and nachos. At that moment, eating healthy wasn't a priority. She wanted something that gave her some happiness. Nachos were a start.

Her drink came right away, and she downed half of it. She leaned forward onto the bar, eyes closed. The first sip was always the best.

This day better end soon. I can't take any more surprises.

Jordan returned to the question posed by Bob and Ben. She could think of three explanations for how GenPhage knew about her conversation with Laurie. One, Laurie had proactively confessed to GenPhage that she'd talked to Jordan and then begged for mercy, signing the affidavit as a further guarantee of silence. Two, GenPhage regularly checked on Laurie and just happened to do so while Laurie was confessing to Jordan. The third option Jordan almost couldn't consider because it seemed too paranoid: she was being followed.

Option one was plausible on its face, but it didn't align with

Jordan's read on Laurie. Laurie was under duress, but she wasn't weak. She also wasn't stupid. Jordan marked that option as unlikely. Option two seemed just too coincidental. Jordan discarded it. Option three, as crazy as it seemed, couldn't be ignored.

Could they really have been following me?

Her nachos arrived, delivered by Travis. This interrupted Jordan's train of thought. She was so relieved to see Travis that she couldn't hold back the tears that had been building. The stress of the day, capped off by the meeting with GenPhage, needed release. Not unlike cracking the cap of a soda bottle to release the initial pressure. Not an explosion but a steady escape.

"Whoa," Travis said. "What's wrong? Is it the nachos? If they're overcooked, I can get you a new batch. No need for tears."

Jordan did one of those laugh-through-tears snorts. Leave it to Travis to change the trajectory of her emotions when she needed it. "Asshole," Jordan said, wiping her eyes. "Can't you just let someone cry without trying to be smart?" Jordan's smile signaled she was happy with his intervention. This was about as well as she handled an emotional thank-you.

"As a bartender, it's part of my job. Probably the most important part. So, what's up? Why the tears?"

"A really shitty day. I went from having one of my best days in recent memory to having one of my worst."

"That's quite a roller coaster. Care to share?"

Jordan took Travis through the week's events, describing the progress she'd made on the GenPhage story, only to have it torn apart in an instant. In front of her editors, no less.

"Wow," Travis said. "That's one fucked-up day you had."

"Yep. One I don't want to repeat."

"Now what?"

"Back to my regular 'who gives a shit' stories. Bob ordered

me to stay away from GenPhage, so there's no way I can find other sources to validate the story. Without the wife and GenPhage, I have nothing."

"At least you didn't get fired."

"True. But there's still one thing eating at me."

"Tell me."

"Bob pointed this out to me, and I don't know why I didn't think of it myself. How did GenPhage find out Laurie had spoken to me and then get her to recant so fast?"

"Did you come up with an answer?"

"I ruled out Laurie confessing voluntarily. It would be risky for her. That leaves surveillance. By GenPhage. On me."

Travis slapped his hand on the bar. "Shit, Jordan, do you really think that's what happened? How much have you had to drink? You're not Jason Bourne."

"I know that, smart-ass. But think about it. What if someone tipped GenPhage off that I was poking around Eric Smith's death? If they really have something big to hide, they might resort to following me or Laurie. When I was at GenPhage yesterday, I saw several dudes who were real security. Not mall cops or high school dropouts. They looked like secret service types. Plus, their head of security was at the meeting today. He didn't say a single word. He just sat there observing us. Come to think of it, he looked like Jason Bourne."

"I think it's a stretch, Jordan. You watch too many spy movies. Besides, you could never prove it."

"Probably not."

But Jordan didn't really agree. If they had been tailing her, wouldn't it make sense to continue? To make sure she did as agreed? If they were concerned enough to tail her in the first place, the smart play would be to continue for a while longer.

"Travis, do you see any new guys in here, ones you haven't seen except in the last week?"

Travis looked confused but humored her and looked around.

"Not that I can pick out right now. But it's busy, and Friday is a day when I would expect a lot of newcomers."

"Do you have security cameras running?"

"Always. We have three in the bar and one covering the front entrance. Why? Do you want to sit and watch the monitors?"

"No, I want to see the parking lot."

"Sorry," Travis said. "I've got no cameras out there. You'll have to go outside and look."

"Save my chair." Jordan grabbed her jacket and headed out the door and into the parking lot. She had no plan but figured she'd just take a walk through the lot and see if there was anyone looking suspicious. Whatever that meant.

The lot wrapped around from the front of the building to the right and then went behind. As Jordan walked outside, she looked at her phone, pretending to be doing something. But she was really scanning the part of the parking lot she could see from the front of the restaurant. The lot had a light in each corner, and Jordan could see the cars parked there reasonably well.

In the row of cars parked right in front, all were unoccupied and none jumped out as being surveillance. Not that she really knew what she was looking for on that front. From her vast movie-watching experience, she was automatically looking for some kind of black sedan or SUV. American made with very dark windows. If she were being tailed by someone in a red Toyota Corolla, she wouldn't catch it.

Jordan had parked her car along the back edge of the lot, about halfway between the front entrance and the far right end. She walked toward her car while looking farther down the row of cars. Nothing in that row looked suspicious. She went to the driver's side and opened the door, pretending to look for something. From here, she could see the three rows of parking that went along the side of the restaurant. One row was next to the building, one was along the back edge of the lot, and between the two was a double row, which didn't continue around behind the restaurant.

As she scanned the back row from her car to the end and then to the right, one car caught her attention. A black Chevy Suburban, parked in the second spot along the right side of the lot. It was parked rear end first, facing her. She could see it head-on, but the front windshield was dark. The lighting was behind the Suburban, making the inside looked black to her. Impossible to tell if there was anyone inside. She needed a view from a different angle but couldn't be obvious about it.

She jumped when her phone rang. She was so focused on the Suburban, she had tuned out the rest of the world. It was Emma. Jordan wondered if she knew what had happened. "Hey, Emma. What's up?"

"Turns out I have no plans this evening and wanted to see if you felt like hanging out?"

She doesn't know what her uncle did today.

It surprised Jordan that she thought she'd enjoy Emma's company. She could also address something that was bothering her. She felt a confession was in order—that she had planned to use the information Emma shared as part of a story. It might not go over well, but since the story was dead, she wanted to come clean. Just in case they became friends. "That sounds nice. I actually just parked myself at the bar I told you about the other day, the one where my ex-fiancé works. Any chance you could come here? We can have some drinks. The food is acceptable for bar food."

"Sure. Text me the address. I can be there in maybe thirty to forty minutes. Later."

Jordan hung up and texted Emma the address. While walking toward the door, she tried to see if there was anyone in the Suburban, but the lighting was too poor. If someone was tailing her, they'd still be there later.

She sat back down, and Travis came by with a fresh drink. "Did you take out the spies and put their bodies in your trunk?"

"You're hilarious. But I saw a car I want to get a better look at."

"Really? Why?"

"Shiny black Suburban. The windows are heavily tinted. It's parked with a good view of my car and the entrance. I couldn't see if there was anyone inside. I need a better look."

"As I said, you watch too many spy movies. If I had a Suburban, it would be black. Other colors just don't work."

"Joke if you want, but I'm going to find out if there are guys in that car following me."

"I shouldn't feed your paranoia, but if you really want to know, just go for a drive. Go to the ATM a mile down the road and come back. If you're being followed, they'll be right behind you. Then you'll have your answer. But I think it's a waste of time."

Of course. You don't have to see them sitting in the car. Just give them something to follow.

"You're pretty bright for a bartender. I'll be back in fifteen minutes."

"If you don't come back, I'll call the FBI."

"You do that." Jordan headed toward the door but turned back before leaving. "By the way, my friend Emma is coming to hang out here. Can you get us a table? Thanks." Jordan didn't wait for Travis to respond.

Jordan returned ten minutes later. She rushed in and came right up to Travis at the bar. "The Suburban's gone. Where'd it go?"

"Come sit down."

They went to a table and sat down across from each other. "So, where did it go?" Jordan demanded.

"It left just after you did, maybe thirty seconds later. Went the same direction. And the windows were dark. I couldn't see anything inside. I can't believe I'm saying this, but you might actually be right."

"I fucking told you so. Did you see them come back?"

"No. But give me a few minutes. I'll bring out some trash and look." Travis went back to the bar.

Jordan contemplated the likelihood she was being followed by GenPhage. It made little sense to follow her because she was looking into a workplace accident. The worst that could have happened to GenPhage had she published her story was some negative press. Maybe a fine. But nothing criminal. At least, not according to the accident report.

She had to admit that the accident report troubled her. Not because of what it said but because there was nothing concerning in it at all. It was so bland that no one would consider it had anything to do with Eric Smith's death. That also meant there was nothing in it to justify following a nosy reporter.

Something else happened that day. Something not in the report.

Her train of thought was broken by Emma energetically plopping herself on the bench across from her. "Hey there," she said. "Long time no see."

"Ha. Twice in one day. What happened to your evening plans?"

"I never really had any. I was just going to stay in and watch a movie, but that felt kind of pathetic. Better to hang out with you."

"What you think is pathetic is my preferred Friday evening. Let's go to the bar and get you a drink. You can meet Travis."

"Your ex is here tonight? I can't wait to meet him."

"He's almost always here. He's a co-owner. This place is his baby."

At the bar, Jordan caught Travis's attention with a quick wave. He came over with his trademark smile. "So, this must be Emma? I'm Travis. Pleased to meet you. What'll you have?"

"Hmm. I think a vodka and cranberry would hit the spot."

"Coming right up."

Travis brought Emma's drink, plus another gin and tonic for Jordan. "Here you go."

"Travis, can you get a menu for Emma?" Jordan said.

"Absolutely," he said and handed her one.

They each ordered a burger with a salad on the side.

Jordan dreaded having to tell Emma that she had misled her. If she handled this well, they might get the chance to become friends. She also didn't know if her uncle Neil had told her about what had happened earlier. Having this discussion could clear that up.

"Emma," Jordan began. "There's something I need to tell you."

"Oooh. Sounds serious. Go for it."

"This isn't easy. You can ask me anything you want, but give me a few minutes to get it out. It's about Eric Smith."

Emma leaned back. "Take your time."

"There was more to my request from Investor Day than what I told you. It was true Laurie Smith wasn't given a lot of detail about what happened to her husband and that I told her I'd share anything I learned. But I was also tipped off that GenPhage was hiding something about Eric's death. I thought there was a story. As it turned out, the accident report was pretty straightforward and didn't support a motive to cover anything up." Jordan reminded herself this was basically the truth. The next part would have to be more vague.

"I also thought I had a source that could support some of what I've learned, but that fell through. This was all brought to a conclusion when your uncle, and the GenPhage legal team, which somehow suspected there was a story brewing, suggested to my editors there wasn't one that could be published without risking a libel suit. That was probably true. So we scrapped the story. That's it. I hope you're not too mad. I didn't intend to use you for this. I think we could be good friends. But when I saw you at GenPhage, I couldn't resist asking you for help."

Jordan stopped. That felt like enough. She held her breath and looked at Emma for some reaction.

"Well," Emma said. "Good confession. While no one likes feeling used, I can appreciate the situation you were in. It must have seemed pretty lucky to meet me when it was coincidentally helpful for a story you were working on."

How could she not be pissed off? She should be. At least a little.

"You don't seem upset. Are you just hiding it really well, or are you about to let me have it?"

This time, Emma paused and avoided Jordan's gaze for a moment, looking down briefly and then back up at Jordan. "I also have a confession to make. Last week, my uncle Neil said he learned of a new reporter covering the local biotech space. He asked me to get to know her. That reporter was you. I figured he wanted me to get an early read on something you knew or to help keep GenPhage in a positive light. It's common for the senior folks at drug companies to maintain relationships with those in the press, so I didn't think much of it. But when I looked at your background and the stories you published, it was clear you weren't a biotech reporter. Knowing my uncle, I read between the lines and figured he wanted me to get to know you for some other reason. But I never asked him directly. With what you said, it all makes sense. He must have known about your GenPhage story and thought I might learn something. It never got to that point, and now it looks like it won't."

Jordan processed this on the fly. She was caught totally off guard. "Damn. Meeting you wasn't a coincidence. I didn't see that coming."

"I'm sorry too," said Emma. "I didn't know you were really working on a story about GenPhage and never even thought to tell anyone we looked at the accident report for Eric Smith. For what it's worth, I also think we hit it off really well."

Jordan felt a huge sense of relief. They had lied to each other, but with no real harm done. Almost like offsetting penalties in football. "I can live with this. As a reporter, I'm used to asking people for things without full disclosure, but I shouldn't have done that with a friend."

"Thanks, Jordan. Clean slate?"

"Absolutely."

As Jordan leaned back on the bench, she glanced up toward the bar and saw Travis heading their way with Emma's food.

"Emma, your food has arrived," he said.

"It looks great."

Just before Travis turned to go back to the bar, he caught Jordan's eye. He mouthed, "They're back," exaggerating the movement to make sure Jordan got the message.

She gave a shallow nod of acknowledgment.

I was being followed. I'm still being followed. What the hell have I stumbled into?

20

Charlie loved New York. But he had to admit that he'd been more than a little bored the past two days. He usually enjoyed conferences, but this time, he found the speakers lacking in their ability to engage the audience. They were way too academic, even for academics. He was thankful when Friday's sessions ended. He wasn't planning to attend any sessions on Saturday and would head home instead. The drive was several hours, and he would get an early start.

The organizers of the conference had planned dinners at a few different locations each night. This allowed the attendees to see more of the city and meet with colleagues less formally. In hindsight, Charlie thought two days of networking sessions would have been more useful. There were people from every continent in attendance. There were doctors from major urban centers and rural outposts from some of the most dangerous places in the world. At least in terms of infectious diseases.

Charlie knew the CDC organizer for the conference well and had made two requests. One was for Charlie to have a scheduled dinner with doctors from Africa, since this was the continent that endured the worst infectious diseases. The second was for it to be at a good Mexican restaurant. He lucked out on both fronts. He would be having dinner with a host of doctors from Africa at Dos Caminos, a great Mexican restaurant with enormous margaritas.

Charlie was in a group of about thirty doctors. They occupied three large tables in a reserved section of the restaurant. There were doctors from five different African countries, plus a few from Europe, South America, and India. Being with doctors from Central Africa gave him a chance to nurture his fascination with Ebola. The virus was elegant in its ability to hide for years and then strike with high lethality. If it was a more resilient virus, able to survive airborne, humanity would be in big trouble.

Dinner was much more lively than any of the events of the past two days. Maybe because it was the last night. Maybe it was just the margaritas. Nothing like a few strong drinks to relax a crowd. At one point, Charlie looked around almost in awe. Many of these doctors were on the front lines of treating horrible diseases or were leaders in trials to develop new treatments. He had an important job himself, but working with infectious diseases in the United States just didn't compare to what his peers from developing nations experienced.

Toward the latter part of dinner, Charlie overheard a snippet of conversation about a new antibiotic treatment that used bacteriophage as a vehicle to deliver genes directly to bacteria. The genes were those specifically needed to combat one or more defense mechanisms that bacteria had developed to resist antibiotics. If perfected and optimized, the approach would provide a flexible technology platform that could be refreshed with different genes to counter future mechanisms of antibiotic resistance.

The general sentiment of the conversation was positive. The technology platform impressed the doctors. Some had even seen results firsthand because they either worked out of a site participating in the clinical trials or they knew of patients who were taking part.

But a couple of doctors expressed concern. They worried that introducing genes to counter antibiotic resistance could speed up the ability of bacteria to evolve new and better defenses.

Charlie wanted in on the conversation. "I couldn't help over-hear your discussion on this new antibiotic treatment. Did I hear someone say they saw patients on whom the treatment worked?"

A tall, thin, and distinguished-looking black doctor responded. "My name is Dr. Mbosi. I have a clinic about an hour outside of Nairobi. I have personally seen several patients with multi-drug-resistant TB recover with no trace of infection. They would other-wise have had a long, slow death sentence, along with the constant fear of infecting their loved ones. Their recoveries were exemplary."

A short, older white doctor, speaking with an Afrikaans accent, joined in. "I, too, have witnessed similar recoveries in my clinic in Cape Town. I've seen nothing like this before. At least for TB, this treatment appears to be revolutionary."

"That sounds exciting," Charlie said. "I'm Charlie Choi.

Do you know the name of the company that developed the treatment?"

Dr. Mbosi responded. "It's a new company named GenPhage. I think they're from Massachusetts."

Charlie almost choked on his margarita and had to fight through a coughing spell.

"Are you all right?" Dr. Mbosi asked.

"Yes," Charlie replied. "Just forgot to swallow. Are you sure that's the name of the company?"

"Yes. I met some of their clinical research team back when they were selecting sites. Do you know of them?"

"Actually, I have heard of them. But I didn't realize they were developing a treatment like this. So they're pioneering this approach?"

The Cape Town doctor jumped in to correct him. "It may be the first treatment for this company, but the use of bacteriophage to treat infection goes back more than a hundred years. It's only now that we have the technology to do the required genetic manipulations and to produce it in sufficient quantities for mass treatment."

"They can directly target antibiotic-resistance genes?"

"Yes. But the real value of the treatment is that they can adapt it as resistance evolves. As you know, resistance genes in bacteria change as bacteria evolve. We need to adapt the treatment as this happens. Bacteria double about every thirty minutes, and each new generation is an opportunity to evolve. That means bacteria can show signs of evolutionary changes over days, weeks, or months. When an evolutionary change results in a new resistance mechanism, we have to be able to respond with a new treatment."

Charlie knew this, but the comments emphasized that a treatment that could evolve as bacteria evolved could be of vital importance to global public health.

"What's the downside of the treatment? Is there a concern that it may trigger faster evolution of defense mechanisms than if we did nothing?"

Another doctor joined the discussion. He was short and thin, his white hair in complete contrast to his very dark skin. "I coordinate care for patients across several rural clinics in Ethiopia. There is one clinical trial site that I know of in my region. I have seen patients whose TB has been cured. But there were patients whom I thought were taking part in the trial who went into septic shock and died of multiple organ failure. I tried to confirm with family members of these patients that they were in the GenPhage trial, but they said I was mistaken. I'm not an investigator in the trial and have no access to any records, but I would bet my medical license these patients received the GenPhage treatment."

"Do you think these patients possibly died because of a side effect of the treatment?"

"I know nothing for sure, as I have no access to records. Remember, people in my country get sick and die regularly from diseases and infections that aren't really a concern in developed countries. They may have been exposed to something else with no connection to this treatment. But, theoretically, it's plausible that the treatment approach doesn't just have an effect on TB cells. Bacterial-resistant mechanisms are many and complex. Genetic manipulation of bacterial resistance could have unintended consequences. Including those that harm humans."

Charlie followed the logic, and his epidemiologist radar was pinging. He could sense something here, and he focused on holding his excitement at bay. "The cause of death you mentioned for these patients. How often do you see this happen?"

"It occurs occasionally but is not too common in the clinics I cover. It's more common in the larger clinics and hospitals, primarily because the facilities aren't able to treat the number of patients that need help. The facilities are not as sanitary as they need to be."

"How many of these patient deaths seemed suspicious to you?"

"There were three that I know of."

"Were there any autopsies or investigations for these deaths?"

"This is not the United States. People die in my country at a much higher rate than you would believe. We don't have the resources to worry about individual causes of death."

"Wouldn't three cases of septic shock with multiple organ failure be a signal of some possible outbreak, something to investigate?"

"Not in Ethiopia. Three deaths are not even noticeable. These people are basically invisible. Besides, the families had no desire to question the deaths. They're used to moving on when someone dies."

"If they were part of the trial and died, even if not from the treatment, the trial database would record the deaths. Right?"

The Ethiopian doctor shook his head and gave a knowing smile. "Record keeping in much of Africa is not as thorough as it is here or in Europe. The records submitted from trial sites in Africa, at least for those countries I have knowledge of, are in some fashion at the discretion of each site investigator. If there are details the sponsoring company wouldn't want included, then it's simple to bribe the site investigator to exclude them. Records of trial patients who've died have often disappeared. A few dollars for the doctor and even less for the family, and a patient was never in a trial. As I said, people are invisible. No one really cares."

Charlie looked around at the other doctors. "Have any of you seen this?"

"Not in this situation," said the Cape Town doctor. "But I know for a fact that such patient-record disappearances happen. It's been happening as long as drug companies have been doing clinical trials in Africa."

The doctor from Kenya, Dr. Mbosi, looked around hesitantly. The honesty of his peers seemed to give him the courage to share. "I have not witnessed this personally with this treatment, but I have a staff member whose sister is a nurse at a clinical trial site in Kisumu. She told me that she knows of at least four patients from the GenPhage clinical trial who have died from septic shock. Someone wiped their records from the clinical trial database."

Charlie shook his head in disbelief. "I can't believe this happens. I guess I'm naïve about how things work over there. Does anyone ever speak up?"

"GenPhage isn't the first drug company to take advantage of people in Africa, and it won't be the last. Speaking up is a good way to get yourself killed. You'd need very conclusive evidence to even consider trying to stop one of these companies. Corruption runs deep."

Charlie turned to look at Dr. Mbosi. "Your staffer's sister. Would she be able to get documentation that any of the patients who died from septic shock were on the GenPhage treatment? It doesn't have to be an actual clinical trial record. Anything that links a patient who died to having received at least one dose of the GenPhage treatment."

"What you ask is dangerous. Someone at the clinic, probably the site investigator, must be expunging records of patients who die while on treatment. This means he is being paid by GenPhage. Companies that engage in corruption in Africa have more resources than just money. Some would kill to protect their business."

"Is this true? Do you have proof?"

"Proof? No. But when you live there, you don't need proof to know it's happening. You just need to pay attention."

"So you don't think it's possible to connect GenPhage to patients who died?"

"I didn't say it wasn't possible, only that it's dangerous. What I can do is confirm the nurse in Kisumu has access to dosing records from the last few weeks. If she does, which I believe to be the case, then if any of those patients died of septic shock, I can get you whatever documentation she finds."

Charlie looked around, nervous people nearby might overhear their conversation. He lowered his voice as he continued. "If this works, it might be enough to expose GenPhage. I know a reporter who's investigating the death of a GenPhage employee. I think he somehow got exposed to this treatment. If we can establish a link to the deaths in the clinical trials, we might be able to stop the use of this treatment."

"Perhaps," said the doctor from Cape Town. "But that would also remove a potential treatment for TB patients who have tried all other drugs. It's a difficult trade-off."

"I agree," said the doctor from Ethiopia. "But I'm torn. These patients are destined to die from TB. Having a high-risk option may be better than no option at all."

Charlie nodded. "I understand. If I had multi-drug-resistant TB, I might opt to give this a try. But right now, I bet these patients don't know there is such a risk. Experimenting on unsuspecting patients in countries where deaths are easily swept away is inhuman. Doing it in the name of trying to save lives doesn't make up for it."

"You're right, of course," Dr. Mbosi agreed. "We all have high hopes for this treatment. I hope that there's a way we can make science do what we intend. I'll contact my staffer's sister. Give me until Tuesday to investigate. You should hear from me by the end of my day, maybe lunchtime for you."

"Thank you very much," Charlie said. "If she can do this, I'll make sure we finish the job."

NEIL WAS surprised by the call from Carter.

"Yes," Neil said. "This must be important, given the time. Good thing I can't sleep worth a damn."

"It's important," said Carter. "My team on Charlie had an interesting night."

After getting the update, Neil ended the call.

A situation he appeared to have dealt with effectively had shifted yet again.

Jordan Reed had started a fire that continued to smolder. Every time Neil thought he'd put it out, it sprang up again. He needed to extinguish it. Once and for all.

21

J ORDAN TOOK ADVANTAGE OF HER S ATURDAY MORNING BY SLEEPING in. A rare event. She should have hit the pool, but the activity of the past couple of days had sapped her motivation to exercise. That and an evening of drinking with Emma. She felt relieved that she'd shared her deception with her and was actually glad Emma had her own deception to share. It balanced their relationship equation and took the sting out of what she'd done. Now they could just be friends with no ulterior motives.

Before rolling out of bed, she checked her phone, a bad habit she couldn't kick. As the screen came to life, she saw several texts from Charlie, beginning at one a.m.

"I learned something big and have to share it in person"

"It's about GenPhage"

"Will come to your place tomorrow...be there by 1"

"I'm leaving now...see you soon"

The last text was sent at eight a.m.

What the hell? I thought he was at some conference. How did he learn anything about GenPhage?

The string of texts had her wide awake. Her GenPhage story disaster came rushing back in an instant. Now Charlie said he had something big.

Jordan was tempted to call Charlie and tell him to forget about GenPhage. To just drive home to Burlington. But that wouldn't really satisfy her. She needed to know what he'd learned but forced herself to be patient.

If Charlie really had something big, Jordan would need help to figure out what she should do. Going to one of her editors with this would be career suicide. She needed the advice of someone who could see the big picture and tell her what she needed to hear. Charlie was now part of the story, so he would stay involved. But she needed someone whose opinion she could trust 100 percent and who knew her well. That meant Travis. It always meant Travis.

Despite their past, he was still the person she counted on the most. She texted him to see when he would be at Darcy's Pub. He said his usual time, sometime around 11:30. She texted Charlie to meet her there and gave him the address. The three of them could digest all of the facts and figure out what the best play would be.

Jordan tried to put the whole mess out of her head until she learned what Charlie knew and talked it over with him and Travis. But setting things aside wasn't her strength.

The bar had only been open for forty-five minutes when Jordan got there at 12:15. It was mostly empty. That would quickly change as the sports crowd poured in for the day's games. Jordan took her preferred seat at one end of the bar. Travis was on the opposite side and came around when he noticed her taking a seat.

"Hey," he said. "You're becoming a real regular. I wasn't expecting you so soon. Hell, maybe not at all if the bad guys had gotten you." Travis grinned slyly.

"Not funny, asshole. Remember, you saw them come back last night. You know they're following me."

"All right. I agree it's strange that they left came back right after you did. It certainly looks like you're being followed. Is that why you're here? You need a safe place to hide? You know I don't have a gun."

"I'm not hiding. But I need to get another opinion on this whole freaking mess. And, believe it or not, you are the best person to give me that."

"No shit. But I'm surprised you're asking me. What exactly do you need an opinion on?"

"Big picture, what I should do next. If anything."

"I thought they put you on the sidelines as far as GenPhage is concerned."

"They did. Unless I happened to come up with some amazing new lead."

"I'd be totally impressed if you've done that since I saw you last night."

"I didn't." Jordan paused and looked directly at Travis. "But I think someone else may have."

"Someone else? Is there someone else from the *Courant* working with you?"

"You know there isn't." Jordan had to tread delicately here. Travis didn't know about Charlie, and she didn't want to begin their meeting with unnecessary tension. "I think I mentioned I know someone who works for the CDC. He helped me get access to Eric Smith's death certificate. He also talked to the doctor who treated him in the hospital."

"Is this the big new lead?"

"No," Jordan said. "I don't know what it is yet. Charlie, my friend from the CDC, texted me last night from New York. He said he learned something big about GenPhage and that we had to talk. I told him to meet me here around one."

"You know him from another story you did?" Travis asked, hiding his real question behind one about her job.

"More or less. He helped me on that Ebola stuff."

"Oh. So why meet here?"

"I need you both. If he has something huge, then I'll be in a jam. My editors don't want me anywhere near GenPhage. Even with a brand-new angle, I bet they think I would somehow screw it up. Given my recent crash and burn, I don't totally trust my judgment either. That's where you and Charlie can help. If what he has is just crap, then we can forget it and drink the afternoon away. But if he has something I can't ignore, then I'll need help."

"I live to serve you. But you already knew that."

"Don't be a baby. You're no fun when you're sulking."

"I'm not sulking. I was just stating a fact."

"Fine. How about a drink, though? No matter what Charlie has to say, I think it'll go down better with a gin in my hand."

"That's my job." Travis's look told Jordan what he thought of her having a drink so early. She didn't care.

Travis brought Jordan's drink over. She took a long sip, savoring that first, instant sensation of relief she felt when she really needed a drink. She sometimes wondered if she was an alcoholic. In her own mind, she knew she could still pass on a drink if she needed to. Maybe she was pre-alcoholic, if there was such a thing. She could live with that.

"There's one more thing that happened you might find interesting," Jordan said.

"Oh yeah? What's that?"

"I got a call yesterday. From the guy who stuck that obituary on my door."

"You're shitting me. Someone admitted to doing that? Did he tell you why?"

"He didn't exactly answer a lot of questions. He gave me some bullshit about wanting to do the right thing in stopping whatever Neil Foley and GenPhage were up to. Said he knew Foley and somehow helped him get where he is today."

"But why pick you?"

"That was the surprising part. He evidently knew that my mother died from side effects of the breast-cancer drug that

Foley's company tested. This guy, Ben, eventually learned that Foley and their company covered up the side effects, and knows Foley is now doing something wrong again. He connected Foley to my mom and then to me. Since I'm a reporter, he figured he could sic me on him."

"Damn, this keeps getting better. Did he tell you anything else?"

"Only that Eric Smith can't be the real story. There must be something bigger going on for GenPhage to make such an effort to shut me down."

"Now I see why you're considering getting back on the story. You know you could get fired, right?"

"Yeah, I know. I'm not a complete moron. Let's see what Charlie has to say."

"Sure. Let me know when he gets here."

22

Jordan checked her phone. Nothing from Charlie. She assumed he'd gotten her message and wasn't able to respond. She was lifting her glass to take another sip of her drink when he walked in. He wiped his feet on the doormat and unzipped his jacket, looking around for Jordan. She raised her arm and gave a little wave as his gaze swept in her direction. His big smile told her he saw the wave. He hustled over to the bar.

"Hey there," he said, giving Jordan a quick hug as she stood up. "I made great time today. There was almost nobody on the road. I can't remember the last time I-95 was so smooth."

"It must have been fast. I wasn't expecting you for at least twenty more minutes. Want a drink?"

"Just a seltzer. I had more than my share last night and need to detox today."

"Let's take care of that right away." Jordan saw Travis and gave him a wave, which he picked up in the mirror that ran behind the bar.

"Travis, this is Charlie," she said as Travis came over. "Charlie, Travis."

"Pleased to meet you," said Travis. "You must be Jordan's friend who works for the CDC."

"That's me."

Jordan's impatience prompted her to interject right away. "Charlie needs a seltzer. Maybe a menu too."

"You got it."

"Travis," Jordan said, "we'll grab a table. Join us when you can?"

"Absolutely."

Charlie looked puzzled. "You want the bartender to join us? I thought you'd want to hear what I learned about GenPhage."

"I do." Jordan spoke deliberately. She needed Charlie and Travis to focus on her problem and not get distracted because they each had some kind of history with her. "I'll catch you up on the last two days, but they've been crazy. And not in a good way. Travis isn't just a bartender. He and I go way back, and he knows most of what has gone on with me and this GenPhage story. If you drop a bombshell, I'll need some trusted help in deciding what to do. That includes you as well. After the week I had, I need as much help as I can get."

"Sounds like I missed a lot."

"That's an understatement." Jordan took advantage of the fact that Travis hadn't come over yet to share the headlines with Charlie.

"Wow," he said after Jordan had finished. "That's a shitty couple of days. But do you really think you're being followed?"

"It seems like it, though I'm sure Travis doesn't want to believe it."

"Well, we can come back to that. Once I tell you what I learned, you'll want to reopen the story."

"I'm not sure I really want to. I can't afford to screw up again."

Jordan saw Travis approaching. "It's about time. Did you get lost?"

"You know I have real work to do to keep this business running. I should charge you for my break."

"Are you a manager here?" Charlie asked.

"Co-owner, actually. It belonged to an uncle, and when he died suddenly, I bought a stake from my aunt and agreed to run the place. When I'm forty, it'll be a hundred percent mine. If I can keep it going that long."

"That's great. I have a lot of respect for people who run their own businesses. It's a lot harder than working for someone else."

"Damn straight it is. Thanks," Travis said. "Jordan told me you have some kind of big news on her recently deceased story."

"Ha ha," said Jordan.

"I do. And when I heard it for myself, I nearly choked on my drink."

Jordan couldn't wait any longer. "Just fucking tell us already."

Travis and Charlie exchanged one of those looks that guys exchange when they think a woman needs to be handled cautiously.

"OK, calm down," Charlie began. "I've been at a conference on infectious diseases in New York. Last night a bunch of us went out to dinner, and I sat with some doctors from all over Africa. At one point, the conversation turned to some new antibiotic treatment that was being tested for TB. You know, in clinical trials."

Jordan and Travis both nodded, and Charlie continued.

"This treatment is supposedly some kind of new gene therapy that targets bacteria to overcome antibiotic resistance. This resistance is a big problem that's only getting worse. For TB, it can be a death sentence. Anyway, one minute they're talking about the promise of the treatment and the next they're talking about patients who got the treatment and died."

"So what?" Jordan said. "I'd expect patients dying wouldn't be too surprising in Africa. Especially for patients with serious infections."

"Sure, but these patients were taking a treatment that these doctors had seen work. All of these doctors saw patients who responded. But get this. They didn't die of TB. They died of multiple organ failure. Septic shock. Sound familiar?"

Jordan's mouth dried up, and her jaw dropped. "Are you saying they died of the same thing as Eric Smith?"

"We can't know for sure without autopsies, but it's one hell of a coincidence. But that's not all. These doctors also told me there are no records of these patients being in a clinical trial. They were sure these patients were in the trial, but the records to prove it vanished. They told me that in Africa it was easy and common to have a patient record disappear if someone didn't like the result. It's like Africa is just one big petri dish for pharmaceutical companies."

"That's disgusting," Jordan said. "With the money these companies make and how much they pay their executives, you'd think they couldn't get away with shit like this."

"It's not just drug companies," Travis said. "Corruption itself is like a virus over there. In countries without a lot of checks and balances, it's how business works. Hell, the restaurant business in Boston has its own share of corruption."

At this moment, Jordan didn't really give a shit about global corruption or anything else she couldn't change. She needed to know the GenPhage connection. "But where does GenPhage fit in?"

"The clinical trials were for the first GenPhage treatment," Charlie said. "The one they're manufacturing in Lexington. Where Eric Smith worked."

"Holy shit," Jordan said.

"Does that mean he got infected there?" Travis asked.

"Maybe," Jordan said. "He had responded to an accident at work three days before he died, but the report didn't mention anything dangerous. There's no obvious reason he should've gotten that sick."

"Right," Charlie added. "An otherwise healthy person doesn't just die of organ failure. There has to be some kind of specific cause. Commonly, there's some underlying infection or a significant trauma. Eric Smith was apparently healthy, so there's no clear reason why he got so sick."

"Did these doctors from Africa know what it was about the GenPhage treatment that caused the deaths?" Jordan asked.

"That's the real unknown here. According to these doctors, the treatment seemed to work well for patients with drug-resistant TB. But there were some who got sick and died of multiple organ failure. And it happened quick."

"But it only happened to GenPhage patients?"

"That's what these doctors believed. No one would talk about the patients who died. Not even the families. The doctors think there was something about the treatment that caused non-TB bacteria to proliferate and become dangerous. The infections didn't respond to any antibiotics. Maybe the GenPhage treatment transformed otherwise normal bacteria into strains that were highly resistant to treatment. For all we know, they designed it this way."

Jordan thought this shouldn't have been a surprise. "Wouldn't they have seen this before? In some other trials?"

"Maybe, but earlier trials would have been small, and they might have missed this. Still, though, it would be a surprise if GenPhage had no idea this was possible. And if they're behind hiding the deaths of these patients, they definitely know now and aren't stopping the trials."

"What do you think, Travis?" Jordan said. "You're good at figuring shit out."

"Let me try laying this out to see if I understand," Travis said. "We have GenPhage conducting clinical trials in Africa on a treatment to cure TB. Their treatment cures TB but also triggers multiple organ failure in some patients. GenPhage probably knew about this and is now hiding the deaths. Am I keeping up?"

"So far so good," Charlie said. Jordan nodded in agreement.

"At the same time, Eric Smith, who worked in the nearby GenPhage manufacturing plant, died of multiple organ failure. But the company accident report doesn't suggest anything that explains his illness. Since he died in the same way as those patients in Africa, you think the cause is the same. Which means the company is covering up that there's something very wrong with their treatment."

"Bingo," said Jordan. "Plus, GenPhage was quick to get a settlement to the Smith family. Companies don't do that unless they want to keep something quiet."

"Do you think Eric Smith's family knows what really happened?"

"I talked to Eric's wife twice. Neither time did she seem to know how her husband had really died. Plus, there's Eric's obituary that a third party wrote and stuck on my door."

"Wait. The wife didn't write the obituary?" Charlie said.

"She said she didn't publish one. Her agreement with GenPhage stipulated saying nothing in public about his death. Laurie didn't know who wrote it. But a guy named Ben called me yesterday and claimed that he put it on my door. He probably wrote it."

"Did this third party tell you why he did it?"

"The short version is that he has a connection to Neil Foley and wants me to stop him. My connection to Foley via my mother's death was why he picked me."

"I'm feeling like we're in a movie."

"I think it's the opposite. It feels more real every day. Is there anything else you picked up from those doctors?"

"Yeah. Probably the most important thing. The doctor from Kenya, Dr. Mbosi, has a connection to a trial site there. I believe it's the sister of someone on his staff. He thinks she can get her hands on records of patients that recently died of multiple organ failure who received the GenPhage treatment. If GenPhage is directing site investigators to destroy records of patients who've died, then there's possibly only a small window of time when this nurse could find useful records. He said he'll let me know by Tuesday what they can provide."

Jordan couldn't believe it. To get actual evidence linking a patient death to GenPhage would be like winning the lottery for her. "That's freaking unbelievable," she said. "If this doctor can come through, then not only do I have a story again, but it's a hell of a lot bigger than I ever thought. It's certainly bigger than a single worker's death."

Ben was right.

"That sounds good," Travis said. "But before we get too caught up in taking down a big, evil company, let's all take a deep breath before deciding to do anything rash."

This was exactly why Jordan would have preferred to be doing this by herself. She didn't appreciate Travis putting the brakes on her excitement. That was so like him. Always hesitant to take action. Afraid of what could go wrong.

"We don't need to take a deep breath. We need to decide the best course of action and take these bastards down." Jordan noticed she was almost yelling. "Sorry," she said, looking down at the table. "This story feels way more important than I expected."

"No need to apologize," Charlie said. "I agree, it feels like something big, and we're in a position to expose it."

"We're on your side, Jordan," Travis said. "We want to help. You're the tough reporter. Charlie's a medical expert. I don't want to stop you or slow you down. I want you to figure this out and find the truth. But these guys at GenPhage aren't stupid. I don't think we've seen their bad side yet."

Jordan looked at her two companions. One a former lover and fiancé, and the other a friend who wanted to be more than a friend. The looks on their faces gave her no doubt they were on her side, driving home a sliver of guilt. Good thing she was used to feeling guilty. "Fine, you win. What do you recommend?"

Travis took a deep breath. "OK. Here's what I think. First, we need to prove that the GenPhage treatment is dangerous, that it can lead to organ failure. Second, we have to show that GenPhage knew of the risk. Third, we need to show that GenPhage acted to cover up the risk. If we can do that, you definitely have your story."

"Sure," Jordan said. "Three simple steps. Piece of cake."

"I'm glad you think it'll be easy," Charlie said. "These may be the pieces of the puzzle, but none of them are easy."

"Maybe not," Jordan said, "but we know what we need. Let's focus on each piece individually. First, there's documenting the danger of the treatment. Let's assume the Kenyan doctor can provide proof that at least one patient on the GenPhage treatment died of multiple organ failure. This is probably a best-case scenario, but let's pretend it's doable. We also have Eric Smith dying similarly, though we don't know why. Maybe GenPhage does. That provides two avenues that could show the danger of the treatment."

Both Travis and Charlie nodded. "Keep going," Charlie said.

"The question, then, is whether GenPhage knew of any treatment risk. This is where our story is the weakest, at least in terms of what we can prove. The settlement for Eric Smith's family may help prove the cover-up, but it doesn't mean they knew exactly what happened. They can claim they were just taking care of an employee's family."

Travis looked at Charlie. "If the Kenyan doctor comes through and proves GenPhage patients died of organ failure, do you think the documentation they share would also show that GenPhage knew something was wrong with their treatment?"

"I doubt it. The best I can expect is a record of a patient being administered the GenPhage treatment who eventually died of organ failure. To support what you're suggesting would require a list of all patients actually enrolled in the clinical trial and then a document that showed the patients reported to be in the trial. Patients that were in the first list but not the second and died of organ failure would be good evidence. But that'd be hard to do."

"OK. I didn't think it would be easy, but now it seems impossible. We'll need to look closer to home to find evidence that GenPhage knew of the danger. This is where we will need Jordan's reporter magic."

"So I get the hard part?"

"You're the star reporter. We're just your minions," Charlie said.

"But we're here to help. You just have to point us in the right direction."

Jordan was thinking about options to get the evidence they needed, but nothing that came to mind seemed easy. "OK, minions. I don't like these options, but let me know what you think. There must be documentation within GenPhage that proves they knew of the risk. We could try to hack their systems and search for what we need. Travis, how are your Mr. Robot skills? Do you think it's possible?"

"Maybe if we had the real Mr. Robot," said Travis. "That's definitely out of my league. I could hook us up with someone, but it would be risky."

"OK. The hacking approach isn't at the top of the list. Another option would be to get into GenPhage's headquarters ourselves and search for copies of any documents that show they knew of the risk. This also feels like a long shot, but if we could get in there for a few hours, we may have a chance. Thoughts?"

Charlie jumped in first. "It sounds good, but companies like this have a lot of security. Just getting in will be challenging. If we could knock their security system or cameras offline, we might be able to pull it off. We'd need a company badge to unlock doors. Difficult but not impossible."

"And let's not forget that GenPhage is probably following

Jordan. You can bet they won't let her get anywhere near GenPhage."

"I didn't forget, but thanks for reminding me," Jordan said. "I don't know how far they'd go to keep me in check, and I really don't want to find out. That leaves us two long shots as options. Anything else?"

"How about your friend Emma?" Travis asked.

"Who's Emma?" Charlie asked.

Jordan was hoping not to have to consider that option. Emma was someone she felt a real connection to and just wanted to have a normal friendship with. Even if her uncle was the devil. Lord knows she didn't have a lot of friends and could use a good one. "She's someone I met who works for GenPhage. We didn't exactly meet by accident, and I kind of used information from her without telling her. Not exactly a great way to become friends. Oh, and her uncle is the GenPhage chief operations officer, Neil Foley."

"Holy shit, Jordan," Charlie said. "You know someone connected to the top of the company? You can bet that if GenPhage is really doing what we think they're doing, then this Neil Foley will be at the center of it. In a small company like this, he must be all over everything they're doing."

"Oh, he is," Jordan said. "He was part of that nice little meeting I had with my editors and the GenPhage lawyers yesterday when they threatened to sue the paper. He just sat there with one of those shit-eating grins on his face, thinking he had buried my story. I'd like to teach him a lesson."

"That's all very interesting, but back to my question," Travis said. "Can we get Emma to help?"

Jordan thought about how easily Emma had offered to let her see Eric Smith's accident report because she thought it would help Eric's family. Emma seemed to be someone who would do the right thing. But would she knowingly help get information that could cause her company to get shut down? A company where her uncle was an executive? If their roles were reversed, Jordan wasn't sure even she could do it.

"I don't know, guys. Emma seems like a good person, and I think she'd want to do the right thing. But to go against her own company? I really don't know. And if we let her in on our story, then we have to live or die by her decision. It's a big risk."

"There may be another avenue we can pursue," Charlie said.

Travis and Jordan both looked at him. "What are you thinking?" Jordan said.

"GenPhage must have had a signal of the risk before getting to phase III. Either they hid it or the FDA didn't notice it. That means there're people in the company who know. Probably not many. I don't expect current employees to cooperate, especially if it puts them at risk. But there may be former employees who knew something. All we need is one person with a conscience to confirm our hypothesis. If they can tell us what to look for, then maybe we bring in Emma or try to get inside ourselves."

"That's not bad," said Travis. "That should be low risk for us, and if we can find someone who knows something incriminating, we can figure out how to get the evidence Jordan needs for her story."

"I like it," said Jordan. "I can do the research to find potential former employees. Tracking people down is something I'm good at. Charlie, I might need you to talk with people."

"I agree," said Charlie. "I think it's most likely going to be a former company scientist that can help us, and I can speak to them on their terms. But this can't be perceived as a CDC investigation, because it isn't. I'm just a doctor trying to learn about a possibly dangerous treatment being tested."

"Charlie," Jordan said, "I think it makes sense to stay in town, if you can. I bet I can get some leads today. With luck, we'll find a talker by tomorrow, so if you stay here, we can make progress fast. What do you think?"

Charlie didn't hesitate. "Not a problem. I have nothing

urgent this week. The few things I need to do can be managed remotely. I should be good at least until Wednesday."

"Perfect. I have a sofa bed you can use. It just happens to be in what passes for my office. On the plus side, you'll be close to everything I know about this story. I have it mapped out on a big whiteboard on the wall."

"What about me?" said Travis. "I'm feeling kind of left out here."

Travis positioned his statement in a lighthearted manner, but Jordan knew feeling left out bothered him more than he let on. She definitely didn't want to leave him out, but since he was local and tied up with his bar, she hadn't immediately thought about including him in the hunt for a former employee. "Sorry, Travis. I didn't mean to exclude you. I just thought you'd be busy with the bar."

"I'm the owner. Well, part owner. I can get away when I need to."

"OK, then. I propose we hunker down at my place for the next couple of days and work together until we either prove GenPhage knew their treatment was dangerous or hit every dead end possible. By Tuesday, we'll know if this Dr. Mbosi can come through for us."

"Now you're talking," Travis said. "Nothing like some good old-fashioned teamwork. I'll make sure my staff covers the bar and will be at your place by six. I'll even bring food and an air mattress."

"Works for me," Charlie said. "I haven't had a good sleepover since medical school."

"All right, then," Jordan said. "Travis, you finish up here. Charlie, you can take my keys and head to my place. Grab a nap if you need one. I know you had a late night and a long drive."

As they split up, Jordan experienced a new feeling. She took a moment to recognize what it was. She was part of a team. And it felt kind of good.

23

ELEVEN P.M. AS FAR AS CHRIS COULD TELL, IT DIDN'T SEEM LIKE anyone was planning on leaving. He had parked his vehicle across the street from Jordan Reed's apartment and had a good view with his scope. He couldn't see them at the moment, but all three of them had passed through his field of vision several times. That Chris and his team were on heightened surveillance told him that someone had underestimated Jordan Reed. He also realized they should have planted audio or video surveillance in her apartment. Chris knew Carter wouldn't like the update coming his way.

"Go," said Carter.

"All three of them are in Reed's apartment. Charlie got there first, followed by Jordan and then the bartender, Travis. They've been there all evening. From my vantage point, there are no signs they're leaving anytime soon. It looked like Travis brought an air mattress, so I think they're all going to spend the night there."

"I guess Jordan Reed shouldn't surprise me anymore. It's time to escalate."

JORDAN, Charlie, and Travis worked well into the night to identify potential informants who used to work at GenPhage. Charlie was the first to fall, crashing around two a.m. Jordan and Travis kept going until four a.m. when they both realized that they couldn't look at a computer screen for one more minute. Jordan woke up around eight a.m. and made a fresh pot of coffee. They would all need some serious caffeine after their short night of sleep.

With her first cup of coffee in hand, Jordan grabbed her laptop, sat back on her sofa, and surveyed the output of last night's work. They had a list of eight potential informants. All of them had worked at GenPhage in the past eighteen months, and seven of them were from the medical side of the business. Two were from the medical affairs department, while three looked like they had roles within the clinical-development team. Two listed their GenPhage jobs as research scientists, with their job descriptions relating to bioassay development. This didn't mean much to Jordan, but Charlie said it was common for a company to create new scientific assays when they were developing a new product. Existing assays often weren't specific enough if a company was developing something new.

Charlie suspected these scientists could have been working on a way to quantify how well they could deliver genes to the target bacteria. The eighth person might have worked directly for Neil Foley himself. He had been the head of manufacturing operations. Based on the roles these people had at GenPhage, there was definitely a chance that at least one of them knew something about what could be wrong with their flagship treatment.

Now that they had their list of names, they needed to move from planning to action. As if on cue, Charlie rose from the sofa bed in the office and slowly walked to Jordan's small kitchen. He may have been walking, but his drooping eyes suggested he was barely awake. "I think I smell coffee in this direction," he said, his voice hoarse. "I'll join you as soon as I grab a cup and wedge my eyes open."

"Take your time. Travis is still out."

Charlie came over and sat on the small sofa, putting his coffee down on a beer coaster on the table. "What time did you knock it off?"

"I think it was around four. We were on a roll, and I wanted to get down to a list of people we could work with before sleeping. We have eight names, and their GenPhage jobs look promising."

"Eight should be easy to manage. How do you want to handle the outreach?"

Just then, Travis rolled off his air mattress and came over, showing no signs he'd only gotten four hours of sleep. "Hey there. I see the coffee's already flowing. Let me get a cup and join you."

"How can you be wide awake already?" Charlie said.

"Practice. I'm used to sleeping four to five hours a night. I get home late from my bar, and I use the mornings to tackle everything else in my life."

"You should find a way to package and sell that," Charlie said. "It'd be a gold mine."

Jordan's impatience made its first appearance of the day. "Enough useless chitchat, boys. Let's focus. We have to convince one of these people to help us. Ideally today."

"Don't get too far ahead, Jordan," Travis said. "It could be the case that none of these folks know anything useful. If we hit that dead end, then I'm not sure we really have another play."

"Always the pessimist, Travis. Have faith."

"I prefer realist. In the real world, the good guy doesn't always win."

Charlie stepped in to steer the discussion back on track. "Let's review the list of names, what they did at GenPhage, and

180

then how best to make contact. Jordan, get the names on your whiteboard."

"Finally," she said with a touch of fake frustration in her tone. They all took their coffee and retreated into Jordan's small office. "Have a seat." Charlie and Travis each grabbed a folding chair and sat down facing the big board while Jordan cleared space to write the names they had identified.

Jordan drew a large table and created a row for each of the eight names. She then captured when each had worked for GenPhage, for how long, and what type of job they had.

Jordan finished filling in the table and turned back to Charlie and Travis. "Here's what we have to work with. One of these people has to know something. Do you think we can find an informant before we hear from Charlie's Kenyan doctor?"

"I don't think time's our enemy here," Charlie said. "The hard part will be getting someone to respond at all. We'll be reaching out cold, so there may be no one willing to talk. We've got to at least get some kind of response before we can even ask any questions."

"He's right," said Travis. "Most people won't be inclined to respond to a stranger inquiring about a former employer. Unless they really have an axe to grind."

"What do you guys think is the best approach? We could be direct and say we'd like to talk to them about a former employer. Or we could say we're doing a biotech employer survey and use that pretense to ask some pointed questions. Other options?"

Charlie weighed in first. "It depends on how we reach out. If we do it via LinkedIn, then I think we need a less direct approach, like a survey. If we think we can get a face-to-face meeting or a phone call, even a short one, we can be more direct."

"Are they all still in the Boston area?" Travis said.

"Mostly," Jordan said. "Are you thinking of trying to meet with them in person?"

"Yes. I think we'll have better luck if we can talk to them face-to-face."

Jordan liked where this was going. "I'm with you. If we get them in person, it will be easier to probe them about GenPhage."

"Jordan, let's see where these people work on a map."

Jordan opened Google Maps on her laptop and entered the locations of the current employers of the eight candidates. They were all in the greater Boston area, within a twenty-mile radius. Two of the eight, the medical affairs workers, were at the same company. The former manufacturing operations leader was at a company five miles away from these two. In the Cambridge area was one scientist plus two of the clinicians. The third clinician and the last scientist were at companies southwest of the city. They were all within reach.

"They're all close enough to talk to in person," Jordan said. "I really want to talk to this guy who may have worked for Foley. I bet he either loved him or hated him. If it's the latter, he could be our ticket."

"So what's next?" asked Charlie.

Jordan had already given this some thought. "I'll reach out through LinkedIn. That way, they'll know I'm a reporter. I'll request ten to fifteen minutes to ask them some questions about GenPhage. I can pitch it as part of a bigger story on local biotech companies in case they're hesitant. Based on who replies, we can then plan to meet them."

Travis and Charlie both nodded in agreement. "Can we get some breakfast first?" said Charlie. "All of this thinking is making me hungry."

"I second that," said Travis.

"Fine," said Jordan. "Let's hit a diner. I can draft the messages while we eat."

24

THE TRIO ATE A BIG BREAKFAST AS JORDAN LED THE CRAFTING OF the messages for the eight former GenPhage employees. Before leaving the diner, the messages were on their way. In the days prior to LinkedIn, it would have been practically impossible to reach out to people so easily without knowing their email address or phone number. Now, it was simple to send a message to a stranger under the guise of professional connection or courtesy.

Next came the waiting game.

They walked in relative silence back to Jordan's apartment. The combination of full stomachs and the completion of a task dampened the energy needed for conversation.

They entered Jordan's building, and she unlocked her door.

A wave of strange scents greeted the trio as Jordan opened the door. Something was wrong.

There were multiple overlapping smells. Some floral and pleasant. Some harsh and acidic. Jordan stepped inside to a complete mess. Items were strewn everywhere, furniture tipped over.

"What the hell?" Charlie said.

"Oh shit," Travis said. "You've had company."

"A break-in?" Charlie said.

"Looks like it," Jordan said. "Let me look around." Jordan didn't own much of value, but she had a few pieces of jewelry in her bedroom that might interest thieves. A check of her jewelry box revealed that nothing was missing. Her television wasn't taken, implying whoever did this wasn't looking for electronics. Or they thought her television was a piece of crap. She called out to Travis and Charlie, "I don't think this was a burglary. Nothing seems to be missing."

Jordan left her bedroom. "Come into the office," Travis said. "I think I know what your uninvited guests were looking for."

Jordan and Charlie entered the office, and the first thing Jordan noticed was the bare wall where her whiteboard had been. Someone had ripped it off the wall. It was now on the floor, covered with dents and holes. Her quasi-organized files and piles of documents were now a huge, gooey mess on the floor. They appeared wet. Jordan realized the pile of papers was the source of one of the strange smells that had greeted them. She bent down to look more closely and saw that something had been poured on the documents that had dissolved the ink. Even if she could separate the pages, they would be unreadable.

"Those motherfuckers," she said.

"Who?" said Charlie.

"Fucking GenPhage. Who else do you think is responsible? We were only gone an hour, so whoever did this had to be waiting for us to leave. Nothing was stolen, but all the hard copies of material I have on GenPhage is gone or destroyed." She looked at Travis. "They're not content to just follow me. Now they're coming into my home."

"I can't argue with that."

"That definitely raises the stakes," Charlie said. "This isn't the kind of thing I picture drug companies doing." Charlie said.

"Don't be surprised," said Travis. "A drug company is just another corporation. They all take security seriously. If this company is willing to kill people during their testing, there's no telling how far they'd go to protect themselves."

"So now what?" said Charlie.

"Same as before," Jordan said. "We've contacted our eight candidates, and hopefully some of them will talk to us. We now have to expect GenPhage will follow us, especially since they know what we know."

"Do you think GenPhage will try to keep these former employees quiet?"

"I would. They wasted no time getting Eric Smith's widow to sign an affidavit. They might not have great leverage over these folks, but they'll try to keep them quiet."

"Should we call the police?" Charlie asked.

"I don't see the point. I don't want them getting involved in this, at least not until I can connect all the dots. Besides, there wasn't much real damage done in terms of value, so there's not much they'll do."

"We may as well clean up some of this mess while we wait," Travis said. He went to the kitchen to get a couple of garbage bags. He picked up the soggy documents and papers on the floor of the office. Charlie joined him.

Jordan cleaned up the rest of the mess, though she was only going through the motions, moving items from one place to another. She knew she should feel afraid or intimidated. Instead, she was angry. No one had any right to violate her home and interfere with her doing her job. The more she thought about it, the angrier she got.

Jordan's phone was in her back pocket, and she heard the tone indicating she had a new message.

Could someone be responding already?

She pulled out her phone and looked at the screen. Sure enough, she had a message from Stephen Calhoun, the former head of manufacturing at GenPhage. She unlocked her screen and went to the LinkedIn app to read the message. "Guys, we might be in luck. I just got a message from the manufacturing guy."

"Already?" said Travis. "What did he say?"

"He's willing to talk. Actually, he seems more than willing to talk. He seems excited. Let me read it."

Jordan,

Thanks for reaching out. You're correct that I used to work for GenPhage and moved on to another local biotech company just over a year ago. I would be more than happy to answer your questions as best I can. As part of my severance agreement with GenPhage, I signed a nondisclosure agreement. There are certain things my NDA prohibits, but if you ask the right questions, I should be able to enlighten you. Message back and we can find time to meet.

Regards,

Steve Calhoun

"I'll be damned," said Travis. "You're right. He wants to talk. We might pull this off."

"Not 'might.' We'll break this wide open and then watch GenPhage crumble."

"Get back to him before he changes his mind," Charlie said.

"Right."

Within five minutes, Steve Calhoun had provided his phone number.

Jordan touched the phone number in the message and made the call. After three rings, someone answered.

"Steve here."

"Mr. Calhoun, this is Jordan Reed. I received your message. I'm calling to find time to meet."

"Call me Steve."

"Thanks, Steve."

"So, you're doing a story on biotech companies, are you?"

"Yes, but I should tell you up front it's not some fluffy profile piece telling everyone about great local companies and their battle to treat diseases. My angle isn't positive. I'm trying to peek under the covers and understand if the public images these companies portray really reflect how they operate. I'm specifically interested in GenPhage."

"You want to dig up some dirty laundry and share it with the world?"

"Only if it's true."

"I'm game. I was at GenPhage for five years. I worked my ass off for them when they had more work to do than they had people or money to do it. They definitely cut corners. Maybe more than that. So, yes, I can answer questions, but no recording devices. I can meet with you in person if we can figure out a time."

"Perfect. What's your schedule like?"

"Well, I'm traveling to Paris tomorrow for vacation. Unless you have time this afternoon, we can meet when I get back."

"Let's meet today. How about three or four? I can meet you anywhere."

"I can meet downtown at four. How about at Joe's at the Waterfront?"

"I can do that. Thanks a lot, Steve. See you at four."

Jordan set down the phone and immediately fell back into her recliner, the chair flexing as it absorbed Jordan's slim frame. She had a stupid smile on her face, like she'd just eaten the last piece of chocolate cake. Charlie and Travis watched her with expressions that were not quite awe, but close.

"Don't tell me he'll help?" Charlie said.

"Oh, he will. And he sounds like he has things he wants to share."

"Holy shit," said Travis. "I wonder what he knows. He might be our very own Deep Throat."

"I can't believe it's me saying this, but let's not get too excited," Jordan said. "He may be a pissed-off former employee who wants to vent and maybe generate some bad press. Yeah, he wants to talk. But he may not know what we really need."

"You're right," said Charlie. "There're likely only a few people who really know what we need to know. His job at the company was one where he may have seen or heard something that would help us. We won't know until we ask him."

"But we have a chance here," Travis said. "Plus, we still have seven other people who might help. Maybe GenPhage has pissed off everyone that used to work there, and they all want to take a shot at them."

"Remember, that's not why we're doing this. We're trying to show that this company knowingly exposed workers and patients to something dangerous. Let their HR department sort out the other shit."

"I know. I only meant that if the culture at this company is toxic, we may learn more than we expected."

"Well, we now have our first contestant, and with a little luck, we'll get a few more." Jordan stood up and walked over to what was left of her office. Having her apartment trashed made the story more personal.

It would take a lot more than a mess in her apartment to get her to back down this time.

25

"You're not going without me," Travis said.

"Shit, Travis, relax. It's not any more dangerous now than it was before."

"Maybe technically it's not. But these guys are escalating things. They made the jump from following to breaking in. Violence is the next step on the ladder. If you're going to meet with someone, I'm going to be right beside you. I may not be a great fighter, but my size is enough to make most people think twice."

"Travis, I need someone who can speak science. I need Charlie."

"That won't matter if they try to hurt you, or worse. I'd make a better bodyguard than Charlie." Travis turned to Charlie. "No offense, man."

"None taken," Charlie said. "Jordan, I agree with Travis. There shouldn't be anything too complicated from Steve. If you really need me, just put me on the phone with him."

Jordan looked at the two men. She knew they meant well. But not being able to freely make her own decisions was frustrating. One of the things she liked about being a reporter was the lone-ranger aspect. Travis and Charlie were seriously cramping her style.

"Fine. I don't have the energy to fight with you two. Let's go, Travis."

"I'm driving," Travis said.

"What? No. You've already forced me to change my approach. You're not going to drive."

"I am. GenPhage knows your car. You're too easy to follow. They'll have a harder time following you if you're in a different car. Plus, I have a curveball we can throw them."

"Oh, what's that?"

"We can stop at Darcy's Pub on the way. Then we take the van. They sure as hell won't know that vehicle. Even if they follow us there, we can slip out the back and get to the van without being seen."

Jordan was thwarted again. While she hadn't seen much reason to have Travis instead of Charlie, she had to admit Travis's idea was pretty good. If they did it right, the GenPhage guys might stake out the restaurant all evening.

"You win again. Now, let's go."

Even with the detour, Jordan and Travis arrived downtown about fifteen minutes early. Traffic and parking availability were unpredictable. Jordan made sure they had time to spare. Charlie stayed behind at Jordan's, monitoring her LinkedIn account for replies from any of the other former GenPhage employees. If any of the remaining seven contacted Jordan, Charlie was to set up a meet or, if that wasn't possible, do a quick interview on the phone. Charlie knew what to ask, but Jordan still left him with a list of key questions. Just in case.

Jordan's phone binged as Travis parked the van. She had a new text message. "It's from Steve," she said. "There's a change of plans. He said some guys from GenPhage were just at his place and that they told him not to speak to us. We're now meeting at Starbucks on Atlantic Avenue."

"Shit," said Travis. "These guys are all over us. How did they know we'd talk to Steve today?"

"They saw the names we had on the board, so they're probably just going through them one by one. Doesn't change what we need to do right now. We can regroup later. Starbucks is less than ten minutes away by foot, so we may as well walk."

They got to Starbucks at 4:05. No one inside looked like the photo of Steve. Travis bought three coffees, assuming Steve would want one. They grabbed a few sugar packets and found a table at the far end of the cafe where they could easily see both entrances.

At about 4:10, Jordan saw a man enter who looked just like the photo of Steve on LinkedIn. He must have recently updated his photo. He looked like your typical middle-aged professional. Overweight, with an air of past fitness visible on his frame. He had well-maintained short hair, graying on the sides and windswept from the walk over. His face was red, either from the wind or perhaps from hauling ass to get here quickly. He surveyed the cafe as he entered and looked toward Jordan and Travis. Jordan did a quick wave. Steve came over and sat down without removing his jacket.

"You must be Steve," Jordan said. "Thanks for coming. It looks like the situation has evolved since this morning. I really appreciate your willingness to still meet." She motioned toward Travis. "This is my friend Travis. He has been helping me with the research."

"Nice to meet you," Travis said, extending his hand.

"Sure," Steve said, shaking Travis's hand. "Just so you know, I told my GenPhage visitors I wouldn't speak with you. I snuck out the back of my parking garage, so I don't think they followed me here. I hope you weren't followed. Which reminds me, how the hell did they even know we were meeting?"

"Interesting story," Jordan said. "After we researched some possible people to interview, we summarized them all on a whiteboard in my apartment. We went out for breakfast and sent the messages to these individuals, including yourself. When we got back, my apartment was trashed. They ruined any sort of documentation or research I had on the story. It was probably the same guys who came to see you. I assume they must plan to visit everyone on my list."

Jordan saw Steve tense as he took this in. "If I had known that fact, I might have listened to those guys. They looked like they could seriously hurt someone if they wanted to. If they had no hesitation breaking into your place, they probably wouldn't object to a little violence to make sure they got their way. Good thing for you I don't like being threatened."

"I totally understand. I'm pissed at the violation of my home. If I can make them pay, I will. But for them to threaten you tells me you know something that could incriminate GenPhage. This company isn't the mafia. Violence can't be part of their normal business tool kit. You can help expose them, and I'll never reveal you as a source. I promise."

"I'm here now. Even if they find out I met with you, I don't think they'll believe me if I tell them I didn't say anything, so I may as well help. Lord knows they deserve what's coming to them."

"I'm glad that's your decision," Jordan said. "Let's start with your job at GenPhage. What did you do there?"

"I managed all clinical-supply manufacturing and the scale-up for commercial production." Steve must have seen the confusion on Jordan's face and elaborated. "Think of it this way. Whenever a pharmaceutical company is doing clinical trials for a drug, they need to have a manufacturing process that regulators like the FDA approve. For the GenPhage treatment for multi-drug-resistant TB, we had a small-scale manufacturing facility that the FDA approved to supply the drug for the clinical trials. I oversaw the design and implementation of that process and also was in charge of the day-to-day operations of the facility. All the product that we produced from that location was my responsibility."

"You knew every step of the process and everything that went into the product?"

"Yes. Plus, I oversaw the quality checks on the final product before they allowed us to ship it to the clinical trial sites. Any problems with production quantity or quality came to me. We shipped nothing unless my team approved."

"So you'd know if there was anything wrong with what GenPhage shipped for their trials?"

"Absolutely. But every shipment that went out met every quality check. Period. We sent nothing that didn't match the specifications we manufactured against."

That puzzled Jordan. She had assumed, maybe incorrectly, that there must have been some quality control problems that were overlooked and that the product used in clinical trials was therefore not safe. If they did all the QC checks correctly, then what Steve was saying invalidated Jordan's assumption. "Let me get this straight. All the product manufactured that was under your oversight met the required specifications?"

"Yes," Steve said with a sly smile.

"I don't get it, then," said Jordan. "What was wrong with the product?"

Steve couldn't hold back his expanding smile. "You're not asking the right question. I said what we manufactured met specifications. But you didn't ask about the specifications we had to match. There were multiple sets of specifications."

"What do you mean, 'multiple sets'? I thought there was only one treatment?"

"That's what I thought. At least at first. One product should have one set of specifications. But when we developed the scale-up process to move into clinical supply, they gave us multiple sets of specifications. We were to cycle through variations of the product based on a schedule we were provided. Each variation followed the same process, except the starting stock was different."

"I'm no scientist, but this doesn't seem right."

"Good intuition. I asked why we would use different cell stocks when we should only use one. Initially, no one wanted to answer the question. Then, one day, I met one of our clinical-development scientists at a company party. She was drunk, so I chatted her up, asked about the different stocks. It surprised her we were using multiple stocks for clinical manufacturing because they needed only one for the trials. She said that in the lab there were many variants being tested. She seemed skittish but said she thought some were for the Department of Defense. She wasn't exactly sure of their purpose, but she saw that the genes they were targeting differed from the TB treatment. She had learned from one of the research scientists the sequence and identity of one of these genes. She researched its function. It was a gene that would enhance bacterial resistance. In fact, she said she saw data on some cell variants that looked like they could turn on all the most common drug-resistant genes." Steve paused and looked at Jordan and Travis. "You know what this means, right?"

Jordan looked at Travis, and he shrugged. "They had a way to create resistance to antibiotics?" Travis said.

"Bingo," Steve said, too loudly. He took a quick look around, saw that no one was paying much attention to them, and continued. "Not only were these bastards trying to develop treatments for drug-resistant bacteria, they were also engineering ways to create bacterial resistance. That's a biological weapon."

The words almost didn't register in Jordan's mind, they were so far from anything she had considered. It took her longer than it should have to process the information.

"Do you really think that's what the other stocks were for?" Jordan said.

"They had to be. Why else develop bacterial-resistant genes?

And then produce enough to be used in people? These genes could silently make common bacterial infections resistant to any antibiotic. People could die from a simple infected cut. Or from childbirth. Or from strep. And no one would know exactly why. At least not for a while. You could wipe out towns or villages. And if the resistance spread, you could kill millions. It would be a very effective weapon. Let people get infections, like they do every day. Treat them like we always do. But they wouldn't respond. Health-care resources would be diverted to fight the infections. Many of these people would die. Then others would get sick. Infections would keep spreading, and before you knew it, there'd be an untreatable epidemic."

Jordan processed this as Steve spoke. Now she wished Charlie were here. He had spoken with the doctors in Africa, and what Steve was saying could explain what they were observing.

"Let me make sure I'm following. GenPhage has a technology or process that allows them to develop treatments that would work against drug-resistant bacteria. Sounds great. On the side, they were also doing the reverse. Developing some kind of biological weapon that would make bacterial infections resistant to drugs. While the notion of this disgusts me, if the military supports it, does that mean the government also approved? Am I missing something?"

"I've no idea when it comes to the military. I'm sure this started out as one of many partnerships that the Department of Defense has on the go. They're probably doing all kinds of shit that is illegal or immoral. But ask yourself this: How do you really test a biological weapon?"

Jordan had never thought about anything like this before and didn't really know the answer. But she could take a good guess. "Get this weapon into real people. See what happens."

"You got it. And where would you do something like this, if it were up to you?"

The pieces came together in an instant. "I would test it somewhere where I could hide what I was doing. Where the people would have no clue and there was unlikely to be any real oversight. Where I could control the trail of records. I would go to a place where corruption was the norm and I could find people to bribe. There are a lot of countries in Africa that fit the bill."

"Give the girl a prize," Steve said.

Travis was also putting the pieces together. He turned to Jordan. "This explains what Charlie learned from those doctors he met."

"Who's Charlie?" Steve said.

Jordan fielded the question. "Charlie's a friend who happens to work for the CDC. He was just at a global infectious-disease conference and met some doctors from Africa. They thought the GenPhage treatment was causing patients to go into septic shock and die of multiple organ failure."

"That's fucking it." Steve pounded his fist on the table, bouncing their coffee cups and drawing stares from the few people in the Starbucks. "I knew GenPhage was manufacturing different batches of the treatment and sending them to clinical sites in Africa. The batches were all coded based on the particular source material used, but I never knew how to break the code. But if people on the GenPhage treatment were dying like that, then for sure they were getting one of the weaponized strains of the treatment. You need to get proof. If you can do that, not only will you have your story, but you'll expose GenPhage for the lying bastards they are."

"Believe it or not, there's a doctor trying to get proof that some patients who died were on a GenPhage treatment. He knows a nurse at one of the trial sites."

"You need to get that proof. Otherwise, the only way to get what you need is to break into GenPhage, decipher the codes for the weaponized strains, and find their shipping records. The weaponized strains aren't approved, so records of them going to clinical trial sites would be enough to get them shut down."

"We'll know soon."

Steve took one more sip of coffee and pushed his chair back from the table. "I think we're good. I gave you enough to know what GenPhage is really doing. The rest is up to you. And remember, I'm not coming forward for this. We won't be speaking again." Steve stood up to leave.

"Wait," Jordan said. "I need to ask about Eric Smith."

"You mean the one who died recently? Does it matter now? The real story is what GenPhage is doing in Africa."

"Yes, it fucking matters. Eric Smith is the reason I'm even here. He was the first piece of the puzzle for me, and I owe it to his family to find out what really happened."

For a moment, Steve didn't move.

"Fine." Steve sat back down. "Remember, I'm not going to speak about this again. I'll tell you what I know. Then I'm out of here."

"I'll keep you out of it. What really happened to Eric Smith?"

"Remember the coding I mentioned for the different strains of the treatment? Well, Eric was a production supervisor and developed the production schedules to meet the demand plan he was given. One day, he asked me if he could share something he'd noticed. It turned out there were a handful of trial sites in Africa where he had to send product batches from different source strains. But for every site outside of Africa, he only had to provide one strain. He didn't know why there were different strains, since every trial site had to follow the same protocol. I told him not to worry about it, that there were likely slight variations of the product needed in Africa because of the higher levels of infectious disease there. I didn't know if that was the reason, but I hadn't given it much thought. My job was to make sure the trials had product when they needed it."

"Hang on," Jordan interjected. The timing wasn't tracking

with her. "But that would have been over a year ago. Eric just died. The timeline doesn't make sense."

"Let me finish. I was about to say we didn't talk about it again while I worked at GenPhage. But about a month ago, he called me out of the blue. He said he didn't know who he could trust at GenPhage. I guess he figured that since I hadn't left voluntarily, I wouldn't rat him out. He told me he learned that some product strains did the reverse of what they were supposed to do. He thought they were some kind of weapon, even though he had no real proof. He wanted to see what I knew."

"Did you tell him anything?"

"Indirectly. I said there was only one product strain directed against drug-resistant TB. He thought there were multiple strains being used in trials that didn't match what was approved for testing. Anyway, he said he had to do something, because whoever was allowing this was putting the company at risk. I cautioned him against this, but he said he had to do the right thing and take it to Neil Foley. Can you imagine that? For sure, this was all done because of Neil fucking Foley. I told Eric his plan was risky, but he said he had met Neil once and thought he was a stand-up guy."

"Do you know if he actually went to Foley?"

"Not for a fact. But he said he would do it the next day and would let me know what happened. Five days later, I heard from a friend at GenPhage that Eric was dead. Apparently, there was some kind of incident that Eric responded to. He was even taken to the medical facility on-site. And then he went downhill fast."

"Quite a coincidence," Travis said. "If I were a betting man, I'd say your stand-up guy Foley had Eric removed from the equation. Did your friend share anything else?"

Steve had his hands crossed on the table and was squeezing them together so hard that his fingers were turning red. "This is really going out on a limb, OK? My friend said he saw Eric being taken to the medical facility, but that Eric protested. Said he wasn't exposed to anything. Anyway, guys dressed in hazmat suits took him forcefully. He never came back to work. I think they gave him a weaponized variant and exposed him to a bacterial infection to make sure he got sick. To Eric, it might have looked like he was getting a simple IV."

"Shit," Jordan said. "They fucking killed him. That all makes sense. I'm sure Eric had no idea. There's no sign he told anyone. That also explains the bland accident report we saw."

"If this is true, we're all in more danger than we thought," Travis said. "If they crossed that line, we're not safe."

"All the more reason to expose these bastards." Jordan turned to face Steve. "What about the guys who came to your place? Any description?"

"Not much. Athletic, clean cut, black jackets."

Jordan turned to Travis. "Want to bet it's the same assholes who trashed my place?"

"It's got to be the same guys," Steve said.

As if on cue, Jordan, Travis, and Steve all looked around Starbucks, just in case the three thugs had snuck in. There was no sign of them.

Steve broke the momentary silence, shaken by the conclusion they reached. "Time to go. I'm leaving for vacation tomorrow. Don't call me again unless it's after you publish your story and we're all still alive. Good luck."

Steve zipped up his coat and headed for the door that opened to Atlantic Avenue.

Jordan and Travis sat in silence for a moment. "Do you still want to go through with this?" Travis asked.

"What do you think? There's no way we can back down now. Those fuckers are killing people. They nearly got me fired. They violated my home. I'll show everyone what they're doing."

"All right. I just hope we don't end up dead first."

Jordan and Travis put on their coats. They could hear a car gunning its engine.

"Someone's in a hurry," Travis said.

As Jordan was about to speak, there was the sound of an impact, followed by that of a car speeding away. "Did a car just hit something? Or someone?"

"If it did, it didn't stop. Let's look."

Jordan and Travis rushed out of the Starbucks and looked left and right, trying to figure out which direction the sound had come from. They didn't have to look long. To their right, they heard a person yell. "Someone call nine-one-one. There was a hit-and-run."

Twilight was fast becoming night, but there was enough light to see a person about fifty yards to their right, standing over an object in the road. Travis sprinted ahead of Jordan.

They approached an older man. He was leaning over someone on the road. "Did you see what happened?" Travis said.

The man appeared frozen, in a state of shock or disbelief. He was holding a mobile phone in his right hand. Travis came in beside him and put a hand on the man's shoulder. "Sir, are you OK? Did you see what happened?"

The touch of Travis's hand brought the man out of his daze. "I heard a car speeding up, and when I turned to see where the sound came from, I saw it hit this man. The car just kept going. I think it actually accelerated right into him. Look at him."

Jordan stood beside Travis as they looked down at the man on the street. "Holy shit," she said.

Jordan recognized Steve Calhoun right away. But only because of his jacket. His face—in fact, nearly his whole head—was crushed. Kind of like an apple that had been dropped from a building. His head was at an unnatural angle from his torso, and his left arm and leg both appeared broken in multiple places. He wasn't breathing.

Travis gently grabbed the witness's left arm and helped him to fully stand up. "There's nothing you can do. He's gone."

Under Travis's guidance, the man returned to the sidewalk. "I can't believe he just died. Right in front of me."

"We heard the car from Starbucks. There was no way anyone was going to survive an impact like that."

"It wasn't a car. It was a black Suburban. Tinted windows. I don't think it had any license plates, and I saw no lights. It was as if it was trying to hit this guy."

Jordan's breath caught in her throat as the man's words registered. GenPhage just killed her best source of information. Right in the street.

They could hear sirens, and moments later, both police and EMTs arrived. Jordan, Travis, and the witness who'd called 911 moved out of their way. The first responders began their work in vain.

"You know GenPhage did this," Jordan whispered to Travis. "Because of me. It's my fault. If Steve hadn't talked to me, he'd still be alive." Her tough exterior cracked. Tears filled her eyes.

Travis enveloped her in his arms, letting her bury her face in his shoulder. "It's not your fault. These guys are doing whatever it takes to keep their secret."

They stood together for a long moment. Jordan silently cried. She forgot how safe she felt with Travis. Her guilt at breaking off their engagement came back again. He'd do anything for her. Why couldn't she commit to the one person who loved her?

Jordan realized they might have to give statements to the police. She pulled back from Travis and wiped her eyes. "We can't tell them we just met with Steve. If the police get involved in the GenPhage situation now, GenPhage will shut down what they're doing and they'll get away with everything."

Travis looked confused. "Are you serious? A man was just killed here. Someone we just met with. We can't lie to the police. What if they find out? We could go to jail."

"They have no reason to suspect we knew Steve at all. I bet they won't even ask if we know him. We were just at Starbucks down the street and came over when we heard the car. We didn't even see the Suburban. We won't have to lie. Just act like bystanders."

"This doesn't feel right. If they knew what we knew, they might be able to tie GenPhage to this. It's still murder. You may not get your big story, but you'll still get a good one, if that's what you're worried about."

"Is that what you think? I'm worried about my story? I already walked away from it once and could do it again. Think about the big picture. GenPhage is testing a biological weapon on unsuspecting people in Africa. Now they're murdering people here in the US to keep it covered up. Even if the cops could tie Steve's death to GenPhage, they won't be able to get any further."

"They could if you helped."

"Once they get their murderer, they won't give a shit about what's happening in Africa. Besides, you heard the guy who saw

Steve get hit. The Suburban had no plates. There's no way to prove who did it. I bet that vehicle is on its way to disappearing."

Jordan expected Travis to continue to fight to tell the cops everything. For someone who had broken his fair share of rules in the past, he had become quite a stickler for doing the right thing.

"Fine," he said. "We'll do it your way. For now. But for the record, I think we should come clean with the cops."

Jordan smiled and gave him a quick squeeze on his arm. "Duly noted. We'll nail GenPhage soon."

27

JORDAN WAS BARELY ABLE TO SLEEP. SHE FELT IMMENSE GUILT OVER the death of Steve Calhoun and couldn't get the image of his smashed body out of her mind. Not even five minutes after their meeting and he was dead. Run down in downtown Boston with no obvious connection to who did it. Except for Jordan and Travis.

She knew if there was any chance of bringing the GenPhage story to light, it was up to her. Knowing something that could help the police bring Steve's killers to justice made her guilt worse. She had to keep reminding herself that if the police were to walk into GenPhage and ask them to provide the names of the goons working for them, GenPhage would line up their lawyers and not say anything. When they eventually had to cooperate, they could just deny that there were any such people. If GenPhage execs were as smart and prepared as they seemed, these security guys were likely not anywhere on GenPhage's books. They wouldn't leave so much as a vapor trail.

Jordan smelled fresh coffee brewing and could hear voices, talking low. Her blinds were closed, so she couldn't tell if the sun was up yet. She rolled over to grab her phone from the night table. It was 6:30.

No sleeping in today.

When Jordan and Travis had returned the previous night, they caught Charlie up on the events with Steve. Everything from the last-minute change of venue to the shocking conclusion about GenPhage testing a biological weapon in Africa and finally Steve's brutal death. Charlie seemed to be in shock as he listened, unable to believe GenPhage killed Steve on purpose.

Jordan dragged herself out of bed, yawning, stretching her arms in the air. Not a good sign for her day that she was already tired. She headed into the kitchen, where Charlie and Travis were standing with their backs against the counter, drinking coffee. "Morning, boys. I guess you couldn't sleep either?" Jordan poured herself a cup of coffee and sat on one of her two kitchen chairs.

"Not really," said Charlie. "I feel like I'm in shock, and I didn't even see what happened."

"We didn't see it either," said Travis. "But the aftermath was bad enough. I can't imagine what it would have been like to see that Suburban run him down."

"You think it was the same guys? Hit-and-runs are often accidents. Many people leave the scene when they hit someone."

"Not a chance. We heard the vehicle speed up, hit something, and speed away. The guy closest to the accident confirmed it. Plus, it was a black Suburban with no plates."

"Let's not forget the other important facts," Jordan said. "First, I was being followed by someone in a black Suburban. Second, that someone broke into my apartment, and third, three thug-like guys threatened Steve just before we met with him. Too many violent acts in a row for his death to be a random accident."

"OK," Charlie said. "I'm convinced. I hope the decision not to tell the police what you knew doesn't come back to haunt us. They may never be able to find these guys anyway, but we know information that could help. We better wrap this up fast."

"That's where your doctor friend comes in. When do you think you'll know if he can help?"

"Good news. He sent me an email this morning. He said he contacted the nurse, and she said she'd be able to get some information tomorrow. He didn't specify exactly what the nurse could get, so we'll have to wait and see."

"Shit, that's awesome," said Jordan. "For the record, I'm not remotely superstitious, but I'll be crossing my fingers."

"That gives us something for tomorrow," Travis said. "What's the plan for today? I need to get to the bar to receive deliveries, so maybe I'll head there this morning and circle back with you later today."

"OK by me," Jordan said. "What about you, Charlie? Are you good to stay in town until you hear from Dr. Mbosi, or do you need to head back?"

"I'm good to hang here. I can use the morning to get caught up on a few things for work."

"Perfect. I need to decompress and think about what to do if whatever Dr. Mbosi provides isn't able to help. We may need to find a great hacker in case we need the plan B Steve suggested."

"What was that?" Charlie asked.

"Simple. We get a list of the different strains GenPhage has made. We get the codes that identify what's in each strain so we can know which ones GenPhage weaponized. Then we get shipping records of what they sent to the clinical trial sites in Africa to prove that they sent weaponized material there."

Charlie let out a fake laugh. "Hilarious, Jordan. That's about as far from simple as you can get. It's probably impossible. We know nothing about how and where they'd keep information like this that's supposed to be secret. We might find shipping information, but it would be useless without knowing what they shipped."

Jordan stood up to pour herself another cup of coffee. As she reached for the pot, she heard her phone pinging from the bedroom, notifying her of a new text. She considered ignoring it, but with all the crazy shit that had happened over the past couple of days, she figured she should take a look.

She walked back to the kitchen, phone in hand, looking down at the message. "It's from Emma. She wants to meet me for lunch. Says it's important, that she has a question she needs to ask me. About GenPhage."

"Uh oh," Travis said. "I feel a new twist coming. I'm not sure we can take another surprise."

"Relax. I'm sure it has nothing at all to do with our story. I never told Emma anything about what we knew, other than I was trying to help Eric's widow learn more about his death. Nothing about what we think is going on."

"Nothing would surprise me anymore."

"Are you going to meet her for lunch?" Charlie asked.

"I should. I don't think she knows anything. But you two are making me paranoid, so I better see what she wants to ask me. But if I see a black Suburban, I'm out of there." Jordan forced a smile that didn't hide the kernel of fear she felt.

JORDAN MET Emma at a new seafood restaurant on the waterfront. Emma had gotten a table before Jordan arrived and waved her over when she walked in.

The restaurant was less than a year old and had a cozy New England feel to it, unlike the high-end Manhattan-style restaurants that were becoming more common. Their dark cherry oak table had a red-checkered tablecloth covering all but the corners of the table. The silverware appeared well polished, and the accents on the walls made you think you were on a ship.

Emma stood to greet Jordan as she approached the table. She was wearing a blouse the color of a rich Cabernet Sauvignon, buttoned up to her neck, paired with a long, slim black wool skirt. "Jordan, glad you could come," she said, giving Jordan a quick one-armed hug.

"That's the advantage of not having a social life. I'm almost always free. Not to mention I'm between stories at the moment."

They both sat down and pulled in their chairs. "Sorry to hear that. I'm sure you'll be busy soon enough."

"You're probably right. It's good for my line of work that people just can't find their way to do what's right. Every time a politician, public servant, or corporation doesn't do the right thing, I have a potential story. I'm sure someone, somewhere, is setting up a story for me right now."

Jordan was on edge after the events of the past thirty-six hours, making her unsure of what to expect from Emma today. Whether she cared to admit it, she found herself slightly on guard. Jordan didn't get a negative vibe from Emma, but she couldn't take anything for granted right now.

The server came with menus, mentioned the specials, and took their drink orders. Emma ordered an iced tea. Jordan wanted a gin and tonic but opted for a soda and lime instead.

There was a brief moment of awkward silence. Jordan knew well that when someone wanted something, they would eventually find a way to ask. She played the waiting game to see what Emma would say. It took less than thirty seconds.

"So, Jordan," Emma began, "there's something I want to ask you about. It's about GenPhage, and I'm not sure how to bring it up."

Jordan leaned back in her chair, yielding the space for Emma to speak. "It's best to just get it out. Less chance of a misunderstanding."

"Right. Good suggestion." Emma paused and took a deep breath. "I caught up with my uncle at work this morning. You remember him. Neil Foley?"

"How could I forget? He's practically in charge, right?"

"He's chief operations officer, so yes. It's the most important leadership role for a small biopharma company looking to get its first product approved. Anyway, this morning he asked me, out of the blue, if you were working on a story about GenPhage. Something about the safety of our lead product. He caught me by surprise, and I told him I didn't know about anything you were working on. GenPhage or otherwise."

Jordan wasn't expecting this. She hoped she concealed her surprise. With as plain a face as she could pull off, Jordan said, "That's surprising. Did he tell you why he was asking?"

Emma looked unsure. "He did, but I don't think he was being totally honest with me. He said he heard from some colleagues that there was noise GenPhage was doing something illegal. That maybe you had picked up on that and were writing a story about the company. I asked him which colleagues told him this, but he said that it was more like informants than colleagues. Who knows how he heard." Emma paused and looked Jordan right in the eye. "So, is it true? Are you writing a story on GenPhage?"

All of Jordan's journalism instincts told her to deny this. Nothing good could come from Emma knowing what she was working on regarding GenPhage. But the look on Emma's face convinced Jordan that something worried her. Jordan got the distinct sense that Emma suspected or knew there was something illegal or illicit going on at GenPhage.

"You already know what I was working on, but the sources didn't come through. In the end, there wasn't enough there." Jordan left out that Neil knew damn well what she was working on because he and his team of lawyers had shut her down in front of her bosses. Jordan wasn't sure if Emma knew that. If she didn't, then Neil hadn't included her in his inner circle. "Did he tell you anything else?"

"No. He assured me there was nothing going on at GenPhage I needed to worry about. Based on what you said, I guess he wanted inside information, to find out if you were still working on the story. It sounds like you're done with that now, right?"

Again Jordan used a partial truth. "Right. That story was a stretch, and it turned out to be a ghost."

Emma looked relieved. "That's good. I was worried there was something else you weren't telling me."

"Why? Because I might have found something about GenPhage you may not have known?"

"In part. But there's more."

Not that Jordan wasn't paying close attention to everything Emma said, but her ears perked up at this. She leaned forward, her forearms resting on the table. "Can you tell me?"

Emma fidgeted in her chair, looking uncomfortable. "I feel like I need to tell somebody, but a reporter isn't the best option."

Jordan offered Emma some reassurance. "We're one hundred percent off the record. Just two friends talking. I won't use anything you tell me without your permission. So if you want to talk, I can listen."

"Thanks, Jordan. I appreciate it. OK, here goes. After my conversation with Neil, I called a colleague I know, Dan, who works on our quality control team. I told him I heard rumblings that our product may have safety or quality issues and asked if he knew if there was any truth to the noise. He took a long time to answer, and when he did, he sounded like a different person. Almost like a robot. He said there was absolutely nothing wrong with our product and that anything I was hearing was inaccurate. He pressed me pretty hard on how I'd heard this."

"What did you say?"

A smile crossed Emma's face. "I told him I saw it on Cafepharma."

"Cafepharma? What's that?"

"It's this rather nasty chat site where people working in pharma, sales representatives mostly, share all kinds of stuff. I'm sure eighty percent of it is utter crap, but there's often some truth. Anyway, he dismissed the rumors as nonsense because of the source."

Jordan didn't see where this was going. She thought Emma had stumbled across something, but apparently not from this guy. "I assume something else happened to worry you?"

"Yes. I didn't believe Dan told me the truth, so I took a more direct approach. I went to his office, closed the door, and confronted him. I told him that Neil let it slip that the product had some liabilities and that, given my role in the company, I needed to know what was up."

"That's aggressive. How did he respond?"

"He didn't know what to say. We don't work together, since our areas of responsibility don't overlap, but we have a good relationship. He wasn't expecting me to come to his office and challenge him. I could see the sweat beading on his forehead. He tried to deny it, but I put my hand up and told him I wouldn't take any bullshit. He caved in and said he'd tell me but that I couldn't say I'd heard it from him."

"He knew something? Good instincts on your part."

"Thanks. I can read people pretty well. Anyway, he tells me to sit down, which I did. Then he tells me there's nothing wrong with our product. Nothing at all. But he said GenPhage is testing other versions of the product that aren't for TB. He said he didn't know the details, but it didn't matter because the actual product was safe. The rest wouldn't matter and wouldn't affect the approvability of the product."

"Did he tell you anything else about the other versions of the product? I'd think there might be a potential risk there."

"No, he said he didn't know anything else. But I haven't seen or heard of GenPhage doing any other testing, and we aren't running other clinical trials, so I'm not sure what's going on. But whatever it was sure made Dan nervous."

Jordan took this in. It lined up with what Steve had said, and it looked like as though this Dan guy knew something about the military versions of their product. "That's interesting, for sure, but it doesn't seem like you know enough to do anything. Are you going to pursue it?" Jordan hoped Emma would drop it. Having someone poking around, even if she worked for GenPhage, might panic them into shutting down what they were doing. She needed GenPhage to keep going a bit longer.

"I thought I'd approach Neil about this tomorrow. He doesn't need to know exactly what I learned or how, but I want to hear from him what's going on. I'm an employee and shareholder in the company, and I deserve to know if there's something wrong."

This wasn't what Jordan wanted to hear. "That sounds risky. How do you think Neil will respond?"

"I'm not sure. In executive committee meetings, he has this amazing ability to absorb stressful situations and remain calm. But I also know him as my uncle and as a member of our family. He has a temper. And not a mild one. He can explode. I've seen him tear into his wife until she was in tears. It's a bit of a gamble."

"I'm not sure it's worth getting on his bad side, family or not. If you knew something specific, then you'd have some leverage, but he can play the denial game all he wants right now. I wouldn't approach him unless you had something concrete."

"Maybe you're right. But I can't get it out of my head that there's something bad going on. Neil's comments and Dan's strange behavior and cryptic answers tell me they're hiding something. Something big."

Emma's body language was open, almost as if she were asking Jordan to help figure out what was going on at GenPhage. If only Emma knew what Jordan knew. Jordan could get her uncle fired, along with anyone else who was in on their weapons program. Jordan's experience told her it would not be a good idea to bring Emma into the story. She was too close to the target and would have conflicting interests. Emma may want to stop what was going on, but Jordan suspected Emma wouldn't approve of Jordan's approach of making this a public story that could take down GenPhage. Emma would likely prefer to air it out internally.

Jordan was comfortable keeping Emma out. As long as the Kenyan doctor came through with the information that connected GenPhage treatments to patients dying from organ failure. Even if they didn't explicitly link these deaths to weaponized versions of the product, the correlation alone should be enough.

The problem was that Jordan didn't have a backup plan if Dr. Mbosi didn't come through. There would be no proof to connect the most important parts of the story. That would mean they'd have to consider a high-risk break-in, either a real one or a virtual one, to get documents from within GenPhage. This would be hard, maybe impossible.

As Jordan watched Emma, she thought that if Emma wanted to help, or wanted Jordan to help her, then Emma could be the wild card they needed. Emma would know where to look inside GenPhage for the proof they needed. She may even have access. If Jordan let Emma in on her research, should she let her all the way in? It would be a risk. Jordan could wait until they heard from the Kenyan doctor, which would be soon. But with Emma sitting right across from her, she felt pressured to decide on the spot. Logic said no, but her gut told her Emma wanted to know the truth and would help. They could figure out the exact end game later, but Jordan wouldn't let it get handled internally at GenPhage. She went with her gut.

I can at least tell her part of the truth.

Jordan took a deep breath. "Emma," she began, "you're right. There is something going on." Jordan was staring hard at Emma, holding her gaze. Emma returned her stare.

"What? I thought you said your story was a dead end? There's something going on? What the hell, Jordan?"

"Hang on for a minute and relax. It's true that my original

story died. I thought I had uncovered a conspiracy to hide the cause of Eric Smith's death, but the sources became compromised. Then I learned of something different. Something huge. Front page of the *Washington Post* huge. I think I have most of the pieces of the story but will know for sure soon."

"What is it? You have to tell me something."

"I can't. I've already been derailed once. If it happens again, I'll be out of a job. Maybe even out of a career."

Jordan couldn't read Emma's look. It had an element of consternation, for sure. Rightly so. She should feel conflicted at the prospect Jordan had raised. But there was something else.

Is that excitement?

"Can't you give me something? A crumb, at least?"

The request was fair. But it put Jordan in a bind. Could she share something that didn't significantly compromise her story?

There was one thing she could share.

"All right. I'll tell you this. I have evidence GenPhage is hiding something big. It could ruin the company if it got out. Some men who work for the company broke into my apartment and trashed it. They either took or destroyed everything they could find that might have to do with the story. Fortunately, I keep digital versions of everything, so I didn't lose much. If you believe me and want to help, then you can come to my place and I'll tell you more. But only if you agree to help."

Emma's look changed to one of satisfaction. Was it because Jordan had shown some good faith by sharing?

"It's a deal. You've shared something important. Something about my company. If whatever they're doing is as bad as you say, I really should help. I should do what's right. I'll come by your place. When should I get there?"

"How about seven?"

"I can do that."

"Good. But there's one condition."

"What's that?"

"Agreeing to help. We may need more information from GenPhage, depending on what I learn in the next day or two. I don't know for sure yet if I'll need information from you, but I might. If I need you to help get inside information, and if I tell you what I already know, will you help?"

There it was. Jordan couldn't believe she'd put this out there. She was effectively asking Emma if she would steal from her company. Would she do it?

Jordan could see from the look on Emma's face that she hadn't been expecting this. The decision wasn't easy. It was one thing to go against your company when it was breaking the law. But when it involved a family member, loyalties were more conflicted.

"Let me make sure I understand. You might have all the information you need. But if not, you want me to help you get what you need from GenPhage? As in steal it?"

There was no way to sugarcoat this one. "Yes. You can think of it as stealing, if you want. But what GenPhage is doing has to be stopped."

"Do you think people are getting hurt because of what they're doing?"

An image of Steve Calhoun's smashed body lying in the street flashed through Jordan's mind. "I'm absolutely certain."

Emma exhaled, almost as if she had been holding her breath. "All right. If what you say is true, if you need my help, you'll have it. But I'll need some convincing."

I can't believe she's actually agreeing.

Jordan smiled and put a hand on Emma's hand. "Thank you. My place. Seven p.m."

Emma relaxed into her chair. "OK. I'll be there."

"Great. Let's eat."

28

As Jordan walked up to her car, parked in the lot of a CVS two blocks from the restaurant, she couldn't help but notice a silver Audi A8 parked such that its driver's side was beside her own. It was so close, she could barely squeeze between the cars and open her door. As she wriggled between the cars, Jordan jumped, startled by a man sitting in the A8 driver's seat. He was looking right at her.

Jordan got into her car and started the engine. As she buckled her seat belt, she saw that the man in the A8 had rolled down his window and was motioning for her to do the same. She didn't recognize the man at all and couldn't think of a reason to follow his instructions. She put her car in reverse and was just about to back out of her parking spot when she noticed the man was holding something in his hand. It was a sheet of paper with one word written on it in black ink: GENPHAGE.

What the fuck is this?

Jordan put her car in park and rolled down her window. "What the hell is that about?" Jordan said, pointing at the sheet of paper still in the man's hand.

"I needed to get your attention."

"Well, you have it. For thirty seconds. What do you want?"

"I thought it was time to check in on how your GenPhage investigation is progressing."

This has to be Ben.

"Nice of you to show your face. But you don't need to check in. We're not working together. Apart from giving me some cryptic information, you haven't been much help."

"As I said before, my position is such that I can't personally get involved. But it seems like you're making progress."

"How the hell would you know? Are you following me as well?"

"I prefer to think of it as monitoring a situation of interest. Just a light touch to estimate how this will turn out."

"From where I sit, this is none of your damn business. Unless you want to do something useful."

"Remember that it was me who tipped you off on this story."

"Oh, I remember. But that doesn't prove you give a shit about helping me. For all I know, you're doing this to save your own ass." Jordan looked up and down the length of the A8. "Or maybe to make money somehow."

"I'm involved only because I played a part in Neil Foley getting to where he is today. Period. Speaking of Neil Foley, it surprised me to see you having lunch with his niece."

"It's called investigative reporting. She works at GenPhage and may be able to help. Unlike you."

"How well do you know Emma?"

"Well enough. Why?"

"Let me offer a word of caution. Whatever negative adjectives you use to describe Neil Foley, Emma is those in spades. She may appear sweet and act like your best friend, but everything she does is to make money and advance her career. Nothing else matters to her."

"How do you know?"

"I know Neil and Emma well. Trust me. They're cut from the same cloth."

"Thanks for the warning, Ben. I'll judge Emma based on what I see and not take the word of a complete stranger."

"Fair enough. But don't say I didn't warn you."

"Anything else? I need to go."

"One last thing. Don't underestimate Neil. He won't let anything or anyone prevent him from getting what he wants. There's little he won't do. Remember that."

"Well, he's never had to deal with me before. Don't bother me again."

Before Ben had a chance to say anything else, Jordan started her car and drove off. She quickly checked her phone before she left the parking lot. She had turned off the ringer before having lunch with Emma and was surprised to see that she had several missed calls from Charlie, all within a few minutes of each other. While debating calling him back, she received a text from Charlie asking her to meet at Darcy's Pub. He must have joined Travis for lunch.

WHEN JORDAN ARRIVED, Charlie and Travis were almost giddy with excitement. She thought that wasn't a good look for grown men. "We tried calling you," Travis said. "Didn't you hear your phone?"

"Shit, sorry, guys. I had the ringer off and forgot to turn it back on. What's up?"

"So that means you didn't check your email or LinkedIn account either?" Charlie said.

"No, why? Did someone else reply to our request?"

"Kind of."

"What the hell does that mean? Either someone replied or not."

"Well, we heard from someone because of the messages you sent, but the person who replied wasn't one of the original recipients. This person who reached out said they know one of the scientists who received one of the messages you sent through LinkedIn. They also said they know some things about what's going on at GenPhage and may be willing to talk."

"Damn," Jordan said. "Is there nothing straightforward with this story? Everything has to have a twist or complication. We know there's something wrong there, so if that's all they have, it's not exactly a news flash."

"She wouldn't say any more to us, only to you. She gave us her number, and she's expecting a call at six p.m., which is three for her, since she's in California. I told her you'd call."

"Thanks for that. Did you get a name?"

"Yes. Madeline Jacobsen. She worked in clinical development at GenPhage and managed supplies for clinical trials. She said she's a good friend of a guy from clinical development who we messaged. He called her after he got our message. She felt like she should talk to us."

"I wonder if she knew Steve Calhoun?"

"If she managed clinical supply, she would have worked with Steve and his production team. It's a small company."

"She probably doesn't know what happened to Steve yet." Jordan directed a question to Travis. "Do you think we should tell her about Steve?"

He thought for a moment, wiping his hands with a towel. "I wouldn't, unless she seems like she's committed to bringing down GenPhage. That we know Steve is dead raises some questions about how we know. We shouldn't attract unwanted attention. If she seems like a true ally, tell her. It could help build trust."

"Way to take a stand, Travis. But I know what you mean. I'll see how the conversation goes."

The group lapsed into one of those moments of silence where no one knew what to say next. Travis seemed to remember why Jordan hadn't answered Charlie's calls. "What happened at lunch with Emma? Just girl stuff, or something more serious?"

"More serious." Jordan took a few minutes to recount the details of what Emma had shared with her, including Emma believing there must be something going on at GenPhage that was some combination of bad, illegal, and dangerous.

"Interesting," Charlie said. "Do you think she'll take action, maybe challenge her uncle?"

Jordan had left out an important part of her conversation with Emma. "Funny you should ask," Jordan said. "She's going to join our little team." Jordan let that new fact hang in the air and watched the two men, gauging their reactions.

Travis spoke first. "Damn, Jordan, that's your worst idea yet. She works for GenPhage, and her uncle practically runs the place. There's no way you know her well enough to trust her that much. Remember, these guys play hardball. If Emma lets anything slip, we'll be in serious trouble. The kind that leaves people dead."

"I'm with Travis," Charlie said. "This is a big risk. Plus, if Dr. Mbosi comes through, you'll have everything you need to expose GenPhage. We won't need any more help."

Jordan had expected the resistance. "I know, I know. I had the exact same worry. But you guys didn't see how concerned she was at the thought of GenPhage and her uncle doing something terrible. But for me, the real reason I'm including her is more selfish. If Dr. Mbosi isn't able to get what we need, then we'll have a hole in the story and no easy way to fill it. I told Emma that if I tell her what we know, she'll have to get us inside information. She'll have to contribute if we need her to. That's part of our agreement."

"She went along with that?" Travis asked.

"She's close. She just needs a bit of convincing."

"Do you believe she'll be able to help?" Charlie asked.

"She's got a better chance than we do."

"All right, then," Travis said. "When do we meet her?"

"Tonight at seven. She'll come to my place."

"Great," Travis said. "Right after you talk to Madeline. This'll be one hell of an evening."

"I hope so. Let's head to my place. It's getting close to six."

29

JORDAN CALLED MADELINE AT SIX P.M.

"Very punctual, Ms. Reed. I appreciate that."

"Please call me Jordan. Is it OK if I call you Madeline?"

"It is," Madeline said. "So, you must wonder why I wanted to speak to you?"

"I'm sure it's to tell me something about GenPhage. But since you weren't someone I had reached out to, it surprised me to get your message."

"I'm good friends with someone you contacted, and as soon as he got your message, he called me. I honestly think it was because he wanted no part in anything to do with GenPhage. But he remembered that I saw something I shouldn't have seen."

Jordan loved to hear a sentence like that. Madeline knew something significant, and for her to reach out meant she thought it was worthwhile to share. "I assume that since you wanted to talk, you'll share what you know?"

"That depends. I don't know anything about why you have this interest in GenPhage. I suspect it's because you have some insight that there's something rotten there. If that's the case, then I'll share what I know. But maybe you or your newspaper are buddies of Neil Foley and are trying to protect him. If I think that's the case, then you can go to hell. Convince me."

"I'm not on GenPhage's side here. I've learned some things that make me believe they're hurting people on purpose. And that they'll go to great lengths to cover up what they're doing."

"OK. That helps. So, what have yo found out? Tell me something that will show me you're on the right track."

This wasn't starting out as expected. Someone had to trust the other, at least a little, and Jordan didn't want to go first. "Not yet. For all I know, you're trying to set me up and report back to Neil and GenPhage. I won't jeopardize this story. It's too important. You'll have to trust that I'm not protecting GenPhage. That I plan to expose what they're doing."

The line was silent for a moment. Jordan held her breath, hoping Madeline would cooperate. She thought she'd done enough to make Madeline feel comfortable talking to her. Jordan let the silence continue for what seemed like minutes.

"I can live with that for now," Madeline said. "But consider me anonymous. I won't go public or otherwise go on the record with what I'll tell you. If Neil and his little security team found out that I shared this, I've got a feeling I'd be putting myself in real danger."

An image of Steve Calhoun's crumpled body flashed through Jordan's mind again. "Are you talking about those thugs in black jackets who drive around in black Suburbans?"

"Yes. Have you seen them?"

"More than once. They've been following me and broke into my apartment. I think they may have done worse than that." Jordan stuck to the plan and didn't bring up Steve.

"Well, don't fuck around with those guys. I know someone who had a run-in with them, and this person thought they'd actually hurt him. You know, mafia kind of stuff. Not something you'd expect to happen in the drug-development world."

"That's what I thought until I started investigating

GenPhage. I guess when a company has something it really needs to hide, all bets are off. I don't think your industry is immune to the corruption, intimidation, and violence that you hear about in industries like finance and construction. They're just better at keeping it under the radar."

"You've got that right. So many people in the drug business act altruistic, like they only care about curing diseases. But in the end, it's just a business, and they have to generate profit to survive. If they can get a drug approved that's a blockbuster, you can guarantee at least a decade of strong revenue. So imagine how people in charge would react if someone jeopardized that. That's where GenPhage is right now. On the verge of having a blockbuster and going public and making many people very rich. But there's something strange going on there, and while I don't know all the details, I'm sure it would be enough to take down many at the company."

Jordan couldn't wait any longer. "What do you think's going on at GenPhage?"

"As I said, I don't know exactly what they're doing, but I've seen signs that tell me they're breaking the law."

"In what way? Tell me more."

"Well, at GenPhage, I managed the day-to-day shipping of clinical supply product to all sites where GenPhage was running clinical trials. Based on the clinical trial plan, we had estimates of the number of patients that each trial site would recruit, and I made sure we had an appropriate amount of product ready to ship. Not technically very complicated, but we took supply management seriously, and we had to account for every vial of product we shipped. When sites were first coming online, the supply management was simple, as there weren't a lot of patients. But after the first few months, as the volume increased, I noticed some irregularities."

"What kind?"

"For the phase III trials, we shipped product based on the

estimated number of patients for each trial site. In the shipping summary, there was one line per trial site. But after a while, I noticed that someone split the patient estimates into two lines for each site. Remember, we were only testing for one indication, so regardless of how many patients we expected, they should have been accounted for on one line of the shipping summary. The split wasn't necessary."

"Was there anything else that changed?"

"It wasn't exactly a change, but I noticed that the patient numbers were much lower in the second line of the patient estimates. Again, this made little sense, since all patients would have had drug-resistant TB, and we only had one treatment."

Jordan was out of her depth here. A supply-chain management expert she was not. But she knew business well enough. "Maybe it was for accounting? Maybe some tax regulation or loophole GenPhage wanted to take advantage of? Or maybe there was a customs reason? Did the shipments for the patients in the two lines go together, or were they separate?"

"They were shipped together, and the shipping manifest for customs just listed the total number of vials shipped for each clinical trial site. There was no further breakdown."

"They based the shipments on the total number of patients per site, not the breakdown into two lines of patients. I'm with you. It doesn't make sense to me either."

"Right. So I did an impromptu inspection of one of our shipments for a site in Africa before it went out. And sure enough, all the labeling was for the same GenPhage product. At least it appeared that way."

"What do you mean?"

"The labels on the vials were all identical, but all the vials weren't exactly the same."

"What do you mean not the same? Different size? Different colors?"

"Nothing so obvious. There was only one strength and

dosing regimen for the product. GenPhage manufactured the product at the same concentration and packaged it in one-hundred-milliliter vials. Every vial should have been identical. But when I inspected them, I noticed something different on a few of the vials. In fact, it was only by accident I even noticed it at all. When I was repacking the vials after inspecting them, I dropped one. It didn't break, but when I picked it up, I noticed something catch the light on the bottom of the vial. When I examined it, I saw letters etched into the glass itself. The etching was tiny, and I needed a magnifying glass. The writing was a three-character code. One letter followed by two numbers."

"Really? Was that normal?"

"Not at all. This wasn't part of the approved package labeling. I went through the entire shipment and checked the bottom of each vial. Guess what I found?"

"That they all had a code on the bottom?"

"Nope. Only about a quarter of them had a code."

"That seems strange."

"That's not the strange part. The number of vials that had the etched code was an exact match to the number of patients estimated on the second line of the shipping summary."

A light bulb went off in Jordan's head. This was how GenPhage got the weaponized product to the trial sites. Mixed in with the real product in plain sight. The doctors at the other end must know the codes, or at least what to do with the coded vials. She doubted Madeline knew this. "There must have been something different about what was in those vials that GenPhage wanted to keep separate. Any idea what?"

"No, but there's one more thing about the codes. There were four different codes, and each version was present in the same amount. So whatever was actually being shipped in these coded vials, I think there were four different versions. And my guess is that it wasn't the same product that was being tested in the clinical trials. Otherwise, why go through the effort to isolate these vials?"

Unless you're testing a biological weapon.

"Do you know how many times GenPhage added these coded vials to shipments, or to exactly which sites?"

"No. When I discovered this, it was for a shipment to a site in Kenya. I didn't know what to do, and I didn't know whom to trust. Only a few people could have pulled this off. I figured it was in my best interest to get the hell out of there. I resigned the next day and went to California to be close to my folks. I was lucky enough to get a job at a big company in San Francisco."

Jordan needed to get ready for Emma, and it seemed like Madeline had shared all that she knew. "I have to say, what you discovered was new information for me, and it lines up with other information I've gathered. Is there anything else you remember that might be useful?"

"That's about all I have. What are you going to do next? I know you must have a lot more than what I shared. Do you have enough to expose GenPhage?"

"I can't say too much yet, but I'm definitely close. I have a couple more dots to connect, and I have a plan to connect them. I'll let you know once it's published."

"I look forward to it. But remember, I don't want to see my name anywhere in your story. I absolutely want to help, but I don't want anyone to come after me."

"Don't worry. Your help will remain anonymous. I promise."

"Good luck. I can't wait to see what happens. But from a safe distance."

"Thanks again, Madeline."

Jordan ended the call and smiled at her two partners. "One more piece of the puzzle."

30

JORDAN HAD TIME TO BRIEF CHARLIE AND TRAVIS BEFORE EMMA arrived. They agreed with her that the coded vials must have contained weaponized product and that the concealed coding on the vials, coupled with the shipping records manipulation, was how GenPhage got the material out of the country. Unless someone did a detailed vial-by-vial inspection, they wouldn't have discovered what was being shipped.

They were ready for Emma.

At 7:05, Jordan's doorbell rang. She opened it to see a smiling Emma waiting on her doorstep. "Hey there," she said. "Only a few minutes late. Is that pizza I smell? I haven't eaten since lunch and am about to pass out."

"Hey yourself. And yes, that's pizza. Got here about ten minutes ago. I don't cook much and figured we could use some food."

"Oh my God, yes. I assume you're still OK with our little deal from lunch?"

"Absolutely. As long as you're OK with possibly helping to expose whatever is going on at your company. We're close to being able to connect all the dots, but we may need you to help with any open questions we have. Besides, we can always use the extra brainpower."

"I can rationalize having to do something I don't like as long as it's for a great reason. If what you told me is true, then something has to be done." Emma seemed to just remember something Jordan had said a moment before. "Did you say 'we'?"

As Emma entered the apartment, Travis and Charlie stood up. "Hi, Emma," Travis said.

Emma looked surprised. Her feet seemed to stop moving forward as she saw these two men, but the rest of her body kept going. She realized this too late and wasn't quick enough, stumbling and almost falling. Travis still retained most of his former athletic prowess, reacting quickly and catching her by her left arm, steadying her while she regained her balance.

"I'm sorry. I didn't expect anyone else to be here. Sorry for being clumsy."

"No, it's my fault," Travis said. "I didn't mean to startle you. Are you all right?"

"You remember Travis, right?" Jordan said.

"How could I forget all those muscles," Emma said, smiling.

"And this is Charlie," Jordan said. "He's a good friend who works for the CDC."

"Pleased to meet you," Charlie said.

"Same here. So, Jordan, I think there's something I'm missing. I thought you and I would be by ourselves."

"Not on this one. I said I'd let you in on what I know about GenPhage. But it's more like I'll let you in on what we know. Travis and Charlie have been helping me piece this together, and I guess we've formed a little team. I trust them with anything. You have nothing to worry about. I hope this doesn't change things for you."

"No, the team approach is fine. More brains, better ideas."

"Glad to hear it. Let's grab some pizza."

The group went into the kitchen, where two pizzas were

waiting in unopened boxes. One was a Margherita pizza targeted for the ladies, while the other was a meat lovers for the men. Travis had ordered the pizzas and admitted to being 100 percent stereotypical in his selections.

They all stuffed their faces without saying a word, satisfying the hunger they all felt. After finishing her first slice, Jordan took a second and sat on the sofa. The rest of the group followed, with Emma joining Jordan on the sofa, Charlie taking the recliner, and Travis choosing to lean against the wall.

Jordan had told Travis and Charlie in advance how much she would share with Emma. This included what they had learned from Laurie Smith and the bits of information that highlighted the inconsistencies of the facts around his death. Jordan would push the theory that Eric Smith's death may not have been accidental and that GenPhage had covered its cause up. The nondisclosure agreement and settlement to the family practically screamed cover-up.

Jordan then had Charlie take Emma through what he'd learned from the doctors he'd met at the conference, in particular the Dr. Mbosi As Charlie summarized what he'd learned, Jordan could see Emma becoming uncomfortable. Hearing how her company had recklessly endangered patients must have been a shock. Whether her discomfort was because of the clear lack of ethics or the impact this could have on the viability of GenPhage, Jordan couldn't tell. She assumed it was the blatant breach of common ethical behavior.

Up to this point, the story could have been one of aggressive carelessness. GenPhage had developed something that could help patients but could also kill them. Not to mention what could happen to others exposed to the treatment.

The next part of the story made the leap from carelessness and negligence to breaking the law and committing murder. Jordan and Travis together told Emma what they'd learned from Steve Calhoun, but they were careful not to share his fate. At least not right away. Emma continued to look uncomfortable, but Jordan had expected her to seem more shocked. This should have been a big revelation.

Last, Jordan shared what she'd learned from Madeline, that other vials had been hidden among the actual product vials being shipped out to clinical trial sites. Emma sat silent, unmoving, taking it all in. She looked to be processing everything she heard, piecing together in her mind what Jordan, Travis, and Charlie had already figured out. The look on Emma's face reminded Jordan of Neil Foley.

Travis brought over one of the pizza boxes and placed it on the table. "I find I can handle shocking news better with a good slice of pizza. It can't change what happened, but it gives the brain something positive to enjoy."

"No, thanks," Emma said. "I think better when I'm not eating. And this information definitely gives me a lot to think about."

"Sorry to hit you with this all at once," Jordan said. "But so far, it hangs together and points to GenPhage testing a weaponized version of their treatment, with no approval or oversight at all. And they're doing it on people who're already suffering and who think they're getting a treatment that can cure them of TB."

"Not to mention that what they're testing is not in any way benign," added Charlie. "What GenPhage is doing leads to multiple organ failure, a painful way to die."

"I get it," Emma said. "It's shocking what you've uncovered. I still can't believe it, though I know there is logic in the facts you've gathered. And you think this is all linked to Eric Smith's death?"

"As far as we know, yes. I had walked away from the story when my source was compromised. Even with what Charlie learned, I wasn't sure there was anything there. Then I figured out I was being followed, even though Travis thought I was being paranoid." Jordan shot Travis a quick "I told you so" look, to which Travis shrugged his shoulders. "But when I did a little test at the bar to see if it was true, Travis confirmed that two dudes in black jackets followed me out when I took a drive down the road. Within ten minutes of getting back, the two guys also came back. I figured if people were following me, then I had to be on to something. Had GenPhage left me alone, I probably would have stayed away. Too bad for them."

"What's next?" Emma asked. "It sounds like you have a good base of facts and information. Do you have enough to publish?"

"Not quite. For Eric's death, we don't have the direct link to the GenPhage weapon. We're pretty sure what caused his death, but 'pretty sure' isn't enough to base a story on. The Africa piece of the story is tighter. We have multiple sources that say there was a weaponized version of the treatment. What we really need is to link patients who died to having received the GenPhage treatment. Several doctors in Africa believe GenPhage patients died because of something that GenPhage provided. But the clinical trial records of these patients were cleansed."

"I assume you have a plan for this?"

Jordan looked to Charlie, who nodded. "We do," he said. "One doctor I met from Kenya has a colleague whose sister works at a trial site where patients died. He asked her to find any documentation that these patients received a GenPhage treatment before they died. We might even get proof that these patients had their records expunged from the clinical trial. That would be icing on the cake."

Emma's eyes opened wider as she listened to this, apparently surprised or impressed that there was a plan to connect deaths in Africa to GenPhage. "When will you know if the doctor from Kenya can come through?"

"Hopefully tomorrow, before noon. He said he would have something, but wasn't sure exactly what until he saw it. The benefits of a digital world. We would have had no hope of pulling this off ten years ago."

Emma set down the piece of pizza she'd been holding but not eating. Her expression had the look of someone who had taken in all they could.

"It sounds like you're close to having enough to go public. Where do I come in?"

This was the moment of truth. Jordan took a deep breath.

No time to beat around the bush. Just tell her what you need.

"There are two areas where you could help. First, in case the Kenyan angle doesn't pan out, we need an alternative way to connect the GenPhage weapon to testing in Africa. Can you find any records that show a weaponized version of the treatment was developed and then used in Africa?"

"Wow," Emma said. "That's one hell of a request." She paused a moment and leaned forward, resting her forearms on the table. Jordan could imagine her brain churning through options and scenarios. "First, I'm setting aside whether I'd be able to do it. That would take some digging."

Jordan nodded. "Go on."

"Second, I think what you need is possible. If what you've told me is true, then GenPhage would have periods of time when they're manufacturing the weapon and not the actual product. There would have to be documentation somewhere to prove this. Maybe production batch records or some communications with the DoD. Worst case, we could consider intercepting an actual shipment destined for Africa. It would be a stretch to pull off, but it can't be impossible."

"OK," Jordan said. "You think there are options. That's good."

"You said there were two areas where I could help. What's the second?"

Don't back off now. Just spit it out.

"Eric Smith. His whole story just doesn't hold water. He knew how to do his job, and there's nothing in any report that suggests how he got sick. I don't believe for an instant his death was an accident, especially because he died the same way as the patients in Africa. Someone 'helped' him get exposed to the weapon, knowing he'd be dead in days. There aren't many people who could make that happen." Jordan paused before finishing, glancing quickly at Travis and Charlie. "I'd put your uncle at the top of the list of likely suspects."

Emma stood up, nearly spilling the drinks on the table. "Are you kidding me? You think Neil ordered some kind of hit on Eric Smith? Like a mobster? Not a chance. He's a tough businessman who knows how to succeed, but he's not Tony Soprano. You're way off base." She walked into the kitchen and poured herself a fresh gin, her posture rigid, her back angled to the group. The message was clear: back off.

Jordan knew this would be tough for Emma to believe. Jordan didn't know how strong Emma's relationship with Neil was, but based on the one interaction she'd observed between them, it seemed to be good. Jordan had one more piece of information at her disposal. While it didn't prove Neil was a killer, it made such a proposition seem possible.

Jordan looked to Travis and mouthed, "I'm going to tell her."

Travis had just grabbed another slice of pizza. Jordan caught him off guard. He moved over to Jordan. "Tell her what?"

"What happened to Steve."

"No way. You know we're witnesses to what happened, even though we told the cops we saw nothing. If they learn we lied, they could charge us. We need to keep this to ourselves."

Jordan shook her head. "No choice. She doesn't believe Neil could be a murderer. What happened to Steve comes close to proving he must be. If nothing else, it should create some significant doubt."

"I'm with Travis on this one," Charlie said. "Whether or not Emma believes her uncle capable of murder, it isn't worth the risk of bringing her in on this."

"So, this is gang-up-on-Jordan time? Man, you guys just won't take any risk at all. Did you both put on your old-man underwear this morning? Trust me. Once she sees there's a real possibility her uncle is a murderer, she'll help us. She'll hope it's not true, but her curiosity will be impossible to ignore. She's too intelligent not to want to find the truth."

"You better be right," Travis said. "It's my ass on the line as well." He turned to face Charlie. "At least you're in the clear. You weren't part of lying to the cops."

"True. But if they ask me anything, I'm sure I'll crumble like a stale cookie. I don't do well with authority figures."

"Don't worry, tough guys," Jordan said with a grin. "I'll make sure you're both safe if things fall apart. But they won't. Trust me."

Emma was still in the kitchen but had turned around, her back no longer facing the others. "Emma," Jordan said. "There's one more thing you need to know."

Jordan couldn't read Emma's expression. It almost looked like she was angry.

"Do you know Steve Calhoun?"

"Steve? From operations? Sure. We didn't interact a lot since our jobs were different, but I knew him. He's a good guy. A hothead, but he worked hard and spoke up when he saw something that needed to be fixed. He got into some personnel trouble, and we had to let him go. I heard he found a new job soon after. Why are you asking?"

"He's dead."

Jordan watched Emma closely as she delivered the message. She expected her to show an immediate reaction of surprise, shock, disbelief, or some combination of the three. Emma's immediate reaction was unexpected, but Jordan couldn't place it. But it only lasted an instant, quickly replaced by the look of shock Jordan had expected.

"What do you mean dead? How did it happen? How do you know?"

"Travis and I were there. You remember what we learned from him?"

"Yes."

"We met him at a Starbucks downtown. He told us three guys came to his apartment and threatened to hurt him if he spoke to me. I'm sure these were the same guys who are following me and who trashed this place. You couldn't know, but I used to have a big whiteboard and some file cabinets in my office. You must have noticed the holes in the wall and the stains on the floor? It was a gift from the guys following me."

"I just assumed it was typical for a reporter. Sorry."

"Fair point," Jordan said, taking in the less-than-tidy appearance of her apartment. "Yeah, I'm messy. Anyway, back to Steve. After our meeting, he bolted. He said he was going on a vacation. While Travis and I were getting ready to leave Starbucks, we heard a car speed by, followed by the sound of an impact. When we got outside, we could see someone lying in the street further down the block. We also heard a vehicle speeding away. When we ran up, we saw that it was Steve. He was dead. The was another man there who said he saw a black SUV speed up and run right into him. He said it didn't slow down at all. It looked to him like it was deliberate."

Emma now looked concerned, a more normal human reaction. Maybe Jordan had misread her earlier expression.

"You're sure he was dead?"

"No doubt about it. His head was at an angle that no one alive could tolerate. I'm sure he died on impact."

"And the vehicle that hit him. How sure are you it had anything to do with GenPhage? Maybe Steve had crossed someone else? Maybe it was just an accident?"

Jordan gave her a look of incredulity, strode away from the kitchen, and turned around to face the group, hands planted on her hips. "An *accident*? Think about the fucking sequence of events," Jordan said. "I find out that there are guys following me and that they drive a black Suburban. The next day, my apartment gets trashed and someone takes or destroys everything I had on GenPhage. Then three guys, who probably work for your uncle, visit Steve and tell him not to talk to me. They did this with an 'or else.' Within an hour of that and within minutes of Steve talking to me and Travis, he's dead. Hit by a black Suburban. Did someone leave a GenPhage calling card by Steve's body? No. But our explanation makes a hell of a lot of sense."

The tension in the room rose noticeably with Jordan's comments, her patience frayed. Emma walked over to the sofa and fell onto it, closing her eyes as she leaned her head back. After a moment, she shifted forward, placed her hands on her legs, and looked at Travis. "What do you think? You were there and heard and saw the same things as Jordan. Do you buy this explanation?"

Travis walked over to Emma and sat down on a chair. "You know, as farfetched as this seems, it's the only thing that makes sense. If GenPhage is doing what we think, something so bad it could end the company if word got out, then they have everything to lose. It's not a big leap to go from killing patients in Kenya to running someone down in Boston. What Jordan said about these guys in the Suburban is true. I was with her when we did the little experiment that proved she was being followed. Hell, I bet they're somewhere in the neighborhood right now. So, yeah, I believe it."

"How about you, Charlie?"

"I wasn't with them for this event with Steve, but GenPhage wouldn't be the first drug company to illegally test drugs in developing countries. It's easy to hide the evidence with a few well-placed bribes, and it's hard for regulators to monitor them. As horrible as this sounds, it's a possibility."

"Well, this is a real fucking mess, then. The company I work for, and one that is practically run by my uncle, is testing some kind of biological weapon when it should focus on getting our breakthrough TB treatment approved. Worse, people are being experimented on without their permission, and people have died. So I have to choose between my company, which includes my family, and doing the right thing. There's no upside here."

Jordan wasn't sure which way Emma was leaning, but she needed her to decide. The clock was ticking, and it was only a matter of time before the GenPhage goons would step in and shut this down for good.

"What's it going to be, Emma? Are you in or out?"

"Wow. The biggest decision of my life, and I only get two minutes to decide? You sure know how to turn the screws."

"Sorry, but we don't have a lot of time. I need to know what you'll do."

"Fine. I'm in. Is that what you want to hear? I'm in. Let's get this over with already."

Jordan smiled and fell back onto the sofa. "All right, then. Let's finish this pizza so I don't have to eat it tomorrow."

31

It was at least an hour before sunrise. Chris was Carter's lead for the surveillance operation, and his team was around the corner from Jordan Reed's apartment. They had spent the night taking turns dozing in the back seat. Once Travis had left the apartment the previous night, it was clear there wouldn't be any more action. Chris had told the team to take advantage and rotate getting rest.

Based on the instructions from Carter, they would have to conduct an intervention to separate some incriminating evidence from Jordan Reed's team. Carter had told Chris that Charlie would receive information from a doctor in Kenya. Most likely, he would receive it via email or text. Either way, they would have to take the device and destroy whatever was sent. Carter said a team in Kenya would make sure that information couldn't be sent again.

Chris was on point when he thought he heard some rustling come through the audio feed from Jordan Reed's apartment. There were no voices. It sounded like someone was moving around. After a moment, he heard a door close. It sounded firm, like it was the apartment door and not one inside the apartment. It didn't make much sense for someone to be going outside so early. Maybe Charlie had to get something from his car. If that was the case, Chris should hear whomever it was come back in a minute or two.

Almost five minutes passed without Chris hearing another sound. He was debating whether they should get eyes on the apartment when he noticed someone on the opposite side of the street heading toward the Suburban. It looked like someone out for an early-morning run. "Crazy bastard," Chris mumbled to himself.

Chris was going to ignore the runner, but as he passed under a streetlight in front of the Suburban, Chris thought the runner looked to be of Asian descent. His size was close to the size of Charlie. As the runner passed by the Suburban, Chris could see he was wearing black-framed glasses, just like Charlie's. Chris realized the sound he'd heard from Jordan Reed's apartment was that of Charlie heading out for a run.

Chris couldn't believe their luck. He grabbed his phone and called Carter.

"This had better be good," Carter said as he answered the call.

"Oh, it is," Chris said. "Remember the individual we're expecting to visit today?"

"Yes, why?"

"The idiot just went by us on a morning run. Alone."

Carter came to the same conclusion as Chris. "Do you think he has his phone with him?"

"I don't know for sure, but would you be out on the streets in the dark without your phone? It doesn't matter, anyway. We have his number. I can call it and watch to see if he answers."

"Perfect. If it's him, pick him up and take him to our location. Do it clean. No witnesses. Have the backup team take over surveillance of Jordan Reed."

"Got it. We'll provide an update once we know if it's Charlie."

Carter ended the call.

Chris needed to get the team going. "Time to move," he said.

Chris stepped out of the Suburban and looked back, trying to pick out the runner. He thought he was out of sight, but then he saw a figure turn right under a streetlight. He was three blocks away, heading east. Chris climbed back in on the passenger side, getting another team member, Pete, to drive. "Slight change of plans," he said. "Turns out today's target is out for a run all by himself. If it's him, we'll pick him up now to avoid trying to grab him in daylight."

He directed Pete to make a U-turn, drive two blocks, turn right, and go eight more blocks. They parked on the side of the street. This would put them in a position to spot the runner in about a minute. Chris told Pete to take up a position that would allow him to grab the runner if it was Charlie. If the runner was Charlie, Chris would flash the parking lights, and Pete would grab him.

Chris grabbed a burner from the glove box and looked up Charlie's number from the data packet his team had prepared. As Chris looked ahead, he saw that the runner was right on schedule, just coming into view as he crossed their street from left to right. Chris dialed Charlie's number and waited. About two seconds later, just before the runner went out of sight, he slowed, then stopped and reached into a pocket of his hoodie. He pulled out an object, looked at it, touched it, and lifted it to his ear. On his open phone line, Chris heard someone say, "Hello."

"Hello," Chris said. "Is this Charlie?" Chris couldn't remember his last name. It didn't matter.

"Yes, it is. Who's this?"

Chris quickly flashed the high-beam lights of the Suburban. Charlie turned and looked in his direction.

"Would you believe a secret admirer?"

"What? No. Really, who is this?"

As they spoke, Chris could see Pete walking toward Charlie.

He'd be there any second. "You'll know soon enough." Chris hung up as Pete put Charlie in a choke hold. Within a minute, Charlie was out. Pete tied Charlie's hands together while Chris drove the Suburban up. They loaded Charlie in the back, took his phone, and searched for any other devices he might have with him.

As they headed to their designated location, Chris texted Carter that they had Charlie. They'd sit on him until the message came through from the Kenyan doctor.

JORDAN SAW the sky lightening and popped out of bed.

Today's the day.

Despite not being able to get to sleep until well after midnight, even with a healthy dose of her preferred adult beverage, Jordan got moving. The day would be unpredictable, and she needed to be ready for anything. Besides the different activities already planned for the day, she needed to find time to actually work on the story. There was some writing and technical work to do. If there were more gaps, she'd have to deal with them.

Jordan walked to the kitchen to microwave some of yesterday's coffee. She remembered Charlie saying he'd start his day with an early-morning run. Jordan didn't see him when she got up, so she assumed he'd gotten a predawn start. He was expecting to hear from Dr. Mbosi by noon, giving Jordan some time in the morning to work on the story.

Emma was to be at the GenPhage office today as she normally would. But unlike her typical day, she said she would look for documentation that could prove what GenPhage was doing at their trial sites in Africa. A key piece of information needed was any link between Eric Smith and the GenPhage product. Emma would also look for documentation that would support GenPhage testing unapproved material in Kenya. Before Emma had left the night before, she said there were several possible sources she could check. She'd provide an update in the afternoon.

After forty-five minutes, Jordan wondered where Charlie was. She knew he sometimes ran for more than an hour, but given he had been gone when she'd gotten up, she figured he should have returned by now.

He better bring me a fresh coffee.

Jordan worked for another thirty minutes. Still no Charlie. She wasn't worried, not exactly. But this felt off somehow. She couldn't tolerate something going wrong today. They needed Dr. Mbosi to come through, and Charlie was the only connection to the doctor. Jordan hoped Charlie hadn't gotten cold feet.

Time to call him. I don't give a shit how early it is or how important his morning run is.

Jordan grabbed her phone and called Charlie. It rang and then went to voice mail. Jordan hated leaving voice messages, but she needed to know where he was. "Charlie, this is Jordan. Where the hell are you? I assume you went for a run, but that was over an hour ago. Stop fucking around and get back here. Or at least call me back. Today's a big day, and I need you here."

Jordan lay down on the sofa, propping a pillow behind her head. A feeling that something was wrong began to take hold. And she had no idea how to handle it.

WHEN SOMEONE REMOVED the blindfold from Charlie's head, it took his eyes a moment to adjust to the bright fluorescent lights. He was seated in a foldable metal chair, the kind you might find in an old church hall when they set up for bingo or a bake sale. His arms were zip-tied behind his back and his torso was taped to the chair with duct tape. In theory, he should've just been able to stand up and walk while attached to the chair, but something connected the chair to pipes along the wall behind him. He wasn't going anywhere unless someone cut him loose.

When his eyes adjusted to the lighting, Charlie took stock of his location. He was in a large room with a concrete floor and cinderblock walls. The room was at least fifty feet square. It had no windows but had six rows of fluorescent lights running the length of the ceiling. Furnishings were sparse. There were two more chairs set up like the one he was in. Against the far wall were two old brown leather sofas. In the corner to his right were two foldout cots. The opposite corner to his left had a makeshift kitchen. It was really just a counter with two cupboards, a fridge, a stovetop, and a sink. There was a door to what appeared to be another room off to his left. Probably a restroom. The large room itself seemed clean but had the musty smell of dirty clothes. Probably no shower facilities. Or the room's occupants had no desire to shower.

Charlie now focused on the three other men in the room. The one who'd removed the blindfold was walking toward the other two, who were stretched out on the sofas. All three had short, neat haircuts, and they all wore identical black jackets. The man walking toward the other two appeared to be over six feet tall. They all looked muscular, and Charlie figured they had some military or police training. No one had spoken to him yet, but Charlie figured they had to be the guys who had been following Jordan. Meaning they were also the ones who'd trashed her apartment and killed Steve Calhoun.

Charlie opted to break the silence. "Are you guys going to tell me what's going on? My family isn't rich, so I know it isn't for money."

The tall one looked over with a smug expression, the kind a star quarterback would give the captain of the chess club. "You're a smart guy. Figure it out."

Charlie was sure it was because of GenPhage, but he didn't

know why they wanted him and not Jordan. "You're the guys working for GenPhage, right? The ones who trashed my friend's apartment?"

"Look at you putting pieces together. I guess that really does make you the smart one."

"But why me? If this is about the investigation my friend is doing, I'd think she'd be a more likely target."

"So you think we should have taken her instead of you? That's definitely not cool." The man looked at his colleagues. "It's official, guys. Chivalry is dead."

That drew a chuckle from the other men in the room.

"That's not what I meant," Charlie said, stammering just a little. "I meant that if you want to get her to stop, it would make sense that you confront her and not me. I can't control what she does. If you knew anything at all about her, you'd know she does what she wants."

"You don't think she'd give up this little witch hunt to save you?"

"Maybe, but you wouldn't have to go through taking me hostage to find out."

"So you don't think there's another reason we took you? No other benefit you offer?"

Charlie thought about it. The adrenaline coursing through his body was making it hard to concentrate. His arms and hands trembled under the pressure of their forced position. His field of vision seemed reduced. "Not off the top of my head. I don't decide anything. I just help sort through technical details."

A ringing phone interrupted their conversation. Unless one of the three guys also had *The Walking Dead* ringtone, Charlie knew it had to be his phone. But it wasn't in his hoodie or any other pocket. As he tracked the sound of the ringing phone, he saw the tall guy reach into his jacket pocket and pull out an iPhone. Charlie recognized it. The tall guy didn't answer it and set it down on the table in front of the sofas. About thirty seconds after it stopped ringing, it beeped, indicating a voice mail.

The tall guy brought the phone over, holding its screen in front of Charlie. The phone was an iPhone X, and Charlie had set up Face ID. He tried to turn his head to prevent the phone from unlocking but was too slow to react.

"Thanks," the tall guy said.

"You're not welcome."

The tall guy found the voice mail and put the phone on speaker. Everyone in the room listened to the message Jordan had left wondering where the hell Charlie was.

"Looks like you're missed, Charlie. How sweet. Especially on a 'big day' like today."

A light bulb went off in Charlie's head. Somehow they knew about the Kenyan doctor and that he was supposed to contact Charlie today. His situation was more dangerous than he'd originally thought.

The tall guy looked at him as if he saw the light of Charlie's epiphany. "I bet you figured it out now, smart guy."

Charlie hung his head, acknowledging defeat. "Yes. You know about the doctor from Kenya."

"Bingo. Now we're all on the same page."

"So you want to know what he has to say?"

"Close. If he has something to share that wouldn't be welcome by my employers, then I'll need to destroy whatever it is. I can only do that if I have you and your phone. Whether he calls, texts, or emails, we need to have it. It's simple."

"And then what? I get to leave?"

"That's one option. Not the most likely one. I guess it'll depend on how cooperative you promise to be."

"I see. And what if I'm not cooperative?"

"Do you really need to ask?"

Charlie knew he didn't. "But what if the doctor from Kenya sends me the same thing again? I can't really stop him."

246

"Nothing you need to worry about. We have that contingency covered."

The meaning of this comment hit Charlie immediately. They were going after Dr. Mbosi. That was the only way to make sure he didn't send anything again. Charlie hoped they'd offer him money and not do something violent. But somehow, he felt things had gone too far for money to be the method of dealing with uncertainty.

32

BY MIDMORNING, JORDAN WAS BEYOND KNOWING WHAT TO DO. SHE had called Charlie twice more without success and had called Travis to see if, by some strange stroke of luck, he had been in contact with Charlie. He said if she hadn't heard anything by noon, she should come over to Darcy's Pub and they would decide what to do.

There was no plausible explanation for Charlie's disappearance that Jordan liked. If he had gotten cold feet about the whole GenPhage thing, he wouldn't just bolt without telling her. Jordan's gut told her something had happened to him on his run. It was possible he had some kind of accident and needed medical attention and couldn't get a message to her. But Jordan used her contacts at the paper to search the morning's hospital ER admissions for pedestrian accidents. There was nothing from her neighborhood involving anyone even closely resembling Charlie.

In Jordan's mind, that left only foul play, with GenPhage being the most likely suspect. But why would they take Charlie and not her? If they really wanted to stop her, then either threatening her or eliminating her would make the most sense. These guys were smart and organized. Taking Charlie must have been for a specific purpose. If they planned to use him as leverage over Jordan, then they would have contacted her by now. He was only leverage if she knew he was in danger. If not leverage, then what? Why was Charlie so important?

It hit her like a slap in the face.

Oh shit. I'm an idiot. They know about the doctor from Kenya. That he's supposed to send Charlie information. That's the only explanation that makes sense. Those fucking bastards.

Jordan went from worried to pissed off in an instant. It still scared her that Charlie was in danger, but knowing why only made her mad. Mostly at herself. She had asked for his help, and he hadn't hesitated. Now his life was in danger, and she had no obvious way to find him or help him.

Not that it mattered at the moment, but Jordan wondered how GenPhage had found out about Dr. Mbosi. Only four people besides the doctor knew about this. And they only ever talked about it in her apartment. She may have had notes on her whiteboard, but she knew for certain she hadn't written the specific date they expected to receive information from him.

This pointed to two possibilities. One, Emma had told someone last night. Someone like Neil. The second option she hesitated to even think about. It seemed as farfetched as being followed had felt.

What if GenPhage had bugged her apartment? They could have done it when the GenPhage crew had broken in.

The Emma option raised all kinds of questions about their new friendship. If it was her, then Jordan was finished. Just the thought made her nauseous. But this wasn't something she could tackle right away. Such a challenge would have to be done face-to-face, and she wouldn't see Emma until later.

Option two she could at least address. If they had bugged her apartment, she could look now while waiting to hear from

Charlie. This would have the extra benefit of keeping her mind focused on something other than an old friend being in danger or a new friend deceiving her.

She didn't know exactly what she was looking for, but she figured any listening device would be tiny and in a place where it could easily pick up conversation. She prioritized her office, living room, and kitchen, deciding to look at the undersides of tables and chairs first. Then she would check in and around the ceiling light fixtures. She assumed that the undersides of sofas and beds wouldn't be great for audio. She'd do those last, if at all.

As Jordan searched, she felt stupid. At least she was alone and no one could witness her paranoia in full flight. She used a flashlight to make sure she could see every angle. She wouldn't chance letting something hide in a shadow. After spending about half an hour searching what she thought were some obvious and reachable locations, she found nothing but dust. She grabbed her step stool to check around the ceiling light fixtures. Her apartment was ancient and predated even the notion of recessed lighting. Each room in her apartment had an old and cheap ceiling light fixture, most with a glass enclosure.

She started with the kitchen lights, both the one over the sink and the one centered in the kitchen ceiling. Having two lights in a twelve-by-twelve-foot kitchen was overkill, in her opinion. But the landlord compensated by putting in 40-watt bulbs. Nothing out of the ordinary as far as she could tell.

Next, she moved to the living room, which had the biggest light fixture in the apartment. It was brass colored and from the center spread out into three distinct arms, each with a small shade around where the light bulbs were screwed in. Nothing fancy, but it was an attempt to make the living room seem somehow more formal. As if her rundown apartment had any chance of appearing formal. Or even nice.

But that had nothing to do with whether she should search it. In fact, there were places on the fixture where one could hide a small object and it would be impossible to notice. Unless you got above the small glass light shades.

She saw nothing on the first two lights of the fixture. But when she got to the third one and looked inside the light shade, she saw a small silver object attached at the base, near where the bulb screwed in. She didn't know what she was looking at, but when she tried to remove it, she couldn't. She had to get a small flathead screwdriver to try to pry it off. This required removing the shade from that light. After a few tries, she pried it off.

The object was small and round, less than a quarter of an inch in diameter, by her estimation. It had a flat surface with some type of adhesive on it. The top was dome shaped with several tiny holes on the surface. Jordan figured this was to enable audio capture. There was a small red light in the device's center, faint in intensity. She wasn't sure what it meant, but she didn't care. This was how the GenPhage goons knew so much.

She almost forgot to search the other rooms. She would be some kind of idiot to think that finding one listening device meant she had found them all.

That turned out to be a good idea. There was one more in her partially destroyed office. It relieved her to find nothing in her bedroom or bathroom. That would have been too creepy.

With two listening devices, GenPhage would have overheard everything they talked about. Including last night's conversation when Emma was here. GenPhage knew everything.

I made it too easy for them. They just had to sit back and see what I would do next.

On the plus side, this reminded her that finding these devices addressed her other concern. Emma. She didn't want to think Emma would have set her up, but it had been a possibility. But for her to do so went against the positive vibe she got from

Emma. Such behavior just didn't seem to be part of Emma's makeup. But without locating these listening devices, it would be hard to find another explanation. At least she had one sliver of good news.

Jordan paced around her apartment holding the two listening devices in her left hand. She wasn't sure what to do next. At a minimum, she had to tell Travis what she'd found so they could figure out what it meant for Charlie. The morning was getting late, and she was due to call Travis soon anyway.

As she walked circles in her apartment, she noticed Charlie's bag lying on the floor against the back wall of her office. She hadn't paid it much attention before, but she saw that his laptop was sitting on top of the duffel bag. Judging by the stickers on it, it was his personal laptop.

Jordan's mind sprang into motion. If Dr. Mbosi had any documentation of GenPhage patients dying in Kenya, and their deaths being hidden from their records, then he would have to send Charlie what he had. He may also call him or send him a text, but it was likely that he would send the material via email. If so, Charlie's computer could access the email. GenPhage may have Charlie and his phone, but Jordan still had a chance to get what they needed. If GenPhage realized she could intercept the communication from Dr. Mbosi, she might have leverage to help Charlie. GenPhage didn't need to know she didn't have Charlie's password. But she would need someone who could break in and access his email. That was the key to getting Charlie released. Good thing she knew such a person.

Travis had picked up serious hacking skills while in under-grad. Jordan had seen him break into computers before. She was pretty sure that in school he'd made a fair bit of coin on the side from his hacking activities. She had never pressed him for a lot of details.

Now her mind was racing. Could Travis break into Charlie's computer in time to help him? Would Dr. Mbosi send what he had via email? Too many unknowns. Jordan needed Travis. She grabbed Charlie's laptop and practically flew out of her apartment. Travis usually went in around eleven, so she should get there at about the same time. She didn't know how much time she had, but she knew she had none to waste.

33

CHARLIE HAD GIVEN UP ON FURTHER DISCUSSION. HIS CAPTORS weren't especially chatty and seemed content to wait for the doctor from Kenya to reach out. They made him keep his phone unlocked so they could monitor texts and emails. As far as Charlie knew, nothing of interest had shown up yet. Twice, the taller guy went to another room, probably to make a phone call, but Charlie could hear nothing of what he said.

Charlie wasn't sure exactly what time it was when he heard his phone ring. His hunger told him it was almost noon. The guy who was closest to the phone, not the tall guy, picked it up and looked at the number that was calling. The man seemed puzzled. "I don't know what this is," he said.

The tall guy came over and took the phone. "It's a Kenya country code. A mobile number and not a landline." He walked over to Charlie. "Showtime. Conduct this conversation like nothing's wrong. Otherwise, something will be wrong. I think you know I'm serious."

The tall guy opened the call and put it on speaker, holding the phone in front of Charlie's face.

"Charlie speaking."

"Charlie, this is Dr. Mbosi. We met at the recent conference in New York."

Charlie didn't react well under real stress, in particular the life-and-death kind. It took a concerted effort to speak slowly and clearly. "Dr. Mbosi. It's very nice to hear from you. How are you doing?"

"I'm very well. How are you?"

"I'm doing well." Charlie wished he could appreciate the irony.

"That's good to hear. I very much enjoyed meeting you and the discussion we had."

"Me too. I assume your call means you've made progress in finding evidence of what we discussed."

"That's correct. As you may recall, the sister of a close colleague is a nurse working at a clinical trial site for the GenPhage TB treatment. I spoke with her immediately upon my return to Kenya. Let me say our hypothesis was correct."

"Really," Charlie said, still surprised they were actually right. "Are you saying she found documents that linked the GenPhage treatment to patient deaths?"

"Better than that. It looks like corruption cuts both ways. The nurse overheard several conversations that could only be explained by GenPhage paying the site investigator to destroy records of patients who died. In particular, those who received product not part of the trial. But she also knew that while the investigator destroyed the records from the trial database, he kept a separate record himself. This was to protect him in case GenPhage tried to one day blame him for anything that leaked to the press."

"I'd say that's unbelievable, but you can't trust a cheat. GenPhage should know that better than anyone." Charlie looked up at his captors as he said this, enjoying a small bit of satisfaction.

Charlie could hear Dr. Mbosi chuckle. "You're absolutely correct."

"So was the nurse able to get any specifics?"

"Any specifics? No. All specifics? Yes."

"What? Are you saying she got all the records?" Charlie was so surprised he almost forgot he was a prisoner.

"Of the patients who died? Yes. It turns out the site investigator wasn't very diligent. Or perhaps he was too arrogant. Nevertheless, he didn't encrypt or digitally protect his files. The nurse easily found and copied them."

"Do you know how many patients died from what GenPhage did?" As Charlie said this, he looked at his captors again, catching the gaze of the tall one, who seemed to be the one in charge. Charlie may have been the one who was trapped, but he wanted to make sure these goons had some idea of whom and what they were protecting.

"I couldn't bear to look for myself. But the nurse estimated there were maybe twenty deaths. Just from this site. I don't know how many other sites there are like this one, but that number alone is staggering."

Charlie knew that to be true. "I've never heard of that many deaths from a trial site. It backs up our theory they were testing something lethal. This has to stop. It's inhuman."

"That's why I'm helping you. I just sent the files to your email account. You should have them at any moment."

"Thank you so much, Dr. Mbosi. We'll make good use of this information and stop what GenPhage is doing."

"I look forward to hearing how this comes to its conclusion. Please keep me informed as best you can. I should be going. I feel like I need some quiet time and a nice glass of Scotch."

"Thanks again, Dr. Mbosi. There's one more thing." Charlie hadn't planned on what he would do next, but as soon as the idea came to him, he knew he had to do it.

"What's that?"

"Run! You're in danger, and they're coming for you. Get out of town before—" Charlie never got to finish his sentence. The butt of a pistol smashed across his face, knocking him out cold.

———

JORDAN RACED into the parking lot at Darcy's Pub. She could see Travis getting to the front door, reaching to unlock it. Her wheels squealed as she pulled into a parking spot near the front, drawing a "what the hell" look from Travis. Jordan jumped out of the car and sprinted over to him.

"Whoa, slow down," he said. "What's gotten into you? Did you hear from Charlie?"

"No. Everything. And no," Jordan replied to Travis's command and questions. Breathing hard, she paused beside Travis as he opened the door to the bar. "They've been listening to us. I don't know for how long, but probably since they broke in. They know everything."

"Who? Do you mean GenPhage? How do you know?"

Jordan reached into her jacket pocket and pulled out the two listening devices. "Because I found these."

Travis took one from the palm of Jordan's hand. He held it close and turned it around, looking at it carefully.

"I think they—" Jordan started to say. Travis put a finger in front of his mouth, motioning for her to stop talking.

He took the second device from Jordan and went inside. Jordan followed as Travis went behind the bar, filled a glass with water and dropped the devices into it. He then took the glass into his office.

"What did you do that for?" Jordan said.

"Because they were still transmitting. Didn't you see the red lights?"

"Oh shit. I didn't even think of that. I'm an idiot."

"It's all good. They shouldn't pick up anything now. Where were they?"

"I found them in light fixtures. One in the living room and one in the office."

"I'll be damned. This shit is right out of a spy novel."

"Maybe a bit. But it doesn't matter now. I need you to help with Charlie. He's unreachable, and the Kenyan doctor was supposed to contact him today with the information we need. You've got to break into his computer."

Travis looked unsure. "Do you think that's a good idea? I mean, he works for the CDC. Is the laptop his or the government's?"

"It's his. I think GenPhage took him. They would have heard everything about the Kenyan doctor. It's the only explanation for Charlie disappearing. Just get into his damn laptop."

"OK, OK. I'll do it. With what we've seen the past few days, it wouldn't surprise me at all if they grabbed Charlie. Give it to me."

Jordan handed Travis the laptop, and he sat down at the bar.

"For the record, you're taking the blame if Charlie gets mad."

"I'm pretty sure he won't mind."

34

CHARLIE FOUGHT TO OPEN HIS EYES. HIS HEAD FELT FUZZY, LIKE the wiring was out of whack. He got his right eye open a crack, followed by his left. The fluorescent brightness of the room overwhelmed his vision. After a moment to allow his eyes to adjust, Charlie saw that there was a bright floodlight aimed straight at him, perhaps five feet away.

Initially, he couldn't make out anything else in the room, but after maybe thirty seconds, he saw two figures, one on each side of the light. He recognized the one on the right, but it took a moment for his identity to register. One of his captors. The taller one. The rest came back in a flash. Charlie had been talking to Dr. Mbosi from Kenya. Then he'd warned Dr. Mbosi. And then everything had gone black. Based on the pain on the side of his face, the tall guy must have hit him and knocked him out.

A voice broke the silence, one Charlie didn't recognize, coming from the man on the left. "I see you've decided to wake up. Thank you for that."

Charlie sensed that this new individual was really the one in charge, the other men deferring to him. He wasn't sure how much he should engage in conversation, but given recent events, he couldn't make his situation much worse. "A drink of water would be nice. And maybe some Advil."

"Yes, I'm sure you must have a bit of a headache." The man motioned for someone to get what Charlie asked for. "But you brought that on yourself. All you had to do was talk to the Kenyan doctor, confirm what he would send you, and say good-bye. Warning him wouldn't help either of you."

One of the men brought a bottle of water and two Advil. Charlie swallowed them without taking a drink. The tall captor undid the clip on the strap around his hands so he could grab the bottle of water. "Aren't you afraid I'll overpower you and make my escape?"

"Not even a little. But go ahead and try. I could use a workout."

It was the leader's turn to speak again. "So, Charlie, what should we do with you?"

"I guess you got what you needed, so there's no need to keep me here. We don't have a story without that Kenya evidence. We can all go our separate ways."

The leader shook his head. "That's only partly correct. We got the email from the Kenyan doctor and deleted it from your account. And by the time the Kenyan doctor might consider needing to resend you the information, it will be too late. So, yes, we accomplished our main goal for the day. But you're wrong about all of us going our separate ways. While Jordan Reed's little team of troublemakers may not have enough information to expose GenPhage as planned, you, in particular, know more than enough to create a significant inconvenience in our lives. You've seen all four of us and likely even know some of our names. Not to mention that we have technically kidnapped you, which is a federal crime. From my vantage point, you're a liability. One I can't ignore."

Charlie's vision had finally adjusted to the bright light in his face. The newest arrival to the kidnapping clan walked over to a table against the far wall to Charlie's left. His back was to Charlie, but it appeared he was doing something with an object on the table. When he turned, he was holding something in his hand. Charlie's first thought was that it must be a gun, but he quickly saw that it was much too small. But it looked shiny, almost metallic, catching and reflecting light. As the man returned to his starting position, Charlie could see that he was holding a glass ampule with a gelatinous liquid inside.

Charlie's brain processed this observation, trying to divine what was in the ampule and for what purpose. It likely contained something lethal. Perhaps a drug or poison. But whatever it was, Charlie prayed that it wasn't the GenPhage weapon. There were a lot of horrible ways to die, and multiple organ failure was a very painful way to go.

The man held up the syringe. "Do you know what this is?"

Charlie hesitated to answer. He feared the worst and really didn't want to know the truth. "No, I don't, but I'm sure you'll tell me."

"This ampule contains what you and Jordan Reed have been searching for from the beginning, even if you didn't realize it. It's perhaps the most effective city-scale biological weapon, highly infectious with a high kill rate. The initial symptoms often resemble the flu, but as you may guess, that is a function of exactly what bacterial infection accompanies use of this material. It will respond to no known antibiotic treatment and will rapidly stretch health-care and emergency-response resources past their breaking point, forcing towns to shut down or self-destruct."

Charlie was only partially registering what was being said. His brain was grappling with the growing certainty he wouldn't be able to get out of this situation alive. But despite his primal instinct to survive, his scientist persona couldn't help but be intrigued by what he was hearing. And while he was adamantly against the development and use of any weapon of mass destruction, he felt an odd sense of respect for the science behind the off-the-books GenPhage treatment. To take an ancient life-form and use it as a genetic delivery vehicle to insert any of a number of different genes into a host was elegantly simplistic. At least as a concept.

If Charlie's captors wouldn't let him live, then maybe he could at least learn why GenPhage was doing this. "What's the real point of all this? I mean, for GenPhage. They've harnessed an amazing technology that can be used to treat many diseases. At the same time, they can make a fortune. Why the weapons angle?"

The team leader pondered the question a moment, seeming to consider the risk of explaining the rationale to Charlie. He must have concluded that the risk was low, likely because Charlie's days, or minutes, were numbered. "You're asking the wrong person. I'm a soldier, not a businessman. I leave that to the experts."

"Like Neil Foley."

"Yes."

"But you must have some idea why GenPhage is doing this?"

The answer wasn't at all what Charlie was expecting.

"In part because they can."

Charlie didn't know how to respond to that. As a scientist, it made little sense. "Are you serious? They've created a messenger of death just to test what they're capable of?"

"Neil has always been someone who didn't accept not being able to accomplish a goal or rise to a challenge. He's a very competitive individual and has high career aspirations. About five years ago, the Department of Defense quietly provided some initial seed money to develop and test the first prototype of the technology. Once a meaningful proof of concept was demonstrated, GenPhage sought serious financing via several rounds of private equity funding. They secured enough investment to fund the development of the technology as a disease treatment. But the DoD still had a financial interest in GenPhage. They challenged Neil to develop a weaponized version of the technology."

"That's all it took to make someone develop a terrible weapon? This sounds more like middle school than corporate America."

"The two are more alike than you think. But let me finish. As I said, Neil doesn't accept failure. He knew the science and what this technology platform could do. But as a businessman, he knew a commercially successful drug treatment was worth billions, while DoD funding was only millions. GenPhage would not get huge compensation from the DoD with a successful weapon, at least not compared to what it could make in the medical market."

"That's true. But there must be more to it than Neil responding to a dare?"

"Very intuitive," the leader replied. "There were actually two important incentives for Neil. The first he shared with me, and the second I learned of through back channels. First, DoD promised Neil ten million dollars in a variety of financial assets. He didn't say much about how that would work, but I've heard of similar deals over the years. There're no shortage of financial back doors in our government that enable transactions like this. The real motivation was the second incentive, one that is much loftier. Neil is very discreet, but his career ambitions are much bigger than to be CEO of some company. He has his sights set on the White House."

"He wants to be president?"

"That's what I've learned. He comes from a well-connected family that has a lot of old money. Apparently, there's a team behind the scenes, working on generating the support he'll need. He wouldn't be the first leader from the pharma industry to take a run at the White House. GenPhage is just a stop along the way."

"Typical. Greed and power."

"Never forget how enticing these two motivators can be."

Charlie didn't know what to make of this. It was so far afield from anything he had considered that it didn't compute. Corporate negligence was easy to believe. Corporate and individual greed were also easy to swallow. But the notion that this was all tied to someone's future presidential candidacy was off the charts for Charlie. Perhaps he shouldn't have been surprised, given some of the men that had held high political positions in his lifetime. But to develop and test a biological weapon on a human population as a path to becoming president made Charlie feel sick.

"This is all just a power trip," Charlie said. "Curing disease, helping people, all just sideshows on the way to the real goal. Money and power."

"That's the American way. Few people can increase their wealth by ten million in a single shot. With this weapon program, Neil gets richer and helps his path to the most powerful job in the country."

Charlie could now more easily absorb this reality. Wealth and power. These drivers of human behavior were as old as the human species. And Jordan stumbled right into it. "So what do you get out of it?"

"Me? Just money. I'm a simple guy. I'm the best at what I do, and I get paid very well by my clients. And I take care of my team. I couldn't care less about what people like Neil think about power. Real power is being able to do anything to anyone whenever I want. That's my power. I worked hard at it and owe no one for my success. Not like most of these spoiled millionaires who don't really know what it means to struggle."

Charlie saw a thread he couldn't resist pulling. "So you and Neil don't go to the same country club?"

"I prefer public courses. Look, Neil is a smart and driven individual and works hard in his own way. But we're not friends. He pays me very well for my services, and I respect the professional relationship we have. Nothing more, nothing less."

"What's next?" Charlie asked, though he was sure he knew.

"This part of the story is almost complete. GenPhage knows the weapon platform works and can be scaled up. I expect Neil will get his commission and continue to put the pieces in place to plan his political future. Such aspirations take many years. They've almost completed the clinical trials, and their treatment should be approved within a year. My team now needs to finish cleaning up the mess. You and your friends have no story without the information from Kenya. Your disconnected facts, bits of information, and accusations won't be believable. We'll encourage Jordan Reed to let this story die once and for all. We have many ways to motivate someone, and I'm sure we can find one that works for her."

"I was asking more specifically about me. Right now."

"I know that. Your part of the story is over. You know too much and have seen too much."

"Am I going to get the same fate as those patients in Africa?"

"You think I'll infect you with this?" the leader said, holding up the ampule. "That's not the plan. We don't have days to sit around and wait for it to run its course. Besides, this is the only sample I could acquire. I may need it one day. No, unfortunately, you were attacked and killed while out for your morning run. The attacker did a good enough job of hiding your body that it wasn't found until the evening."

The leader turned to the tall captor. "When I give you the word, you know where to leave him. Use a burner to call in a tip as soon as it gets dark."

"Got it. Are you going to keep his phone?" the tall man asked.

"Yes. I need to make sure there's no trace of what the doctor sent. I'll also watch to see if anyone else sends him something critical in the next few hours. Just in case. Once you're done, your team will roll off for some downtime while we let things quiet down. Good-bye, Charlie."

Charlie sat in silence, head down. There was really nothing to say. He knew there would be no persuading these men to let him live. They were doing their job. Not a job Charlie could rationalize. But a job.

As his captors packed up and prepared to take him to wherever they planned to leave him, Charlie had one overriding thought.

Jordan better check her email.

35

Jordan watched as Travis got to work on Charlie's MacBook Pro. First, he forced it to reboot in recovery mode. Jordan stood behind him on his left side, resting a hand on Travis's shoulder.

"Will this take long?" she said.

"It shouldn't. I'd be more worried if it were a CDC laptop. That would have some extra security."

"Good. We really don't have a lot of time. We might already be too late to intercept an email from Dr. Mbosi. We've seen firsthand how GenPhage deals with human obstacles."

"I remember. I'm going as fast as I can."

Jordan watched Travis intently.

She generally took his computer skills for granted, even though he was her de facto IT team. He was always tinkering with her laptop, making some adjustment or upgrade. She had no idea exactly what he did, but she was grateful he looked after it for her. Travis regularly assured her she'd have no worries about security or loss of data.

Jordan watched Travis make quick work of accessing and changing the administrator password and gaining access to Charlie's keychain, which kept track of all his account passwords. Within a few minutes, and following another computer reboot, Travis announced success. "That should do it."

"That was easy," Jordan said. "You know, you never really told me exactly what got you suspended from college. Which, given our circumstances back then, wasn't very cool. Was it this kind of stuff?"

"Not even close. This is a piece of cake when the computer doesn't use advanced encryption. Let's just say I had friends who were going to fail some courses. If they did, they'd lose their scholarships and their spots on the basketball team. I helped improve their academic records and used the money I made to pay most of my tuition. We got away undetected, and that should have been the end of it. But one of my friends opened his big mouth about how well he did, and someone at the university got suspicious. That spelled the end."

"I can see how the school wouldn't appreciate that. At least you haven't lost that skill set. Remind me to get you to help me with my next story."

"If there is a next story."

"What the hell is that supposed to mean?" Jordan said, slapping Travis across the back of his head.

Travis glanced over his left shoulder, not daring to look Jordan in the eye. "You know. In case we end up like Steve Calhoun. Or if this blows up in our faces and you get fired. It's not like we've got any guarantee of success here."

"We're close. But if we don't find Charlie and hear from the doctor in Kenya, I may as well head over to Target and apply to work there."

Travis had logged in to Charlie's computer. He opened a web browser and went to the email website. As expected, when prompted for the login and password, the keychain filled them in and Travis could read all of Charlie's email. "Bingo."

"You're in? His email account?"

"You bet your ass I am. Let's look."

Jordan grabbed a chair and sat down next to Travis. "I can't remember the doctor's name, so let's look at each message."

Fortunately, they were only looking for messages from today, and likely messages received in the past three or four hours. There were only about forty messages showing for today, so it didn't take long to scan them. Travis scrolled down the list as Jordan read the subject for each message. Travis made sure not to select any messages. That way, any messages Charlie hadn't read yet would show as unread.

They finished scanning the messages from today. Nothing at all from a doctor in Kenya. In fact, there appeared to be nothing having anything to do with GenPhage. "Shit," Jordan said, pushing herself back in her chair. "Not a damn thing. Are we too late? Was nothing sent?"

"Hang on," Travis said. "Let me check the trash and junk folders. Maybe the message went there."

Travis selected each of these two folders in turn. The result was the same. Nothing.

"What if it was a text and not an email?" Jordan asked.

"Well, if it was from someone with an iPhone or other Apple device, then we'd see it in iMessage."

Travis quickly checked iMessage but again found nothing. "I don't know where else to check. There may be nothing to find. This doctor may have sent nothing at all. We knew he was planning to send what he found by noon today, but what if something went wrong?"

"I don't believe that. Charlie said the doctor confirmed he'd have something. It must have been deleted already. Go back to his inbox."

"What're you looking for now? We already went through this."

"Something caught my eye the first time through, but I didn't pay attention. Scroll down to around ten a.m. this morning."

Travis scrolled about half a screen and stopped. "OK, now what?"

"Look at the messages. Of all the messages received after six thirty, only one was read." Jordan pointed to a message from 10:50. "A message saying Charlie could lower his insurance rates. Why would only one random message have been read, hours after Charlie went for his run? It makes no sense."

"I think it does. Let me show you." Travis pulled out his laptop and went to his email account, which happened to be from the same provider as Charlie. "See that I have about ten unread messages? Let me pick one in the middle. See how it loses the bold typeface once I select it?"

"Wow, Travis, you're brilliant," Jordan said sarcastically. "I never knew that."

"Just follow my lead. Watch what happens when I delete it." Travis hit delete, and the message disappeared. The next message in line was selected. Now it appeared to have been read.

"Shit, of course," Jordan said. "Someone must have deleted the message that was ahead of the one that looks read. The next message in the line, the insurance one, then became marked as read. GenPhage used Charlie's phone to intercept the Kenyan doctor's message and delete it from his account."

"What do we do next?"

Jordan stood up and paced around Travis's office. "Let me think a minute."

"While you do that, let me say I still think we need to tell the cops. We're not going to find Charlie by ourselves. We've got no idea where he is, and the guys who took him are pros."

Jordan turned to face Travis. "I know why you're saying that. But think about it. If we bring in the cops, what do we tell them? Everything? We don't know anything to help them find Charlie quickly. The cops will probably want to start asking questions at GenPhage. They'll clean up their mess before the cops even know what they're looking for. They'll get away with what they're doing, and we still won't be closer to finding Charlie."

Travis laid his head on the desk. "I'm an idiot." After a moment, he lifted his head back up and typed something on Charlie's computer.

"What is it?" Jordan asked.

"Charlie might make his location history available to his account. If he does, then there'll be a timeline for his phone's location. I should have thought of that right away."

"Yeah, you should have. Some fucking hacker you are."

"Give me a break. I'm out of practice."

"Fine. What do you see?"

"I don't believe it. Look."

Travis showed Jordan the screen. It was a map view of the Boston area, roughly centered on her neighborhood. There were many small circles, each one a location for Charlie's phone.

"Zoom in on my apartment," Jordan said.

Travis zoomed in, and they could see several of the small circles on Jordan's building, plus several others around the neighborhood. Jordan pointed to what appeared to be the last one in what looked like a path from her place out in a big loop. "What's the time of that location?"

Travis clicked on the circle and got the details, including the time and address. "That was at six twenty-two this morning. Looks like about a half mile from here. Maybe a bit more."

"That was Charlie on his run. I know he left before six thirty. I bet if you start at my place, you can trace his path with the first few circles." Jordan pointed at them, and Travis followed, confirming Jordan's assessment.

"You're right. But then they stop."

"Zoom out again."

They watched as Travis zoomed out the view. There was no obvious pattern they could see right away, but they both noticed a cluster of circles. "There," they both said at the same time.

At what must have been about five miles away was a cluster of circles in an area Jordan knew to be full of warehouses and old buildings.

"How long was Charlie's phone there?" Jordan asked.

"It looks like several hours." Travis looked at the different location circles. "Last one was about forty minutes ago."

"That has to be where they took him. There's no other explanation that makes sense."

"I can't argue with that. But where is he now? There should be more recent information if he's still there."

"Maybe his phone battery died. Or maybe the GenPhage guys turned it off."

"Or maybe Charlie isn't there anymore."

"Fuck, Travis. Are you trying to find the worst possible explanation for everything, or does it just come naturally?"

"I'm trying to be realistic here. You seem to think everything will just fall into place, no matter how bad things have gone in the past. You need to face reality. We're in over our heads here and should get the cops involved."

"You know what? I agree."

"Really? About bringing in the cops?"

"Yes. Now we can tell them where to go. They're trained to handle this kind of stuff, so the chances of getting Charlie are better if the cops do it."

"Now you're making some sense. Don't tell me you're willing to tell them everything?"

"Not a chance. Just enough to make sure they take action. Charlie was helping research an important story about corruption. We think the story target knew what we were up to. Charlie went out for a run. He didn't come back. We tracked his phone to an address. That should be enough."

"Maybe for now," Travis said. "But they'll eventually expect us to tell them everything. We probably don't have more than a day."

"That's enough," Jordan said. "We were going to have to pull this together today anyway. Can you make the call to the cops?"

"Why me? What're you going to do?"

"We still need more evidence. It looks like we lost whatever Dr. Mbosi sent to Charlie. I need Emma to come through. I'll call her and tell her we're out of time and need whatever she can get us. I'll head to her office and call on the way."

"Let's hope she can get something."

"I'll let you know as soon as I learn anything. You do the same." Jordan grabbed her purse, jacket, and phone and headed for the door.

"I will." Travis picked up his phone and stood up. "Jordan."

She turned and looked at him. "Yeah?"

"Be careful."

"Aren't I always?"

36

Jordan pulled out of the Darcy's Pub parking lot and called Emma. It went straight to voice mail.

Shit.

Jordan hated voice mail. She wanted to hang up and try again in a few minutes. But time was running out, and she needed to know if Emma had found anything that could help. "Emma, Jordan. We're in some trouble. Charlie's missing, and we have nothing from the Kenyan doctor. It looks like you're our last hope. Call me back as soon as you get this."

Jordan continued on toward the GenPhage headquarters. If Emma didn't call back soon, she'd have to decide if she should turn back. As she considered hitting a coffee shop or diner nearby, her phone rang. It was Emma.

"Emma, thanks for calling back so soon." Jordan thought she hadn't called back quickly at all, given how critical the situation was, but it wouldn't help to get all bent out of shape.

"Sorry I missed your call. I was away from my phone but called as soon as I could. What happened to Charlie?"

As Emma asked, it really hit Jordan that Charlie was in danger. She could feel tears building but held them back. "He never came back from his run this morning. He should've been back hours ago, and he hasn't responded to calls or texts."

"Are you sure he didn't have something else he had to do and just forgot to tell you?"

"Charlie doesn't forget anything. Besides, all of his things are still at my place. Something's happened."

"I'm sorry, Jordan. What are you going to do?"

"Well, Travis and I think we know where he is, so we're going to get the police involved."

There was a moment of silence. Jordan's impatience was in high gear. "Emma, are you still there?"

"Yes, sorry. Just thinking. How did you figure out where Charlie was?"

"Travis hacked his laptop, and we accessed his phone's location. After his run, he seems to have been in a location a few miles from here. He was there for a few hours. But his location hasn't been updated in almost an hour, so he may not still be there. But it's a start."

"Seems reasonable. Is Travis talking to the police?"

"Yeah. They should be on their way by now."

"So is it true that you didn't get the information from the Kenyan doctor?"

"As far as I know. It's hard to know for sure since Charlie hasn't turned up yet. Were you able to find anything? If you aren't able to dig anything up, then we're shit out of luck."

"Then let me brighten your day. I have a definite lead here and will know exactly what I can get you in the next couple of hours. I'm sure that by the end of the day, we'll have this all wrapped up."

Jordan couldn't believe what she'd heard. Emma had come through. Of all people, it was someone from the inside. Someone whose uncle was running the whole operation. "Seriously? You found something? What is it?"

"I don't want to share the details yet. I need to confirm a few things first. But trust me, you'll get closure on this today. I guarantee it."

"Holy shit. I was thinking this was all for nothing, that we wouldn't be able to tie GenPhage to any of the crap we know they're doing. When will you be able to tell me what you've got? Or better yet, show me?"

"Give me a few hours. Definitely by six p.m. I'll call when I finish here and am ready to meet up."

Jordan breathed an audible sigh of relief. "Thanks, Emma. I know this is putting you in a tough spot, but you're doing the right thing."

"True. But I know what's important."

"I'm going to help Travis. I'll wait for your call."

EMMA DIALED a number from her favorites list. After two rings, a familiar voice picked up. "This must be important. You know I'm prepping for our board of directors meeting. We have decisions to make on our IPO, and I have some aggressive views that these stuffed shirts won't like. Why the call?"

"What do you mean 'why the call'?" Emma said. "You know damn well why I'm calling. Your little army of idiots grabbed Jordan's friend Charlie, and in the process, they managed to let Jordan track him down from his phone. Now the cops are on their way to where they're holding him. They might even be there by now."

"Shit. Carter must have fucked up. That's the second problem I have to deal with."

"Really? What's the other one?"

"I'll explain later. But we need to go to the alternate plan. I'll call Carter now. Do you know what to do?"

"Don't worry about me. Just make sure your soldiers don't fuck anything else up."

JORDAN CALLED Travis from her car.

"I wasn't expecting to hear from you so soon," he said. "What's up?"

"I talked to Emma. She said she'll be able to get us what we need to close out this story. That at least solves one problem. But it still leaves Charlie. What happened with the police?"

"I told them what we agreed to. They said they'd send a car right away to the address we identified. They'll also send someone by your apartment within the hour. They want to check Charlie's things and get statements from us. I'll head over now. I've still got a key. Will you go home now?"

Jordan had forgotten Travis still had a key to her place. It had never felt right to ask for it back.

"I should. I just hope they find Charlie and that he's all right." Jordan felt her voice crack a bit as an image of Steve Calhoun's battered body, with Charlie's face, flashed in her mind.

"I know. When you first told me about the story, I would never have guessed we'd be in a situation like this. I'm sorry I didn't take it seriously enough. You know, when you thought you were being followed."

"It doesn't matter now. The cops have got to find Charlie, and we've got to nail GenPhage. Emma will come through."

"About that. Doesn't it strike you as a little strange she wouldn't tell you anything about this information she said she's getting?"

"Maybe. But she is stealing from her company. She's probably just nervous."

"I hope you're right. But I'm not popping any champagne until we know for sure she's going to help."

"Can't you ever be optimistic? Emma said she'll get what we need. She wouldn't say that if she wasn't sure. Give her some time. Don't be such a downer." Jordan briefly thought that Emma had never actually said she'd get what they needed. What she said was that there would be closure. In Jordan's mind, that was the same thing.

"I'm a realist," Travis said. "You should know as well as anybody that life dishes out shit. I'll believe we're good when I see what Emma has. For me, it feels a bit too convenient that she was able to come through that fast."

Jordan did think Emma had made quick progress. But she wasn't going to give Travis the satisfaction of agreeing with him. In the back of her mind, a tiny seed of doubt formed. She didn't think Emma was lying. Not exactly. But not sharing anything? It's not what Jordan would have done were the situation reversed.

"Don't worry about it. I'll manage Emma. Just focus on helping the cops find Charlie. Ideally without giving GenPhage a chance to save themselves first."

"I'll try. If they don't find him or his phone at that address, we'll have to tell them more. A mugger would have left him where he was. It'd be hard to believe he was randomly taken. If the cops ask specific questions, we should answer them."

The more time that passed with Charlie in danger, the less Jordan cared about protecting her story. She wanted to save both Charlie and her story. But she knew she'd sacrifice her story if she needed to.

"You're right. We'll cooperate. First, let's see if they're able to find Charlie. I'll see you back at my apartment soon."

———

JORDAN THOUGHT she'd get back to her apartment before the police. She was wrong.

Upon entering her apartment, she saw one police officer talking to Travis while the other was looking at Charlie's duffel bag. The degree to which Travis towered over the cop in front of him was almost comical. All three turned when she walked in.

"Jordan," Travis said. "You're just in time. This is Officer Jennings. His partner is Officer MacKay."

"Ms. Reed," Officer Jennings said. "Your friend said it would be all right for us to come in even though you weren't home."

Jordan felt sweat running down her neck despite the cold day. Being around the police always made her nervous. She tried to act relaxed but was sure it came across as fake.

"It's fine. I told Travis to make sure he was here for you. Did you find Charlie?"

"Unfortunately, no. The officers that went to the location you mentioned found it empty. It had evidence of someone having been there recently, but whoever was there had left. A forensic team is there collecting evidence. If whoever was there left any prints, we should know something by tomorrow."

Jordan was deflated. The GenPhage thugs had moved Charlie. Or worse. If she had reacted faster to his disappearance, the police might have gotten to him in time to rescue him.

"That's not good. I really hoped you'd find him. I see you found Charlie's things."

"Yes," said Officer MacKay. "I assume you don't object if we go through them? Since he's missing, we need to treat them as evidence."

"Do what you need to do. Everything should be there."

Officer MacKay proceeded to inspect Charlie's things.

"I was just about to ask Travis here about Charlie," Officer Jennings said. "Now that you're here, we can do it together."

"Makes sense."

Having had a moment to take in the police officers, Jordan couldn't help but notice Officer Jennings's good looks. And it wasn't just the uniform effect. His broad shoulders and slim frame was a perfect match for his short blond hair and Tom

Cruise-shaped face. With Scott standing beside Travis, Jordan realized how different these two attractive men looked.

"Travis gave us the basics when he called. That your friend Charlie was helping you with a story you were working on. Charlie was apparently supposed to be getting information from a doctor overseas. That was supposed to happen today?"

"Yes. It would have been sent by email. I think Charlie was kidnapped by the company I'm investigating. By taking him and his phone, they could intercept the information and make sure it doesn't go public."

"That's an interesting theory. I don't recall hearing the name of the company. I need to know."

Jordan glanced at Travis, who nodded his approval.

"GenPhage. The company is GenPhage."

Officer Jennings's eyebrows raised. "Isn't that the company in that new building down in the Seaport?"

"That's the one."

"They're a drug company, right?"

Jordan had opened the door to having to share more information than she would have liked. For Charlie's sake, she had to do it and hope she could still nail GenPhage. "That's right. They're supposed to be developing a treatment for tuberculosis."

"I have to say, I've never heard of a drug company doing anything like what you're suggesting. Especially in Boston. That's organized crime family stuff."

"Well, with what I know, they should want to keep it quiet."

Officer Jennings looked hard at Jordan, as though he was sizing up the accuracy of what she'd said. "Would it be too much to ask what exactly you know?"

"Exactly what I know won't help find Charlie. But it was GenPhage."

"How can you be sure? How did they know about this doctor sending information to Charlie?"

Jordan weighed the pros and cons of answering the question.

Again, Charlie's safety trumped her story. "Because GenPhage planted listening devices in my apartment. When they broke in and trashed it."

Officer Jennings swiveled his head, taking in Jordan's apartment. "I see your office wall is damaged. Where are these so-called listening devices?"

"I have them," said Travis. "In a glass of water at my business. I figured they might be evidence. Sitting in water should prevent them from capturing any conversation."

"I'll need to get those from you. We might be able to get something useful from them. Is there anything else you can tell me that could help find your friend?"

Jordan shook her head. "I wish I did. I suppose you could go and question the leaders at GenPhage. But they'll grab their lawyers, and that'll prevent any discussion. I've had the joy of meeting them."

Jordan recalled that shitty afternoon when GenPhage ambushed her and her editors at the *Courant*. There was one thing she could share. Something useful for the police that didn't immediately impact her story.

"Actually, there is something else. The time when I met GenPhage's lawyers, one of the men with them was introduced as a security consultant. His name was Carter Nash. He looked like an ex-cop or a soldier. If there's anyone who had something to do with Charlie's disappearance, it's that guy."

"That's helpful. We can run his name and see what turns up. I guess that's all for now."

"Really?" Travis said. "What's next?"

"Well, we'll run down any prints we get from that location. As I mentioned, we'll check on this Carter Nash fellow. Anything we learn will guide next steps."

"But you'll keep looking for him, right?" Jordan said.

"Absolutely. We pulled a photo of him from a CDC website,

and it's now part of our missing persons database. We'll let you know of any progress we make."

"Will you question anyone at GenPhage?"

"Not immediately. Let's see if we get some prints and what Carter Nash's relationship is to the company. Questioning someone there won't get us very far unless we have a solid lead."

"There's one more thing, Officer," Travis said.

Jordan looked sharply at Travis, shaking her head.

"Oh? Go ahead."

"Travis," Jordan said. "We don't know. Not for sure."

"Sorry, Jordan. I think we're pretty damn sure." He turned to Officer Jennings. "It's about a hit-and-run downtown. A guy named Steve Calhoun."

Jordan lowered her head. There was nothing she could do.

"Please continue," Officer Jennings said.

"We had met the guy who was hit. He used to work at GenPhage. He told us some stuff that was pretty incriminating for the company. About their clinical trials. Anyway, he was run down right after we met with him. We didn't see the accident, but it's one hell of a coincidence."

Jordan received a not-so-friendly look from Officer Jennings. "You didn't think this was worth sharing with the police?"

Jordan tried to downplay the event. "Look, we didn't see the accident. For all we knew, it was a random accident. Even if it was the same guys, there's no evidence from the accident proving who did it."

Travis interjected before Jennings could respond. "Actually, there may be other evidence."

"What?" Jordan said.

"Steve's apartment. I didn't pay much attention when he said it, but some guys threatened him at his apartment. If any of them were the same guys we think grabbed Charlie, there might be a fingerprint match. Sorry. I really didn't think of it until now."

Jordan hadn't thought of that either. It was actually a good suggestion.

Jennings looked at them both. "That could help make a connection. You two better not be hiding anything else like this. We're all on the same team here."

"There's nothing else we know," Jordan said. "Really."

"For your sake and that of your friend, you better be telling the truth."

Jordan was both angry and relieved. Angry at Travis for not warning her that he was going to tell the cops about Steve. Relieved because it was the right thing to do. In the short term, it probably wouldn't help find Charlie. But it could help with the bigger picture if some physical evidence emerged.

The police officers made their way to the door. Officer Jennings turned to Jordan before leaving. "Take my card. If you remember anything else, don't hesitate to call."

Jordan took the card. She didn't have a real relationship with anyone on the police force. Maybe Officer Jennings could be her first.

"Thank you. I'll definitely call if something comes up."

"I most definitely will be in touch."

Jordan closed her door after the two police officers left. She gave Travis a look she knew he had seen before.

"I know what you're going to say," Travis said. "I should have told you what I was going to do. But if I did, you would have talked me out of it. Knowing the connection to Steve could help the police find Charlie."

"Relax. My first reaction was to be pissed. But you're right. I had forgotten there might be evidence in Steve's apartment. That was a good call."

"Whew. I was actually more scared of you than the cops."

"That's good. Remember that next time."

"Now what?"

"Right now? I need a drink."

Jordan walked over to the kitchen and poured herself a shot of gin.

"That's not the best idea you've had today," Travis said, pointing to the nearly empty gin bottle on the counter.

"I need to take the edge off. I'm agitated and can't focus."

"Whatever. Sounds like the same old excuse."

"Go judge someone else. I'm busy."

They were both startled by Jordan's phone. "It's Emma. Here we go." Jordan answered. "Hey there. Are you calling with good news?"

"Absolutely. Did you doubt me?"

"Maybe a little," Jordan said, giving Travis another look.

"No sweat. I've got more to do in the office. How about we meet at seven?"

Jordan looked at her watch. It was just after three p.m. She wanted to meet right away, but with Emma still in the office and traffic being shitty at this time of day, she figured seven would be fine. "Sure. Do you want to come here?"

"We should pick a different location, just in case there's someone still watching your place."

"Good idea. Just tell me where."

"I'll text you an address. Should take you twenty to thirty minutes to get there."

"Right. See you at seven."

"One more thing. Come alone, Jordan. OK? It's not that I don't trust Travis, but I prefer to share this just with you."

That struck Jordan as odd, especially since Emma must realize Jordan would tell Travis anyway. In the end, it wouldn't matter as long as she got what she needed. "Sure, just me. See you later."

"What was that 'just me' all about?" Travis asked.

"I guess she just wants to show me. It's strange, but I doubt it really matters."

"She has to know you'll tell me. I don't know, Jordan. This feels off."

"Jesus, won't you just relax? Not everything is a conspiracy or a trap. She's probably just being extra careful. After all, she's betraying her company and her uncle."

"Let's hope that's all it is."

"You worry too much." Jordan's phone beeped. "She just texted me the address. I can't tell if it's a business or some kind of office building. Can you look at the area and let me know what this place might be?"

"Sure. Send it to me."

Travis pulled up the location on a map. "Hmm. I'm not sure what this is. It looks like it's kind of close to the GenPhage manufacturing facility, maybe two miles away. There doesn't seem to be a lot around it. Let me do a real search on the address."

Travis typed in the address and quickly scanned the results. "That's a surprise that really shouldn't be. It's GenPhage property. Maybe it's where they did some research or manufacturing in the past. We know where their main manufacturing site is, but this is different. I can't find it listed on their website as an official location."

"Maybe that's why Emma wants to meet there. It'll be private."

"It also isolates you. I don't like it. I should go with you."

"Not a chance. I'm not risking this meeting because you're paranoid."

"Well, growing up black in America has taught me that a healthy dose of paranoia can keep you safe."

"Tone it down for now. This meeting will be fine."

"Just be careful."

37

It started raining while Jordan and Travis were in her apartment. Fortunately, the temperature was above freezing, or Jordan would have been driving in one hell of a snowstorm. In the dark, it was tricky finding the exact address. There were almost no streetlights in the area, and street signs were absent or hard to see in the rain. What should have been about a twenty-five-minute drive took closer to forty minutes.

When she came across a parking lot entrance with the address on a sign chained to a wire fence, she knew she'd arrived. She headed toward what looked like the main entrance. There were three vehicles parked in the spots closest to the doors. The bright-red one she recognized as Emma's. She had no idea about the other two.

What the hell is this? Who else is here? Emma didn't mention anyone else.

As Jordan got close to the parking space that would make her the fourth car in line, her heart skipped a beat. The third vehicle was a black Suburban. She didn't know if it was the one that had been following her, but just seeing one here gave her the chills. She had a moment of panic.

What do I do? Stay or go? If I leave now, I lose the story for sure.

It'll be over. And I need to know what happened to Charlie. I came too far to quit now. Fuck.

Jordan pulled into the parking space beside the Suburban. The windows were so tinted, they were practically black. In the darkness, Jordan couldn't see inside the vehicle at all.

There was no sign of anybody outside, so she went to the front doors of the building. They were glass but had steel bars for added security.

The poor lighting made it difficult to see if there was a buzzer or intercom to gain entrance. After a moment of looking, she saw an intercom box to the right of the doors. She pressed the only button. Nothing. No sound. No light. It appeared not to be working. But a moment later, she heard a buzzer and a loud click, then the door on the left swung open.

I guess it worked after all.

Jordan walked through and opened an inner door. Once inside the building, she paused, taking in the lobby, trying to decide which way to go. The lobby was large but nothing like the cavernous one in the GenPhage headquarters. This one had a long counter in the center with a few chairs behind it. There was a single computer set up, and it appeared to be on. On both sides of the lobby was a quartet of chairs, each centered on a low, square wooden table about three feet by three feet. Everything in the lobby was covered in a thin layer of dust.

While Jordan considered where to go, a man entered the lobby from behind the long counter.

"Jordan Reed," he said. "You're early. I suppose I shouldn't be surprised. Come this way." The man opened the door he'd just come through and gestured for Jordan to go first. She hadn't expected to see anyone other than Emma, let alone this man who looked like a secret agent. Jordan was so lost in thought, the man's words didn't register when he spoke. "Hey, are you with me? This way."

"Right, sorry. I was expecting someone else."

"I know. Emma's waiting for you."

Whatever was going to happen, Jordan knew it would not be what she had expected. Emma had something different in mind. A sense of foreboding began to envelop Jordan. Extra people and a black Suburban wasn't a positive sign.

Jordan went around the counter and toward the door being held open. As she walked past the man, she realized he was taller than he first appeared, at least six one. He was lean but muscular. His attire was simple and black, creating an impression of strength. Based on his appearance, he could easily pass for thirty or younger. Interestingly, she didn't detect either a pleasant or unpleasant scent. She couldn't detect a scent of any sort. This was such a noticeable surprise she assumed it must have been on purpose.

There was a long hallway that seemed obvious to follow, but as Jordan walked by a door on her right, the man told her to open it and take the stairs down to the bottom. Jordan hadn't been the least bit concerned with meeting Emma tonight, but minute by minute, she was becoming more convinced that Travis's concerns were valid. Too late to back out now. In for a penny, in for a pound.

Jordan descended to the end of the stairs, dropping two floors. As she reached for the door at the bottom of the stairs, the man told her to turn right. He then directed her to a room at the end of the hall. It reminded Jordan of a hospital. The walls were painted white, and there were bright fluorescent lights on the ceiling, the kind with the long three-foot bulbs. There was the faint hum of electricity to go along with the sterile smell hanging in the air.

Jordan got to the end of the hall, slowly opened the door, and stepped inside. The room was smaller than she'd expected, maybe thirty feet wide and twenty feet deep. It was mostly empty. She was utterly unprepared for the situation that greeted her.

In what seemed like the dead center of the room was a long foldout table with four people seated behind it. On the far left was the last person Jordan thought she'd see here but the one she most wanted to see. Charlie. He looked fine, albeit with a big bruise on his cheek. He was still in his running clothes. Jordan couldn't see his hands, but they were in front of him, below the table. They may or may not have been tied.

Jordan recognized the man beside Charlie. He was the security guy from the meeting with the GenPhage lawyers who'd never said a word. Carter Nash. He was older than Jordan's greeter but looked no less fit. Next came the only person Jordan expected to see. Emma. She looked calm, as if this was a typical situation for her. Her face wore a hint of a smile. Jordan felt afraid.

Last in the row of people, but not least, was none other than Neil Foley. He too looked relaxed, but in a pissed-off kind of way. He had a sneer to his expression that told Jordan he had more important things to do with his time. There were no other chairs in the room. Jordan noticed that her greeter stood in front of the door she'd come through, blocking any retreat.

Jordan felt like she was on trial, forced to stand in front of this group lined up at their table. Travis was right to have been worried. He would never let her forget this. Never.

Jordan looked over to Charlie. "Hey there. I'm glad to see you're all right."

"Hey yourself." He looked to his left. "I wasn't sure I'd make it this far. I'm glad to be here to see you."

Neil appeared in a hurry for whatever was planned. "If you're done with the reunion, can we get down to business?"

Emma looked at her uncle. "As you wish, Uncle." She turned to Jordan. "It's good you made it. I wasn't sure you'd go through with the meeting. Part of me thought you never believed I'd actually help you and that you'd set some kind of trap. That must make you one of the most gullible reporters alive."

The realization that Emma had been playing her the entire time finally hit home. There had been small signs that she shouldn't have trusted Emma. But Jordan had brushed them off. Emma had acted like she wanted to be a friend. And Jordan could have used one. Their whole relationship had been a fraud.

"Yeah," Jordan said. "I guess I thought you were genuine. Man, was I wrong. You missed your calling by going into business. You should have been an actor. I should have known better than to expect people like you to do the right thing."

"The right thing is subjective," Emma said. "I do what's right for me and the company. If you recall, I did promise closure. Unfortunately for you, tonight won't play out as you planned. Instead, we're going to make a deal that leaves all parties satisfied."

"A deal? What the hell do you mean by that? I won't be part of any deal. I'm done with you. Charlie and I are leaving." Jordan wasn't sure if Charlie could just get up and walk out, but Jordan was playing the role of being in charge and hoped it would be enough to get them out of there in one piece.

"Do you really think that's an option, Jordan? You and Charlie aren't leaving. Not until we say you can leave. Remember who's in control here. We know everything you know. We know everyone you talked to. You're not in a position to bargain."

"You and your uncle make quite a pair. You spent a lot of effort just to shut down a minor reporter."

"Thanks for the compliment, but it really didn't take much effort. You should consider a new career after tonight."

It was Neil's turn to speak. "Enough wasting time. We all want resolution here, and Charlie leaving is only one dimension of the arrangement we need to come to. How about you take a moment to listen to what we propose and then decide if you want to be rash?"

"It doesn't look like I have much of a choice."

"You can make any choice you like," Emma said. "But every choice has consequences. Some for you. Some for others." She looked at Charlie as she spoke that last sentence.

"I'm beginning to see how you all operate. Get as much as you can get and fuck everybody else."

"What world do you live in, Jordan?" Neil said. "Do you think corporate America is based on strong moral principles and high ethical standards? The primary aim is to maximize profits. Why? To make people rich. And not just ourselves. Our investors and shareholders don't give us their money as some form of charity. They expect us to make them more money. The companies that do this the best become leaders in their industry, and their CEOs and executives get rich. Some even get to wield political power and influence. That's why we do what we do."

"With no regard for the innocent people who get hurt or killed along the way?"

Neil stood up and walked around the table, stopping about six feet in front of Jordan. "This is how my industry works, especially for infectious diseases. They're very difficult to develop treatments for, at least treatments that work well enough to garner meaningful revenue. And most of the patients are in developing nations."

"And that gives you an excuse to experiment on them? Putting their lives at risk for your benefit?"

"Their lives are already at risk because of where they live and because of their dismal living conditions. Millions of people a year die because of infectious diseases. The number who died because of our actions is a rounding error. They would have died anyway. The overall good outweighs a small bit of harm. We'll save thousands of lives, maybe even millions, with our treatments."

"Treatments are one thing. But biological weapons are another."

At that comment, Neil's face showed his true contempt. It

disappeared as quickly as it had surfaced. "You're overstating things. The DoD simply wanted to know if the technology could be used for offense as well as defense. The phage platform, in combination with any of an array of potentially dangerous bacteria, can in fact be a potent weapon. If needed."

"Tell yourself whatever you need to hear. Where I come from, the ends don't justify the means."

Neil smirked. "Exactly what I'd expect from someone who can barely pay her bills. Let's stop this bullshit and get down to business. There's a scenario where we all leave this room alive and satisfied. Do you want to hear the terms of the agreement, or would you rather get on your high horse and leave?"

"Go ahead."

"Don't sound so defeated. I'm sure you'll be satisfied when we're done here."

"I doubt that."

"Suit yourself. There are three components of the deal we'll make. First is the matter of Charlie's safety. He knows enough to create problems for us. Not the least of which is being able to identify the gentlemen he spent the day with."

"Don't you mean the criminals who kidnapped him? Probably the same bastards who trashed my place and planted listening devices."

Neil glanced quickly at the man behind Jordan with a questioning expression. "Your choice of words is extreme. As you can see, your friend is perfectly fine and can leave with you tonight."

"So what's the catch?"

"Simple. He agrees to let what happened today become a thing of the past that requires no future action or discussion. No harm, no foul. And you immediately call off the police. Charlie wasn't missing. He got lost and then got mugged. The muggers knocked him out and took his phone. With no phone, it took him a while to get back."

"That sounds too simple. What am I missing?"

"That's tied to the second component of our arrangement. You agree to drop this and any future investigation into GenPhage. Unless you want to praise our success when we have our first treatment approved and take our company public."

"Really? I'm a fucking reporter. I don't give free passes. Let Charlie come with me, come clean with the authorities on testing something unapproved, and I'll drop the current story. Clean slate all around. That's a deal I can make."

"Sorry, but that's not going to happen. Plus I don't really trust you. You were supposed to back off once before and never really did. Remember? Besides, you don't really have a story at the moment. Do you?"

Jordan didn't have a comeback for that one. "You're asking too much. I can't do my job if I agree to give people like you a free pass."

"You didn't let me finish. There's more to this second component of the deal. In fact, it's the best part."

"Let me guess. You'll give me a job at your company?"

"No. Truth be told, I never want to see you again after this evening. But I'm referring to something financial."

"Your big idea is to bribe me?"

"Call it what you like. I prefer to think of it as compensation. Let me ask you something. How much money do you have in savings and investments? Across everything? Bank accounts, retirement plans, stocks, piggy banks?"

Jordan had a general idea but wouldn't admit it to him. "I don't know for sure. It's not a lot, but I'm young. I've got a long runway to save for my future."

"Let me answer that for you. Less than two thousand dollars in your checking account. Your retirement account, small as it is, has been nearly emptied. And you have no stocks. Basically, you live month to month."

"That isn't a crime. Hell, for many, that's the American dream."

"And how about your father? Still strapped with all those medical bills? It's a shame he lost his house and still hasn't been able to pay off your mother's cancer treatments."

Jordan clenched her fists and glared at Neil. "You fucking bastard. Leave my family out of this."

"If you listen to me, you'll see how my offer will help. In exchange for forgetting about GenPhage, there are two pieces of financial compensation I'll give you today. The first is a check that covers actual and related costs to the property damage that resulted from the recent act of vandalism at your apartment."

"Which you had nothing at all to do with."

"Of course not." Neil held an envelope for Jordan. "You'll see this more than compensates for any possible value of possessions in your apartment. It may even buy you a new place to start fresh."

Jordan had never had a meaningful amount of cash in her life. It surprised her how tempted she was to grab the envelope. But she left Neil's hand and the envelope hanging in midair.

Neil looked offended and lowered his arm. "In addition, I want to make sure you enjoy the prosperity of GenPhage. While you may not appreciate it at the moment, we're poised for great success. When we take the company public, our internal shareholders will all make a significant amount of money. As part of our arrangement, I'll give you twenty thousand shares in GenPhage. We have not set our IPO price yet, but expect it to be around fifty dollars per share. The only condition, and it applies to myself and Emma as well, is that you hold the shares for twelve months after the IPO date."

Jordan was good at math, and the calculation was simple. A million dollars. Her mouth went dry. That amount of money was so large it didn't compute. It could get her father out of debt. Assuming she'd actually help him. Jordan hadn't considered this scenario.

"I assume by your silence you're at least considering my offer."

Jordan didn't want to appear thankful. It was a bribe, plain and simple. It just happened to be an extremely lucrative bribe. "It's certainly a very large bribe. But you mentioned three components to the arrangement. What's the third one?"

"You have something of high value I need. An email. I need the email and your phone. There can be no trace of this particular email."

Jordan was confused. She couldn't think of any email she'd received that would be so important that Neil or anyone else would need to take her phone to make sure they deleted it. Especially for the GenPhage story. She didn't use email as much as text and sometimes went hours without checking. She racked her brain to figure out what Neil was referring to. She couldn't remember when she'd checked her email last. With the crazy day it had been, she realized she hadn't checked since early in the morning.

"You're going to have to be specific. I can't think of any email I received that you'd find very important."

"Have you checked your email today?"

"Not since this morning. I've been kind of busy."

Jordan noticed Charlie lower his head. She didn't know what that meant.

"As I suspected. Take out your phone and look through the messages you received today. Don't open or read any of them. Just look at the sender and the message subject. You'll know the message I'm referring to when you see it."

Jordan pulled her phone out of her jacket pocket. Out of the corner of her left eye, she noticed the man who'd greeted her in the lobby move to stand to her left. No doubt his job was to make sure Jordan did as they instructed and didn't actually read the message in question.

Jordan looked at the day's emails, starting from the most

recent message at the top. She looked at each sender, many of which were junk. She made a mental note to unsubscribe from all of this shit when she had a chance.

As she scanned the messages, she almost missed the one from Charlie. It had come around 10:45 in the morning. That made no sense. Charlie had been spending quality time with his new GenPhage friends at 10:45. She was pretty sure they wouldn't have let him send any messages. But the message wasn't originally from Charlie. It had been forwarded. From Dr. Mbosi. And it had an attachment.

Holy shit. Dr. Mbosi's information. Somehow Charlie forwarded it to me. How the hell did he pull that off?

Jordan's jaw dropped ever so slightly.

"I see you found what I'm looking for," Neil said. "It turns out your little friend here had set up an automatic forwarding rule to send any message from Dr. Mbosi directly to you. Lucky for us, we checked his sent email and saw that this occurred. Otherwise, we wouldn't have known and would have mistakenly thought we had erased all trace of this message."

Jordan looked at Charlie. "You should have told me you set this up. I would've seen it, and then we wouldn't be in this position."

"I just thought to set it up this morning before going for my run. I must have had a premonition or something. Still, though, you really should check your email more often."

"Let's move this along," Neil said. "If you hand me your phone, I'll take that as an acceptance of the terms of our deal. In exchange, Charlie can leave with you, and you'll notify the police immediately that Charlie isn't in fact missing. I'll give you the two envelopes we discussed. Your journalistic interest in GenPhage will cease immediately. It's up to you."

"No offense, but this seems too clean. You buy what I have so I can't expose what GenPhage has done. I agree not to look into GenPhage anymore. Which, by the way, isn't really a big problem for me. You're all insane. Plus, I get to take Charlie with me. How do you know I won't change my mind in six months?"

"There are two things you need to know. First, a million dollars of future GenPhage stock is peanuts to me if it means ending this mess. Second, while I know you and your family aren't on great terms, I'm willing to believe you'd like them to stay safe. As long as you do your part, they won't be harmed."

Jordan knew there had to be some extra insurance for Neil. This was it. Not very original, but effective. "You'd make a good gangster."

"A good gangster is always a good businessman. What's your decision?"

Jordan was out of time. She had to decide. If only she had checked her email before coming here. If Jordan didn't agree, they'd take her phone anyway, and she and Charlie may not leave this place alive. Travis would be a loose end they could either deal with or just ignore. He wouldn't have any evidence to prove what GenPhage had done.

Thinking of Travis triggered a memory from when she'd first received the obituary. He'd mentioned an upgrade he'd made to her computer. An upgrade that might actually save her story. She didn't know exactly what Travis had done, but it she might not be done with her story. Regardless, her current situation was no-win. She had to take what was being offered and hope for the best.

"I guess I'll have to take your deal. This isn't how I expected the evening to go, but it's not a total loss." Jordan gave Charlie a quick smile, but it did nothing to alleviate the confusion on his face.

"Excellent. Hand over your phone and we can conclude our business."

Jordan closed her email and walked toward the table, stopping in front of Emma. "Here."

"Your password?"

Jordan spelled it out, and Emma made sure it worked. "It's correct."

Neil reached back and grabbed two envelopes, holding them up for Jordan. "Remember. You can't engage in any reporting on GenPhage. Someone free her friend."

Neil and Emma started to walk away.

"For the record," Jordan said, "I know about OncoThera-peutics."

Neil stopped and turned back to look at Jordan. "Yes, I believe you referred to that before. So what?"

"The breast-cancer study you led, the one that failed, was personal for me. It was what killed my mom. That was an interesting fact I uncovered as I dug into your background. In fact, without knowing that bit of information, I may not have made it this far."

Neil's face betrayed that he had never made the connection. He knew Jordan's father was buried in medical debt from his wife's cancer, but he must not have connected the family with the trial he'd run.

"Does that mean you see our arrangement as some long-deserved justice?"

"Not exactly. I just wanted to make sure you knew one reason why I never gave up. When you cause people harm, when you put them in jeopardy, expect it to be repaid."

"I don't dwell on the past. Neither should you. Don't forget the envelopes."

Jordan looked at the two envelopes. Carter Nash approached. He spoke so softly only she could hear him. "If you break the rules, we'll know. And you know how we deal with transgressions."

The scene of Steve Calhoun's death came rushing back.

Neil and Emma reached the door. "My men will escort you out in a few minutes," Neil said. "Make sure our paths don't cross again."

Emma looked over her shoulder as she was leaving. "Ciao, Jordan. It's been great. I'd say we should catch up again real soon, but that would be a lie."

Jordan scowled at her. "You wouldn't like the outcome if we did."

"Atta girl. Still fighting, even though you lost."

Five minutes later, Jordan and Charlie were in the parking lot. She grabbed him and hugged him as hard as she had hugged anyone in recent memory.

"I'm glad you're all right. Knowing what they did to Steve Calhoun, I thought they might kill you."

"They almost did. When they realized I auto-forwarded the email from Dr. Mbosi, they changed their plan. They needed me alive."

"That was a smart move. Sorry for not knowing."

"You should be." Charlie's smile made the jab perfectly acceptable.

38

THE DRIVE WAS ONLY ABOUT TWENTY MINUTES. THE RAIN HAD stopped, and Jordan's adrenaline rush had accelerated her driving speed. When she and Charlie walked into her apartment, Travis was practically bouncing off the walls.

"Travis," Jordan said. "I need you to check something for me."

"I'm way ahead of you. I've already checked your email backup." Travis apparently just realized Charlie was with her. "Good to see you, Charlie. I'm glad you're OK. Sorry about that bruise."

"Happy to be here. Even more happy to be alive."

"Yes, we all agree," Jordan said. "Charlie being safe is the most important thing. What did you find in the backup?"

"The email Charlie forwarded to you."

"No shit? But why didn't you think to check earlier?"

"Seriously? What with the police being here and you getting ready to go meet Emma, my brain hadn't had time to think. Once you left and I thought through the sequence of events, I knew the email must have been backed up."

"I didn't know you could do that. At least not on a personal computer. I know the *Courant* has automated email backups, but I never thought about it for me."

"That's why you should always let me manage your computer. When your hard drive crashed a couple weeks ago, I looked into some options to make sure you never lost any data. At the same time, I found a great application that automatically backs up your email. So, yeah, you have the email."

"Let's see what's in it," Jordan said.

Jordan and Charlie joined Travis at the kitchen table, where he had his laptop set up. They could see that Travis had a PDF file open and was going through it.

"This Dr. Mbosi got real records of patients from a GenPhage trial site."

"We kind of expected that," Jordan said. "What are the details?"

"His email said to compare three files. One was the documented clinical trial patients as collected by GenPhage. I guess these would be part of their official documentation."

"Yes," Charlie said. "Every patient who enrolled in a clinical trial must be accounted for and reported to health authorities like the FDA. There would be a list for each site."

"Got it. The second file looked like it was a bunch of individual records that showed patients who received an infusion of something provided by GenPhage. I guess a doctor or a nurse kept the proof of every patient who received an infusion. Anyway, if you compare the names from the two lists, not a single patient from the second list is in the first. That means they received something from GenPhage but weren't part of the official trial documentation." Travis looked to Charlie. "What does that mean as far as GenPhage's clinical trial goes?"

Charlie thought for a moment. "Well, if someone approved GenPhage to conduct a trial to support one treatment, say for TB, then they must show the FDA, or whoever will approve the treatment, the records for every patient who received the treatment. What you just described is against guidelines and illegal. It violates the integrity of the trial and guarantees that their treatment shouldn't get approved. At least not by the FDA or a similar agency in another country. It's one thing to fail to include actual patient records. It's worse to test something not approved for testing. Such as a weapon."

"Travis, what's in the third file?" Jordan asked.

"The third one is also a bunch of separate documents combined into a single PDF file. It has information, sometimes a newspaper obituary, sometimes a death certificate, of people who died. I was doing a quick check of the names. While there are far fewer names in the third file, every name there is on list two."

"Every one?" Jordan said. "So, of the people this nurse has identified as having received something from GenPhage, the ones who have died are only from the second group? That's consistent with testing a weapon. GenPhage put some patients in a real trial. Others were given the weaponized version."

Charlie asked the most important question. "Travis, how many names are on list three?"

"I counted sixteen."

"Jesus," Jordan said. "How many on list two?"

Travis swallowed hard, his throat apparently going dry. "Forty-two."

"Mother of God," said Charlie. "They're prepared to kill dozens of people to test their weapon." Charlie looked at Jordan. "I assume you're sticking to the original plan and not the deal with Neil?"

"Deal? What deal?" Travis asked.

"I'll explain later. It won't matter once the news gets out. GenPhage will sink faster than the *Titanic* hitting two icebergs. Before we put this story together, I need to call Officer Jennings. There's no need to look for Charlie anymore."

"You asked the cops to find me? Really?"

"Yes. Once we realized that you had to have been taken."

Charlie smiled, tears welling. "Thanks. Thanks a lot."

"Anytime. Let's get cracking, if you're up to it. I think it's going to be an all-nighter."

"I can't think of a better use of my time. Other than a hot shower and a cheeseburger."

JORDAN WAS RIGHT. It was an all-nighter and then some.

Even without having to stop working while Officer Jennings and his partner took their statements, it would have been a long night. The more than an hour of police questions just guaranteed sleep wasn't going to be an option.

It took until late morning to put the story together to the point where Jordan could take it for review. That meant getting it in front of Tom and Bob.

The last time Jordan had sat in Bob's conference room was a low point for her. She was embarrassed and had nearly lost her job. Since then, she'd done the one thing he'd told her not to do. Now she was back to tell her editors she'd disobeyed. Only this time, she had a team with her. Though they both protested, Travis and Charlie sat beside Jordan. Travis looked relaxed. Charlie couldn't figure out what to do with his hands.

Tom opened the door and entered the conference room, with Bob right behind him. Jordan had hoped to run this by Tom first. If she could have convinced him, he would have helped sell it to Bob. Now she'd have to sell them both at the same time.

"Who do we have here?" Tom said, his tone sending the message that outsiders weren't welcome for story reviews.

"I think you met Travis before, at the Christmas party two years ago?"

He looked at Travis. "You look familiar. That must be it." Tom gestured toward Charlie. "And over here?"

"This is my friend Charlie Choi. He works for the CDC."

"Pleased to meet you," Charlie said, extending his hand. Tom took it and gave it a quick, firm shake.

Bob was an impatient person, and this meeting didn't change that characteristic. "So, what's this about, Jordan? We haven't seen you in a few days and figured you were off licking your wounds after that GenPhage fiasco."

Jordan made sure she was sitting upright in her chair, trying to look calm and confident even though she felt the complete opposite. "Funny you should mention GenPhage. That's why I wanted the meeting."

"You better be fucking kidding," Bob said. "If you tell me you disobeyed my orders to drop your story, I'll fire your ass right now."

Jordan had prepped for this. She planned on using a tried-and-true American approach: getting off on a technicality.

"Actually, the original story was on the role of GenPhage in the death of Eric Smith. The story I want to review today is how GenPhage is killing innocent people through its illegal testing of a weapon."

Tom jumped in. "You're splitting hairs, Jordan. This is still about GenPhage. I thought we were clear about leaving them alone."

"You were clear about dropping the story I was working on. I did. But I learned, I mean, we learned," Jordan said as she gestured to the men flanking her, "that patients in a GenPhage clinical trial were dying. And that GenPhage was hiding it."

"All right," said Tom. "And how did you come across this interesting set of facts?"

"Charlie met a doctor from Kenya at a conference who said he knew of patients who were getting a GenPhage treatment and then dying. The doctor also said someone paid the trial doctors to make sure these patients didn't appear in the official records."

"Wait," said Tom. "Did you say this doctor was from Kenya? Does he work in the US?"

"No. He was referring to patients in Kenya."

"All right. I'm just trying to keep the facts straight. So GenPhage patients in Kenya died. And doctors hid this?"

"Yes. We have records to show there were patients who received a GenPhage treatment who were not part of the official clinical trial records."

"Does that mean the company did something wrong? Couldn't the patients have received something else?"

Jordan looked to Charlie. "Can you help?"

"Sure, Jordan. The short answer is no. GenPhage has no approved treatment in any country. They're working on their first one. And they only have approval to test for one indication. Therefore, any patient who received anything from GenPhage should have been part of the official trial. Many patients weren't. That's a violation in any country."

"That helps," Tom said. "So we've got some major manipulation going on. That's newsworthy. What about these patients who weren't part of the trial records?"

Jordan took over from Charlie. "Many of them have died. From multiple organ failure."

"Shit, Jordan. Are you sure? Do you know what they received?"

"I'm sure. We've got records that confirm the deaths of sixteen of them. What they received is the really nasty part. The evidence trail points to GenPhage testing a weaponized version of their treatment. For the military."

"Whoa. That puts this in a different league. What do you have to support it?"

Jordan walked Tom through the interviews and what she'd learned. How all the pieces pointed to testing something other than what GenPhage was approved to test. The result, many dead, supported the weapon hypothesis.

Tom looked at Bob. "This is big. We'll have to sit with legal. Especially on the military angle. But this will rock the industry."

"And it will sink GenPhage. They'll never survive this as a company."

The ensuing pause was broken by Travis. "You should tell them everything."

"There's more?" Tom said.

"Um, yeah." Jordan didn't really want to share the rest. It raised questions about her judgment. But she had no choice. The police were already involved. "There were a couple of incidents. Bad ones."

Tom lowered his head "Just tell us."

Jordan shared details about the death of Steve Calhoun, the kidnapping of Charlie, and the surveillance of her and her apartment. She also included the interactions with the police. The only thing she left out was the prior night's confrontation with Neil's team. And the supposed deal they made. Jordan had never intended to honor the deal; she'd just said what was necessary to save Charlie.

"Jesus," Tom said. "If I had known any of this, I would have stopped it immediately. I don't know what the hell to do with you."

"You can thank me. This will be one of the most important stories of the year. I didn't break any laws. Not really. And I negotiated to save Charlie. I wish I could have done something to save Steve Calhoun, but that was before I knew how serious things were."

"You've got some—" Tom started.

"It's fine, Tom," Bob interrupted. "Yes, she should have kept us in the loop. At least a little. But you can't argue with the end product."

"So you agree to run it?" Jordan said.

"Damn right," Bob said. "Do you agree, Tom?"

"I do. I'll get someone from legal. Jordan, find a couple of the external medical experts we have on retainer and go through this with a fine-tooth comb. I'll make a call to an old friend who used to work at the FDA and get his perspective on how to engage the right authorities. We'll get crucified if we make a mistake, so let's not fuck it up. I want to see what we have before five p.m. If we're good, we can consider reaching out to GenPhage for comment."

"Let's get this done, Jordan," Tom said. "No rest yet. But your friends can go. Thank you both."

"There's also the police element," Jordan said. "I owe them some follow-up."

"Do what you've gotta do," Bob said. "But we're not holding the story unless someone files an injunction."

As the group began to disperse, Jordan looked at Travis and Charlie. Both appeared to be at least as tired as she felt. Like her, their adrenaline levels were probably dropping now that the danger and chaos were behind them. Charlie looked particularly tired, the bruise on his face reminding Jordan that he almost hadn't made it.

Jordan realized that, as important as the story was to her, Travis and Charlie had come first. As much as she liked to be her own boss and call her own shots, she wouldn't be sitting in a conference room with a career-defining story without them. At her core, Jordan may have been a loner. But she realized even a loner needed a little help now and again.

JORDAN WAITED for Officer Jennings at a pizza shop around the corner from the *Courant*. She knew the mom-and-pop joint to be a popular place for lunch but was surprised to see how quiet it was in the evening. Despite her hunger, she held off grabbing a slice. Just in case Officer Jennings also wanted to eat.

Jordan had called Officer Jennings after the meeting with Tom and Bob. She'd explained that the story would be published but that she needed the afternoon to finish it. With a police investigation ramping up, Jordan knew he'd be in a hurry to know the impact of the story. She was thankful he agreed to wait. He said his shift ended at six but he'd meet with her when she was ready.

Officer Jennings entered the pizza joint at 6:15, still in uniform. He spotted Jordan right away.

"Hello, Ms. Reed." He set his hat down on the table. "I know we need to talk business, but I need to grab a slice. I'm starving. Do you want one?"

Jordan was caught off guard. Her read on Officer Jennings was that he found Jordan's actions, and maybe her herself, frustrating. She expected a very tense meeting. What she saw was the complete opposite.

"Um, yeah. That would be great. A cheese slice is fine."

"Hang on. I'll be right back."

Officer Jennings returned with three steaming slices and two bottles of water. "Here you go."

"Thanks. I see you're hungry."

"I am. I didn't have time for lunch today."

"Don't let me stop you."

They ate in silence, Officer Jennings downing both slices in the time it took Jordan to eat one.

"So, Ms. Reed, you came very close to getting on my bad side."

The remark didn't surprise Jordan, but the officer's friendly tone did. "I probably can't blame you. I could have been a better citizen."

"That's an understatement. For example, when I was at your apartment, you gave no hint you'd be meeting with that group from GenPhage."

"On that one, you knew what I knew. I had no idea that would happen either. No one was more surprised than me when I saw who was waiting for me."

"For real? You didn't know?"

"Nope. I was even more surprised to see Charlie there."

"When do I get the complete picture? I know there're details you haven't told me."

Jordan set an envelope on the table. "The story's inside. It needs some editing, but the facts are all there."

Officer Jennings looked at the envelope. "I'll read it tonight. What do I need to know that I don't already know?"

"The only missing pieces for you are what GenPhage was doing in Africa. Testing a weapon on unsuspecting patients. You know about Steve Calhoun, Charlie's kidnapping, and the break-in at my place, the three things that I'd think are most relevant to you. Not to mention that the death of Eric Smith probably wasn't an accident."

"I won't be surprised by some other crime in Boston?"

"Nope."

"I hope you're telling me the truth."

"I am. This time." Jordan's smile was returned. "There's one more thing inside. It'll be worthless soon, but it's part of the evidence trail. The bribe from GenPhage."

"Really? There's a check in there?"

"Nope. Company stock. Or at least stock units. I don't know how that stuff works."

"I'm sure you know they're technically evidence, but didn't you consider keeping them?"

"Nah. They'll be worthless. Just paper."

But I'm not turning over the other piece of the bribe.

"You're something else. Can I give you some advice?"

"I thought you might feel obligated to do that at some point. Go ahead."

"Don't take risks like the one you took yesterday. You and your friend could have easily left the building in body bags. The next time you think it's a good idea to go by yourself to meet with actual or potential criminals, call me."

"Thanks for the advice. But you know reporters don't like to bring the police along. You cramp our style."

"Then don't call me as a cop. Call me as someone who can watch your back."

"Officer Jennings, I'm not sure that's appropriate."

"Call me Scott. And if it means saving you from getting killed one day, I can live with any fallout at the precinct."

Jordan was at a momentary loss for words. He genuinely seemed like he cared. Despite Jordan not having been exactly transparent with him.

"I might take you up on that. I still have your card. And call me Jordan. That 'Ms. Reed' crap makes me feel old."

"It's a deal, Jordan. But take my personal number. I'm always reachable."

"I should get going. I missed a night's sleep and have an early start tomorrow."

"Oh? Another big story?"

"No way. But I've got some unfinished business with this one."

"Off you go. Remember, call me if you get into trouble."

"Thanks, Scott."

As Jordan left, the look on Scott's face made her think he knew exactly what she had planned.

39

JORDAN WAITED OUTSIDE THE GENPHAGE HEADQUARTERS. THE morning was crisp, with the temperature just above freezing. Winter would be here before she knew it.

She didn't know exactly what time Emma typically arrived at the office, but today she knew it would be before eight a.m. Jordan had called Emma's assistant the day before, pretending to arrange for a delivery that required her signature. The assistant said eight a.m. would be fine. So Jordan arrived at seven a.m. And she waited.

Despite good advice to the contrary from Scott, Jordan had told no one what she was doing. Tom and Bob had their own tasks related to the story to take care of. Charlie had no reason to go near anyone from GenPhage ever again. Jordan should have told Travis. He'd be extremely pissed if he ever learned what Jordan was about to do.

Ironically, the one person Jordan had considered calling was Scott. What she planned to do wasn't a police matter. But something about the way Scott had offered to help her if she needed it had connected with her. No doubt he would have tried to talk her out of it. So, in the end, she did what she wanted. With no one to give her a hard time.

At just past 7:30, Jordan saw a car she recognized. She watched as Emma pulled into a reserved parking spot. She didn't know Emma's title, but it must have been high for her to score one of those spots. Jordan was about 150 feet away from the entrance, past where Emma parked. She walked toward Emma's car, slowly, since she could see Emma still gathering her things before getting out. As Jordan got to within about twenty feet of Emma's car, the driver's door opened and Emma stepped out. She had a small laptop bag in her left hand and a Starbucks coffee in her right hand. She closed her car door with her hip and started for the entrance. She was not paying attention to anyone around her and didn't notice Jordan.

Jordan was looking forward to this. "Hey, Emma. Hold up."

Emma froze. Then she slowly turned around. "What the hell are you doing here? What part of our arrangement said you can stalk me at work? You got your friend back, and you're a million-aire-to-be. Now get the fuck out of here or I'll call security. And not those mall-cop types that just stand by our doors. The real ones. You know who they are."

"Is that any way to talk to a fellow shareholder? I think you need to brush up on your public relations training."

"Don't give me that crap. We both know you'll be a share-holder until you're allowed to cash out. Hell, I might even buy you out before we go public. I'm sure you need the cash."

"Wow. I really misread you. You are one self-important bitch. I can't believe I thought we had something in common. Man, was I off on that."

"Get over it, sweetheart. We have nothing in common. Now get lost." Emma turned and continued toward the entrance.

"Don't worry. I wasn't planning on staying long. I just wanted to tell you to make sure you go see Uncle Neil this morning. I think he'll want to talk to you right around eight oh five."

Emma stopped and turned around for the second time. "Why would you say that? What's happening at eight oh five?"

"At eight a.m., he'll be asked to comment on a story being released at noon. It's about how a local company killed patients while conducting clinical trials in Africa and tried to cover it up. It even suggests that this local company was testing a biological weapon. My guess is, as soon as Uncle Neil declines to comment, he'll want you in his office. You know, to figure out what the fuck to do."

"You stupid bitch. Without the email from that doctor in Kenya, you have no story. Anything your shitty paper publishes will be libel. We'll sue you into dust."

Jordan sauntered up to Emma, stopping a foot in front of her. "About that. I have to admit it was stupid of me not to check my email when your goons took Charlie. If I had checked, then I could have handled the situation differently."

"If you're a smart girl, you'll learn from your mistake. But deciding to publish a story without proof tells me you're not as smart as you think."

"You're right. I'm not that smart. But I have a great friend who's really smart. So smart he did something that came in handy. Do you want to know what he did?"

"Do I have a choice?"

"No, you don't. You see, he's a bit of a computer geek, something I'm not. He takes care of my computer for me. Makes sure it's up to date. Deals with problems. Anyway, he figured it would be good to have an application that automatically archived my email. Not daily, or every few hours. But every time there was a new message. You know, just in case I do something stupid and lose my phone or lose an important email."

Emma's eyes widened. "You're bluffing. You would have never thought of something like that."

"You're right. But I don't deserve the credit. If this had been left in my hands, I'd have nothing. Just like you think. Good thing I have friends."

Jordan had been holding an envelope during their conversation. She handed it to Emma, who set down her laptop bag to take it. "In case you still don't believe me, take a look. It's everything from Dr. Mbosi in Kenya. Plenty of evidence that GenPhage tested something unapproved and killed innocent people. Start looking for a new job, bitch."

"You really don't want to do this. If GenPhage goes down, your shares will be worthless. The company has to go public for you to cash in."

"I already gave that envelope to the police. It should help them with their investigation. Turns out they have questions for Uncle Neil and his security team. Something about Steve Calhoun. You remember him, right? Not to mention a kidnapping."

Jordan watched as Emma's jaw dropped, her eyes opening wide. Jordan could see her adversary process that GenPhage was done. Maybe her career and freedom as well.

"You're really willing to walk away from becoming a millionaire? How stupid are you?"

"Probably very stupid. But I'll be able to live with myself. Time to go. The proofs of the story will be ready soon, and I don't want to hold things up."

Jordan looked back at Emma as she walked to her car. Emma hadn't moved at all, still holding the envelope from Jordan in her left hand.

———

JORDAN WAS EXPECTED back at the *Courant*. But she had a detour to make. An important one. As with her visit to Emma, her detour was not open to sharing with others.

After a thirty-minute drive, Jordan parked on the street in front of Laurie Smith's house. There were two cars in the driveway, and the lights in the kitchen were on. Laurie was home.

Jordan hated to disturb her, but she deserved to hear the news firsthand.

Jordan walked to the front door and rang the bell. After a few seconds, she saw Laurie peek through a window. The main door opened a moment later, followed by Laurie opening the screen door. Her face was a mix of curiosity and concern.

"Hi, Laurie," Jordan said. "Sorry for the early-morning visit. I hope it's not too inconvenient."

"I guess it's fine. I sure didn't expect to see you again. If you need to ask me more questions about Eric, you can save your breath. I've told you all I can."

"Not this time. No questions. Just something you should know."

"Really? About what?"

"GenPhage."

"Oh. Should we go inside?"

"It'll only take a minute, and I don't want to intrude any more than I already have. If it's all right with you, we can talk right here."

Laurie stepped out onto the porch. She had on furry slippers and a thick sweatshirt, sufficient to handle the cool morning for a few minutes. "Go ahead."

"Thanks. First, you should know my paper will publish a story on GenPhage in a few hours. It will detail how they manipulated clinical trials and exposed patients to something deadly. It appears to have been some kind of biological weapon. Many people in Africa died."

Laurie was taken aback. She stood up straighter and crossed her arms in front of her body. "Really? Is it true?"

"Without a doubt. We received information from a doctor in Kenya that proved this was happening. GenPhage will probably have its operations halted, and there'll be a criminal investigation. As a company, they're finished."

"I don't believe it. Eric was always sure the company would be a huge success."

"If they had stuck to trying to help patients, maybe that could have been the case. For some reason, they thought they could test a weapon and not get caught."

Laurie paused, not seeming to be sure if she could ask what had to be on her mind. She looked down at her feet and spoke quietly. "How did they die?" Another pause. "Was it similar to how Eric died?"

"Yes, it was. I think it was exactly the same." Jordan answered the next question so Laurie wouldn't have to ask it. "Whatever killed the patients in Africa was likely the same thing that killed Eric here. He must have come into contact with it at the manufacturing plant." Jordan really believed that Eric hadn't been exposed accidentally. But telling Laurie that wouldn't do her any good.

Laurie lowered her head again. Jordan knew she didn't want her to see the tears welling up in her eyes. "I guess that's it, then. Whatever GenPhage did that got Eric killed has come full circle. Serves the bastards right. I wish whoever was responsible could feel what Eric felt. Someone should suffer like he did."

"I couldn't agree more." Jordan had one more thing to do. "Laurie, I know you can't talk about the settlement you have with GenPhage, but can you tell me how they pay you? They may have to declare bankruptcy. That would affect you and your family."

Laurie wiped her eyes with the sleeve of her sweatshirt. "I almost forgot about that. Funny how them getting what they deserve may hurt my family again. After the initial settlement payment, which I already got, the arrangement is for us to get a payment once per year for three years. Every December thirty-first. I assume I have to show them I can keep my mouth shut all year before they pay me. I hope I can at least get this year's payment before they go under."

Jordan had one of the two envelopes from Neil. The one she didn't give to the police. It had a bank draft made out to Jordan for $250,000. Neil was right in that it could have almost gotten her a new place. Maybe not in Boston, but somewhere. Jordan had confirmed she could endorse the draft so that another person could cash it. Laurie needed the money more than she did.

Jordan handed Laurie the envelope. She was aware that action could constitute breaking the law, but Laurie deserved anything she could get from GenPhage. "This won't make up for what you may not get paid from GenPhage, but it should help as you figure out what you do next."

Laurie took the envelope but didn't look inside. "Are you sure? I can't take your money."

"It was never mine. Let's just say it was for a deal I decided not to honor. I have no intention of returning it to its source. But that doesn't mean you and your family can't have it. Consider it an advance on your GenPhage settlement."

Laurie stepped toward Jordan and embraced her. "Thank you, Jordan. For everything."

40

CARTER AND NEIL WERE AT THEIR TYPICAL SEAPORT PARK BENCH one more time.

Carter knew they had reached the end of this assignment. A source inside the company had told him something bad was coming and that Neil Foley was at the center of it. For all Neil's careful planning, he had been undone by the same motivators that had made him a success. Greed and self-preservation. At least one site investigator had covered his ass, keeping copies of records he either should have destroyed or shouldn't have had at all. Just in case. It reinforced a truth Carter had come to learn well. There was always a trail.

"It's time to pull the plug," Neil said. "This is about to blow up, and knowledge of your team will make a bad situation worse. I have kept your name and your team off the company books, but I can't control for the people who saw you. As long as the story is about GenPhage and the clinical trials, your role might slip through the cracks."

"That would be best. We have a protocol in place for situations like this. I'll activate it."

Carter didn't believe he and his team were in the clear. Not at all. Too many people could identify them, in particular Charlie.

But Carter was confident that Charlie wouldn't be too keen to find his kidnappers. After all, he'd gotten away unscathed. Plus, he wasn't the type to put his friends at risk. As far as it concerned Carter, there was an equilibrium with Charlie that could be maintained indefinitely.

Carter's concern was Neil. Despite his bravado and apparent camaraderie, Carter knew all too well that when people were put under extreme pressure, they would act to save themselves. When law enforcement inevitably put Neil under duress, he might just offer up Carter and his team. Especially if it could save him jail time.

Neil stood up, followed by Carter. They shook hands. "I'll be in touch," Neil said. "It may be a while."

"You know how to reach me."

Carter watched Neil walk back toward the GenPhage headquarters. Out on the street, Carter could see that Chris had parked the Suburban as they had discussed.

NEIL KNEW how the day would play out. The story would break. The executive team would have an emergency session. The board of directors would convene separately. They would fire many or all of the company executives. Technically, these employees would be asked to resign. But that was just a nicer way to fire people. Most of the executives would be shocked by what the company had been doing. Even the CEO had no idea. But he knew enough to know Neil had to be behind everything.

That's why Neil had already resigned. He did this right after the paper called him to ask for comment.

Neil headed toward the headquarters building, but he didn't go inside. Instead, he went to his car, a Porsche Cayenne Turbo. He unlocked the doors before reaching the car, confirmed by a quick chirp from the vehicle. The doors would have unlocked automatically when he put his hand on the handle, but he just didn't like waiting the extra second.

He grasped the handle to open the door. "Shit," he yelled, jerking his hand back, shaking it in the air. "What the hell?" Neil looked at his left hand. There was a cut just at the base of his middle two fingers, almost an inch long. Like most cuts to the hand, it bled freely. Neil went around to the passenger side. He opened the front door and grabbed a small packet of tissues from the glove box. He took out a few and put them on the cut and closed his hand into a fist to stop the bleeding.

He went back around to look at the door handle. It was tough to see, but it looked like someone had damaged the handle. It was scraped and gouged. He could see an edge of metal about an inch long protruding on the inside of the lever. Neil wondered how the hell this happened. Probably some asshole trying to break in.

———

CARTER ANSWERED HIS PHONE. "Go," he said.

"It's done. He cut his hand as planned."

"Good. And the material?"

"Sealed in a metal case. It'll be incinerated."

"Nicely done. Rendezvous in two weeks."

———

JORDAN HAD ONE MORE STOP, albeit not one she had planned or really wanted to make. Ben had called her after she left Laurie Smith's. He wanted to touch base. Jordan told him she had no interest in doing so, but Ben said he'd make it worthwhile.

She pulled into a grocery store parking lot and drove to the northwest corner, as Ben had directed. She spotted his car and pulled into a spot beside him. As they'd done the last time they spoke, they rolled down their respective windows.

"Why did you want to meet? You said it would be worth it for me, so let's get it over with."

"Still no thanks? I shouldn't be surprised."

"Are you serious? You may have stuck an envelope on my door, but it was me and my friends who did all the work. Hell, one even got kidnapped."

"I didn't know that. Sorry. I hope he's OK."

"He is. So why the meeting?"

"Two reasons. First, I heard a rumor that you cracked your story. Is that why you went to see Emma at GenPhage this morning?"

"How the hell did you know I was there?"

"You should have figured out by now that I'm well connected. There are several people in GenPhage with whom I talk. One called to tell me Emma was very upset when she arrived at work. She said it had something to do with a reporter. Shortly after that, news that Neil Foley had resigned spread through the building."

"Well, based on what you know, I suppose I can confirm that the story will come out today. You need to keep it quiet until it's public."

"No worries on that front. I want to see the headline in public as much as you do. And let me congratulate you on your success. This was a difficult story to crack. I'm certain it bodes well for your future."

Jordan softened her demeanor, finally accepting that Ben may not be such a bad guy after all. "Thanks. I guess it wouldn't have been possible without you."

"As you said, I just stuck an envelope on your door."

"You mentioned two reasons to meet. What was the second?"

"I owe you an explanation. I'm not just a bystander who saw something that needed to be exposed."

"I never really thought you were. What's your real role in this?"

"I work for Newman Brothers."

"The investment firm? One of the GenPhage backers?"

"That's right."

"Well, sorry this cost you guys a shitload of money."

"That doesn't really matter. We can always make more money. But I have a more direct connection to Neil Foley. I met him when he worked at the company that tested the cancer treatment your mother took. My firm had invested in that company as well, though it went bankrupt not long after the trial was halted. Lucky for us, I suppose. Anyway, Neil had impressed me, and at the time, I didn't believe he personally knew about the risks of the treatment. In hindsight, I'm sure I was mistaken. When that company folded, I brought him to work at Newman Brothers. GenPhage became a company we got very excited about, and I thought it would be beneficial to move one of our own into the company. That's how Neil got there."

Jordan absorbed this in silence. She wanted to assign some blame to this man for her mother's death, but it wasn't justified. But she could blame him for handing Neil a company he used as a weapon.

"What about the Department of Defense? Did you know about their arrangement with GenPhage?"

"I knew they had helped early on with the development of the technology, but that happened before Neil got there. He must have had a connection we didn't know about. Someone who supported the weaponizing of the platform."

"Your hands are pretty dirty after all. I hope you're losing sleep over this. You're part of the problem."

"I can't deny that. That's why I approached you."

"Don't expect any thanks. Next time you want someone to clean up your mess, don't call me."

Jordan started her car and left the parking lot. She realized that, as bad as Neil Foley was, he was just pond scum. The pond was still there.

———————

JORDAN SAT in the conference room at the paper, where they reviewed the final version of the GenPhage story. In the room with her were her unofficial teammates, Charlie and Travis, plus her immediate editor, Tom. He displayed the story, which was scheduled to go live on the paper's website in minutes, on a large flat-screen TV.

This was by far the biggest story of Jordan's young career. Ironic that after years of trying by herself to land "the big one," she'd needed the help of two non-journalists to pull it off. That's not how she had envisioned getting here. It showed how little she knew about what it took to succeed.

Travis broke the silence. "I'm glad this is over. I'm not cut out for it."

"You're right about that," Jordan said. "Imagine if *you* had been kidnapped?"

"Don't you mean 'allegedly kidnapped,'" Travis said. "There's no proof it happened."

"Really?" said Charlie. "What do you think I did that whole day?"

"Running. Aren't you training for some kind of marathon or something?"

"Not one that would have me go for a twelve-hour run."

The ribbing was casual and frivolous. The tension in the group had dissolved now that they'd finished what they'd set out to do. Jordan had never played a real team sport like hockey or softball as a kid. But she had a feeling this was a lot like a locker room after a hard-fought win.

"So, what are you heroes going to do to celebrate?" Tom asked.

"I think Jordan will take us all out for a nice dinner and an open bar," said Charlie. "Rumor has it she came into a few dollars, so I think she's good for it."

"What's that about?" said Travis. "Jordan, are you holding out on us?"

"Yes and no. Part of the deal I made with Neil included some compensation for damaging my apartment."

"Nice. Sounds like a five-star dinner is coming our way."

"Let's shoot for one star. There was someone who needed the money more than me. But I promise, the next time I get bribed by a millionaire, I'll take you all out for a five-star dinner. Deal?"

The men looked at each other. "Deal," they said.

FOLLOWING the publication of her story, Jordan became a minor news star. At least for a week or two. She found herself on the receiving end of questions from other reporters and news personalities. She quickly got tired of answering what became the most common question: How did she feel about taking down a company?

As if that was the most important question. The story wasn't about her. It was about a monster operating in complete disregard for human life, from a position that should have been focused on saving lives. After her fourth interview where she was asked that insane question, she refused to do another one.

She preferred to sit back and be a spectator.

Jordan watched the news of GenPhage's fall from grace spread like wildfire. Their use of clinical trials to hide the testing of a weapon rocked the medical community and the pharmaceutical industry. The US Attorney General launched an immediate investigation. Manufacturing was halted, and GenPhage's clinical trials were shut down.

Jordan was content to let other reporters cover the fallout. Like the resignation of the entire GenPhage leadership team. Which was followed by an announcement of several investors cutting ties. At least as much as they could. All discussion of an IPO vanished. About the only good news for anyone in the company was that their technology platform had value. A midsize pharma company was rumored to have made a very low offer to buy out the company.

The only real disappointment for Jordan was that after the second day, the biological weapon angle never got much traction. The Department of Defense came out with a quick statement denying any connection with weapon testing, which was challenged for about twenty-four hours. Then the pressure on the DoD let up. Completely. It was like someone had declared the topic off-limits.

Almost lost in the news was the fact that GenPhage's chief operations officer had died within days of the story breaking. Family was quoted as saying that Neil Foley had been fighting illness for months and that his body had finally given out. Jordan noted that the time frame between her story's publication and Neil Foley's death was remarkably close to how long it had taken Eric Smith to die once he had been exposed to the weaponized treatment. Jordan had no doubt about how Neil Foley really died.

The one loose end Jordan couldn't track was Emma. She wasn't mentioned in any news coverage. According to Scott, she had been wanted for questioning, but the police were never able to find her. She simply disappeared.

More than once, Jordan wondered if their paths would ever cross again.

EPILOGUE

JORDAN HAD BROKEN THE STORY TWO WEEKS AGO. THE GENPHAGE manufacturing site had not produced a batch of anything in more than a week. With trials halted and an interim executive team in place, there was no reason for anything to be manufactured. The bioreactors had been formally shut down. Partially used starting materials had been disposed of. Materials that had potential for some future use were stored.

In the quiet state of the GenPhage manufacturing site, there was no need for anyone to be there. Except for a pair of security guards. There was always a risk of vandalism, after all.

So the arrival of two black cube vans would have seemed out of place. Factoring in a time of two a.m., "out of place" was elevated to "highly suspicious."

Each van had a team of three men, all of whom entered the main building without being challenged. Had their faces been visible, at least one would have looked familiar to Jordan. Had she been there.

Within thirty minutes, the men made five trips back and forth between the building and the vans. The boxes and containers they loaded ranged in shape and size. A few even appeared to be emitting steam. A closer inspection would have revealed the mist to be evaporating nitrogen from the liquid used to keep biological materials frozen.

When they were done, with hardly a word spoken the entire time, the men climbed into the vans and left.

From the passenger seat of the first van, a tall, muscular man made a phone call.

"Yes?" answered Ben.

"It's Chris. We have the material."

"Very good. You know where to take it."

JOIN THE GILLIS CLAN

Why join the "Gillis Clan?"

Members of the Gillis Clan will get the Jordan Reed novella *Mercury Shock* for free. It will only available to those who join the Gillis Clan.

Members of the Gillis Clan will also have exclusive access to "The Story of the Story" content for the books they buy. This is where I will share my thoughts and motivations for each Jordan Reed novel. This will also include additional information related to the story and will be exclusive to the Gillis Clan.

Members will always be the first to hear about new Jordan Reed mysteries, as well as other writing projects, including as new series. And there will be more!

It's completely free to join the Gillis Clan and you will never be spammed by me. You can easily opt out whenever you want.

Ready to join? What are you waiting for. Click the link below.

Join the Gillis Clan

DID YOU ENJOY THE BOOK? PLEASE LEAVE A REVIEW

Reviews are one of the most important tools to help authors generate interest and attention for their books. Independent authors lack the scale and resources of big publishing houses and rely heavily on our readers to provide honest reviews. These reviews help other readers find books they might enjoy.

If you've enjoyed this book, I would be very grateful if you could take just a few minutes to leave a review on the book's Amazon page. If you do, feel free to drop me a note at kevin@kcgillis.com.

Thank you in advance!

ACKNOWLEDGMENTS

I must give credit to an extended team of professionals, without whom this novel never would have made it to publication. A special thanks to my editors Aja, Michelle, and Kate. I truly enjoyed working with them on this novel and would have nothing worth publishing with them.

Every book has a cover, and Stuart Bache's team of professional book cover designers at Books Covered developed a superb cover for my Jordan Reed debut. I hope it caught your eye!

I would also be remiss not acknowledging other professionals from Reedsy, Findaway Voices, BookFunnel, Draft2Digital, IngramSpark, and Kobo Writing Life. Each one played an important role in moving from manuscript to completed novel.

Let me also thank you for choosing to invest your time getting to know Jordan Reed. I hope you enjoyed her first story as much as I enjoyed writing it.

Jordan Reed will return!

ABOUT THE AUTHOR

K.C. (Kevin) Gillis is the author of the Jordan Reed mystery series. Despite being a lifelong lover of stories and books, writing took a distant back seat as his professional career travelled through the Canadian Air Force, a decade as a chemist, followed by a long and continuing run in corporate America. With writing no longer in the back seat (but not quite yet in the front seat), Kevin now has the Jordan Reed series well under way. His personal interests focus on endurance and water sports. Having grown up in the Canadian Maritimes, he now lives in the US northeast.

Kevin can be found online at www.kcgillis.com. You can connect with Kevin on Twitter at @kcgilliswriter, on Facebook at www.facebook.com/kcgilliswriter, and you can email him directly at kevin@kcgillis.com.

Information on all of his books can be found at kcgillis.com.

facebook.com/kcgilliswriter
twitter.com/kcgilliswriter
instagram.com/kcgilliswriter

ALSO BY K.C. GILLIS

Mercury Shock

A Jordan Reed novella that takes a glimpse into her backstory. Learn how Jordan earned her job at the Boston Courant while dealing with more than one personal challenge. Experience her first real taste of corruption and greed and how it nearly killed an innocent teen. This book is available for free for those who join the Gillis Clan, the virtual community that will be the first to hear about all things Jordan Reed, not to mention having exclusive access to the "Story of the Story" that will accompany each new Jordan Reed mystery.

Jordan Reed Mystery #2

Coming in April 2020!! Stay tuned for preorder details.

Printed in Great Britain
by Amazon